MW01245258

Return
to the Eyrie

KATERINA DUNNE

HISTORIUM PRESS
U. S. A.

This is a work of fiction. All characters, locations and events in the narrative – other than those clearly in the public domain – are products of the author's imagination and are used fictitiously. Any resemblance to real persons, living or dead, is entirely coincidental and not intended by the author. Where real historical figures, locations and events appear, these have been depicted in a fictional context.

All rights reserved. No part of this book may be reproduced in any form or by any electronic or mechanical means or used in any manner without written permission from the author, except for the use of short quotations in a book review.

For more information:

www.facebook.com/Katerina-Dunne-Writer-107262811794150

Contact: katerinadunnewriter@gmail.com

Book design by White Rabbit Arts

Original cover artwork (illustration and borders) by Paddy Shaw

HISTORIUM PRESS

Macon GA 31211 U. S. A.

www.historiumpress.com

First paperback edition April 2024

Copyright © 2024 by Ekaterini Vavoulidou

(under the pen-name Katerina Dunne)

ISBN (paperback) 978-1-962465-32-8

ISBN (eBook) 978-1-962465-33-5

Table of Contents

GLOSSARY   5

July 1479   7

Chapter 1: 'Freckle-Face'   10

Chapter 2: The Mentor   22

Chapter 3: The Gift   37

Chapter 4: The Runaway Bride   46

Chapter 5: The Wedding   60

Chapter 6: Setback   67

Chapter 7: The Plea   76

Chapter 8: Husband and Wife   83

Chapter 9: A Time of Pain   89

Chapter 10: The Return   100

Chapter 11: A Broken Man   104

Chapter 12: Baptism of Fire   110

Chapter 13: A Daring Plan   126

Chapter 14: The Ruse   136

Chapter 15: Some Useful Advice   147

Chapter 16: A Painful Decision   152

Chapter 17: A Dangerous Journey   162

Chapter 18: Homeland   173

Chapter 19: The Test   182

Chapter 20: Meeting the Devil   195

Chapter 21: On the Battlefield   205

Chapter 22: Chasing a Shadow   217

Chapter 23: Tears   227

Chapter 24: The Awakening   233

Chapter 25: The Incident   240

Chapter 26: The Way In   252

Chapter 27: On the Inside   259

Chapter 28: Revelation   267

Chapter 29: The Night Visitor   277

Chapter 30: The Prisoner   291

Chapter 31: A New Destiny   297

Chapter 32: The Human Side of a Monster   312

Chapter 33: Breakthrough   321

Chapter 34: Fighting the Ghosts   332

Chapter 35: Justice   351

Chapter 36: Best Laid Plans   358

Chapter 37: The Confrontation   368

Chapter 38: A Funeral Long Overdue   378

Chapter 39: The Mystery Knight   382

Chapter 40: A New Life   392

ACKNOWLEDGEMENTS AND THANKS   396

AUTHOR'S NOTES   397

APPENDICES   401

GLOSSARY

In Hungarian, all letters in a word are pronounced. They have the same pronunciation no matter where in the word they are. For example, the *i* is always pronounced as in *sit,* the *e* always like in *get* and the *g* always like in *give.* The accent above the vowels prolongs them. There are two exceptions to this rule. The first is *a*: without the accent, it is "closed" and pronounced between *a* and *o* as in the English word *call* (in the transcription below I note it as *aw*) With the accent, it is "open" and pronounced like in the word *father.* The second exception is *e*: without the accent, it is pronounced as I showed above. With the accent, it is pronounced between *e* and *i* as in the word *café* (in the transcription I note it as *eh*)

Bácsi (ba-chi): an informal way of addressing an older male; also means uncle

Csillag (chil-lawg): star—in the novel, this is the name of Margit's horse

Dolmány (dol-maɲ; the letter *ny* is pronounced like the Spanish ñ): Dolman; a long upper garment of Turkic origin, worn over a shirt. In its Hungarian version, the top part and sleeves were usually tight-fitting; it became looser below the waist and reached down to the knees

Drágám (dra-gam): my dear, my precious

Galambom (gaw-lawm-bom): my dove

Huszár (hu-sar; the *u* like in *put*)—plural **Huszárok**: a light cavalryman in medieval Hungary, Serbia and Croatia

Jóisten! (yow-ish-ten): My Goodness! (literally: Good God!)

Kedves (ked-vesh): dear, favourite—**kedvesem**: my dear

Kincsem (kin-chem): my treasure

Madárka (maw-dar-kaw): little bird

Mente (men-te): a short fur-trimmed coat, usually with short sleeves, worn over the dolman

Naszád (naw-sad)—plural **Naszádok**: a single-masted gunboat—smaller than the galley, which had two masts

Sárkány (shar-kaɲ, *ny* like the Spanish *ñ*): dragon—in the novel, this is the name of Endre's warhorse

Sasfészek (shawsh-feh-sek): eyrie (literally: eagle's nest)

Szívem (see-vem): my heart (used as a form of endearment between lovers)

Úristen! (oo-rish-ten): My God! My Goodness! (literally: Lord God!)

Zora (Serbian word): dawn—in the novel, this is the name of Endre's mare

July 1479

The glaring sunshine jarred Margit and brought a sting to her eyes and nose. As her vision cleared, scenes of chaos unfolded before her: castle guards rushed about, shouting and scrambling to take their posts.

Her regained freedom and thirst for retribution propelled Margit forward. Through groups of soldiers, she jostled and elbowed her way to the smithy.

Adnan jumped up from his stool, relief flooding his face. "Margit! You're free. God is great!"

"I need weapons! Now!"

He pointed at a counter.

She grabbed a sword, strapped a knife to her right leg and placed an open-face helmet on her head. "Come with me. Time for revenge, at last."

Heart racing, she ran to meet her destiny.

An eerie silence hung about the unguarded keep. Margit and Adnan barged in, blades at the ready, and slammed the heavy door shut.

"Secure the door to the great hall," she ordered him.

"What the devil is going on?" Her cousin's voice came from the floor above. He stood on the wide step at the turn of the staircase with Balog by his side, both with their swords bared.

Márton's face hardened as soon as he saw her. "Dóczi was meant to deliver you in chains."

"Well, he's not on your side anymore."

Both hands clenched around the handle of her sword, Margit assumed a fighting stance. Let him come. She was ready.

But instead of Márton, Balog attacked her first.

"I'll take him," Adnan said, drawing the castellan away.

Her cousin had not moved but simply watched from above.

No time to waste. She must capture him now, or else...

With sure strides, Margit charged up the stairs until she came to the step below him. "Give yourself up, cousin. The voivode's army is outside."

"I know I am a dead man." The wicked glint had returned to his eyes. "But I shall take you with me. Since you rejected my proposition, I shall never let you have Szentimre."

Holding the weapon with steady hands, she took the final stride onto the wide step. "I *do not* intend to die today, cousin."

Márton withdrew momentarily and then lunged at her.

Raising her sword just in time, Margit parried his hit, but its force made her stagger backwards.

Steel rang out as blades crossed in a deadly clash. Crippled left hand notwithstanding, her cousin displayed impressive fighting skills. Margit continued to block and evade his strikes. But little by little, she was driven back towards the edge, her heels barely balancing above the lower flight of stairs. One wrong move, one slip, meant a bone-shattering plunge.

Damn these steps! How did I end up so cornered?

Her mind raced, seeking a solution while blows rained down. One foot braced on the lower step, then the other, she retreated carefully.

Halfway down, Márton suddenly kicked out instead.

Agony exploded in Margit's stomach as his boot connected

with brutal force and drove the air from her lungs. In a blinding flash, the sword fell from her numb fingers, and the world spun wildly as she tumbled down the unforgiving steps. Each one struck like a hammer blow, wrenching another ragged gasp through her shattered ribs.

At the bottom of the staircase, she scrambled to crawl away through shrieking pain, elbows scraping against the floor.

A feral snarl rent the air and sent fresh terror through her veins. Teeth bared in a madman's rabid hiss and eyes ablaze like hellfire, he launched at her.

Is it truly going to end like this?

1

'Freckle-Face'

July 1470 – Nine years earlier
Nándorfehérvár (Belgrade), Kingdom of Hungary

Margit planted her feet on the Danube's muddy shore, left leg bent forward and right one a step behind. Under a sky heavy with dark clouds, the dank air always made her nose twitch, but she was used to it now. Away from the main port, this area of the riverbank was her and her mates' playing ground because it was less frequented, except for the occasional fishing boat moored at the rickety wooden pier nearby.

Margit tossed her braid over her shoulder, brushed stray strands of hair from her eyes and stole a glance down her bruised legs, bare up to the knees. Those long skirts had better stay tucked under her belt.

Although not perfectly smooth or straight, her staff was sturdy. She clenched it tight, diagonally across her body; left hand close to her hip and turned inwards, right hand in the middle of the stick and turned outwards.

The Serbian boy opposite was twelve—her age—but stood half a head shorter.

Margit smiled to herself. An easy target.

She had already beaten the other five boys in mock combat.

Their taunts and jeers were reduced to fading whispers in her mind while she waited for the signal, eyes on the prey. Though but a children's game, she would do her utmost to win.

"Go!" the group leader shouted.

Her opponent stepped forward and swung his stick at her head. Margit arched backwards as far as she could bend. The rush of air whipped only a finger's breadth from her cheek.

The boy growled and tried again.

Margit sprang upright to block.

The weapons collided mid-air with a loud crack. Gritting her teeth, she slid her staff across his, swung it in the opposite direction and struck him on the shoulder.

A cry of pain burst from his lips, his feet sliding on the slimy mud.

Perfect!

Bending her knees, Margit swiped the staff against his legs. He lost his balance and crashed on his backside.

A sudden hush descended upon the group of children. At length, the mud-soaked boy got back on his feet, red-faced and with his mouth twisted in disgust. Huffing and mumbling to himself, he retreated towards the group leader and complained.

Margit relaxed her shoulders and thrust her weapon into the sodden ground. Arms crossed and chin raised, she watched the boys form a circle and whisper like conspirators. They would surely conjure an excuse to taint her victory.

"Hey, freckle-face!" the leader called, inciting a roar of laughter from his mates. "Come hither."

She stuck her tongue out. Enraged, he lunged at her. Margit drove her foot up into his groin.

He collapsed in agony, his choked cry painfully high-pitched. "The Hungarian wench must pay!"

Margit curled her lip. He had certainly got his just deserts.

But her satisfaction was short-lived. The boys pounced on her like a pack of hungry wolves.

A slap stung her cheek, then her braid was pulled from behind. A fist collided with her nose. She tottered on the slippery earth, arms flailing and hands searching for something to hold on to. There was nothing.

Her face smacked on the ground, the inside of her mouth scraping against her teeth. The taste of filthy water made her retch. From the corner of her eye, she glimpsed a foot swing towards her. She curled into a defensive ball, hands covering her head.

The kick found her ribs and knocked the wind out of her. She bit down hard on her lip. She would neither cry nor beg.

Thankfully, a woman's shrill-voiced rebuke echoed from somewhere nearby. The boys dispersed; their squelching footsteps faded away.

With immense effort, Margit pushed herself to her knees and gasped for breath. She spat out blood and dirt. How silly of her to think the boys would accept her as their equal. Sure, they tolerated her while she was small and weak; they used her to do their bidding: squeeze through narrow openings, steal things for them or run errands. But as soon as she grew taller and stronger, everything changed.

She clambered to her feet and wiped the blood from her face with her soiled sleeve. The raindrops and the light wind blowing from the Danube cooled her burning cheeks but did not quench the fire raging within. She stomped her foot in a puddle. And cursing this cruel world, she turned at last towards home.

"For the love of God!" Erzsi's hands settled on her hips, her voice pitched high in their native Hungarian. "Have you been rolling with pigs? The stink of you!"

"Cheaters," Margit mumbled, reluctant to meet her god-mother's gaze. "So unfair."

Erzsi exhaled loudly. "How many times must I tell you not to play with those street urchins? You always promise, but the moment I leave the house to earn a living, you skip your lessons and sneak off to the port. What will Endre think of you? Will you look at me, child?"

As Margit raised her eyes, Erzsi paused her rebuke and crinkled up her dainty nose, obviously offended by the smell. "Sit down."

Margit slumped onto a stool by the hearth.

While concern darkened Erzsi's usually bright countenance, she cleaned Margit's face with a wet cloth and stuffed a little ball of wool into her right nostril to stanch the bleeding. "You've inherited your lord father's red hair and passion for the fight. You should've been born a boy."

Margit sighed. She observed the worry wrinkles which furrowed her godmother's face, and the grey-streaked honey-coloured ringlets curling from under her linen coif. Poor Erzsi must have regretted telling her about the misfortunes that befell her family. Since that moment, something had changed inside Margit. Unable to accept fate's unjust treatment, she became angry, disobedient, restless. She constantly picked fights with the boys at the port and often came home with bruises, cuts and even a broken finger once.

How could she not be angry, though? She only remembered glimpses of her earlier life in Sasfészek. According to Erzsi's descriptions, that eyrie of a castle in the mountains of Transylvania sounded like a fairy-tale. Lofty walls, well trained soldiers and, above all, her father's love had kept Margit safe until that fateful night, eight years prior. But now, living in exile amongst strangers who spoke a foreign language, all she had for protection was the rough stone walls and reed roof of this humble dwelling: a former bookbinder's workshop with one room downstairs and one upstairs, given to her and Erzsi out of charity by her betrothed's Serbian grandfather.

"The water's heated now," her godmother interrupted her thoughts. "I'll help you wash."

The rain stopped, and the summer sun peeped through the parting clouds. All clean and smelling like a lavender bush in bloom, Margit left behind the muddy alleys, fishy odours and gruff voices of the port and elbowed her way through the throngs of people, animals and carts as she crossed the gate into the upper town of Belgrade.

But what was the point? She had already missed the Latin lesson. She shrugged her shoulders, smoothed down her kirtle and continued at a slower pace on the hay-sprinkled cobbled streets. Now and then, she stopped to peek at the merchants' colourful stalls, inhale the aroma of freshly baked bread and pies, pet a dog or a horse and try to guess the multitude of languages and accents that crammed the air.

By the time she arrived at her betrothed's house in the burghers' quarter, the tutor was leaving. The man cast her a disapproving glance as he walked past.

Endre stood at the bottom of the porch steps, tying back his shiny blonde hair. His usually sandy-coloured complexion took on a reddish hue as his olive-green eyes narrowed at her. "Where have you been? My father pays good money for these lessons."

Although only thirteen years old and a hand shorter than her, her future husband was so pleasing to the eye that Margit sometimes forgot how much she resented their betrothal, arranged by her late father when she was but four years of age. Perhaps it was Endre's fine features—he took after his Serbian mother rather than his Hungarian father--that made her heart flutter.

Margit cleared her throat to dispel the warm but awkward feeling. "Will you practise today?"

Skirts gathered in her hand, she skipped after him to the back of the house, where an open-air shed served as a combat training area.

Endre pulled a blunted sword from the weapon stand and balanced it in his hands. Then gripping the hilt tighter, he hit a pell covered with animal hide.

How agile he looked! One day, he would certainly become a skilled warrior like his father. Or as strong and valiant as her own father.

How Margit wished to lay hold of such a weapon! Hands clasped under her chin, she stepped towards Endre. "Let me practise with you."

His eyes sparkled with amusement. "You may hurt yourself."

"I've gone past that." She pointed at the dried blood from that morning's grazes on her face.

"Oh, I see." He chuckled. "At the port again, picking fights? Women are not meant to fight."

Margit lunged forward and delivered a hard kick to his kneecap.

The sword fell from his hands. "Why did you do that?" he squealed.

"To show you I can fight." She crossed her arms and turned her nose up.

After several winces and some intense rubbing of his injury, Endre straightened himself. "Very well, freckle-face. My father is in the stables. Let us talk to him."

Margit's balled fists landed on her hips. "Don't call me that! Unless you want your other knee kicked, too."

Margit twined her fingers behind her back and tapped her foot on the straw-strewn floor of the stable. Her eyes fixed on Imre Gerendi—a tall, broad-shouldered man in the fifty-fourth year of his life.

Leaning on the wooden post of his black rouncey's stall and absently scratching his greying brown beard, Endre's father took an eternity to respond to her request. "Out of the question!" he said, at last, eyebrows drawn together, his face stern as a judge announcing a death sentence.

Endre drew close to Margit's ear. "I told you so."

It might as well have been a death sentence. She clenched her hands and scowled at the man. "Why, Imre *bácsi*? I wish to learn." Tears of frustration stole into her eyes. "I must avenge my father."

The man's face softened. "I promised your father I'd look after you. I don't intend to let you come to harm. You're too headstrong, like your poor brother. Do you forget what befell him?"

Margit's arms fell to her sides. Her chest heaved as she fought to swallow the lump that rose in her throat.

"Calm yourself, child," Imre said and patted her shoulder. "You're my dear friend's daughter, and I care for you like my own, but—" His eyes met hers. "As the rightful heir of the Szentimre estate, you must wait another two years until you're wed before we can plead with the king to return your inheritance."

Two years? How am I ever to wait this long?

Margit's exasperation raced to her cheeks.

But before she opened her mouth, Imre raised his hand to stay her protest. "Patience, child! We'll prove your father wasn't a traitor. I promise. Until then, don't draw attention to yourself. After all, your cousin and his wily mother may still be looking for you."

Fuelled by an urge to vent her vexation, Margit poked at Endre's arm, making him recoil. "So, I must marry *him* to take back what was stolen from me?"

Imre shot her a reproachful glance. "It was your father's wish; and the only way you can inherit landed property."

"Because I'm a girl!" Margit spun around, seething at the injustice.

Just then, a male servant rushed through the stable door, sweating and gasping between panicked breaths. "Master!"

"What is it?" Imre said.

"Three men at the port. Looking for you and the young lady. Hungarian. With accent like yours."

Imre's face turned ghostly white. "Transylvanians. From Szentimre, surely."

"Again?" Margit gasped and grabbed onto Endre for support.

"Take her to the cellar," Imre ordered his son. "Don't come out until I return."

He ran to rally the servants while Endre dragged Margit down the cellar steps.

In the damp underground chamber, she fervently clung to him amidst the pungent wine racks, barrels of tangy fermented foods and smoky cured meat.

Margit shivered in the faint rushlight, her mind reliving her ordeal during a moonlit night, three years prior, when she had fled with Erzsi along the riverbank. A hooded figure seized upon her with brutal strength, the white of his eyes glinting beneath his cowl—an image forever branded in Margit's memory.

But just when all seemed lost, Imre appeared and drove the man through with his blade. Blood spurted from the stranger's screaming mouth.

Thankfully, Imre also slew the rogue's companions and threw their bodies into the Danube to be taken by the currents to the sea, far away in another land.

And now, the enemy had found her again.

The meagre light soon died. Moments dragged like years. The cellar's dank walls closed around Margit, awakening unspeakable horrors. Who would protect her if those men bested Imre this time? Was she to cower, waiting to be saved or slain?

If only she could fight!

The trapdoor's grinding flushed fresh terror through her veins. As heavy footsteps descended, Endre shielded her with his body. Breath frozen in her chest, Margit squeezed his arm and peeked over his shoulder.

Lantern light formed menacing shadows on the rough walls until a familiar voice, grave yet reassuring, said, "You can come out."

Imre's tunic was stained—with blood, surely—and he still held his sword. "They'll trouble us no more."

Later that night, Margit sat on her pallet with knees bent and drawn against her chest, staring into the blackness. The echoes of her terrifying experience still plagued her sore head, awakening a wave of unease.

Forbidden from handling weapons and training, how was she to protect herself?

Imre is concerned I might hurt myself?

She snorted.

What nonsense!

She carried the blood of a strong and brave warrior; a man who had defended Hungary against the Ottoman onslaught time and again. She would not hide like a coward. If she could fight, she would deal with any threat. And she would kill Márton and Anna. Yes, they were her relatives; but they had stolen her land and castle by slandering her father. Perhaps they even had a hand in his death. Margit searched her memory, desperate to remember the night of her escape from Szentimre. Only images of fear haunted her mind: candlelight trembling on the walls of a bottomless shaft; the heavy breaths of frightened people; her face buried in a man's shoulder; her tears staining his clothes; cold and dampness penetrating her skin. And then the frantic gallop of a horse as she clung to the same man: Imre, her saviour.

Her knees pressed against her growing breasts as she crouched on the thin mattress, raising another dreaded thought. After her first blood three months prior, her body had started to change. This scared her. She loathed the notion of being treated like other noble women: forced into marriage and a lifetime of obedience and childbearing to secure a husband's protection.

Yes, she was grateful to Imre and Endre for shielding her from the perils of the world. But she would not live like a falcon locked in its mews. There was only one way to avoid that fate. Though she could not become a man, she would do her best to look and behave like one. Having spent so long in the company of those street urchins, she had learned to imitate the male gestures and gait. If Imre had refused to train her, she would practise on her own. And when the right time arrived, she would dress as a boy and escape to her homeland.

Beside her, Erzsi's light snoring issued from her pallet.

At last!

Margit slid off her own pallet, tiptoed out of the chamber and then down the creaky staircase to the ground floor living area. On the bottom step, she paused and clenched her jaw to chase away a sudden doubt.

I can do this... I must do this.

In the meagre light of an oil lamp, she found Erzsi's scissors. Silent as she could, she took off her linen chemise and laid it on the table. Naked and shivering, she measured two hands' width, then cut a strip along the hem. She wrapped it around her bust and tied the ends under her left arm, wincing as the fabric's frayed edges cut into her flesh above and below her breasts.

Satisfied, she looked down her traitorous body.

I shall not let you grow.

2

The Mentor

Margit crept through the town, all her senses on alert. Although the threat to her safety had been eliminated, yesterday's terror still gripped her heart as she cautiously reached the blacksmith's backyard. At the edge of the town and far from prying eyes, it was the ideal place.

No longer would she cower defenceless. Skirts tucked under her belt, she scaled the chest-high wall. The yard stood deserted. After many failed attempts to open the sealed wooden crates which lay about, she found an unlocked one. Half a dozen brand new swords gleamed temptingly within. She picked one and weighed it in her hands. Lighter than her staff, its slick steel blade flashed in the sunlight. A shiver of delight tingled through every limb, quashing all fear of getting caught and being punished.

Margit pulled a crate against the wall. Standing on it for support, she glanced about to check that no one was passing by and then climbed out. Pleased with the success of her little adventure, she smiled to herself and smoothed down her kirtle.

The old oak tree around the corner from the smithy served as her pell. She swung her pilfered sword at it, hitting the right side with the edge of the blade and then switching to the left, just like she watched Endre do. With each strike, her heart pulsed with exhilaration. In her mind's eye, the thick trunk took the shape of those she hated. She did not remember their faces, but it did not matter. One day, she would find them and make them pay.

Sweat trickled down Margit's back. Her dampened hair stuck to her throbbing temples. She paused to catch her breath, muscles aching and burning. The binding around her breasts increased the discomfort. No matter, though, it was only something else she needed to get accustomed to.

But with no one to instruct her, she would need months, perhaps years, of practice. Was she even doing it right? A prolonged sigh escaped her.

After casting the sword aside, she pulled the knife, which was secured under her belt. Surely, she would endure Erzsi's reprimands for destroying the newly sharpened kitchen utensil. But Margit did not care.

Determined to defy all who opposed her, she threw the knife at the tree with all her might. It hit flat against the trunk, bounced and dropped to the ground. She picked it up and continued throwing until, at length, the point of the blade lodged into the bark; shakily, but it stuck.

"Yes!" She raised her clenched fists. It was pure luck, but she had done it.

"Here's the thief."

Margit halted and turned on her heel. "I'm no thief!"

She beheld her mysterious accuser: a short but brawny man with the most prominent cheekbones.

The stranger folded his arms. Surprisingly, his demeanour was not aggressive but one of merriment. His large moustache twitched as curiosity played in his narrow black eyes. "I pity that poor tree."

Long leather apron, smoke smudges on his face, tools hanging from his belt... Margit slapped her forehead. Of course, he was the blacksmith.

He retrieved the sword while paying her an accusatory look.

"I only borrowed it," she muttered.

With puckered lips, the man examined every inch of the weapon. "You scratched it. Will you pay for the damage?"

Embarrassment stung Margit's cheeks. "Of course. I'm no rascal."

Seemingly satisfied with this promise, the blacksmith inclined his head in her direction. "A girl who wants to fight. How odd."

Only now did Margit notice his heavily accented Serbian. Imre bought swords and axes from this man, and she remembered him saying the blacksmith was a former Ottoman prisoner who had fought in the siege of 1456.

A great notion sprang into her mind. "I can fight with the staff. But I want to use proper weapons. You were a soldier before. Will you teach me?"

Without saying a word, the blacksmith walked towards the tree and pulled the knife out. He returned to where Margit stood and threw it with a fluid movement, sinking it deep into the trunk.

"Deadly!" Margit shrieked and clapped her hands.

"I served the great Sultan Mehmed for many years."

Her jaw dropped. "Really? Do you not miss the soldier's life?"

"No." He chuckled. "I'm too old now, and I've a son to look after."

At that moment, a boy appeared from around the corner of the yard wall. Slender, olive-skinned, with short black hair; around

Margit's age, perhaps a year younger?

"Anyway," the man said, "my name is Ahmed. And this is my son, Adnan."

The boy stood beside his father, grinning at her.

"Margit." She gave the young lad her best indifferent stare.

"A Hungarian name?" Ahmed said.

She nodded but revealed nothing more. "So, will you teach me how to fight with a sword? And how to throw a knife?"

The man's face turned serious. "No time. Much work to do."

Margit clasped her hands in front of her face. "Please. I shall pay you."

Just as Ahmed shook his head, the boy tugged at his father's sleeve.

"What is it?" The blacksmith leaned towards his son, who whispered in his ear. "That's what you wish, son?"

Adnan bobbed his head eagerly.

The man, however, frowned. Switching to what Margit guessed was the Turkish language, he spoke to the boy in an abrupt tone. But his son continued to plead until Ahmed relented and turned to Margit. "Very well. Adnan also wants to learn, so I won't take your coin. Come back tomorrow."

***

The interior of the forge felt as hot as the fiery mouth of a dragon. Rivulets of sweat streamed down Margit's brow. Despite the ear-splitting noise, she stood mesmerised, watching Ahmed transform a plain piece of red-hot metal into a thin, deadly blade.

"Father's a skilled craftsman," Adnan shouted into her ear. "I'm learning, too. I'll be as good."

With a wave of his hand, Ahmed signalled for them to go outside.

Once in the yard, Margit crossed and uncrossed her arms several times and paced to and fro, fiddling with the strings of her coif. But it was not just impatience for the smith to finish his work that made her restless. Glued to her, the boy's chestnut eyes followed her every move while a giddy smile played across his face.

"How did a soldier become a blacksmith?" she broke the awkward silence.

Adnan's head jerked as if someone tossed cold water at him. "Ummm.... He...he was captured in the siege. My Serbian grandsire bought him as a slave to help in the smithy. Father learned the craft so well that my grandsire freed him and let him marry my mother."

"Marry your mother? Even though he's an infid—" Adnan's glare made her swallow her words. "I mean...from a different faith."

The boy's expression softened. "Yes. He makes weapons for the city guards. They need him, so they let him keep his faith. And me too."

"Oh?" Margit twitched, a little uneasy. "You are not Christian either?"

"No. My mother was, but Father wished me to follow his religion."

Tension spread over Margit's shoulders. Should she trust these people? They seemed kind, but they were still strangers. And *infidels* too. She felt bad for using this word, but that's what Erzsi and Imre called anyone non-Christian before hurriedly crossing themselves.

In any case, Margit was only interested in learning to fight. She would keep her new friendship secret. Otherwise, Erzsi would lock her in the house.

At that moment, Ahmed appeared, holding two wooden swords. "I made them for me and Adnan, but you can have this one."

Margit snatched the weapon and swung it around eagerly, following the movement with her body. It whistled through the air until she tripped on her skirts. Weapon dropped, her outstretched arms broke the fall but stung with pain against the hard ground. A burning flush spread over her cheeks as she scrambled to her feet.

"You can't fight in woman's clothing," Ahmed stated the obvious.

Margit bit her lip and straightened herself. She grasped the hem of her kirtle and underclothes and thrust them under her belt.

Adnan's mouth dropped, his eyes nearly popping out of their sockets.

"Cover yourself," the blacksmith said sternly and blocked his son's view with his hand. "I only show you the moves today. Tomorrow, I give you boy's clothes for lesson."

***

Margit strained her eyes, tugged at the string of her coif and bit the top of her stylus, trying to solve the mathematical problem the tutor had assigned her and Endre. The shaft of sunlight reflecting on the polished surface of the table kept moving farther away. She writhed in her chair and swung her legs back and forth. It was taking so long to finish this accursed exercise.

The day before, Ahmed had shown her a mounted archer's beautifully crafted recurve bow, made of wood, bone and sinew. The thrill of touching it made her heart skip. Her mentor often spoke longingly about his younger years with his nomadic Tatar tribe, when he had mastered horseback archery and knife-throwing. That was before the Ottomans raided his camp and took him prisoner. But his fighting skills had saved him from slavery and secured him a place in the Sultan's army.

Because Margit had been such a diligent student for three entire weeks, Ahmed promised to show her how to use the bow that day. Her mind flooded with thoughts of only this.

"Finished," Endre announced, his face beaming with pride.

Margit eyed him with equal measures of envy and admiration. He was always the clever one, paying attention to his tutors and absorbing every bit of knowledge.

She craned her neck to steal a glance at the boy's wax tablet, but he lifted it from the table and handed it to the tutor.

The man read silently and nodded. "Well done, young master! Now, let us see your answer, young lady."

Grimacing, Margit turned her incomplete calculations over to him.

The tutor shook his head. "Ah! Let me explain it to—"

"You need not! I must go. I have an errand to run for my godmother." She jumped off the chair and hastened out of the room.

Scarcely had she descended the stairs to the entrance hall

when Endre grabbed her from behind. "You're a terrible liar, Margit."

Heat rushed to her cheeks. She yanked her arm from him. "What do you mean?"

His brow frowned in ironic disapproval. "You must do an errand for Erzsi?"

She inclined her head, quizzically.

Endre's frown turned into a smug smile. "Have you forgotten today is Wednesday? Erzsi is here to help my mother and grandmother with the spinning and weaving. Let me ask her about that 'errand'."

Stupid me!

Ensnared by her own forgetfulness, she spat out the next words which came to her mind, "I meant I must do some chores in the house."

Endre did not look convinced, but Margit did not care. Her mind was elsewhere already.

The summer breeze rippled across the vast golden fields of wheat to Margit's left. To the right, distance dwarfed the lofty walls of the city. The flat, barren land in-between still bore the scars of a battle which, although long gone, had not been forgotten.

Margit ran her hand along the bow, feeling its smooth curves and the polished bone plate in its centre, where the arrow would rest. Five paces ahead, a round target stood on a wooden tripod, its centre marked with a black circle.

Under Ahmed's keen eye, Margit held the bow in her left hand, arm stretched out, and slowly raised it. Beautiful as it was, it was also difficult to draw.

Deep breath. She pulled the string, yet it barely moved. She tried again. "It's so tight! My fingers hurt."

"I'll help you."

Ahmed placed his thick hand over hers and pulled back with her. The glare of sunlight blurred Margit's vision. The light air brushing across her face conjured a mysterious presence to her side: that of a tall and powerful knight in armour.

Margit shivered. Who was that man? Her father, perchance, approving her actions? If so, his strength and skill seemed to take possession of her miraculously. The string moved easily until it anchored at the side of her mouth. Margit blinked. Her eyes cleared, and the image vanished.

"Now, release," Ahmed whispered.

The string sprang forward and whipped against her forearm. "Oooh!"

Adnan burst out laughing.

Margit rubbed her arm. "It's not funny."

"Trust me, I know," the boy said. "Let me see."

He took hold of her wrist and folded back her sleeve. Gently and lingeringly, his fingertips trailed along the red mark on the inside of her forearm. "Don't fret. It'll heal soon. It won't leave a scar."

Despite the boy's impropriety, Margit sighed. Whether owed to his light touch or the breeze caressing her skin, the burning pain slowly subsided. She was in no rush to snatch back her hand.

"I was also hurt the first time," Adnan said, his face reddening as he finally let go of her arm. "Father wants to teach us a lesson. You need a—" He turned to the man, "What's it called?"

"Leather bracer, son." After fixing the boy with a stern look, Ahmed pulled one of those from the sack lying by his feet.

Again and again, Margit practised drawing and releasing the string until she could do it by herself albeit using the more secure three finger draw instead of the thumb grip favoured by the Tatar and Ottoman archers.

"Now I show you to nock arrow and aim," Ahmed declared, looking pleased with his pupil's progress.

By the time they returned to the smithy, the sun was on its descent, and church bells called worshippers for vespers. Margit smiled as father and son walked ahead of her, driving the mule and cart with the equipment into the front yard. Although she had known them for only a few weeks, they had become more than just her training companions. They were, indeed, her friends.

Oh, I must change into my kirtle. Erzsi can't see me in these clothes.

She started after them but barely took two steps before someone grasped her wrist from behind.

Margit spun around, coming face-to-face with Endre.

He frowned, his lips pressed into a thin line. "So, this was your 'errand' and your 'chores'."

Margit exhaled through clenched teeth. "How did you know to find me here?"

"I followed you after you left my house. Then I waited until you returned."

Of course. That's why he did not raise any objections earlier.

Still clutching her hand, Endre drew closer. "I worry about

you." Despite his serious countenance, his voice was soft and laden with concern. "It's not safe to roam around on your own. What if your relatives send men after you again?" His eyes drifted in the direction of the smithy. "And being friendly with the infidel? My father will be angry if he finds out."

His tight grip hurt her, and she wrested her hand free. "Then make sure he doesn't!"

Dismay grew on Endre's face. "You don't look like a girl anymore. Why are you in a man's clothes? Who gave them to you?"

"Margit, is something amiss?" Adnan's voice startled her. "D'you know this boy?"

He was now standing beside her, eyeing Endre warily. He did not understand Hungarian, so he must have thought she was in trouble.

"Yes, all is well," she replied in Serbian, annoyed at the intervention.

Though she liked Endre, she enjoyed teasing him. Never would she let him treat her as a little girl who needed protection.

"As your betrothed, I must guard your honour," Endre whispered close to her ear, his warm breath tickling her skin in an unexpectedly delightful way.

With that, he turned and walked away.

"He likes you," Adnan said, a smirk playing at the corner of his mouth.

Margit did not know where to look. "What makes you so sure?"

"Easy to tell when a lad has feelings for a girl," he blurted before retreating in haste.

"Feelings? What do you mean?"

Fired by disgust and curiosity, she pursued her friend to the smithy. But he ran from her before she had the chance to speak to him.

A little later, Margit was smoothing the creases on her kirtle and adjusting her linen coif in front of her house when the door swung open. Imre rushed out with a grave expression on his face.

"Greetings, Imre *bácsi*."

No answer. He just hurried past as though he had not seen her.

Margit shrugged her shoulders and stepped inside.

"What's the matter with him, godmother?"

Despite her diminutive figure, Erzsi appeared menacing as she stood with hands on hips. "We need to talk."

Margit cocked her head towards the woman. "Talk?"

"About you sneaking out to fight."

"Of course!" Margit exhaled sharply. "I assume Endre told his father. I should have expected this from the little traitor."

"Don't call him that! He cares about you and is respectful. He could take any other wife, but he agreed to marry you, honouring your father's wish."

Margit's swelling anger infused her clenched fists. "So, must I feel grateful for that?"

"You must stop what you're doing. It's not right for a Christian noblewoman to befriend infidels." Erzsi crossed herself. "And this business about wearing men's clothes and binding your breasts—"

"How did you know about my—"

Erzsi crossed her arms. "I've seen the tattered hem of your chemise and the strips you hide in your trunk at night. Don't take me for a fool. This must stop now."

Margit stamped her foot on the floor. "Damn, Erzsi! You can't tell me what to do. You are not my mother."

The woman's face flashed red. A slap exploded across Margit's cheek, leaving a mighty sting.

"Impudent child!" Erzsi hissed although her eyes brimmed with tears. "You aren't the only one who lost everything when your lord father died. We all saw our lives turn upside down. The moment we left Sasfészek, carrying you in our arms, our safe and comfortable existence was no more. You know how much I toil all day. Cleaning, washing, scrubbing, spinning, weaving, mending—all to put food on the table and make sure you've clean clothes to wear."

Erzsi paused to dry her tears. "And Imre pays the tutors because your father wanted you to have an education and learn how to run your estate. We're both trying to protect you so that you can reclaim your land when the time comes. This is the right way; not swinging swords. A good marriage to a good man who will fight for your inheritance."

Margit bit her tongue, her fingers twisting the fabric of her kirtle. Her godmother had never raised a hand against her before. She must be in so much distress inside.

Erzsi inhaled deeply and looked her in the eye. "Don't you understand? It's not your place to fight. Think of Imre. The poor man has a price on his head for helping you escape. And yet he would still give his life for you."

Margit winced. She brought her hand to her forehead and lowered her eyes. How could she behave so hurtfully to the woman who had cared for her all those years?

Shame upon me.

She flung herself into Erzsi's arms. "I'm sorry, dear godmother. I just resent that my parents made me a girl."

"Your parents didn't 'make' you a girl." Erzsi's voice became calm and comforting. "It was God's will that you were born female. I know it's hard for you, but you must understand that sometimes life can't be the way we wish it to be."

Margit pulled away and grasped Erzsi's arm. "I shall never be rude to you again. But I beg of you, let me continue the training. It's the only thing I love doing in my life. And yes, Ahmed and Adnan follow a different faith; but they are my friends. I can vouch they are good people."

Erzsi looked appalled at these words. She turned away, rubbing her brow. At length, she drew a deep breath and peered at Margit. "Why do you wish to fight so ardently?"

Margit clung tighter to the woman's arm. "To protect myself, of course." It was only half the truth. Her godmother would never accept the notion of her beloved girl taking bloody revenge. "What if my aunt and cousin try to abduct me again? I can't always rely on others."

She searched Erzsi's face for signs of agreement. But the woman's expression remained blank.

"Imre and Endre refused to instruct me," Margit continued. "I needed to find another way. If you are so concerned about my safety and reputation, why don't you accompany me? No one will question my whereabouts if we are together. We shall say we went to the market or to collect herbs or wild fruit."

At length, Erzsi bobbed her head. "Very well. But we must keep it a secret."

Margit's heart leapt in hope. "So, you will let me continue?"

"I'll allow you only once a week. And you mustn't skip your lessons again."

"Of course." Margit let go of her godmother's arm now. "On Saturdays we have no lessons, and Imre spends the afternoon practising with Endre. We can do it then and return before vespers."

Erzsi stroked Margit's cheek while a loving smile graced her face. "I can't say 'no' to you, *galambom*. No more than I could to your lady mother. You remind me of her... Oh, how I miss her!"

3
The Gift

March 1471

The rhythmic pitter-patter of rain on the window reverberated like thunder against the absolute hush that descended upon the office of Endre's grandfather, the city clerk.

The quill fell from Vuk Lazarević's grasp, ink spilling all over the charter he had just begun to write. His blanched face and gaping mouth evinced his astonishment.

"What?" Vuk's normally deep voice come out as a squeal while the thick vein on his forehead looked ready to burst. He pointed at Margit. "She is related to the king?"

Margit squirmed in her seat.

"Her father was a third cousin of Erzsébet Szilágyi, the king's mother," Imre explained.

"You told me she was the daughter of some deceased minor noble who had been the victim of false accusations." After fixing his son-in-law with a ferocious glare, Vuk addressed Imre's wife. "And you, daughter! You deceived me for so many years?"

Dragoslava—Endre's Serbian mother—a slender woman of thirty-five years, still clinging to her youthful beauty, reddened and dropped her gaze to the floor, one hand twitching at her veil and the other squeezing her son's forearm.

Imre stood up. "My lady wife isn't to blame. I asked her to keep quiet. We left my lord's estate on the night he was killed, escaping to save his daughter from her relatives. Her identity must remain secret, for her safety and ours." He pointed at several parchments which lay on the writing desk. "They're all the documents which prove who Margit is. You'll also find the betrothal contract her father and I signed. Now that the children are old enough to give consent and promise to wed in a year's time as her father wished, we need an engagement contract."

Vuk inhaled deeply. The anger ebbed from his face and, at last, was replaced by a broad smile. "So, my grandson is to marry a relative of King Mátyás."

Dragoslava raised her head and exchanged a surprised glance with her husband.

The elderly clerk rose from his desk and approached Margit. Despite his cracking arthritis, he took a deep bow. "I am honoured, Lady Szilágyi." He grunted with the effort of straightening his joints. "I sincerely apologise that the dwelling I provided does not befit your rank. Had I known," he glanced at Imre, "I would have invited you to share my residence. You are most welcome to do so presently."

Margit's face twitched at his formality of speech. Until that day, Endre's grandfather rarely spoke to her. He had accepted the betrothal, though begrudgingly as it did not benefit him in terms of wealth or status. Often, he even complained to Imre about spending money on Margit's education.

"We'd rather leave things as they are," Imre interjected. "At least till we've met with the king, and her safety's been guaranteed."

"Why, Imre *bácsi*?" Margit whimpered, but Erzsi cleared her throat loudly, cutting her short.

It would have been better to live in a proper house and enjoy the comforts of a burgher's life instead of huddling in a tiny converted workshop. That said, in her betrothed's family residence, Margit would have been watched constantly, unable to sneak off and practise with Ahmed and Adnan. The sacrifice was necessary.

"Very well," Vuk said and returned to his desk. He unfurled a fresh roll of paper and picked the quill. "Let us confirm and seal this agreement."

***

The golden evening sunshine of the next day made Margit shade her eyes as she followed Imre to the stables. Her breath quickened in anticipation of her betrothal gift.

It must be a horse. Dear God, let it be a horse!

Endre already had his own chestnut mare, Zora, and Margit was jealous.

Her knees wobbled when the most exquisite animal was brought to her: his coat the purest white; his muzzle the colour of pale flesh. Set on a thin and elegant face, his alert brown eyes regarded her keenly.

"A rare one," Imre said, lead rope in one hand and stroking the horse's forehead with the other. "Some nobleman sold him to pay gambling debts. He was his young daughter's mount." And turning to Margit, his usually stern face opened into a paternal smile.

"Only a two-year-old, so he'll grow up together with you."

"Mine?" Margit shrieked with delight.

"Yes. Already gelded. He'll give you no trouble."

Trembling from sheer joy, she slid her hand down the animal's neck and threaded her fingers through his silky mane. "You are such a beauty; your coat so bright. You shine like a star. I shall name you Csillag."

The horse nuzzled her shoulder, neck and face. The warmth of his breath and the wetness of his nostrils prickled her skin.

"He likes you," Imre observed.

"And I love him already."

She cuddled Csillag's head and kissed him under the eyes. He snorted in response and scraped the ground with his front hoof.

"Will you teach me how to ride, Imre *bácsi*?"

"Of course."

The man beckoned the stable boy to take the horse to its stall.

But while walking away, Csillag looked back at her, like saying farewell.

Margit sighed, her heart melting. "Can I take him with me?"

"Where are you going to keep him?"

"In the storage shed next to the house. Erzsi and I will make space for him."

Imre chuckled. "Are you sure you can look after him?"

"Oh yes, Imre *bácsi*. I shall wash and curry him every day. I shall make sure he is well fed and watered; keep him warm at night with blankets. Please, let me take him."

"And how will you afford all this?"

Margit's heart sank. She had not thought of that. The only grazing land was outside the city. As for drinking water...

Imre squeezed her shoulder. "Don't fret. I'll send him to you in the morn with the stable boy and two servants. They'll help you prepare the shed and set up a water trough. And I'll make sure enough fodder is delivered to your house every week, and that his waste is removed regularly."

"Oh, thank you, Imre *bácsi*."

The man's face became serious. "Come. I've another gift for you. In the house."

Margit followed him, her thoughts still with her horse, the rides they might take, the wind blowing through her hair.

Once inside the house, out of sight and earshot of everybody else, Imre produced a beautifully carved oblong wooden box.

Margit opened it with impatient hands. An ecstatic cry burst from her as she unveiled a shiny cross-hilted dagger, its double-edged blade etched with her family's coat of arms: a mountain goat rising from the flames against three peaks; the sun and moon of the Transylvanian Székely people hovering above.

Her fingers traced the smooth blade and the precious stones adorning the black leather scabbard which rested beside the dagger. How well would this masterfully crafted weapon fit her grip and protect her in a time of need.

Margit had no words as her heart swelled with awe. She threw one arm around Imre's neck, the other firmly wrapped around the box.

"Your father was to give this to you on your wedding day." The man's voice cracked. "Only this dagger and your papers could I grab when we left the castle. It'll help you never forget you're a Szilágyi."

A massive lump climbed to Margit's throat. With the box held tight to her breast, she ran into the garden. She remembered so little of her father; but seeing the dagger brought back a new, though faint, memory of him holding her in his arms. She could still feel the safety of his presence and the love in his embrace. "I shall not let you down, Father." She looked up towards the sky. "You will be avenged."

In the lambent glow of the oil lamp, Ahmed traced a thumb down the flat of Margit's blade, carefully like touching a precious gem. "Beautiful," he murmured.

"Will you show me how to use it?"

Fixed on the etching, Ahmed's eyes narrowed, and his forehead wrinkled as though his mind was caught by a distant recollection. "Where did you find this?"

Margit swallowed back down her sudden apprehension. "Why do you ask?"

"You didn't steal it, did you?"

"No!" She snatched the dagger from Ahmed's hand, placed it back in its box and slammed the lid shut. "It's mine." She wrapped her arms about her precious possession.

"Why are you so angry?" Adnan ventured but shrank back at once, cowering under her fierce gaze.

"Forgive me," Ahmed said. "I don't know the family, but I remember the coat of arms."

Margit's stomach tightened. "You do?"

"An old story. Some other time. You don't keep Erzsi waiting outside."

He waved Margit away, but she let the canvas bag with her

other gifts drop from her shoulder. "Erzsi will not mind waiting. Please, tell me."

Ahmed cleared his throat. His eyes wandered away to times long past. "When Sultan Mehmed besieged Belgrade fifteen years ago, I fought beside Janissaries against Hunyadi's army—"

"General János Hunyadi? The king's late father?" Margit interrupted him, eyes wide open with excitement.

The general was her own father's overlord. Hungary's bravest protector as Imre always referred to him, tearing every time he uttered his name.

Ahmed nodded. "Yes. His defenders trapped us in the town. I killed many but then saw this tall and skilled knight. No shield; just a sword in one hand and axe in the other, slaying Janissaries like untrained peasants." He pointed at Margit's box. "He wore this coat of arms. I thought I must stop him. I attacked. But I never fought anyone like him. By Allah, he had no fear; didn't care if he lives or dies."

He paused, fighting some emotion which seemed to overcome him. "Although shorter, I held my ground." His voice trembled. "I made him angry. He growled and screamed at me. We had a long fight till I slipped and dropped my sword. He slammed the axe on my chest. I fell to my knees, in big pain. He stood over me. I thought my end was near and prayed to Allah. It was an honour to die in battle, but fear froze me. He could take my head, but he stopped. Just hit my face with the axe handle, and I fainted."

"He spared your life?" Margit breathed. "Why?"

"I don't know. Next morning, I was bound with other Turkish prisoners in the square. Place full of soldiers and city people, but everyone quiet. I saw that knight sitting with his men; helmet off, but still wearing the tabard with coat of arms. When women went to him with food and drink, he let his men eat first and then took whatever was left."

"And this was his coat of arms?" Every part of Margit's body shivered upon the realisation that Ahmed was more than likely talking about her father, who had fought in the siege.

"Yes, I swore I'd never forget. I kept in my mind, hoping I'd have a chance to thank him some day. And, by Allah, I'd recognise him even now. So different from the others. So tall, with hair the colour of copper...like yours—"

"He let you live out of respect. Because you were a worthy opponent, and he was an honourable man." Margit slapped her palm against her lips. She had said too much already.

Ahmed stared at her curiously for a moment before continuing, "I watched him encourage the men and speak with respect although he was their leader. And then he looked up to the sky and cried. I swear the tears weren't for pain, but sadness."

A swell of emotion caught in Margit's throat.

Because he had lost his beloved son in the battle.

Ahmed's narration was becoming more and more unbearable to listen to. "I must go!" she snapped. "It's late, and Erzsi is waiting."

She hurried away, box clasped against her heaving chest.

No sooner had she put her hand on the front door than she remembered. How silly of her to storm out and leave her bag there.

She hastened back but stopped in her tracks upon hearing Ahmed speak to his son behind the heavy cloth-hanging, which separated the workshop from the living area. "Will you promise to protect her?

"Yes, Father. But why?"

"I think she's related to the knight who spared my life. I prayed for so long to repay his kindness. And now, Allah sent that blade as a sign."

Bag forgotten, Margit rushed into the street and ran all the way home, ignoring Erzsi's pleas to wait for her.

She went straight to bed, still clutching the box. An eerie feeling stirred in her heart. Her father was a warrior, trained to kill the enemy; yet he had let Ahmed live in such a fierce battle. And, out of hundreds of men, why Ahmed? The only one who was now willing to help her. An accident of fate, perhaps? Or God's plan to determine her destiny before she even came into this world?

4

The Runaway Bride

April 1472

A year flew by with the swiftness of a fleeting dream. The seasons changed, but Margit paid little notice. Studying, helping Erzsi with house chores, taking riding lessons from Imre; her life flowed uneventfully. She seized every opportunity to exercise her body, either at home or in the fields outside the city with Ahmed and Adnan but always under Erzsi's supervision.

By the time she turned fourteen, she had developed enough strength to use the bow on horseback. And she was proud of her knife-throwing skills. She would hit the target eight out of ten times. Her swordsmanship was still lacking, but she more than compensated for that by speed and flexibility, thus evading the strikes of her opponent and kicking his feet from under him.

All this kept her mind occupied, and she did not think about the wedding until the week before, when Erzsi sat her down and talked to her about the conjugal relations between husband and wife. As Margit listened, embarrassment scorched her cheeks, and she squirmed as if an army of ants were crawling under her skin. Although she liked Endre, she shuddered at the thought of exposing her body to him.

And what would he think of her? Instinctively, she pressed her hands against her chest. With all those fair noble maidens parading in the city, dressed like bright flowers and flaunting their unblemished faces and full bosoms, would he desire her at all?

Leaving Erzsi mid-sentence, Margit rushed to the bedchamber and slammed the door shut. She slumped on the pallet and buried her face in her hands. Apart from the anxiety she felt about her spindly body, she still resented being forced to marry. She would lose her freedom, caged into a certain behaviour appropriate to a married lady. The notion that her husband would dictate what she could or could not do in her life made her blood turn hot and cold. Surely, Endre would be vexed if he found out she had been training secretly. But what Margit dreaded most was that she would never have the opportunity to take revenge on the people who had caused her father's death. Imre and Endre would try to resolve this in a peaceful way, by pleading with the king on her behalf, while all she wanted was to confront her deceitful relatives head-on and administer the punishment they deserved herself.

"What's the matter, child?" Erzsi called through the door.

The pressure on Margit's chest became unbearable. She stood up, flung the door open and pushed her way past her godmother. "I can't breathe."

She hurried downstairs to grab her bow and arrows.

"Where are you—" Erzsi's shrill voice was lost behind her.

In the street, some distance from home, Margit inhaled the freedom she was about to lose. She hung the bow across her back and clenched the quiver in her hand. She had left her belt in the house, and she still wore her kirtle, but...

Never mind.

There was only one place she wished to be now.

The familiarity of the forge's smells and Ahmed's voice brought some comfort to Margit's heart. She drew the cloth-hanging to the side. "Let us go for train—"

At the sight of Adnan shaking his head in a panic, the words drowned in her throat.

Another man stood in the smithy. Although he had his back to her, Margit knew exactly who he was. Gasping, she staggered backwards.

The man turned around. His face flushed—from surprise or anger, she did not know. "Margit?"

She gulped. "Imre *bácsi*."

His eyes narrowed, penetrating her like a fiery dagger. "What business do you have here?"

Ahmed lowered his head, and Adnan covered his mouth with both hands.

"You're still friendly with them?" Imre's voice clapped like thunder. "You disobeyed me?"

Margit shrank back, clutching the quiver against her chest.

The crackling sound of the furnace increased the tension.

Imre turned his ire to Ahmed. "How dare you?"

"I apologise, sir. But I assure you she's been treated with respect."

"And I assure you I'll never give you my business again!"

Imre grabbed Margit by the hand and dragged her away.

Margit's wrist throbbed. Tears burned her eyes, but she fought them back. She hung her head in shame as people paused in the streets to watch her being hauled along like some animal led to slaughter.

Once back at the house, Imre slammed the door behind them and shoved her into the living area.

"What are you doing?" Erzsi shrieked, rushing down the stairs.

Imre stayed her approach with an abrupt move of his arm. "Did you know about this?"

Erzsi's face turned crimson. "About what?"

"That she still befriends the blacksmith and his son after I warned her not to? And that she trains to fight?"

Margit let her bow and quiver drop to the floor. Despite the searing pain in her chest, she would not let Erzsi suffer for this. "I am to blame, Imre *bácsi*. Godmother didn't know."

Imre whirled around. Never had Margit seen him like this: face redder than the forge's furnace, eyebrows jumping up and down, his bearded jaw snapping like a wolf's bite, spittle flying in all directions as he delivered his angry speech.

Margit averted her eyes and sank her teeth into her bottom lip. The throbbing sting, which came with the taste of blood, and her frustrated heart thudding in her ears blocked most of Imre's voice; yet some of his words still got through: 'shame', 'ungrateful child', 'fraternising with the infidel', 'disgrace to the family name'...

Then silence descended, disturbed only by Erzsi's intermittent sobs.

"I'm sorry for what I have done," Margit mumbled.

"You'll be punished," Imre boomed. "And as for this—" He snatched up the bow and drew his dagger.

Margit's heart faltered. "No, Imre *bácsi*, I beg you!"

Alas, the man cut the string and then stepped on one end of the bow while pulling hard at the other. Unable to break it in this manner, he snorted and threw it into the blazing fire in the hearth, together with the arrows.

Margit lunged forward, desperate to save her only form of joy from the flames, but Imre seized her arm and flung her down to a stool beside Erzsi.

After some moments of angry silence, he exhaled sharply. "Forgive my harsh words and actions. But there's a burden of responsibility that comes with noble birth." He leaned close to Margit. "You can't do as you wish. Do you understand that?"

Margit's dream of freedom perished in the same fire which now devoured her beloved bow and arrows. Despite the tears stinging her eyes, she restrained herself. Her noble blood dictated that she would remain dignified and not show weakness in front of her father's most trusted knight.

During the hours that followed, Margit lay motionless on her pallet. Her mind drifted into nothingness, away from the world around her. Erzsi's knocking on the door, entering the chamber and talking to her felt like a soft murmur lost in the vastness of space.

But after her godmother retired to bed, the events of the day and her dreaded upcoming marriage rushed back and swirled in Margit's head like a dizzying whirlpool until she could bear it no more. Her stomach churned. Bile rose and burned her chest. Her throat constricted as the invisible hand of her looming fate choked her.

I must not succumb. I must escape... Now.

Heart racing, Margit listened for Erzsi's soft snoring. As she slipped out of bed, a loose floorboard creaked underfoot. She froze, straining to hear if Erzsi would stir. The woman mumbled and turned in her pallet. Paralyzed with dread, Margit breathed again only after her godmother's snoring resumed. She tiptoed out of the chamber and closed the door with only a light click.

Downstairs, she donned her male clothing in the dark, silently cursing each fibre that refused to slide soundlessly over her limbs. At last dressed, she looped her father's dagger and her coin pouch on her belt and stole out of the house. Holding her breath, she hung for every sound. A dog barked in the distance. Shuffling footsteps nearby made her back into the wall with a gasp.

When silence fell again, she entered the adjacent shed to find Csillag munching his fodder. He greeted her with his usual nuzzling her shoulder.

This affection momentarily drove away all despair. "*Kedves Csillagom*," she murmured. "You and I shall have a great adventure."

As soon as she saddled him, the horse whinnied uneasily as if sensing her intentions, but she caressed his neck until he settled.

Under the cover of her cloak and swerving to avoid drunkards and other characters who lurked in the darkness, Margit pulled Csillag behind her until she reached the smithy.

She stood below Adnan's bedchamber and threw a pebble at his window.

No response.

She threw another.

At length, the shutters creaked open, and the boy stuck his head out, all yawns and rubbing his eyes. "What are you doing here at this hour?"

"Come down now!"

He was with her presently, pulling a woollen tunic down over his shirt and breeches as he approached. "What's the matter?"

Margit drew him away from the door. "I'm running away and came to say farewell."

"Are you out of your mind? You'll anger Master Imre even more."

"Never mind him. My wedding is next week, but I don't wish to marry."

Adnan stood frozen like a statue. But no sooner had she mounted the horse than he rushed forth and gripped her wrist. "Wait!"

"Let go of me!" she hissed. "You can't stop me."

He released her. After some brief deliberation, he said, "I'll go with you. But let me collect a few things first."

"What?" No, he could not come. She intended to escape alone. Yet it would be wise, perhaps, to have him by her side; especially since she no longer had her bow. Who knows what perils she would encounter on her journey? "Very well. Be quick and make sure you don't awaken your father."

Adnan soon returned, carrying a small bundle.

Margit extended her arm to help him climb onto the horse behind her.

Through the sleeping lower town they rode. The clopping of Csillag's hooves on the cobbled streets and the growling of cats fighting for discarded scraps in the fish market were the only sounds which disturbed the silence.

When they arrived at the port, they found it bustling with people queueing to board the barges: travelling merchants and traders, peasants returning to their villages, messengers, soldiers, priests—all hurrying upstream or across the Danube, eager to reach their destinations.

Margit thrust two copper coins into the hand of a stout Serbian boatman. "We wish to cross the river."

"The two of you?"

"And the horse."

The man measured Csillag with his eyes. "I can't take him. If something startles him, he'll overturn the barge."

Margit produced a few more coins. "I promise he will not do that. He is well-behaved. I shall cover his eyes, too."

The boatman motioned them on with an abrupt gesture and then waved away the rest of the people lining up to board the barge. "We're full. Take the next one."

Heavy with dampness, the wind sent shivers down Margit's back as the barge glided on its slow journey towards the opposite bank. She pulled her hood lower and wrapped the cloak tightly around her. Beside her, Adnan was silent. When she glanced at him, his head had tilted sideways, and his eyes were closed.

What am I doing? I have no plan.

Her hasty escape was fuelled only by defiance of a destiny imposed on her when she barely understood the world around her.

The quivering streak of the moon's silver reflection on the river and the rhythmic lapping of water against the barge gradually lulled her to sleep. She did not know how much time passed, but she jolted awake when the vessel bumped against a wooden pier.

Margit nudged Adnan. "Come on."

They rode north, through hamlets and settlements and then through open countryside.

As Csillag plodded on, Margit felt Adnan's arms slide lower around her waist and his head lean heavy on her shoulder. His soft breath warmed her neck and tickled her skin.

And when Adnan shifted in his sleep, his body hardened against her back, stirring a strange sensation inside her. A flush crept over Margit and turned the warmth of his contact into sweat, slowly trickling down her spine.

She twitched.

With a gasp, Adnan withdrew and relaxed his grip.

As the first light of day seeped over the horizon, Csillag's heavy puffing and snorting worried Margit. "My poor boy is tired. We must stop awhile."

A ruined farmhouse offered them shelter. They would stay here until Margit decided where to go.

"Which way is Transylvania?" she said.

Adnan looked askance at her. "I haven't a notion. But I know it's so far away. Why d'you want to go there? I've heard it's all mountains and full of wolves and bears."

"Because I am from there."

"Oh?"

She had kept her secrets from him for too long. After two years of friendship, he had never given her a reason to doubt his loyalty.

As Adnan listened, his mouth dropped open now and then, and his eyes widened. "Whoa! Twenty thousand acres of land, a town, seven villages, a gold and silver mine, a castle?" He counted these on his fingers as he spoke. "And what's the name of your castle?"

"Sasfészek."

"Sas—what?"

"Sas-fé-szek. It means 'Eyrie' in Hungarian."

He stared at her blankly. "What's an 'Eyrie'?"

Margit threw her arms in the air. "Eagle's nest. You're so ignorant."

"I'm but a peasant to you." He laughed lightly. "Shall I call you 'my lady'?"

"Don't be silly!" She gave him a friendly slap on the head and smiled as Adnan pretended to cower. "It vexes me that the only way I can take back my estate is to marry and let my husband claim it on my behalf."

"But if it's the only way, you must obey."

"I understand that. Yet I do not wish to marry."

"Why?"

"Because my life will change. I shall not be able to do the things I love or be with the people I like."

Before she knew it, Adnan took her hand and gazed at her with dreamy eyes.

A shiver ran through her. "What are you staring at?"

"You're the most beautiful girl I've ever seen."

"Most beauti—seriously?" Margit laughed. "What do you like about me? My red hair or my freckles that everyone makes fun of?"

"Everything," Adnan continued, clearly mesmerised.

Margit froze as his hand cupped the back of her head. He pulled her towards him and set his lips on hers. Gulping, she closed her eyes. Her body felt light, wings sprouting from its sides and lifting her up through the broken beams of the collapsed roof towards the sky.

But the moment passed. Reality dragged her back to the ground.

She pushed Adnan away. "What are you doing?"

He seemed to snap out of the dream. "I'm...so...rry."

"You are supposed to be my friend."

"*I am* your friend. Forgive me." He blushed and dropped his gaze.

Margit fought the stifling air. How could she have been so foolish? Although Adnan's behaviour surprised her, she should have expected it. His face beamed every time he beheld her. He always stared at her with longing eyes. And the way his body hardened as he clung to her when they were riding earlier...

She withdrew to the opposite side of the farmhouse and sat on a mossy rock with her back to him. Whether embarrassed or simply understanding that she needed her space, Adnan did not follow.

Rushing through the frame of a long-gone window, the chilly wind stung her cheeks. Ominous clouds swallowed the morning sun and spread a shadowy cloak over the fields. That single glimpse of the world outside accentuated her own insignificance. The land was vast, the distance unimaginable, the destination unattainable. And despite her willing soul, Margit's body was unprepared, and her mind distracted by the awkward position Adnan had inadvertently put her in.

Or perhaps *she* had put him in this position? After all, she had let him accompany her.

Her journey required a gigantic leap of faith. The unknown

scared her. She was not ready to jump yet.

At length, she forced herself up and returned to him. He still sat there with closed eyes and clenched fists.

Margit coughed for his attention. "I have changed my mind. How ignorant of me to think that all my troubles will be solved by running away. We must return," she said, her heart heavy with guilt as she noticed the distress on the lad's face.

***

The church clock rang for nones when Margit parted with Adnan. She wished to thank him for being by her side during her escape, but they had not spoken at all on their return journey, and the words now drowned in her throat.

After her friend disappeared into the smithy, Margit lingered until Ahmed's furious shouts and Adnan's pleading cries made her hang her head in shame.

Dreading the consequences of her actions, she brought Csillag to the shed and, with shaking legs, entered her house.

Erzsi was sitting at the eating table in floods of tears while Imre loomed over her like a dragon ready to breathe fire. "You should have stopped her, woman!"

"Don't blame me, sir," Erzsi whimpered. "You shouted at her. You destroyed her bow."

"I have returned," Margit bravely interjected.

Erzsi's drenched eyes shot at her. She crossed herself. "Thank the Lord, you're safe, child." She turned to Imre. "I beg of you, sir. Let me deal with her this time."

The man raised his finger threateningly. "Make sure she doesn't escape again. And burn the boy's clothes that she's wearing."

With that, he spun around and left.

Margit could barely look at her godmother, the pangs of guilt already taking hold within.

Erzsi wiped away the tears with the hem of her apron. Margit was expecting an outburst, but the woman spoke softly to her. "You may be a girl, yet you're a lot like your lord father: brave and righteous, but also impetuous and stubborn like a mule. He was always ready to fight; had so much vigour; wouldn't sit still. But unlike you, who only care about yourself, he never shrank from his duty."

Margit winced. "Life has been so unfair to me."

"Life's unfair to all of us, *galambom*. You're your own worst enemy." Erzsi caressed Margit's cheek with maternal fondness. "Your lord father was fortunate to have your lady mother to keep him in check. It's what you need too; an anchor. And Endre can be that. He's respectful, reliable and cares deeply about you. So, give him the chance to be the one who'll keep the balance inside your troubled soul. Trust me, he won't let you down."

Margit sighed so loudly that it threatened to turn into a sob. She ran upstairs and threw herself onto the pallet while a multitude of thoughts struck her mind like arrows. It was difficult to come to terms with the notion of marriage, something that would strip her of her freedom to live life the way she wished.

But, perhaps, this *was* the only way of taking back what she had lost. Perhaps Erzsi was also right in that Endre always stood by Margit's side; her only friend in life—well, until she met Adnan.

By God, he had let her poke him, kick and slap him during her outbursts of temper. Despite herself, she smiled as she relived those scenes in her mind's eye. And how could she ignore his pleasing looks, which dazzled every other maiden when they attended church or strolled in the market?

Yet more importantly, where would Margit be now without the support of Endre's family? Would she have suffered the same grim fate as her father had Imre not whisked her off before her aunt and cousin laid their hands on her? Even if her relatives had not killed her back then, they would have locked her in a convent for the rest of her life or married her off to some stranger—a much older nobleman perhaps, who would only use her to preserve his bloodline.

Though her freedom was limited, she was still alive and healthy because of the sacrifices of those who loved her as their own and indulged her every wish. They had every right to feel betrayed now. Because, by her foolish act of running away, she had insulted them all. She must make amends.

Relieved at this realisation, Margit unhooked the dagger from her belt and ran her fingers along the scabbard, feeling the glassy smoothness of the precious stones and the evenness of the soft leather. Apart from his blood which flowed in her veins, this item was the only part of her father that she still possessed.

I shall honour your wish, Father. I shall wed Endre.

But would she ever love him?

5

The Wedding

Margit stood quietly in the solar of Endre's house, her eyes fixed on the brightly coloured hunting scene depicted in the wall-hanging opposite her. For a moment, she imagined herself in the stag's place: pinned onto the tapestry like a trophy, trapped between hounds and men, resigned to a dark fate. The air brushed cool along her collarbone although she was wrapped in her dark-green woollen gown—open at the bust to reveal the elegant embroidery on her chemise—its fabric gathered around her narrow waist with a brass-buckled leather girdle and flowing in folds down her long legs.

She raised a hand to her throat. Even though she was not facing certain death like the stag, the heaviness of the marriage bond burdened her mind and made her strong body struggle against the weight of her clothes.

"It matches the colour of your eyes perfectly," Erzsi said, stepping in front of Margit. "It's worth the countless hours I spent weaving your gown and embroidering your chemise. You make the fairest of brides—" She broke off to wipe away the tears. "Now, sit down and let me tidy your hair. You've grown so tall already."

Margit absently obeyed as though her mind and soul had abandoned her body. She grimaced as her godmother pulled on her hair and plaited it into a single braid. With smiles of delight, Erzsi coiled the braid inside a beaded caul, fastening it with hairpins at the back of Margit's head.

"One last thing," the woman added.

There came a mist of sweet lavender scent. Margit sneezed. Her godmother giggled. "God bless you, child!"

A knock on the door interrupted them.

"Oh, it's time already, *galambom*," Erzsi said.

Margit rose, smoothed down the creases of her gown and squared her shoulders. "Enter!"

Dressed in his finest, Imre approached. His broad smile mingled with astonished pride. "Why, I see Erzsi has worked a miracle here."

Margit felt a rush of blood on her cheeks. Although she had never received such a compliment from a grown man, she could not help but twitch an eyebrow at the notion that miracles needed to be worked upon her just to be presentable. But then she had never put on such beautiful clothes. Perhaps there was something of worthiness in femininity. She bowed her head. "I thank you, Imre *bácsi*."

He lifted her chin and gazed into her eyes. "Bright green like your father's. The same spark in them." He withdrew his hand but continued in a trembling voice, "And you have the grace of your lady mother, God bless her soul. Had your parents lived, they'd be proud of you now."

The pale sunbeams streaming through the window grew brighter. A wave of warmth surged in the chamber, enveloping Margit in an invisible, protective blanket. It comforted her heart and dispelled her earlier feeling of gloom. A sign from her parents' spirits, perchance, that her future would be as bright?

Her chest heaved. The clothes no longer weighed her down in spirit or strength. She was a noble lady. Such heavy, intricate garments now only added to her power.

Imre extended his hand. "Come, my child. They're all waiting for you."

Margit placed her hand in his and descended the staircase.

At the main hall, she paused, her heart climbing to her throat. Before her, the gathering resonated with whispers of anticipation. The dining table and chairs had been moved against the wood-panelled wall at the back. Rose-scented beeswax candles—specially made for the occasion—burned in the iron sconces, effusing a warm glow about the room.

In the centre, next to a lectern and open prayer book, the elderly Catholic priest conversed with Endre's grandparents in low tones while the house servants gathered in a circle, chirping and chattering like a flock of warblers.

Deep breath, and Margit stepped forward. Her entrance produced a sudden hush and sent everyone scurrying to their respective places, except for Dragoslava, who still fussed about her son's appearance, brushing invisible specks of dust from his clothes and tidying his hair. Imre cleared his throat loudly, startling her. She withdrew her motherly attentions at once and moved to stand by her parents.

Resplendent in a thigh-length red doublet of silk brocade, low-slung leather belt, black joined hose and buckskin ankle boots with brass buckles, Endre cut a striking figure. As he took her hand, Margit inhaled sharply. An unfamiliar thrill coursed through her. Grateful that their assembly was small, limiting public view of her anxiety, she exhaled slowly to compose herself.

In front of the priest, the couple kneeled and squeezed each other's hand. Margit felt Endre shake slightly. Curious, she stole a glance, just long enough to glimpse his flushed face and lopsided grin.

He seemed happy.

But what about her?

All composure evaporated. Doubt and apprehension jostled with the earlier elation. A giant, phantom-like hand pressed hard against her chest. Her heart thundered like a galloping horse, ready to spirit her out of this chamber; out of this prison called marriage.

Dizzy from the fight within, she sought comfort in the familiar faces around her. Every smile, however, flashed like a distorted grimace; teeth turned into the sharpest fangs.

Riddled with panic, her mind muffled the priest's words. Her hand slipped out of Endre's grasp.

"The ring," her husband said, thankfully dissolving the ominous images.

Teary-eyed Imre gave his son the little box, its lid open to display a gold band with the initials of the couple's names carved on the inside.

Endre took her hand again.

Margit's chest swelled as he placed the ring on her thumb, saying, "*In nomine patri.*" Then on her second finger "*et filii*"; and at last letting it rest on the middle finger, "*et spiritus sancti. Amen.*"

Barely remembering the rehearsal of the day before, Margit stuttered her line, "I...take...take you...as my...my husband." To which Endre eagerly replied, "I accept you as my wife."

She bowed her head, staying her racing heart. It was done now. They were wedded. Only death would separate them.

After the priest's blessings and the modest feast flitted by, the couple went outside and sat on a wooden bench, away from family and servants. Margit breathed in the sweet smell of the roses growing against the fence.

"Are you pleased, dear wife?" Endre spoke softly in her ear, his warm breath brushing across the skin of the neck.

Wife. The word and the weight of commitment it carried still frightened her. She shrank back. "Yes, of course."

"I swear I shall love, honour and protect you for as long as I live." He took her hand and held it against his chest. "Shall we be together as husband and wife? My house is yours now, and so are my heart and soul." He blushed as he uttered these words.

Margit twitched. She withdrew her hand and stood up. How could she preserve her independence without insulting her husband?

A shadow of concern darkened Endre's face. He rose too, peering at her and searching her eyes for the answer she had not given.

Margit took a deep breath while contemplating her next action. The boy was obviously smitten with her. Perhaps she could use her charm to make him see her in a different light.

She wrapped her arms around his neck and kissed him on the lips.

Endre did not react at first. But as she pulled away, he put his hands on either side of her face, drew her back towards him and reciprocated in a much more intense manner.

Confused as she was, Margit knew the difference between the way she felt about Endre and Adnan. Sharing a kiss with her friend was sweet while now her body was overwhelmed with a kind of excitement she had never experienced before.

At length, Endre let go. They both gazed into each other's eyes. He coloured again and looked away as if to disguise embarrassment.

Struggling to overcome the unexpected conflict, Margit pondered. Her kiss was meant to enchant him and bend him to her will; yet her own feelings now threatened to taint her power. But in the end, her determination prevailed. "If you truly love me, you must respect my freedom."

His eyebrows shot up. "Your freedom?"

"I am not ready to share a bed with you," she continued. "I wish to remain in my house until we meet with the king and resolve the issue of my inheritance. I shall not rest until my father's name is cleared, and I can face you without shame."

Endre's eyes narrowed. "Is this the *real* reason?" Receiving no answer, he leaned closer. "Or is it because of the blacksmith's son? Don't take me for a fool. I knew you were practising in secret a long time before my father caught you."

Margit gasped. "You knew? And yet you didn't tell him?"

"I understand it's your heart's desire to take revenge on those who wronged you." He exhaled sharply. "So, I looked the other way. But tell me: do I have any reason to doubt you?"

Margit rubbed her neck nervously. "No, you have nothing to fear. When I ran away, Adnan followed me because he wished to protect me. I only think of him as a friend; a training companion. You are my husband, and I shall never betray you." She turned her eyes towards the heavens. "I swear on God's name." And then she looked at Endre again. "You must trust me."

He fell silent, his face hardening as he clearly deliberated. "Very well. I can't say 'no' to you." His expression lightened. "Because if I do, you will kick me in the knee; or worse."

Laughter now dispersed the disaccord.

However, Endre's countenance turned serious once again. "Still, you are a wedded lady now. You can't be seen alone in the company of other men. If I allow you to reside apart from me, do you pledge to cease training with the blacksmith and his son? If you do, I promise I shall convince my father to let you practise the art of war with me instead."

His words rang like the sweetest melody in Margit's ears. She flung herself into his arms, almost knocking him to the ground.

6
Setback

Although the snow had long stopped flurrying down from the grey sky, the lingering frosty wind penetrated Margit's body. She pulled the thick woollen mantle closer around her shoulders. At least, her head was warm in the marten fur hat.

She was grateful that, notwithstanding Endre's protests, Imre had allowed her to cut her hair to just above her shoulders and dress in men's clothes, which were much more comfortable for riding.

Despite the blanket Margit had spread over his rump, Csillag trembled under her while he plodded on bravely, puffing steam out of his nostrils.

After a wait of several months, she, Endre and his father were finally travelling to Buda. Within Imre's saddlebag lay a valuable document: a permit of entry to the palace, addressed to Vuk Lazarević. Instead of Imre, Endre's grandfather was the one who had requested an audience with Mátyás lest the dark cloud of her father's alleged treachery still lingered in the king's memory.

Margit urged Csillag forward with her heels. Endre often taunted her for not wearing spurs. Like most male riders with their horses, he strove to dominate Zora with hard discipline whereas

Margit and Csillag had become the best of friends. The horse responded well to her subtle ways: soft-spoken commands, whistling, a tap of the heels, a slight tug on the reins, a pat on the neck, leaning her body forward or back. Furthermore, thanks to Ahmed's instruction in mounted archery, Margit and Csillag had formed the same sort of bond people of the eastern steppes shared with their horses for centuries.

Endre glanced back in her direction. "Hurry! You are so slow."

Margit stuck her tongue out but regretted it instantly as the icy air stung it with a vengeance.

"Forward, boy!" she prompted Csillag.

His ears pricked forward at her command. Muscles rippling, he surged ahead to match Endre's seasoned mount stride for stride. Like Margit herself, he seemed to relish the challenge.

"Show him who the master is!" Endre ordered Zora. The mare neighed fiercely and butted Csillag with a sideways jerk of her head.

"Leave him be!" Margit leaned over and boxed her husband on the back.

Endre glared at her with eyes barely visible below the fur hat, which had swallowed his brow. "Barbarian! Do you think you can behave like a man because you are in a man's clothes?"

Margit sat tall in her saddle. "Coward!"

"What? Why am I a coward?"

"Because you make Zora attack my boy."

"Attack? She was only playing with him. And Csillag is hardly a baby."

Imre, who was riding ahead of them, pulled his horse to a halt and turned around. "What's the matter with you two?"

"Nothing," Endre replied. "You need not concern yourself, Father."

He spurred Zora forward, splattering Margit and Csillag with clumps of wet snow, which made her sneeze so hard that she nearly fell off the saddle.

***

After ten days of travelling, the hills of Buda finally came into view. Speechless, Margit reined Csillag in to survey the spectacle before her.

Her gaze lingered on the humble town of Pest before sweeping across to the opposite bank of the Danube. Atop a raised plateau, the palace complex sat in resplendent isolation, its crimson rooftops and spires reaching towards the heavens as if these achievements of Man strove to challenge God's omnipotence.

Behind those fortification walls lay Margit's fate; her only chance to redress the injustice committed against her father and reclaim all she had lost. But while colours and shapes vibrated under a brilliant sun which held central place in the azure sky, dreary clouds still darkened her thoughts. Would she succeed, or was she doomed to fail?

Instead of enchanting her heart, Buda's splendour raised nothing but apprehension and a hollow ache within her—an emptiness as wide as the dry moat separating the lofty palace from the elegant half-timbered burgher houses, municipal buildings, shops and churches.

"Magnificent, eh?" Endre's voice pulled Margit out of her

reverie.

She sighed, still uncertain of what was to come.

"Come along, you two!" Imre called them. "No time to waste."

They stayed at an inn on the Pest side. Imre sent a message to the palace announcing their arrival and requested a date and time to visit the king. When the response came that they would have an audience in two days, he talked to Margit and Endre about how they would introduce themselves.

"King Mátyás has agreed to see Endre's grandfather, so I'll pretend to be him. You'll be my two grandsons, whom I plan to present to the king."

Disguised as young Serbian nobles to elude recognition and the potential danger tied to her father's unjustly perceived disloyalty, Margit and Endre needed to use different names.

It was easy for Endre to pick Andrej, which was simply the translation of his own name.

"I wish to be called Saša. Short for Aleksandar, my father's name in Serbian," Margit said, her chest swelling with determination to honour her father.

Imre bobbed his head. "Very well. I'll enter the audience room alone. Only after I ensure there's no danger, I'll summon you in. Margit, you'll hold the bag with your documents, which we'll show to the king to prove who you are and plead for your case."

Though Margit nodded, the spectre of failure haunted her. What if someone recognised Imre before he met with the king? What if Mátyás still deemed her father a traitor and rejected her request to reclaim her inheritance? But she knew she must steel herself and try.

***

They crossed the Danube in the early afternoon. The last few days of sunshine had melted the ice, and the sailing was smooth.

After she passed the dry moat, Margit craned her neck up at the curtain wall, its imposing shadow mocking her insignificance.

Imre announced them as agreed. A stone-faced guard escorted them, together with a large group of visitors, through a cobbled courtyard surrounded by ornate three-storey buildings. The sunny aspect lifted Margit's spirits. She overheard a visitor refer to a previous king's old palace and ceremonial hall. The sense of history and tradition of the past generations was something she proudly carried within and strove to preserve through her claim.

Beyond a second dry moat and gate, another courtyard. The royal chapel, the library and an elegant edifice with an arched portico filled Margit with shame for dismissing the value of knowledge and art over weapons of war. Even if she reclaimed her estate, would she able to manage it wisely?

The small inner court at the edge of the complex was hemmed in by tall buildings and a thin, spired tower which concealed the sky and brought back the darkness of doubt that tormented her mind.

The guard finally led them to the great hall, which buzzed with people waiting to see the king.

Sitting on a cushioned marble niche by a stained-glass window, Margit admired the intricately carved vaulted ceiling and the flags of the kingdom's provinces, which hung on the walls. Their colours and emblems made the otherwise sombre-looking hall vibrant and cheerful, raising a glimmer of hope inside her once again.

Hours passed. Margit, Imre and Endre now waited alone as the chamber grew darker, and the shadows elongated. The chill in the air ran through Margit. A peculiar sense of uneasiness seized her. A strange portent.

She nudged Endre. "When will they light the lamps? I can hardly see beyond my nose."

He dismissed her with a shake of his head.

At that moment, a lantern-carrying page in royal livery appeared and took them through a series of dimly lit corridors to a small anteroom. At least, it was bright here, with an iron wheel of candles hanging from the wood-panelled ceiling. A stern, formally dressed young man was sitting at a desk next to the door of the king's audience hall, which was guarded by two halberd-wielding soldiers.

The clerk beckoned Imre to approach and announce himself. Feigning broken Hungarian, Imre elicited a smile from the man as well as reassurances that there would be a Serbian interpreter present to make him feel more at ease. After he took their details, the clerk opened the door and signalled that they go in.

"Stay here for now," Imre said to Endre and Margit in Serbian. "I'll summon you anon."

It was not long before shouting was heard from the other side of the door. Margit strained her ears, but the thick walls muffled the voices. Within moments, the guards stormed into the audience room, followed by the clerk.

"Something's wrong," Endre said and grabbed her hand. "Run!"

They dashed out into the corridor and rushed through halls, rooms and more corridors until they ended up back in the small courtyard. Here, they hid behind the base of a fountain just as the soldiers emerged from the building, dragging Imre along. The poor man must have tried to fight them because blood streaked his face.

"What happened?" Margit whispered, hand pressed against her chest to still the jumping of her heart.

Endre raised his forefinger to his lips. "Shhh." As soon as the soldiers and Imre were gone, he clutched his head in his hands. "*Jóisten!* What are we to do?"

"We must hide and think of a plan to help your father."

"Where? How?" His breath came out shallow and wheezing.

Margit raised herself above the rim of the fountain. They were right in the middle of the courtyard. Lights shone in many windows of the surrounding buildings. Eventually, someone would spot them. She bent down again as a pair of servants passed by, conversing in low voices.

Then came men's shouts and the clanking of weapons and armour. "Two boys. Find them! Search the inner court!"

Margit held her breath for a few heartbeats. Which direction did they come from? She and Endre needed to move. She turned to him. Still panting, he sat with chin dropped to his chest. Margit secured the leather bag with the documents across her shoulder and clasped his hand. "Come!"

She all but hauled him behind her. Thankfully, the winter darkness and a heavy mist had enveloped the place, obscuring their retreat.

Among the shadows they crept and crossed an unguarded small gateway into the second courtyard.

"The chapel," Margit said. The bells had not yet rung for

vespers, so there would be no one in there. "Even if they find us, we can claim sanctuary."

Thumping, running footsteps approached. Margit shoved Endre into a narrow alley between two buildings. They huddled together until the group of soldiers hurried past them.

Thank the Lord for the mist!

They sidled along the facade of the next edifice and reached the chapel just as more men spilled into the courtyard.

Forced to crouch at the side of a staircase leading to the entrance, Margit felt her heart was about to leap out of her body. It would be impossible to climb the stairs without being seen.

Endre gripped her arm. "Down here."

Below their feet, steps led to a narrow, trench-like path that seemed to encircle the lower part of the building.

The movement in the courtyard intensified with each passing moment. Margit gnawed on her lower lip. They would never make it into the chapel above. This trench could be their only hiding place.

She firmly held Endre's hand as they slid down the steps and crept along the path, which continued at a gradual slope around the building. At the back, it opened into an enclosed cobbled yard in front of what appeared to be a lower level underneath the chancel part of the chapel.

Margit kept her back against the wall while struggling to calm her breathing. The voices now sounded more distant.

Endre tugged at her sleeve. "Look! A door."

Margit rushed to lift the metal latch. "It's unlocked." She stuck her head in. "Another chapel. An old one. Yet it seems it's still in use."

They entered and bolted the door.

Incense clogged the air as scented votive candles burned on a rack below Virgin Mary's statue. In their flickering light, Margit noticed five rows of wooden benches on either side of a carpeted aisle leading all the way to the front of the altar. "I think we are safe here."

Endre slumped on a bench. He buried his face in his hands, his entire body shaking. "Oh, my poor father! What will they do to him?"

Margit's heart ached. She was the cause of Endre's misery. They had come to the palace because of her. She had prayed that the king would accept them without prejudice, but now...

"Forgive me, husband." Her voice cracked. Though she knew the anguish of losing a father, all words of comfort failed her.

Hence, she glided her hand down the curve of his back and pulled him into an embrace. Dreadful thoughts assailed her mind. The chapel offered them temporary sanctuary. For how long though? What fate awaited them tomorrow?

7

The Plea

A multitude of ominous shadows crept along the walls, their twisted shapes mocking her failure and threatening her with foreboding visions of gloom and destruction. Tenebrous, gnarled arms grasped at her while blood-dripping fangs emerged from cavernous mouths, eager to devour her flesh...

Margit's eyes shot open, a gasp ripping through her throat. She frantically searched the unfamiliar surroundings until her memory returned.

Apart from the faint moonlight peeping through the three stained-glass arched windows in the niche behind the altar, the chapel was in darkness. The damp air pierced her to the very core.

Endre's head lifted from her lap, where it had rested until then. "What's the matter?" His voice was hoarse. He yawned and rubbed his eyes. "It's still dark. Where are we?"

"Shhh!"

Hollow footsteps echoed from above. Someone was descending an internal stairwell.

Margit strove to locate the sound. "From there," she whispered. "It must be another entrance." Grasping his hand, she hauled Endre off the seat and shoved him to the floor beside the row of benches. She, too, dropped on all fours just as a latch clicked, and a door at the back of the chapel creaked open.

The light of a lantern spread its vermilion glow about. Face near to the floor, Margit watched the fur-trimmed edge of a cape trail along the floor while a pair of expensively shod feet—one of them slightly shuffling—approached the rack of the now extinguished candles and stopped there.

Warily, she raised her head above the bench.

The man hung his lantern on a wall hook and used a slip of wood to light the candles one by one, uttering a brief prayer for each of his departed relatives: his heroic father, taken away by the plague; his beloved brother, murdered by his enemies; his rebellious but brave uncle, slaughtered by the Turks; his lady wife, who perished in the pains of childbirth; and his newborn son, taken so soon after entering this world.

And then, after a long sigh, for the living ones: asking the Lord to preserve the good health of his noble mother, whose wise counsel was still guiding him through life, and of his beloved lady Barbara, who presently carried his unborn child.

A swell of emotion caught in Margit's throat. This man had endured as much as she had. And yet he carried himself with such dignity. There was undeniably something majestic about him.

She ducked as the stranger moved away from the rack and prostrated himself before the altar.

Curiosity did not let Margit stay still. Only the delicate fibres of pure silk garments would rustle so richly with his every move. She peeked again. A thought raced through her mind: could he be the one she was seeking?

She squeezed Endre's arm. "I think he's King Mátyás."

"How do you know?"

They both stuck their heads above the benches.

The man must have heard them for he clambered to his feet; his movements hampered by an old injury, perhaps, as he hobbled on one leg before straightening himself and turning to look directly at them. His youthful, crystal-clear voice reverberated in the empty chapel. "Who's there? Show yourself! I order you!"

Margit grabbed Endre's arm and pulled him out of their hiding place. They both dropped to their knees.

"Lord King, we mean no harm," she said in a shaky voice.

The man reached towards his left side; but the absence of a sword in the Lord's house must have disturbed him because he took a step back. "Who are you?"

Margit bowed her head and swallowed hard, struggling to restrain the fear inside her. "We are only your subjects who desperately request an audience with you. We have been treated unfairly and hope that you, being so fair and wise, will see that justice is done."

At that moment, two soldiers entered and rushed towards Margit and Endre.

Margit raised her head in panic. "We are unarmed. We claim sanctuary."

With a wave of his hand, Mátyás signalled to the soldiers to stand back.

Though he approached Margit and Endre with slow, cautious steps, his voice sounded calmer now. "What are the names of you two intruders who dared to disturb my early-morning prayers?"

"I am Lady Margit Szilágyi of Szentimre in Transylvania. A relative of your mother's. This is my husband, Endre Gerendi."

Mátyás grimaced. "I see. You must be Sándor's daughter. And I guess this is the son of the knight I arrested yesterday."

"Yes, Lord King." Margit's heart thrashed against her ribcage. "And we beg you to hear our earnest plea."

The king ordered them to rise. "You are both fugitives. Yet you have the impudence to stalk me thus." He pondered before continuing, "But this is the house of God. Let us go elsewhere and talk."

Pain, loss, captivity, treachery, injury, distrust, war—they all had left their marks on the king's face. Despite his thirty years, a multitude of thin lines furrowed the skin around his eyes as he scrutinised his unexpected visitors.

Unnerved by the intensity of Mátyás' stare and unsettled by the soldiers still watching her and Endre's every move, Margit looked away. To distract herself, she studied the royal library around her: floor-to-ceiling bookcases, some stacked with various tomes and others still waiting to be filled, stood against wood-panelled walls. Elegant archways on either side led to further rooms illuminated by hanging oil lamps.

The king coughed as if to draw her attention. Thus obtained, he folded his arms and tilted his head to one side. "So, you are the daughter of a traitor. And you are the son of a man who aided the traitor and then impersonated someone else to obtain access to me. Give me one good reason not to throw you into the dungeons."

"Our fathers are not traitors!" Margit could not stop herself.

Mátyás turned his surprised stare from her to Endre and spoke with a hint of sarcasm, "I see you let your woman dress in men's clothing and talk in your stead?"

Endre bowed. "Yes, Lord King. My lady wife is the one who was wronged the most."

The king's face now assumed a new expression. "At last! You have a voice," he jested, leaving Endre red with either confusion, indignation or both.

"Speak, young lady," Mátyás then urged Margit.

She cleared her throat. "Our fathers fought for Hungary and all Christendom at the side of your Majesty's heroic father. They both came to this city and cheered for you when you were declared king. They both loved you as their lord and fellow Transylvanian. They would never betray you. Instead, they were the ones betrayed by my cousin, Márton, and his mother, Anna, who, I strongly believe, had my father killed and fed you lies for to take my family's land."

Mátyás leaned on a writing desk, seemingly in deep thought. When he, at length, spoke, it was with a kind of musing tone. "From what I remember, Sándor sent me a vile letter, rebelling against my decision to take control of his mine. And when I sent for his arrest, he killed my officer. Isn't that treason?"

Margit sensed she and Endre may be on dangerous ground. She steeled herself and countered, "It would be, Lord King, if it were true. But it is not."

Mátyás chuckled. "How do you know? Were you there?"

"I was not. But all you have is the word of my relatives, which is only one side of the story. As for the letter, it could have been forged. My father would never disrespect you."

The king let out a sneering-like gasp. "You are certainly very courageous and eloquent, dear lady. But you cannot prove anything either. Your aunt and cousin have been loyal to me. I have no reason to doubt them."

A rush of indignant blood shot to Margit's head. "Lord King," she started, and then the words gushed from her mouth like a torrent, "those whom you call 'loyal' harmed my family. Anna married Miklós, my father's younger sibling. She destroyed their brotherly bond and led Miklós to his death as he attempted to kill my father. All because she coveted our extensive and fertile land and our profitable gold and silver mine. Then she placed her son in my parents' care with false pretences. That child tormented my mother with his impudent and cruel behaviour. And in the end, they both came to our castle on the day my father died. But for his loyal knight's bravery, I would have been murdered, too."

"Lord King," Endre interceded, "that knight is my father, Imre Gerendi. He can confirm as a witness what my lady wife claims."

Margit could hardly breathe. She searched the king's face for the hope she desperately yearned for. But Mátyás only raised an incredulous-looking brow.

Dread slowly pooled in the pit of Margit's stomach. Had she just condemned herself and Endre along with poor Imre? Would she ever be able to have the injustice against her rectified?

Tears stung her eyes, but she blinked them back. Sensing there was no alternative, she tried the only thing that might appeal to the king. She fell to her knees. "Please, Lord King, I beg of you as your humble subject. Neither put my husband in jail, nor keep his father there. They were only trying to help me. I alone shall take the blame. You must punish me. But please, let them go."

Silence.

Margit bowed her head and remained still until the king approached and took hold of her arm.

With surprising gentleness, he raised her to her feet. "How old are you?"

Her own incredulous eyes met his unblinking gaze. "Fifteen, Lord King."

"And you, boy?"

"Sixteen."

"Can you fight?"

Endre nodded. "Yes. My father trained me with all knightly weapons."

Mátyás stepped back, his face opening into the semblance of a smile. "I was your age when the previous king took me prisoner. Only the loyalty of my family and friends liberated me. The last thing I wish to do now is inflict that awful punishment on the two of you, who have demonstrated the same loyalty to your family."

He paused. His countenance hardened, and his eyebrows knitted as he fixed his gaze upon Margit. "If you bring me proof that your father was murdered and that he was not a traitor, I shall examine your request."

To Endre, he added, "I shall set off on campaign soon, and I have need of a second squire. If you prove your loyalty to me by serving me and accompanying me to war, I shall free your father. But until then, expect nothing from me. Is that clear?"

"Yes, Lord King," the two said in one voice.

"Report to me here in the kalends of March," Mátyás ordered Endre before summoning the guards to escort Margit and her husband out of the palace.

8

Husband and Wife

Dragoslava's wailing pierced the air like the cry of a wounded animal. Margit shrank back and covered her ears with her hands. Endre's mother rarely showed any affection towards Imre even though they had been wedded for many years. Margit did not know how their marriage was arranged. Strangely, no one had told her, and, out of respect, she had never asked. But now, the woman's heart-breaking reaction to the news of Imre's arrest felt like a hefty punch in Margit's stomach.

Endre embraced his mother tenderly until the crying stopped. He was a loving son, a gentle soul. Unwilling to get involved, Margit retreated to a corner of the chamber and leaned against the wall.

"I don't wish to look at her anymore," Dragoslava whimpered, pulling away from Endre. She glared fiercely at Margit, eyes narrowed and nostrils flaring. "She is not welcome in this house."

Margit looked away. Caught in the grip of both guilt and anger, her chest tightened.

"You must calm yourself, Mother," Endre said softly. "Margit is not to blame. Father did his duty, honouring his promise to his old friend. He did a noble thing, and we should be proud of him."

But his words did not quell the woman's despair. "And now, I shall lose you too because you must serve the king to secure the release of your father. Why must we bear so much for her?" Unable to restrain herself, Dragoslava burst out crying again, her body convulsing as the words came forth in gasps, "You must...now...go to...war...because of her."

Endre put his hand on her shoulder. "Do not weep, Mother. It's the greatest privilege for any young man to be squire to the king. Perhaps, if I serve him well, he will bestow a title upon me and grant me land. Wouldn't this be an honour to our family?"

Margit winced. Mátyás had not promised to make Endre a knight. He had demanded his service and loyalty as the most exacting ransom for Imre's freedom. That was all.

Quietly, she left Endre's residence and returned to her house with a heavy heart. Not only did she hold herself responsible for what had befallen Imre, she also wondered about her own future. The king had given her the chance to reclaim her inheritance; but without Imre or Endre by her side, she could do nothing.

Yet what frightened her more was her husband's fate. How would he survive in the tough and dangerous world of army life? What if he got injured or, God forbid, died so far away from home and from her?

***

Since her return from Buda, Margit's pangs of guilt grew stronger by the day. And to make her misery even more unbearable, time dashed by, and the dreadful moment of Endre's departure arrived too soon.

He came to Margit's house one cold February evening. He

stood with slouched shoulders and sombre face as he reached for her hands and held them gently as though they were precious treasure.

Margit searched his eyes, but he averted them and sighed heavily.

"A company of merchants travels to Buda in the morn," he said, his voice faltering, his tone resigned. "I shall join them. It would be safer this way."

"God be with you, my dear boy," Erzsi said, with tearful eyes. She bowed and retreated to the fireplace at the far end of the room.

Margit wrenched away from her husband's grasp and flung her arms around his neck. She choked around the sob lodged deep in her throat. Endre had always stood by her and been her friend since she could remember. Guilt aside, it was only now she realised how much she cared about him. Too late perhaps? Only this night left before he departed. The hours would doubtless expire in a single breath.

She glanced in Erzsi's direction. The woman was occupied with rekindling the fire. Margit whispered in her husband's ear, "Go to the shed and wait there. As soon as my godmother falls asleep, I shall come to you."

She found him sitting on a bale of hay, in the darkness, and with only Csillag there to keep him company.

Holding a pair of blankets in one hand, Margit hung the lantern on a wall hook. The dancing light chased shadows around the shed.

Endre rose and approached her, his face stern and his gaze distant.

A sudden ache burned through her chest like a stroke of lightning as she beheld her young husband, who would soon leave her. "Are you afraid of what's to come?"

Endre shook his head. "No. Of course not. I'm only concerned for you."

"For me? You needn't be concerned." She lay a comforting hand on his shoulder. "I can look after myself. I know how to fight, remember?"

At last, a smile lit his gloomy face. "Oh, yes. You can fight."

Margit returned the smile and stepped away. She spread the blankets on the floor, one on top of the other, knelt and pressed her open palms on them. They were not very thick, but at least they softened the hardness of the straw-covered stone floor.

She looked up at Endre. "Come lie here with me."

He obeyed tentatively as if trying to guess her intentions.

Margit lay on her side and took his hand. She rubbed her thumb gently against his wrist, struggling to express in words the powerful emotions which raged inside her. "I regret what happened in Buda. All blame is upon me." Her eyes stared into his. "You're always kind to me, but I have been selfish and distant. Let me—"

Words drowning in her throat, she sat up and started to undress with hesitant and shaky movements. Apprehension washed over her, but she took a deep breath to chase away the fear and the shame of exposing her body, with all its imperfections, to a man for the first time.

Endre's eyes widened, but he quickly clasped her arm and

shook his head. The pitch of his voice rang higher than usual. "You...need not...do this."

Margit recoiled from his grip. "I wish to. Who knows what the future will bring, and when we shall be together again?"

Lying on her back, she emptied her mind of all thoughts and waited until he stripped down to his shirt and lay beside her. Lean yet muscular and tense with readiness, his body appeared as pleasing as his fine countenance.

"I hope you know what to do." She let out a nervous laugh.

Endre's stutter evinced his own nervousness. "Yes...yes...I...I think so."

Margit felt her heart was about to melt. Despite the serious face he had struggled to maintain, he was but a boy—inexperienced, innocent and vulnerable. Yet she willed to submit to him with no regrets and no shame.

With trembling eagerness, Endre lifted her chemise above her waist and glided his hand up the inside of her leg. Margit giggled as his touch tickled her until he reached her most intimate parts.

At that very moment, the iciness of a mysterious draft of air pierced her skin like a frozen blade while an oddly shaped shadow spread across the ceiling, inky dark and with a fluid, undulating presence akin to murky water. Her chest hurt as if someone had stamped his foot on it. Her body jerked, and she gasped.

What was that? What happened to me?

Endre withdrew his hand, surprise and worry tingeing his voice. "I'm sorry. Did I hurt you?"

Margit forced a giggle to hide her embarrassment and to encourage him. "No. All is well."

In desperate need to drown the fear raised by that ghastly

vision, she closed her eyes and let her mind drift away, blending into the surroundings: the sweet smell of hay, the oily odour of the woollen blankets, the patter of rain on the roof, Csillag's snorting and munching, her skin tingling from Endre's hot and deep breaths, the swelling of her own heart, the blood pounding in her veins. Grabbing the edge of the blanket, she crumpled it in her fists and squeezed to ease the stinging discomfort caused by his awkward movements inside her.

The end left him out of breath and her lightheaded and queasy.

After he rolled off her, Margit lay motionless until her stomach settled. At length, sensing him stir beside her, she turned and touched his warm face. "Now we are truly husband and wife," she said, caught between happiness and pride.

Endre propped himself up on his elbow. As he leaned over her, his features softened. He slowly raised his hand and traced the side of her face. "Thank you for this, *szívem*. I shall hold on to these moments while I'm far away and count the days until I see you again."

He gave her a light kiss on the forehead before rising and putting his clothes on.

Margit covered her face with her hands. She wished time stopped; she wished they remained there in this shed, hidden from the world, frozen forever…

By the time Endre closed the door behind him, a terrible void had already started forming deep within her heart.

9
A Time of Pain

The wind swept across Margit's face, blowing the loose strands of hair in all directions. High up, on horseback, her lungs drank in the air of the open country; her body brimmed with a vibrant sensation of freedom.

With Endre gone for three months, Imre in prison and Dragoslava shunning her, Margit found consolation only in her friendship with Adnan and Ahmed. Their warm smiles and familiar voices eased, albeit temporarily, the burden of guilt and sadness which weighed down heavier each day on her soul.

Despite feeling unwell for the last two days with dull pain in her lower belly and intermittent bleeding which had reappeared after an absence of two moons, she would let nothing in the world keep her from training. Her menses had been irregular in the past, so she pushed the more obvious—but unwanted—reason for her current discomfort to the back of her mind, vehemently refusing to consider it.

She urged Csillag forward, squeezing her legs against his sides to keep her balance. Long used to the rattle of the quiver against the saddle and to the snap of the release, Csillag responded with the fervour of a seasoned warhorse.

This new bow Ahmed had gifted her was a masterpiece. Margit held it in her outstretched left arm, hand gripping the leather-covered surface of the handle. Arrow nocked, she secured the string with the bone thumb ring and her forefinger, and pulled until it anchored under her chin. She held her breath. At the slightest angle—to avoid a fletch burn on her hand—the arrow flew towards the round wicker target, thrown in the air by Ahmed.

"Hit!" Adnan shouted and picked up the disc from the ground with the arrow lodged perfectly central.

Riding in a circle, Margit wheeled Csillag back towards her friends. Another arrow nocked. Another wicker disc rose in the air. She hit it on the descent.

"Good work!"

Ahmed's voice reached Margit distorted and distant. Searing agony tore through her belly while panic swelled within like a violent deluge, paralysing her.

What's happening to me?

Her numb legs slipped from the stirrups. The bow tumbled from her grip. Sight blurred, she fumbled for the saddle pommel, but her fingers grasped at air. A howl of anguish escaped her as she crashed to the ground, head thudding against the grassy earth. Before she knew it, darkness swarmed up to swallow the world around her.

***

Margit opened her eyes with a gasp.

Where am I?

Despite blinking several times, her clouded vision only allowed her to discern two female figures in the trembling light of an oil lamp.

"Can you hear me, child?"

Margit tried to call her godmother's name, but her lips barely moved.

The dull ache in her belly drained what little strength remained; her body only limp as leaden exhaustion dragged her into the abyss of oblivion.

Margit shivered, floating in frigid sludge. Above, roiling black clouds choked the sun. Foul fumes assaulted her nostrils as she raised her head. She lay in a fetid swamp, littered yonder with rotting corpses, discarded banners and shattered weapons sinking in the muddy banks. Dread slithered around her heart. Was this a portent of her husband's fate? Or of her own, perchance?

A chilling wind moaned, carrying whispers that swelled into tormenting regrets and guilt until she could bear it no more.

Slimy vines extended from the heart of the mire, coiling around her limbs like snakes. The more she thrashed against their tightening bonds, the more ensnared she became.

Help!

Her heart weakened, its beat almost imperceptible. She was fighting a losing battle.

But then, her liquid prison warmed. Strange shapes and shadows fluttered before Margit's eyes until they merged into the image of a woman, flickering at first, then steadying and dispersing the gloom with a glow of ethereal brightness. Hair the colour of straw and loose down to her waist; her face unblemished and radiant; her eyes blue like the summer sky.

"Do not fear, kincsem. I'm here." Her voice rang pure as the light surrounding her glorious form, serene and reassuring.

"Mama? Is that you?" Pangs of remorse spread inside Margit. "Oh, how I've longed to meet you! You gave me life sacrificing yours... Forgive me...please."

The woman's face opened into a tender smile. "Take my hand, dear child."

Sweating and crying, Margit fought against the constricting vines until she broke one arm free and reached out.

Heavy as lead, her eyelids struggled open. It was night for the oil lamp still burned. Damp clothes clung to her drenched body, and every part of her ached.

"She's back. Thanks be to God!"

Erzsi's voice.

With difficulty, Margit rubbed her eyes. "What happened?"

Her godmother nodded to an unknown woman of middle age, who promptly quit the chamber.

Erzsi then helped Margit sit up and change into a clean chemise.

"Will you tell me what happened?" Margit insisted.

Erzsi stared at her with a furrowed brow. "What did you do to yourself?"

Margit twitched. "Do to myself?"

The woman burned into her a look of conflicted disapproval.

Margit could not, however, read her godmother's meaning. "I don't understand. I was practising in the field, and suddenly I felt sick. I don't remember anything after that."

Erzsi sat on the bed. She hesitated as if struggling to find the right words. "Did you...let any man...have his way with you?"

Margit shuddered. "What do you mean?"

"I mean...did you lie with a man?"

Lips clenched, Margit looked away.

"Speak, child! Who was he? That infidel friend of yours?"

Margit turned back to her with a glare. "How dare you? No, it was Endre. I met him in the shed the night before he left."

Erzsi's expression altered in a blink. "Thank the Lord!" She let out a prolonged sigh. "At least you didn't disgrace yourself."

"Disgrace myself? Why do you say this?"

"Because you...you were with child."

A strange sound escaped Margit's mouth, something between a gasp and a moan. The dreaded thought she had dismissed so rashly was the sad reason for her suffering. She pressed her hand against her belly as the truth sank in, cold and merciless. The physical pain had receded, but anguish coursed through her. "Did I lose—" A lump lodged in her throat, choking her words. But she already knew.

"You shouldn't be out there fighting and jumping on and off horses," Erzsi said gravely.

Margit reeled, the grief a crushing weight on her chest. That poor soul was lost because of her carelessness. How could she live with that?

After the torrent of sorrow ebbed, shame flooded in its place. What would Endre's family think of her? Margit grasped both Erzsi's hands. "Please, don't tell anyone."

The woman shook her head. "Too late. Lady Dragoslava knows."

"Why? You could have told her I fell, and not that I was with child. Word might reach Endre and distress him."

"Don't concern yourself with that. You must rest. Thanks be to God, you haven't suffered serious harm. The midwife believes you'll be able to have children in the future. Now, lie down. I'll fetch you some broth."

As soon as Erzsi left, Margit crumbled in on herself, despair and frustration battling within. Once again, she had paid the price of having been born a woman. So unfair. At fifteen years of age, she was still so young, yet forced to bear such harsh punishment.

Erzsi always reprimanded her for thinking only about herself. But on that fateful night, for once, Margit had put her husband's needs above hers, hoping to give him comfort. An act of mercy—or guilt, perhaps—which had come at a terrible cost.

***

Although Margit's health improved, she did not wish to leave the house. Even two months later, she stayed in her chamber all day, plagued by bouts of sadness for the loss of her baby and despair about her situation. Nothing was going well for her. The dream of reclaiming her inheritance had never seemed so far away. Perhaps it would never happen. Was her life worth living anymore?

Her dark thoughts were interrupted by Erzsi, who entered the room huffing. "He just won't go away!"

"Who?"

"The blacksmith boy. He sits outside the house for hours every day. I tell him to leave, but he refuses. In the end, I yielded."

"Adnan." The image of her friend dispersed the heavy clouds in Margit's mind. Her heart skipped at the first ray of sunshine in her gloomy life. "Where is he?"

"Downstairs."

Margit jumped out of bed and pulled her kirtle down over her chemise. She turned to Erzsi with hands clasped in front of her face. "Can I please see him alone, dear godmother?"

The woman exhaled sharply but then nodded and sat on her pallet. "Very well, but only for a few moments. I'll come down if you linger too long."

Margit rushed out of the chamber.

Adnan stood by the fireplace. His face lit up brighter than the summer sun when he saw her. "Are you well? You disappeared for so long. I've missed you."

Unable to resist the sincerity of his words, she told him what had happened. "Until the moment I heard you were here, I wished to die," she concluded.

Adnan took her hand and placed it on his chest. "My heart beats for you. I know you belong to another man. But it won't stop me from loving you and protecting you." His voice was steady and clear as if he were stating the most universally accepted truth.

Margit sighed but withdrew her hand. Why wouldn't he give up on her? Instead, he was making everything so awkward.

"I ask that you come out and do what you like most," he continued.

Just as the stairs creaked under Erzsi's descending footsteps, Margit moved away from Adnan and smiled, for the first time in many weeks. "Yes, I shall. I yearn for a good fight, and I swear I shall kick your backside!"

***

Slowly but steadily, Margit's life returned to some kind of normality. She helped Ahmed in the smithy and did the housework at home so that Erzsi could rest after toiling all day. And, of course, she continued practising with her friend.

She received a letter from Endre at Christmas of 1473, but nothing else came after that until one day in September of the following year.

She and Erzsi were having supper when a knock rapped on their door. No sooner had Margit answered, when her eyes popped wide open at sour-faced Dragoslava, standing stiffly in front of her and holding a parcel.

Before Margit opened her mouth to greet her, the woman swept past and tossed the parcel on the kitchen table. "This is for you. From Endre," she said in Serbian, her sharp tone stabbing Margit. "He sent things to both of us, but the messenger was in a hurry and left everything with me."

Margit unwrapped the parcel with impatient hands: a letter, a gold florin and a linen kerchief embroidered with colourful flowery patterns.

Coin cast aside, she trailed her fingers over the soft material of the kerchief before placing it on the table. She unfolded the paper and read the letter silently, her eyes skipping over any unimportant words.

"What does he say?" Erzsi's voice was full of concern.

"He's well." Margit breathed. "At least, he was when he wrote this two months ago."

Erzsi crossed herself. "Oh, thank the Lord!"

"The royal army has taken many castles, villages and towns in northern Hungary and Moravia. They march into Silesia now to face the Polish forces. The king is pleased with his service. Endre has received his first wages: three florins. He kept one for his expenses and sent the other two to me and his mother."

Her husband's thoughtfulness, even when his own life was in peril, warmed Margit's heart.

"Such a kind soul. God bless him." Erzsi brushed away tears from the corners of her eyes. "Does he say when he'll come back?"

"Sadly, no. He only hopes that with God's help, they will complete the campaign successfully and return to Buda, where he can have his father released from prison as the king has promised."

Margit folded the letter and, holding it against her chest, turned to Dragoslava. "Dear Mother, thank you for bringing his message to me."

Frowning, the woman brought the conversation back to the Serbian language. "You have caused him so much pain."

Margit pressed her lips together. At every turn, Dragoslava reminded her of Endre's life, possibly forfeit because of her. Instead of pressing the issue, Margit merely asked, "Mother, have you written to him about the baby?"

"No," Dragoslava said shortly. "He has enough concerns."

"You are kind."

Dragoslava gaped at her, nostrils flaring. "You jest? You should be ashamed of yourself, you...little whore!"

Margit gasped. "How dare you? I have done nothing wrong. I

did lie with him, but he's my husband. Why does that bother you?"

"God only knows whose that baby was. Did you think you could hide it from me? I know all about your filthy blacksmith boy."

Margit's temples throbbed. She would have lashed out at Dragoslava had not Erzsi spoken first, "Let it go, child! I'm sure the lady didn't mean to speak this way." Even though she addressed Margit, Erzsi's blazing eyes bored into the other woman.

Dragoslava shot a venomous glare at the two of them before storming out of the house.

Margit looked at her godmother. "I swear on my life, Adnan is just my friend."

"I know, *galambom*." Erzsi embraced her tenderly. "Perhaps Lady Dragoslava is concerned about you because of her own misfortune."

Margit pulled back abruptly. "Misfortune?"

"Yes. She—" Erzsi stopped herself and covered her mouth with her hand.

"What do you mean, godmother?"

"Nothing. Forget what I said."

"Why? You started saying something, you must finish it."

Erzsi shook her head. "I'm not inclined to reveal anyone's secrets."

Margit placed her hands on her hips. "You know I shall not leave you in peace until you tell me."

The woman exhaled through clenched teeth. "Very well. I'll tell you. But only because her behaviour towards you makes my blood boil. Many years ago, she got herself with child by a foreign soldier, a complete stranger to her."

"Really? And who was he?"

"Imre, of course. He had the fancy of many ladies back then. They met in this city during the siege of 1456. Five months later, Dragoslava came to Transylvania with a swollen belly, begging your lord father for help. He took pity on her and ordered Imre to wed her."

Margit's chest heaved with a sweet sense of vindication. "So, she is not as saintly as she pretends to be." She pondered this for a moment. "Does Endre know?"

"I think not. But you must not tell him. Do you promise?"

Margit nodded. "I would never do that to him. He thinks so highly of his mother. And if my father chose him as my husband despite knowing the truth, then I shall continue to respect Endre with all my heart."

10

The Return

June 1475

After a balmy mid-summer's day, the last of the sunshine still brightened the western horizon. Its orange glow seeped through the open window, and its warmth touched Margit's cheeks as she sat at the table while her godmother brushed her hair before retiring for the night.

"You're so fair now, *galambom*, with your hair long again." A yearning for happier times echoed in Erzsi's voice. "You're finally turning into a real wom—" Two sharp knocks on the door startled her. "Who could it be at this hour?"

Margit shuddered. "I hope it's not Mother."

Another knock. Louder this time.

"I shall answer," Margit said, slowly rising to her feet.

With hesitant steps, she went to the door and opened it.

A man stood before her, his outline dark against the low sunlight behind him.

Margit squinted. Well-dressed and wearing a hat with a feather pinned onto its upturned brim. A nobleman at her doorstep?

When he uttered *"Szívem"*, her knees buckled, and she stumbled forward. "Endre?"

But for his firm grasp on both her arms, she would have crumbled. Breathless, she leaned on him and straightened herself.

His face, now so close to hers, revealed a broad smile. "May I enter?"

Margit's cheeks burned. "Of course."

"*Jóisten!*" Erzsi hastened to light the two oil lamps on the wall and the thick tallow candle on the table. "You're back, my dear boy!"

He bowed his head. "Mistress Erzsi. I hope you have been well?"

"Yes, yes. What a surprise! When did you arrive? Have you seen your mother?"

"I have, indeed. I brought my father back and took him to the house first. I apologise for coming here so late, but I couldn't wait until morn."

Margit stared at him, her hand pressed hard against her breast to quieten the frantic beating within. After over two years apart, this was not how she had imagined her reunion with her husband. There he stood, dressed in his finest, while Margit was barefoot in her chemise, her hair half-brushed. "Forgive my appearance," she mumbled. "I was preparing for bed."

Endre removed his hat and approached her. "Nonsense. You look fairer than ever before." With his arms around her waist, he drew her towards him, his eyes locking into hers.

She took in a sharp breath. How tall and strong he had grown! Yet his fine features and boyish charm remained unchanged.

"I have missed you, dear wife." He leaned forward and planted a kiss on her lips.

Margit's head spun with sweet elation. Her knees trembled, and she paused, needing a moment to steady herself amidst the rush of emotions.

"You make such a fine couple," Erzsi's voice rang with pride and admiration. And as Margit turned to her, the woman winked. "Don't mind me. I'll go to the shed to water Csillag and give him a good brush 'til you finish your—" she coughed, "conversation." With that, she hastened out of the house.

Endre took Margit's hand. "Come, *szívem*. We have your godmother's blessing."

Endre's warmth slowly loosened Margit's tense limbs. After so long untouched, her skin prickled with uneasy excitement. Though dread lingered in her mind at their encounter's possible outcome, the joy of her husband's return filled her heart. When she flinched as their bodies joined, she clenched her eyes shut to allay her fear. Her thoughts galloped to open fields, where the wind rushed through her hair as she rode Csillag and shot her beloved bow.

No ghastly visions or shadows troubled her this time.

"It felt so good," Endre said after he caught his breath, his voice trembling slightly.

He lay on his back but kept his head turned towards her as if searching for a response.

Margit inhaled deeply, every fibre of her being praying to the Almighty that she would not conceive. "Yes. I'm glad you are home. And your father is finally free. May I visit him tomorrow?"

"Of course. He also wishes to talk to you."

"How is he?"

"Not so well, sadly," Endre said after a long pause. "Two and a half years in a cold and damp dungeon affected his health."

"Alas, all blame is upon me."

"No! You are not at fault. It was meant to happen. It was God's will."

Margit looked away. Despite his reassurances, she doubted that Endre did not feel sad, or even angry, about his father's situation. And now she had to give him more bad tidings. She gathered her courage and turned to face him. With a shaky voice, she told him about the baby she had lost and the argument with his mother.

"She just stood in this house and called me a...whore. I swear on my life, Adnan is only my friend. I was not unfaithful to you. The child was yours."

Endre put his arm around her and held her closer. "Do not distress, *szívem*. I believe you. And I'm sorry for leaving you for so long."

"Yes, I understand. I don't blame you."

"Do not fret anymore. I'm here now, and all will be well."

His comforting words made Margit smile.

He kissed her gently on the forehead. "I must go now. I shall summon Erzsi back here as I leave."

11

A Broken Man

Dragoslava flung her arm in Margit's direction. "Why did you bring her to my house?"

"Calm yourself, Mother," Endre intervened. "She is my wife, and she has every right to be here. Besides, Father asked to see her."

"You are not thinking straight, son. The little witch has seduced you."

Hands on hips, Margit glared even at Endre. "Stop talking about me as if I am not here!"

Dragoslava opened her mouth—to give a nasty response, surely—but Endre cut her short with an abrupt movement of his hand.

He took Margit by the arm and led her to his father's chamber.

At the sight of Imre lying in bed, Margit's hand flew to her mouth. Of the strong and brave knight she remembered, only a shadow now remained: emaciated and pale as death; his hair and beard had completely greyed. He struggled for each breath, and the wheezing coming out of his chest made the hairs stand at the back of her neck.

"Come closer, child." His trembling voice was a mere whisper. "My eyesight fails me."

Margit reached for Endre's arm and held on to it for support as she went to sit on Imre's bed. How could she forgive herself? "I'm so sorry, Imre *bácsi*. You suffered so much because of me."

Even his smile came with evident effort. "Nonsense, my child. I should've thought of a better plan. The king's Serbian interpreter happened to know Vuk and immediately saw I was someone else. Then I had to explain myself, and all hell broke loose. I knew I was a wanted man for obeying your father's order and taking you away. But I thought everyone would've forgotten about me after so many years."

Imre's words cut off as a fit of coughing seized him. When the convulsions finally eased, Endre steadied his father's shaking hand and helped him sip water from a cup. "We shall look after you, Father, and you will get better."

"Oh, I think not, son. I feel I have little time left." He turned to Margit. "I fear I can't help you anymore. You and Endre must finish what we started. You'll go to Szentimre and take back what's yours. This is why I called you here. There are important things to tell you."

And so, in great detail, he described Margit's estate, where it was situated and how they would get there. He also told them of a secret passage, which they had used to flee the castle on the night her father died, and the king's forces took the estate. He revealed to them that he had returned to Szentimre in disguise a few months after their escape to find out the truth of what had happened.

"Anna, Márton and their lackey, Pál Balog, were in charge. The mood was grim. The people refused to say anything to me as a stranger. But I saw the sadness and fear in their eyes. Your lord father was kind to them. He looked after each of them; he even paid their taxes when they didn't have enough coin because of a poor harvest or slow trade. I'm sure if they learn his daughter has returned, they'll be fully behind you. But you must be careful, my child. Your relatives have evil in their hearts, and they won't hesitate to harm you to protect themselves."

Imre paused again, struggling to breathe.

"Don't exert yourself, Imre bácsi." Margit helped him to some more water.

Her heart ached.

All blame is upon me. I caused this.

She brought her hand to her stomach, trying to suppress the queasiness which threatened to overwhelm her.

"Lie down, Father," Endre said. "You must rest."

But Imre ignored him and continued addressing Margit, "My dear child, you must honour your parents. You carry the blood of two of the most important noble families in the realm. I may be a broken man now, but I'd gladly die at this moment, knowing I've helped you survive and not forget your legacy. So, when you're ready, follow the path of your destiny. And remember, even if I'm dead and buried, I'll always be with you in spirit."

Margit waited, sitting on the wooden bench. In the height of summer, the spicy fragrance of Dragoslava's herb garden competed with the intoxicating aroma of the rose bushes. The light breeze checked the force of the scorching sun. The world was in full bloom, in sharp contrast to the gloominess within Imre's bedchamber.

She forced a smile in the direction of her approaching husband. Yet Endre did not reciprocate. His face looked serious and troubled.

"Our situation is simply dire," he said, his voice subdued as he sat beside her. "Mother just dismissed all the servants. We have debts and no money to pay them. Hard decisions must be made."

Margit's back stiffened. "What do you mean?"

"My grandfather's wage will not be enough to sustain us all. He wishes to sell the house you live in. The craftsmen would vie for it to use as a workshop because it's near the market and the port."

Margit twitched. "And what will become of Erzsi and me?"

"You must move here with us—"

"What?" Margit sprang to her feet.

"You must help my mother and grandmother with the house chores, the weaving and the garden."

She shook her head. "I shall not live under the same roof as your mother. She hates me."

Endre exhaled sharply. "Sadly, nobility doesn't always come with riches. You have an empty title."

"Ah, you blame me now? After all your soothing words yesternight? How dare you?" A fiery urge swelled inside her. She discharged it by landing a heavy slap on the side of his head.

Strangely, he did not even flinch. "Hitting me will not solve our problems."

Margit clenched her fists so tight that her hands ached. "Have you forgotten what your father said? That I must follow my destiny?

"He doesn't know how bad our position is. I, too, was unaware until I talked to my mother today. My grandfather's health is failing also, and she is concerned."

"One more reason for me to go to Transylvania and find the

evidence the king requested."

"No, you must wait."

His words pierced her very soul. "What? Why?"

"I can't go with you. I must return to the army. The pay is good. It will clear the debts and sustain us. Perhaps in two-or three years' time, we will have saved enough, and we can go to Transylvania together."

Margit gasped. "Two or three years? I can't wait that long."

A passing cloud cast a shadow across Endre's dejected face. "I feel terrible for saying this, but I can't see any other solution. Soon we shall not be able to afford the basics in life, let alone spend a fortune on a long journey and a stay of unknown duration in a place so far from home."

Margit squeezed her eyes shut, her heart shattering into a thousand pieces. Her life had become an endless battle, each day a struggle against unsurmountable obstacles. Doubts crept in. Did she have the strength to go on? Imre's words rang in her ears; yet the more she reached for her destiny, the faster it seemed to slip away.

"I leave next week," Endre said.

Another blow. Margit shuddered. "Please stay safe. I don't wish to lose you."

His eyes clouded in anguish, he rose, cradled her face in his palm and pressed a kiss to her brow. "Yes, *szívem*, I promise." He embraced her tightly as if to imprint this moment. "Please, make peace with my mother. I know she needs your help although she does not admit it. Will you do this for me?"

How could she not?

"Of course." She clung to him and inhaled his scent, etching every detail into her memory lest this would be their last time together.

12

Baptism of Fire

February 1476

Lumps of ice floated on the water of the Sava, shimmering in the bright moonlight. The snow on the banks rose in drifts while the bitter wind pierced Margit's lungs. Covering her nose and mouth, she breathed into her gloved hand until warmth returned. The brief respite heartened her. At least her bow, kept safe under her woollen cape, was protected from the cold and dampness.

Margit reined Csillag in and waited for her friend to catch up. Poor Adnan had fallen behind as his wretched mule struggled against the deep snow.

"Can we stop awhile?" he said, his voice barely audible. "So tired and cold."

Margit swept her arm towards the surrounding emptiness. "There is no shelter anywhere. We shall freeze to death if we stop. Besides, Szabács is within reach now."

In the distance ahead of them, a ball of fire rose like a shooting star into the night sky, then slowly descended on a curved path and disappeared from sight. Another followed and then another. Across the open plain, dull cannon fire reverberated, and the upstream winds carried the bustle of a siege.

She pointed. "See? Those are the king's catapults. We should reach the camp in two to three hours."

Adnan only grumbled and pulled his fur cap down to his eyebrows. "Why d'you do this? We won't survive a day out there."

An icy gust whipped across Margit's face, making her doubt her rash decision—not for the first time. But only for a heartbeat.

I have trained for this. I can fight. The army pays well. I shall earn enough coin to go to Transylvania.

She turned to Adnan. "I didn't force you to come with me."

"I swore to my father I'll protect you."

"I don't need protection!" Margit snapped. "Even less so from one who complains this much."

With a sharp kick of her heels, she urged Csillag forward.

The groan of wood and clanking of metal floated through the air. As passing clouds peeled back from the moon's face, war galleys emerged from the fog like leviathans chained together, spanning the Sava's banks. Sails furled tight against two soaring masts on each ship, their rigging clattered in the wind and the sway of the current. Rows of lamps glimmered from openings along the hulls like glowing eyes in the night.

Margit's breath stalled in her chest. "Truly magnificent."

A loud "Whoa!" escaped Adnan's mouth.

She chuckled softly. "Even you seem enthralled, my reluctant friend."

Adnan snorted. "An impressive sight, yes. But it changes nothing. We shouldn't be here."

With renewed eagerness, Margit pressed on, her spirit undaunted.

When they arrived at the camp perimeter, they dismounted in front of a wooden wall, which stood at the height of a man. A three-storey watchtower formed part of it just before the wall disappeared into the ever-thickening fog.

The entire area rumbled with constant activity. The air was heavy with smells: sulphur, gunpowder, smoke, cooked food and the stench of human and animal waste floating down the river.

At the entrance gate, a group of guards surrounded Margit and Adnan, swords drawn.

A brawny soldier, who seemed in command, shouted at them in a foreign language, his spit spraying Margit's face. She grimaced in disgust and stepped back.

Beside her, Adnan's teeth chattered—from fear or from the cold, she was not sure because she kept her eyes fixed on the guards.

The man repeated his barking. The language sounded somewhat similar to Serbian. Was it Bohemian, perhaps?

Margit shook her head. "I don't understand you."

He grunted, grabbed a lantern from the hand of another soldier and held it close to Margit's face. "*Mad'arsky?*"

That she did understand. It meant 'Hungarian'. She nodded several times. "Yes! *Magyar*," she said in her mother tongue.

The man gestured to someone else to take over. This other one reeked of ale; but thankfully, he spoke Hungarian. "Who are you?"

"We come from Belgrade." Margit made her voice deeper to match her recently cropped hair and male attire. "Nándor-fehérvár," she hastily corrected herself, using the Hungarian name of the city. "We came to fight the Turks."

The soldier looked her up and down and snorted. "We have enough men here. Why would we need two peasants?"

"We can be useful, I assure you."

The guard spat on the ground and translated to his superior.

The Bohemian snarled an order. Four men grabbed Margit and Adnan and dragged them away. Her desperate protests fell on deaf ears.

Margit's knees trembled as she and Adnan were shoved into a tent. Her pulse thudded in her ears; not because she feared for her life but because both Csillag and her bow had been snatched from her. The soldiers must have thought she and her friend were spies.

Fire roared in two braziers inside this tent, the warmth tingling Margit's frozen face and hands. Her blood flowed freely again.

Clearly taken by surprise, two young male servants abandoned their game of cards and scurried about. Their hurried murmurs in Hungarian filled the air. One lit a large metal lantern suspended from a sturdy beam on the tent's ceiling, and the other went to fetch his master.

A few moments later, a yawning man in a thick night robe emerged from behind the tent partition. Before Margit had a chance to observe him, a hard kick to the back of her leg sent her down on her knees.

"Show respect to Lord István Bátori, the Judge Royal and commander of the king's army!" someone shouted in Hungarian behind her.

Margit grimaced from the pain and the loudness of the soldier's voice. Beside her, Adnan was also forced to kneel.

She took a few shallow breaths and then raised her head to look at the commander. Her eyes were drawn to the coat of arms depicting three dragon teeth in a horizontal position against a dark red background, which was emblazoned on his velvet robe. She knew that symbol.

Of course! Bátori. My mother's family name. Could he be a relative?

But in the current circumstances, it was unwise to enquire such a thing.

Evidently annoyed with the interruption to his rest, the Judge Royal motioned to the guards to stand back and to Margit and Adnan to rise.

Adorned with two glittering rings set in precious stones, the man's hand adjusted a palm-sized wooden crucifix on his neck. His eyes narrowed suspiciously as he scrutinised them, stroking his short beard. "How do I know you are not spies?" He jerked his chin in Adnan's direction. "He certainly looks like a Turk."

Unable to understand Hungarian, Adnan glanced at Margit, confused.

"Do not fret," she said to him; then straightened herself and looked down on Bátori, who was about a hand's breadth shorter than her. "We are not spies, my lord. I swear to all that is holy." She crossed herself to elicit the sympathy of the obviously pious commander. "We came to help. We wish to join the army as mercenaries."

"Mercenaries?" The Judge Royal laughed. "How old are you, boys? What experience do you have?"

Lost for words, Margit pressed her lips together.

"No experience whatsoever," Bátori surmised. "And you still have not proven to me you are not spies."

Margit drew a deep breath, gathering up all her courage. "I beg you, my lord. We are both from Nándorfehérvár. I'm half-

Hungarian, and my name is Saša Lazarević. My companion is the son of the blacksmith who forges weapons for the City Guard."

"I have no time for this," he snapped. "Soldiers!"

Margit raised her hand. "Wait!" How had she not thought of that before? "We have a friend in the royal army. He's here and can verify who we are."

Bátori signalled to the guards to stop. "And who is this 'friend' of yours?"

"Endre Gerendi. He was King Mátyás' squire in Silesia and now serves under Pál Kinizsi."

The commander paused, his brow furrowing. "Yes, I know that lad. Bring him here."

Endre tripped over his own feet on seeing her when he entered the tent. "Mar—" he started, but her ferocious glare made him change half-way. "Freckle-face," he ended up saying, which she did not like either.

Chin raised, Bátori surveyed him with piercing eyes. "Do you know them, soldier?"

"Yes, sir." Endre pointed at Margit first. "This is my...my... cousin, Saša." Then he cast a disdainful glance at Adnan. "And that's the blacksmith's son. His father is well-known in Nándorfehérvár."

"Very well. As you served the king loyally before, I accept your word," Bátori said and then addressed Margit and Adnan, "You can have your weapons back and go with your friend." He flapped his hand towards the tent's exit. "You will be Pál Kinizsi's burden and not mine. Off you go!"

Once outside, Margit heaved a sigh of relief and squealed for joy when Csillag and her bow were returned to her possession.

All around her, a sea of tents sprawled within a palisaded perimeter, creating an impression of a walled town which buzzed with movement, conversation in many languages, laughter, crackling of fires and, now and then, the bellowing of cannon.

Endre dragged Margit away from Adnan. "What in God's name are you doing here?"

"I came to fight. Have you forgotten we are in desperate need of coin for our travel to Transylvania?"

"Have you lost your mind? This is war."

Despite her vexation, Margit recollected where she was and lowered her voice. "I can protect myself. Both Ahmed and you have trained me well."

"And how could you abandon my family and Erzsi? Do they know where you are?"

"I left a note."

"A note?" Endre choked on his reply. "They will be worried to death about you. How can you be so heartless?"

Sudden guilt clawed at Margit's stomach. Once again, she had put her desire for revenge above the feelings of the people who cared for her. With her head hung low, she followed Endre to the section of the camp where he was stationed.

Lying but on a thin blanket on the canvas floor of a cramped tent and disturbed by intermittent cannon fire and the soldiers' snoring, Margit slept fitfully and woke up with a sore head and a stiff shoulder.

She stretched her arms, trying to get rid of the pain, but to no avail. On top of that, her stomach rumbled. Her eyes searched for Endre beside her, but he was not there.

Adnan slept at her feet. She nudged him with her heel. "We have not eaten since yestermorn," she mumbled as he squinted at her, bleary-eyed and yawning. "Let us find some food."

When Margit stepped outside, she was greeted by the cacophony of the camp and the ubiquitous smell of gunpowder. There were soldiers everywhere, crawling like busy ants on the snow-covered ground, each one fulfilling the duty assigned to him.

Straight ahead, beyond a wooden palisade, the defiant fortress of Szabács stood on a peninsula surrounded by marshland and ditches.

Margit rubbed her eyes. "What is this?" She rubbed them again. "It doesn't even have a proper wall."

Unlike most fortresses, Szabács had no stone curtain wall—just a simple wattle frame crammed with packed earth and braced by thick oak beams. Eight watchtowers, also of wood and earth, studded the perimeter with a ninth jutting from the stronghold's centre. At the far end, a stone keep bordered the river's edge.

Mátyás' army had encircled their target on land and water. Cannons, bombards and catapults spewed fire from ashore while galleys and nimble, single-masted *naszádok* blocked access on the Sava. Yet for all the king's fearsome arsenal and two weeks of besieging, the fortress seemed impervious.

On the opposite side, the Ottomans also bombarded the attackers from wooden ramparts atop the wall, albeit sparingly— perhaps knowing they had no chance of receiving fresh supplies soon. Archers on the watchtowers shot at anyone who dared to approach.

"You have awoken at last!" Endre's voice jolted Margit out of her thoughts.

She swept her arm dismissively towards the fortress. "Thousands of men and dozens of ships for a mere...mud hut?"

He chuckled. "Have you become a strategist now? Rammed earth can be as strong as stone. But with time, the walls *will* crumble, and we shall take it by assault."

"And why is this place so important?"

"The Turks launch many raids from here into Southern Hungary and Slavonia. They could even attack Nándorfehérvár. The king wishes to put an end to these violent acts."

Margit's stomach grumbled again. "I'm hungry. Where is breakfast?"

Endre reached for her hand but seemed to change his mind half-way. "Come with me," he said instead.

Although not invited, Adnan hastened after them.

"You brought the peasant with you," Endre mumbled, just loud enough for Margit to hear.

She punched him on the arm. "I didn't 'bring' him. He offered to accompany me for protection. Would you rather I came on my own?"

"I would rather you didn't come at all," he hissed through clenched teeth.

After they filled their bellies with broth and bread, Endre took them to his commander, Pál Kinizsi, a fierce-looking Herculean man with a wild brown beard, whose orders bellowed like a lion's roar over his men.

Kinizsi released a thunderous laugh when he saw Margit and

Adnan. "Your little bows and daggers are useless. Go to the women's camp and wash some pots."

"Sir!" Margit protested. Despite stretching herself to her full height, the top of her head barely reached the base of his thick neck. "We wish to fight."

"Perhaps they could help load the cannons," Endre suggested. "A few of the men are frost-bitten, and they could do with a respite."

Kinizsi dismissed them with a flick of his hand. "Very well. Off you go."

"Loading cannons was not what I had in mind when I decided to join the fight," Margit complained.

"But it's important work," Adnan countered.

She made a face at him, then stepped back and pressed her hands against her ears just as the cannon recoiled with a deafening bang and a smoke cloud, ejecting an iron ball the size of a man's head towards the fortress. The projectile crashed on the elevated timber rampart atop the earthen wall, sending wood splinters and dust into the air.

Adnan was right. This was a siege after all, and the best way to win was to force the Turks into surrender by cutting supply lines and subjecting them to continuous bombardment. They would eventually run out of food and ammunition while their walls would break at many points. How long would it take though? Judging by the size of the king's army, it would need a whole herd of cattle to sustain itself for a mere few days, let alone weeks or even months.

A blinding flash shot up from the fortress, followed by dozens of flaming arrows, which rained on a *naszád*. Swept by fierce currents or overzealous oarsmen, the boat had drifted perilously close to the fortress walls.

And then boom! A barrel of gunpowder exploded aboard the vessel, ripping the deck apart and flinging men skyward and into the Sava's dark waters. Violent flames spread everywhere, hungrily consuming the wooden hull. With a screeching crack, the mast broke in two. Its severed top crashed onto the deck of a nearby ship, splitting it open to torrents of water.

Trapped onboard, soldiers screamed in panic as fire gnawed their clothes. Many plunged into the frigid river, only to engage in a desperate fight to stay afloat, their armour relentlessly dragging them into the depths.

"Those poor souls will die!" Adnan shouted, clutching his head with both hands.

Margit's breath caught in her throat as she watched the soldiers flail about in the water under a wave of Turkish arrows.

"Jakšić!" Kinizsi called one of the Serbian captains. "Send a rescue team!"

A score of men gathered, Endre among them. As he donned his helmet and buckled his sword belt, dread seized Margit in an icy grip. Though her husband had soldiered for almost three years now, in her eyes he remained the tender boy she had lain with in the shed that night. Her stomach churned at the sight of him now grasping his pavise and getting ready to head into slaughter's jaws.

Before she knew it, her feet impelled her forward. She grabbed her bow and quiver. "Captain! Do you need an archer?"

"Are you mad?" Adnan shouted.

His arm shot out to bar her path, but she evaded his grasp. A growl escaped him as he gave chase, bow and arrows in hand, his footfalls echoing hers.

But she would not be deterred so easily.

Endre turned pale and gestured wildly in Margit's direction. "No, no!"

"What is it to you?" the captain scolded him. "The lad offered himself, and he's right. We need an archer to cover our advance."

Endre let out a deep sigh and gazed at her pleadingly. "You have no armour. Please stay near me and don't try anything reckless."

Flanked by Endre and Adnan, Margit was swept towards the battlefield, safe for the moment amidst the royal artillery lines at a distance from the fortress. But then the emptiness of space opened before her: a barren land raked by crossfire. Margit's pulse hammered at this sight. Her knees turned to water. No one could venture on such ground and hope to survive.

Air thick with the acrid smell of gunpowder choked her lungs. The chilling wind lashed her face, its whine mingling with the crunch of snow underfoot—the only sounds that pierced the foreboding silence between bombardments. In her jolting vision as she ran, the last defence loomed: a palisade of wooden stakes impaled in the frozen earth at an outward angle. Screams for help echoed across the water as men from the ravaged ships floundered through the icy swampland. The snow's pure white made the carnage around her even more vivid.

Endre held his pavise before him and Margit as they raced for the palisade with the rest of the rescue group. Arrows flew in their direction. Firearms crackled. With a final push, he shoved her towards the safety of the wooden wall.

"Archer!" the captain shouted.

Margit's hands moved on instinct, drawing an arrow, nocking and aiming at an enemy archer perched on the tower straight ahead. At the same time, a deafening blast of Turkish cannon fire shook the earth.

Pain shrieked through Margit's ears. The bow tumbled from her grip. Before she could react, Endre and Adnan pushed her face-down into the snow, shielding her with their bodies. She thrashed and choked for breath until they rolled off. Gasping and wheezing, she raised herself on all fours and fumbled around frantically for her fallen bow. Only after retrieving it, did she allow air into her burning lungs.

"Everyone alive?" came the captain's voice, still muffled in Margit's ears.

Her eyes swept over Endre and Adnan. By some miracle, neither was hurt. But their luck could not hold forever.

Margit raised the bow again, but her thumping heart and ragged breath unsteadied her hands. She shot hastily and missed.

"Damn!" the officer spat. "You're useless."

Margit grunted in frustration. Despite all her training, she had faltered at the most crucial moment. Endre was right. This was war. The shadow of death hovered, ready to claim her at any moment.

In the corner of her eye, her husband raised the pavise just in time to block a cluster of arrows. The impact jolted him, but he held fast.

Anger and embarrassment burned Margit's cheeks.

"Trust yourself," Endre urged her.

"Forward, men!" the captain ordered. "Use your shields for

cover. God help us."

"I must go," Endre said.

"No, no," Margit mumbled, heart in her mouth. She cursed herself for disguising as a man. Her husband was about to throw himself into the jaws of death, and she could not even embrace him.

Endre's hand brushed down her arm. His face twisted as he passed the pavise to Adnan. "Protect her with your life, peasant!" he said in Serbian.

Off Endre went, crouching after the rest of the soldiers; then squeezing through an opening between two parts of the palisade and making a run towards the river.

"Where's your shield?" came the officer's distant scream.

"I gave it to the archer," replied Endre's distant voice.

"Foolish man! Stay near me!"

Sick apprehension churned Margit's stomach.

I must keep him safe.

Knees planted steadily on the snow, she nocked an arrow. As Adnan momentarily moved the shield to one side, an enemy archer rose into view above the wooden parapet on the fortress wall.

Margit needed to get to him first. An impossible feat—shooting at an upward angle through a narrow opening in the palisade and from such long distance. But she would try.

She drew a quick breath. The enemy soldier was in position. Margit aimed and loosed the arrow. A glimpse was all she needed. The Turkish archer fell backwards just as Adnan covered her with the shield again.

"Hit!" he squealed.

A mere stroke of luck. But it came at the right time. Margit's chest swelled with hope and pride. Quickly nocking again, she took aim at the cannon crew on the ramparts. With two successive arrows, she felled two soldiers. The rest retreated for cover, giving the rescue party precious time to reach their comrades in the swamp waters.

"Shooter on left tower," Adnan directed Margit.

Her next arrows flew swift and sure, hitting target after target. As her friend gave her the exact enemy positions, her quiver soon emptied, and she took his.

The Hungarian cannons behind her provided valuable support. Her accuracy and their deadly force finally suppressed the enemy fire.

Before long, Endre returned with the others, their mission completed.

Though barely an hour had passed, to Margit it felt an eternity.

Back at camp, legs still numb, she collapsed onto a crate.

Commander Kinizsi congratulated her and Adnan for their valour. "Well done, lads. You received your baptism of fire."

Margit nodded nervously while she caught her breath. Her heart was doing tumbles as though it wished to jump out of her chest. The bitter taste of war lingered. But she had survived. This was only the beginning. She knew now that after she overcame the initial fear, she would only improve thenceforth.

Endre interrupted her thoughts as he helped her to her feet and led her into one of the supply tents. "You must go home," he scolded her after making sure there was no one around. "You could have died out there. This is no place for a woman."

"But I didn't die. And I did my duty. You should be proud of me."

A bitter smile formed on Endre's face. "I am proud; but also afraid of losing you. I wish you were less wild and more—"

"Obedient?" she snapped. "Tame? Like a good, dutiful wife, who stays at home and waits for her husband to return from his adventures? No, I can't do that. I shall continue to fight until I earn enough money to go to Transylvania, with or without you."

13

A Daring Plan

Even with her gambeson on, Margit's slender frame was swallowed by the oversized coat of plates, which made an unholy rattle with every movement. Yet her heart brimmed with pride when she wore it together with the sturdy archer's armguards and the open-face sallet, secured under her chin with a strap. Although made up of borrowed and scavenged parts, this was her first armour. She was now a warrior in her own right.

"Pity we must return the armour," Adnan said though he also suffered in the bulky mail shirt borrowed from a wounded soldier.

Accepted into the king's army for two days now, Margit's plan to earn her necessary fortune seemed more attainable, and that filled her with hope and energy.

Bows and quivers on their backs, Margit and Adnan climbed the ladder up the tower and sat on the protruding platform, on guard duty for the third watch of the night.

The camp was eerily still but for the groaning ship masts and the clanging of metal rigging, carried from the river by the breeze.

A welcome mildness permeated the air as thick snowflakes drifted down from the clouded sky, silently blanketing the landscape.

Just then, shuffling and murmuring rose from the far side of the camp.

Margit jumped up.

Adnan likewise sprang to his feet. "What's amiss?"

Glued to the tower railing, she narrowed her eyes. "A night attack?"

Dozens of shadowy figures stole across the snow towards the walls of Szabács. No torches lit their approach. No war cries or orders betrayed their assault until ropes with grappling hooks and anchors whistled aloft.

The shrill sound of an alarm bell shattered the calm. Like an angry giant risen from his slumber, the Ottoman fortress stirred into action. Lights sparked in every direction, and a deafening racket sent powerful vibrations through the night: the clamour of battle.

But it soon became clear the attack had failed. The Bohemian detachment who had initiated it returned decimated.

Margit sank to her knees, the icy hand of dread upon her heart. "The mud hut humiliated the royal army's best." She turned to Adnan. "The siege may last for months. Will they pay us at all until then?" Despair laced her sigh. "Perhaps it's not my destiny to go to Transylvania any time soon. Oh, dear father! I am not worthy of carrying your name."

Adnan knelt beside her. "Why is it so important to avenge him? You've a good life and a good husband. Why throw it all away for revenge?"

"A matter of honour and justice, not merely revenge. The world still thinks my father was a traitor. But this can't be further from the truth." Margit's voice cracked, but she stemmed her tears. "He was a hero and an honest man, loyal to his homeland and to his king. It's my duty to clear his name and destroy those who murdered him. This is more important to me than having a good life and a good husband."

Adnan shut his eyes. His face contorted, fist pressing to his brow as though he battled inwardly. Then, eyes opening, he said, "Just tell me this: the knight who spared my sire's life back then, was he your father?"

Surprised, she nodded. "Yes, I believe so. Why do you ask?"

"It's time to repay the favour." He leaned closer, his breath warming her frozen cheek and her dejected heart. "Don't despair. I'll help you."

"How?"

"The king's army can't win because no one knows what's behind the walls. To take the fortress, we need a man inside."

Of course!

Adnan was right. For all their military experience, the king's counsellors lacked this simple wisdom.

Margit smiled. Was her fortune finally shifting? "Do you have a plan?"

At the end of their watch, Margit and Adnan descended the tower and, elbowing their way through the mass of soldiers lining up for breakfast or hurrying to their tasks, they reached the king's tent.

A group of steel-clad guards blocked their way with halberds. "Halt! State your names and your business."

Margit squared her shoulders. "We wish to talk with one of the king's advisers."

She spoke with such authority that the soldiers hesitated and deliberated among themselves for a moment before rebutting her.

Undeterred, she stood her ground.

"Begone!" a guard shouted, shaking the head of his halberd in her face.

Adnan gripped her wrist. "Let's go. They'll arrest us."

Lips squeezed together, Margit jerked her hand free and took a few steps back. "No, we wait. I know the king's counsellors meet with him at first light every day."

The bronze colour of dawn had spread across the eastern horizon when the commanders arrived for the morning meeting with the king.

"Lord Kinizsi!" Margit called out. "May I speak with you?"

The corpulent commander shot a dismissive look at her. "Don't you see I've been summoned by the king? Talk to my squire." He strode away, following the other advisers into the tent.

Margit stamped her foot and turned to vent her frustration on Adnan. But she came face-to-face with István Bátori instead.

Clearly startled, the Judge Royal squinted at her against the rising sun, his large crucifix swinging across his chest. "I remember you. What is your business here?"

Margit seized the opportunity. "My lord, we know how to take the fortress."

Bátori chuckled. "You are mere peasants. What would you know?"

"We have a good plan. If you bring it to the king and it works, he will bestow more favour upon you. If it fails, we shall take the blame."

The judge's eyes sparkled at the promise of pleasing the king. "Is that so? How?"

"We need a spy on the inside, my lord. Someone who can make the Turks believe he's one of them. And we have the right person for this."

"Hmmm..." The Judge Royal stroked his beard. "Wait here. I shall speak with you anon."

An hour later, the counsellors trickled out of the tent, shaking their heads. Their sullen faces betrayed that their meeting with the king had not gone well.

Bátori approached Margit. "Come with me. The king would like to hear your plan."

"The king?" Margit gasped. Cold sweat beaded on her brow, and her stomach lurched. All she hoped was to speak with the Judge Royal. She did not expect to be brought to Mátyás. What if he recognised her? Would he dismiss her proposal because she was a woman with no experience in warfare? Or worse, would he order her to leave the battlefield?

"Come along now." Bátori waved them on, but Margit hesitated.

Adnan leaned close to her. "Are you well?" Concern tinged his voice.

Margit inhaled deeply to settle her anxiety. Lest her red hair prompt the king's memory, she hastily tucked any stray locks under the fur hat and pulled it down to just above her eyes. "Yes. Let us go."

Inside, Mátyás' tent rivalled his palace, with bear and wolf skin rugs underfoot, atop silk-woven carpets. A thick hanging tapestry, depicting a splendid banquet, partitioned the public area of the tent from the sleeping quarters. Gold, silver and crystal ornaments, lanterns, glazed pottery and cushioned folding stools adorned the space. Beside a trestle table heavy with delicacies and sweet-smelling wine, two male servants and a page stood straight as rods, the haughty expressions on their faces reflecting their coveted positions as the king's personal attendants.

Sitting upon his polished, high-backed carved chair, Mátyás eyed Margit and Adnan with suspicion. Two oil lamps hung from the beams above him, illuminating his grave face.

The Judge Royal approached the king and whispered in his ear.

Mátyás raised his eyebrows. "Speak, soldier."

Margit bowed her head and kept her gaze fixed on the ground. "Lord King. After the failed attempt this past night, I believe the only way to take the fortress is to find its weakest spots."

Mátyás sneered. "I have already thought of this. Do you take me for a fool?"

Heat rose to Margit's cheeks, but she fought the urge to look him in the eye. "Certainly not, Lord King. However, no soldier has ventured into the castle as a spy thus far. Could it be because no one speaks the language well? We are at a disadvantage, not knowing which parts of the fortress remain unrepaired or less guarded because we stand outside. Only an insider could give us this information." She gestured towards Adnan. "My friend here is fluent in Turkish. He has offered to go in pretending he's an escaped prisoner and find the weak points. He will give us a signal on the third night to indicate where to attack."

"And why should I trust you, a mere soldier unknown to me?"

Margit pondered. The king would still remember her husband,

wouldn't he? "You know my cousin, Endre Gerendi. He served you as a squire in the Silesian campaign. He can vouch for me." Her eyes shifted towards Bátori. "And so can the Lord Judge."

At the king's side, Bátori writhed, perhaps surprised at being implicated in the plans of a stranger.

Margit straightened herself, awaiting the king's response.

Mátyás rubbed his forehead and remained silent. But as his eyes searched her face, he twitched. He now stared at her, holding his chin between his thumb and forefinger.

Margit dropped her gaze, silently praying he did not recognise her.

"You certainly put your point across eloquently, soldier," Mátyás finally declared solemnly. "We can try your plan. But if it fails, or if your friend is discovered by the enemy, no one will rescue him."

"He understands the dangers, Lord King, I assure you."

Mátyás jerked his head towards a bemused Adnan. "Why is he silent?"

"He doesn't know Hungarian. I speak on his behalf."

The king nodded. "Very well. I shall send orders anon."

"Your grace is immeasurable, Lord King." Margit took a deep bow.

Mátyás flicked his hand in the direction of the exit.

Adnan bowed, too, and hastened to open the flap and leave the tent.

Margit was about to follow him but stopped to ensure the desired outcome of her proposition. "Lord King, if our plan works, and you take the fortress, would you kindly give us a reward?"

Mátyás frowned. "Why? You would have done your duty to

your king. What is more valuable than that?"

Margit felt the blood drain from her face. "I apologise."

"I jest," Mátyás said, smiling. "If we take the fortress, there will be plenty of rewards for all. But I shall also give you five gold florins each. Is that fair?"

"Yes, thank you, Lord King. You are so generous."

She bowed again and turned to leave, but it was the king who stopped her this time. "Wait, soldier! Turn around."

Margit's stomach tumbled. She wanted to run, but her legs were stone. Hand to her chest, she took a steadying breath and slowly turned to face him.

The king beheld her with narrowed eyes. "Have we met before? You look and sound familiar." A brief pause. He snapped his fingers. "Of course. I remember."

Margit wished the earth would open and swallow her.

"What is it, your Majesty?" Bátori interjected. "Shall I have him arrested?"

"No. This...person is a relative of mine. Remind me your name, young lady."

Though amusement coloured the king's tone, Margit quivered.

"A woman?" Bátori squealed, the high pitch of his surprised voice contrasting with his masculine appearance.

What would she say? She had been caught. It would be unwise to lie to the king. "Margit Szilágyi of Szentimre in Transylvania." Her voice was barely audible. She cleared her throat. "In fact, Endre Gerendi is my husband. My father, Sándor, was a cousin of Lord King's mother. My mother, Margit, was a Bátori of the Ecsed branch."

"For the love of God!" Bátori exclaimed. "It seems I am also related to you. I am of the Ecsed branch. But what in the world is a noblewoman like you doing here?"

Margit gaped at the Judge Royal. Although she suspected he might be her mother's relative, she never gave it any serious thought because there were several branches of the Bátori family.

In a few words, Mátyás explained to the Judge about Margit's situation and the opportunity he had offered her to prove her claims.

"I wish to earn enough coin and travel to Transylvania to clear my father's name and reclaim my land. If the Lord King allows me," she added.

"You are brave, my lady," Bátori commented. "I am glad to be related to you. And I apologise for calling you a peasant." He brought the crucifix to his lips. "God forgive my foul language."

Lightheaded with relief, Margit stumbled out of the king's tent. Even with her disguise uncovered, Mátyás had agreed to her and Adnan's plan. She had proven her loyalty and gained an unexpected ally in her newfound relative, the Judge Royal.

***

In the dim light of the tent's oil lamps, Adnan's countenance appeared as an undecipherable mask. What was running through his mind?

Apprehension filled Margit as she watched him don a Turkish soldier's attire with Endre's help. Her friend was always the cautious one, making sure she did not make any hasty decisions or reckless moves. Yet he was about to throw himself into the lion's den—not for Hungary or for the king, but for her sake. When he had proposed his daring plan, she eagerly agreed, driven by her burning desire to prove her loyalty to Mátyás and earn a hefty reward. But now, after realising the seriousness of the situation, she wished she had declined the offer.

She dug her nails into her palms, willing away the guilt gnawing at her heart.

Endre stepped back, arms crossed. "Are you ready for this, peasant?"

Adnan nodded, his eyes clouded and his gaze distant.

Despite her husband's disapproving look, Margit placed a comforting hand on her friend's shoulder. "All will go well. I believe in you."

She touched the bruises on his battered face where the Hungarian soldiers had struck to make his escape more plausible to the Turks.

He winced and looked away. "I must go."

With slumped shoulders, he trudged out and disappeared into the darkness. Moments later, soldiers shouted and pretended they were giving chase.

Margit strained to hear beyond the tent walls. Only the faintest desperate cry reached her as Adnan begged the fortress guards for sanctuary.

14

The Ruse

For the fourth night in a row, Margit stood on the watchtower, her blanket pulled tight around her body as she observed the fortress, waiting for Adnan's signal. Her teeth chattered, but the bitter cold was the least of her worries. Despite his promise to send a signal on the third night, nothing had happened.

"He has probably failed," came Bátori's voice, raising a wave of dread inside her.

Margit exhaled to relieve her anxious heart. "Perhaps they are watching him. We must give him more time."

The Judge Royal waved a pair of guards away to the other side of the tower and leaned in, reeking of wine. "The king is getting impatient."

Margit crinkled her nose and turned her head in the opposite direction. "I promise you, my lord, he will give us the signal."

Bátori let out a light laugh. "You seem to trust this lad."

"I have known him for many years."

"Your husband lets you befriend another man?" His voice rang of amusement; or was it contempt?

Margit crumpled the blanket inside her fists, fighting the urge to slap the man. That would definitely not help her cause.

Bátori swayed on his feet. "I do not remember your mother

though she was a cousin. She left for Transylvania to wed your father when I was a little boy. What was she like?"

"Alas, I don't know. She died giving birth to me."

"Oh, forgive me for stirring a sad memory." He paused. "My father was killed at the battle of Varna. I believe yours fought there, too."

"Yes. Wounded while covering Lord János Hunyadi's retreat, but he survived. Then in 1456 he and his only son—my brother, István, whom I never met either—defended Nándorfehérvár. Sadly, István died in that siege."

"Your family always did its duty to Hungary. I found it hard to believe that your father had committed treason. I remember the story surprised a lot of the nobles who knew him. I think the king was too busy with other matters and did not investigate the case thoroughly. The only one who would have defended your father's honour would be Mihály Szilágyi, the king's uncle. But he was long dead by then."

With that, Bátori placed his hand on her shoulder.

Margit shrank away.

Her abrupt movement startled him. "I beg your pardon, my lady." He cleared his throat. "I can help you if you wish. As the Judge Royal, I am the third most powerful man in the kingdom."

A friendly gesture and genuine offer of assistance? Or did he have something else in mind for her? Although the latter thought made her stomach turn, she dismissed it. He had no reason to harm her. Perhaps his behaviour was simply the result of drinking too much wine. "Thank you, Lord Judge," she said, hesitantly.

"Come to me after the siege is over, and I shall see what I can do for you."

Just then, a light—weak like the glow of a firefly—glimmered on top of the fortress wall and then disappeared. It shone again briefly and disappeared once more.

Margit threw the blanket off and leaned over the tower's wooden railing. "The signal!"

"Soldiers!" Bátori ordered the guards. "Note the position of that light."

A short time later, the signal twinkled at a different location. Margit followed it with her eyes as it continued to appear at another two spots before all went dark.

"We have what we need," Bátori said. "I shall speak to the king."

Margit heaved a sigh of relief. Not only was Adnan alive, but he had also done his duty. Yet worry for his fate still gripped her. There was no plan for him to escape from the fortress after this. He would lie low and wait for the Hungarian army to make its final assault.

"Dear God," she prayed, back in her tent, "please keep him safe."

A frosty gust bit fiercely into Margit's face as someone's hands shook her awake the next morning.

"Why is it so cold?" Loud noises came from every direction. She sat up and surveyed the surroundings. "What?"

It had barely dawned. The wind rushed through the open flap of the tent. Standing at the entrance, a gruff-voiced officer, legs apart and hands on hips, barked orders to the soldiers to collect their equipment and dismantle the tent.

Endre leaned over her. "Make ready. I shall wait outside."

Still dazed, Margit put on her outer garments, gathered her belongings and stepped out.

The camp was on the move. The wooden wall and watchtowers lay toppled on the ground. Men were breaking down the planks and stacking them; the cannons were dismantled and loaded on carts; the ships lifted anchor; soldiers were pulling down the tents and packing their weapons. Hundreds of sounds blended with the shouts of men, creating a mighty racket.

"Are we leaving?" Margit said to Endre, who stood beside her with a serious face, holding their horses' reins.

"Yes." He handed her Csillag's reins.

Absently, she stroked the horse's neck until realisation hit her. "Why has the king abandoned the siege?" A cold hand grasped her heart. "Adnan!"

"We have orders to move. The king has a plan to fool the Turks."

***

The fog, which had formed over the Sava before sundown, spread farther inland, veiling the movements of the royal army. In the heavy, damp air breathing was a struggle. Marching away from the fortress with the baggage train, Margit felt her throat constrict at the clamour of distant battle.

Several hours earlier, using the feigned withdrawal, the king had dispatched Kinizsi with a sizable detachment to hide in a hilly area at the far side of Szabács. At the third watch of the night, the attack had begun.

Endre's words before they parted still churned in Margit's head. "We shall strike on the northern side of the fortress, at the spot Adnan indicated. The Turks will rush to defend there and will leave the other areas unprotected." His hardened and determined face had softened as he pleaded with her, "You must stay safe, away from the fight. You must promise me this."

Margit had nodded in agreement but only to keep him free of worry. She would not stay idle while her husband endangered his life, and her friend's safety still hung in the balance inside the fortress.

Bringing herself back to the present, she handed Csillag's reins to a groom. "Guard him with your life, or I shall break your neck!" She assumed an icy voice of authority, which made the youth gasp in apparent fear.

Bow across her back, quiver and sword hanging from her belt and knives strapped on both thighs, she defied the darkness and her fear and hastened back towards the fortress.

The ankle-deep snow crunched underfoot. With each breath, the frigid air stabbed her lungs. The oversized coat of plates weighed her down. But she pressed on with all her might and reached Bátori's retinue before long. Farther down the marching column, a lantern illuminated the royal standard. The king was there too.

"Why are you here?" the Judge Royal exclaimed.

Gasping and wheezing, Margit held on to the pommel of his saddle. "I...must...help my husband...and...my friend."

"For the love of God! They are grown men. Why would they need your help?"

"I shall not abandon them, Lord Judge."

Bátori mumbled something under his breath but spoke no more.

The dark mass of the fortress emerged from the fog. Shouts, screams, the clash of arms and the reddish glow of fire... Margit's limbs numbed. Was Endre safe? Did Adnan still remain hidden to protect himself?

Bátori spurred his horse on to reach the king's side.

Despite her frozen and exhausted legs, Margit urged herself forward to keep up with him.

Dressed in full plate armour, Mátyás turned to the Judge Royal. "Is this the right place?"

"Yes, your Majesty. The scouts confirmed a breach on the wall and no one guarding from the inside. The Turks are all defending the northern part."

The king raised his arm and then stretched forward, with his forefinger pointing the way.

Bátori kissed his crucifix. "God protect us."

The ditches were the last obstacle. Although they crossed the marshland at its shallowest point, the water was still hip-deep; a crust of ice had formed on its surface, and the soft ground underneath threatened to give way at any moment.

Margit's body shivered, but her cheeks burned with anticipation, and her fingers clenched around the quiver.

Just as the mass of soldiers surged towards the half-destroyed walls, Bátori dismounted and stayed Margit by the arm. "This is as far as you go. I shall not let you come to harm."

"Of course, Lord Judge."

But as soon as he released his grip, she rushed to join the men as they spilled into the fortress.

"Come back, you fool!" Bátori yelled, his voice fading into the distance.

In the light of torches and braziers scattered about the cobbled courtyard, Margit stumbled her way across the fortress. A burning building straight ahead became her beacon. It seemed to stand right in the centre of the complex. Once she reached there, she would have a better vantage point to search for Adnan.

Around her raged the din of hand-to-hand combat: weapons clashing, arrows splitting the air, men roaring and screaming. The iron stench of blood turned her stomach.

She could not afford distraction. Staying low, she crept close to walls and around the corners of buildings. Her hands grazed against the rough surfaces, but the pulse pounding inside her head drowned the pain. She crouched behind carts, crates or whatever else lay about, waiting for a gap in the fighting. As soon as one appeared, she darted forward to the next point of cover.

At the side of an overturned cart, she knelt and pressed her hand on her heaving chest. How foolish of her to venture into such a dangerous situation. If the king's army took the fortress, all would be well. But what if it did not?

No, this will not happen. We shall win.

Margit gritted her teeth and raised her head, looking for a gap again.

An arrow whizzed past her face. She ducked and jammed her

back against the cart. Blood wet her fingers when she touched her stinging cheek.

She blinked back the tears of pain and turned to check behind, but she was stuck. The top of her bow had caught on something.

No, not now!

Heart pounding, she disentangled herself by sliding under the strap. The bow was useless in a close fight. With an abrupt movement, she unhooked the quiver from her belt. It would also weigh her down. She freed the bow and hid it under the cart, alongside the quiver.

No more time to waste. Margit pushed herself up, only to be confronted by a screaming, blood-spattered Ottoman soldier swinging a sabre at her.

Instinctively, she sidestepped. The blade clanged against the steel plates of her body armour, its force hurling her to the cobblestones.

As the man lunged again, she rolled away. The Turk's sabre struck sparks on the ground where she had just lain.

Urged by instinct alone, Margit clambered up and, knife in hand, slipped behind him and stabbed his lower side. Bone and internal organs crunched beneath her blade, unleashing a sickening churn within her. Doubtless owing to the surprise attack, he wore no armour, only his tunic and trousers. Wailing, he fell to his knees.

Margit pulled the second knife and plunged it into his neck. While he desperately clutched it, coughing up blood, she drew her sword and ran him through with a final bursting thrust.

He collapsed face-down into a widening crimson pool.

No movement.

Margit could not leave her sword there. She tried to pull it out, but it was stuck. She tried again; this time by putting her foot on his back and using it as a lever. The sword finally dislodged.

She staggered backwards and fell on her backside, unable to tear her eyes away from the blood streaming out of the man's body and staining the ground. She had killed Turks before with arrows; but never from so close. Her body shook. She retched. But no... In the middle of a vicious fight, she could not just sit here waiting for death. Endre and Adnan needed her.

Grunting, she forced herself up on quaking knees that slowly steadied. She wrenched the knives out of the dead body and rushed towards the inner fort.

The noise of people and weapons pierced her ears. Amidst the mayhem, she ducked and swerved to avoid being hit by stray blows or heavily armoured soldiers crashing to the ground.

Once Margit reached the centre of the fortress, she frantically searched about for any sign of Endre or Adnan. Some movement to her left caught her attention. In the glow of the timber-framed building consumed by the flames, a group of Bohemians had discovered an underground enemy hideout, and they were pulling the Ottomans out one by one. They shoved them to their knees and made them hold their hands in the air.

Was Adnan there?

Margit rushed forth, near enough to see her friend among the captives. Her initial relief froze in her chest as the Bohemians started to rough up the prisoners.

One of the Turks fought back; he pushed his captor to the ground and jumped up. But before he made another move, a soldier thrust his sword into the Ottoman's stomach.

"Stay down!" Margit shrieked.

Her friend kept his head low and his hands up, but that did not appease the Bohemians. One of them raised his axe over Adnan.

Margit started forward, but a hand shot from behind and restrained her.

"*Zastav!*" Bátori's voice bellowed in Bohemian so close to her ear that she grimaced in pain. "Stop! Stop! He is ours," he continued in Hungarian.

Grumbling a protest, the Bohemian lowered the axe.

The Judge Royal let go of Margit and approached the soldiers. He hauled Adnan to his feet and drew him away from the other Turkish prisoners.

Margit removed her helmet and cast it aside. "Here! Here!" she called, jumping up and down to claim his attention.

Adnan ran to her, and they embraced.

"Thank the Lord, you are unharmed," she said, her hands feeling his chest, arms and sides for any signs of injury.

"I told you to stay back!" Bátori scolded her.

Margit stepped away from Adnan and bowed her head to the Judge Royal. "I apologise, my lord. I wished to find my friend before anyone harmed him."

The Judge Royal shook his fist at her. "Reckless!" Then his anger subsided. "Well, he is safe now. We have taken the fortress."

As daylight was breaking, Margit watched the king's soldiers hoist the royal flags on the towers of Szabács. The siege was over, but hundreds of men lay dead or injured.

The smell of fire and blood gagged her. Bent over, with hands on knees, she struggled to catch her breath. Her first hand-to-hand battle. Terrifying, but she had survived.

Her face opened into a broad smile at the sight of Endre approaching, his sword still in hand. Blood had spattered over his armour, but he was whole and unharmed. They embraced, yet cautiously so.

"You should have stayed back," he said after he re-sheathed his sword, his voice trembling. He pointed at the dried blood on her face. "You are hurt. Did you fight? Why did you put yourself in danger?"

The reply drowned in Margit's throat. She just took hold of his armoured hand and squeezed it against her hip. And turning towards him, her eyes dived into his.

Endre winked at her. "Come with me."

After glancing about as if to ensure no one was watching, he led her away from the boisterous crowds.

Margit's feet barely touched the earth as they moved towards the opposite side of the fortress.

"Here," Endre said and entered the stables. The victors had taken all the horses out already as valuable spoils of war, leaving the building deserted.

They hid in the corner of a stall.

With quick, impatient movements, Endre took off the steel gauntlets and helmet and threw them to the floor. He leaned over and whispered in her ear, "I have never kissed a lady in armour before." Familiar now, his breath tickled her skin and stirred her senses.

Finally at peace, Margit surrendered her lips to his and then nestled quietly in his arms.

15

Some Useful Advice

The winter sun was on its descent over Szabács, spreading a last golden glow over the fortress, which still stood relatively unscathed—a testament to its superior construction. Before long, campfires burned, the mouth-watering smell of cooked meat wafted, and joyous banter in different languages filled the air.

Dividing the plentiful spoils was a smooth process. Every soldier who participated in the final assault received something valuable in addition to his normal wage.

In one of the stable stalls, sitting on a thick layer of hay and still munching the last bite of a delicious roasted chicken leg, Margit shook her canvas purse and smiled at the jingling sound of the ten gold florins held within: her and Adnan's reward, generously provided by the king. And there was more in the two sacks lying by her feet: silver and copper items, arrows, a better-fitting coat of plates and other Turkish-made armour parts.

Csillag's soft snort and Endre and Adnan's sudden shifting alerted her to someone's presence.

A skinny page stepped into the stall. He held a lantern aloft and moved it around as though he was searching for someone.

"Ah!" he said, holding the light in Margit's face. "You're the red-haired one with the white horse."

"For the love of God, lad!" She shaded her eyes from the glare.

The boy lowered the lantern. "The Lord Judge summons you."

Margit wiped the grease from her lips with the edge of her sleeve and stood up. "Mind my things," she said to the men.

Adnan leaned forward. He opened his mouth but did not speak in the end; perhaps hesitant to interfere in her husband's presence?

Endre raised his head. "Shall I go with you?"

Margit motioned him to stay. "Don't fret. The Lord Judge has offered to help me."

She fastened the purse to her belt and followed the page.

Margit entered the Judge Royal's temporary residence in a ground floor chamber of the castle.

Stripped of everything that had likely adorned it before, the room felt cavernous and draughty despite the roaring fireplace and the many candles burning on an iron wheel which hung from the ceiling.

Still in his armour, Bátori sat at a trestle table, having supper. Margit stood straight with legs apart and hands clasped behind her back, just as she had seen other soldiers do when they awaited their superiors' orders.

Pushing, at last, the plate with the remains of his meal away, Bátori raised his eyes to meet hers. He wet his lips and grinned. "My lady."

Margit bowed. "Lord Judge."

"So, how is your friend?"

"He's well. The Turks interrogated him but thankfully didn't cause him any harm. He was fortunate."

Bátori took a sip from a wooden cup. It must have been some strong wine because even from where she was standing, its sweet aroma tickled Margit's nostrils.

"Come closer," the Royal Judge said, and as soon as she stepped forward, he continued, "The king is impressed by the bravery that you, your husband and your friend have shown. He wishes to restore your title and give you land somewhere in Hungary or Transylvania. But it will not be Szentimre."

Margit lowered her head to hide the tightening of her face muscles. Mátyás seemed willing to grant her part of his own land but would not give her back what was rightfully hers. Why? He certainly did not doubt her loyalty any longer. Was it perhaps because he still did not wish to take Szentimre from her cousin and aunt until he had proof of their wrongdoings?

Whatever his reasons, the offer was not good enough.

She raised her head and squared her shoulders. "No, Lord Judge. I can't accept. No favour from the king, no amount of gold or land will ever entice me away from my mission to clear my father's name and ensure the real traitors receive what they deserve. I owe this to all my ancestors who shed their blood for Hungary."

Bátori's smile widened. "Yes, I thought so, too. My dear lady, you have more courage, sense of honour and family loyalty than any of the men I know."

"Thank you, my lord. You have been good to me, and I hope to repay your kindness one day."

"You can host a banquet for me when you reclaim your estate," he said with a light laugh and then continued in a soft, almost paternal voice, "But until then, here is my advice: you must obtain strong evidence of your father's innocence. Find someone who witnessed what happened or holds important information, and who would testify officially and indicate the real culprit. Be careful, though. Some people would say and sign anything for the right price. You must find the one who will tell you the truth and not what you would like to hear."

"Indeed, Lord Judge, this is wise advice."

"When you have all your evidence, bring it to the king. He will examine it and decide. He will probably ask for my advice, too." He winked at her, which gave her strong reassurance that he was on her side. "It will take you time. You may spend months on end in Transylvania looking for the truth. You must also be in disguise lest someone recognises you. And you must be able to support yourself all this time."

"Find employment, you mean?"

"Precisely."

Bátori clapped his hands. A young clerk emerged from the far side of the chamber, with writing implements in his hands.

"My scribe will prepare a letter of recommendation for you. He is at your disposal. Tell him what to write, and he will oblige. Then I shall sign and affix my seal."

The clerk bowed to her and sat on an empty stool beside Bátori. He carefully placed a pen and pot of ink on the table, spread out a scroll and asked for her instructions.

Margit's face eased into a smile. After so many obstacles and frustrations, her luck seemed to have turned. Without thinking, she dropped to her knees in front of the Judge Royal. "My lord, I'm so grateful for your generosity!"

"Stand up, you foolish woman!" His voice rang with

amusement rather than reproach. "A Bátori does not bow to anyone; not even to another Bátori. Do you forget that we of the Ecsed branch are descended from a dragonslayer?"

Letter clasped in her hand, Margit hastened outside. Elation rushed through her blood and sent her head into a spin. Enveloped in the heavy cloak of darkness, the fortress was quiet. Her overjoyed heavy breathing resounded in the open air.

Going around or stepping over drunken and sleeping soldiers, dying embers and extinguished lanterns, she returned to the stables.

Endre lay on his side, sleeping soundly with one arm under his cheek instead of a pillow and the other embracing a sack filled with spoils. His blanket had slid off his body, so Margit gently pulled it back over him.

Adnan raised his head from the hay. "All well?"

"Yes."

After hiding the letter in Csillag's saddlebag, Margit lay down beside her husband. She cast a glance at Adnan across from her. How much she wished to tell him she had feared for his life; how ashamed she felt for almost sending him to his death; how grateful she was for his friendship and loyalty. But a lump rose at the back of her throat, choking her words.

She pulled the blanket over her body and head and forced herself to sleep.

16

A Painful Decision

Late May 1476

Eyes closed, Margit inhaled the fragrant air and relished the light breeze's touch on her face. Birds chirped in the trees, full of life and vigour. After the morning rain, the soft grass blades moistened the tips of her shoes.

But the muffled crying of mourners nigh reminded her why she stood in the city's graveyard. While the world awakened to spring's warm embrace, the cold and merciless clutches of Death had snatched Endre's grandfather away two days prior.

Among moss-covered headstones and decaying wreaths hanging from weathered crosses, Dragoslava's sniffling and her mother's sobs only reinforced the bleak reality which had surrounded Margit since her return from Szabács. Aside from the king's coin earned for her part in the siege, all she had achieved was slipping away. Doubt and uncertainty crawled anew into her mind. Although her spirit willed to embark on her quest for justice and retribution, her body, heavy with the worries of everyday life, grew powerless. She needed to leave this miserable place, these sad people and their grudges and sorrows.

Though Margit blamed herself for what befell Imre, she did not wish to look after him or watch him slowly perish. And while she cared for Endre, their marriage weighed on her more and more as a burden which Fate had forced upon her. She still was not ready to be a wife and mother. Selfish as it sounded, she could bear it no more. Staying any longer would completely crush her spirit.

While relatives comforted Endre's grandmother at the graveside, Dragoslava stood alone, her shoulders quivering and her gaze glassy, lost in the distance. She looked so forlorn that Margit pitied her.

Whether only for Endre's sake or for the need of all the help she could get, her mother-in-law was a different woman now. Gone were the contemptuous remarks, the abrupt words, the bitter stares. Nor had she chastised Margit for still befriending Adnan or for leaving the family to fight in the siege.

"Here. Lean on me, Mother," Margit said, offering her arms.

With a sigh of thanks, the woman accepted the comfort. As their embrace lingered, a horse's heavy hooves and snorting interrupted this rare, tender moment.

Margit glanced over Dragoslava's head.

Still in his martial attire, Endre swung his leg over Zora's neck and leapt to the ground. Blots of dried mud stained his face and armour. "Forgive me, Mother, for being so late."

Dragoslava pulled away from Margit and flung herself into his arms, sobbing loudly. "Oh, my son! My beloved son!"

Margit greeted her husband with a slight bow of her head and a soft smile but kept her distance while he consoled his mother.

***

That night, Margit was awakened by Endre's voice sending Erzsi out of the bedchamber.

He stole into her bed and enveloped her in his tender embrace. As his face brushed against hers, the touch of dampness made her shiver.

"Are you crying, husband?"

He did not reply. Yet by the way he clung to her, she sensed that he sought solace in her body. Was he mourning his grandfather's passing or the loss of his own adolescence? As the head of the household from now on, responsibility had fallen heavily on his shoulders before they broadened like a grown man's.

"You are my love, my heart, my hope, my life," Endre spoke at last. His quavering words raised a wave of sadness within Margit.

What comfort could she give him?

Gently, she ran her fingers through his hair and endeavoured to dab the tears from his face. But when Endre drew her closer, an overwhelming wave of that same inexplicable fear crashed over Margit again, rendering her powerless. Her limbs turned to stone, and she could only shut her eyes as his lips pressed upon hers. With mounting passion, he climbed onto her; his touch both dreaded and inevitable until, ultimately, he entered her body.

Unable to engage in the moment, Margit's mind retreated to a strange world. Yet not a world of comfort, but dark and ominous, where a shadowy figure usurped her husband's place and was about to throw her down a bottomless abyss.

Endre's heavy breathing burned the side of her face. His hard pushing inside her became unbearable. At last regaining control of her limbs, she shoved him away. "Stop!"

He choked on his impassioned breath. The words stumbled

from his mouth as if in disbelief. "Have you...lost your mind?"

Shivering, Margit hastily pulled her chemise down over her naked body. What an eerie vision! Was it the manifestation of her fear of conceiving or a sign of terrible things to come?

She chose the first notion. "Forgive me. I just don't want a child."

"What?"

"Believe me, I do wish for us to have children. Lots of them." She sat up. "But not until we are the lords of Szentimre. Before that happens, I can't let anything distract me from my mission."

"Why didn't you tell me earlier?" Laden with a mixture of sadness and anger, Endre's voice trembled. "Before we started... You...you have insulted me...as a man and as a husband. You can't treat me like this."

To disguise the tears wetting her eyes, she turned away. "Forgive me."

"So, I am a distraction to you? I have given you nothing but love and support, and this is what you think of me?"

Margit looked at him again and shook her head. "No, of course not. I care about you very much, believe me. That's why I don't wish to drag you with me. You must look after your parents. I shall go to Transylvania and take back my land. And when I have done that, we shall live a decent life together. A better life than this. I owe so much to you and your family for raising me and protecting me all these years."

Compelled by guilt and fondness, she leaned forward to kiss him on the cheek.

Before she knew it, his hand cradled her face and drew it close to his. "You are my world. I would give my life for you. And yet you wish to run from me."

Oh, why was he so loving and devoted? If only he were harsh and unkind, it would be so much easier to leave him behind.

"I'm sorry," she replied, still struggling to contain the turmoil inside her. She moved away from him. "But this is *my* battle, and I shall fight it on my own. Do not fret. I am now stronger than ever, and I shall win."

"I have no doubt, *szívem*. Still, as your husband, I can't let you fight on your own. It's my duty to protect you." Anguish shadowed his words. "The world out there is grim, cruel, brutal. You know this already, don't you?"

Margit nodded. After experiencing the horrors of the battlefield, the 'world out there' scared her, too. She did need Endre beside her but...

She pressed her hand on his. "Your duty is to your parents above all for they gave you life. We now have enough coin and valuables. You can afford to stay home awhile. And I shall give two of my gold florins to Erzsi so that she doesn't burden your family with her expenses."

After a pause, Endre's words came forth with evident difficulty. "At least, take the peasant boy with you."

Margit's mouth fell open. "Adnan? You would allow this?"

"The thought does not please me. But I would feel some comfort if you had someone trustworthy by your side. Of course, he must swear on his life and on his Holy Book that he will treat you with respect."

Tears of joy and relief now filled her eyes. "You have my eternal gratitude, dear husband."

***

Ahmed's brow creased while wrinkles formed at the corners of his narrowed eyes. A father's worry. The fear of losing his only child.

Margit lowered her head. She had no right to separate him from his son; even less so after having convinced her husband to stay at home and look after his parents. Had her desire for revenge left her in want of compassion? Although she prayed that Ahmed would allow Adnan to accompany her to Transylvania, she needed to prepare herself for a negative response.

"Son," Ahmed started, his countenance more serious than ever before, "it pains me to let you go. But you're a man now. Your life's yours. You decide what to do with it."

"I shall not demand this of you," Margit addressed Adnan. "Whatever favour your father owed to mine for sparing his life has now been repaid."

Adnan's face darkened. He closed his eyes. His mouth moved from one twisting shape to another. His clenched fist pressed hard against his forehead.

Margit had seen him like this before: on the night he offered to go into Szabács as a spy. Without a doubt, a battle raged inside him.

At length, Adnan lowered his hand and opened his eyes. He stared at her, his gaze determined. "I'll go with you." He took a steadying breath and turned to Ahmed. "Forgive me, Father."

Tears trembled in the corners of the man's eyes. "May Allah light your path, son, and protect you on your way."

***

At the dawn of the eighth day of June, Margit—hair cut short to just below her ears and dressed as a man—knelt at Imre's bedside. She knew she would not see him again.

When the veteran knight's skeletal, trembling hand touched hers, she shivered. She swallowed back the wave of sorrow surging within.

Clearly mustering whatever traces of strength remained in his ailing body, Imre smiled. "God be with you, my child," he said, his words staggering through his lips. "I feel I'll see my good friend in the next life soon, and I know he'll be proud of you." He feebly squeezed her hand, and Margit's heart twinged.

After leaving the bedchamber, she inhaled deeply to compose herself. The eagerness to right the wrongs committed against her and her family quickly chased away the sadness.

She parted from Dragoslava with a hug and a kiss in the entrance hall of the house and then stepped into the front garden where Endre waited for her, holding Csillag's reins.

Beside them, Erzsi whimpered, her cheeks wet and swollen. Margit pulled her into a tight embrace. Another parting which made her heart bleed. Tears burned her eyes, but she willed them not to fall. "Don't be sad, dear godmother. Be healthy and wait for me. It will not be long before we meet again."

"I'll leave you to say farewell to your husband," Erzsi said, sniffling.

Margit gently drew away from the woman and turned to Endre. Not bearing to meet his mournful eyes, she lowered her gaze. "The map?"

"It's in your saddlebag. Adnan will be here soon with the donkey to carry your baggage." He passed the horse's reins to her. "At a moderate riding pace, and given that you don't know the terrain, it should take you ten to twelve days to reach Szentimre. You must find a safe place to spend each night and to rest and eat during the day."

Margit nodded. She pulled the wedding ring off her finger, removed her father's dagger from her belt and handed them to Endre. "Keep these safe until I return."

His face twitched. "Of course." His voice bore a whisper of resignation.

She stroked Csillag's neck and absently threaded her fingers through his mane. How she yearned for a warm embrace and a tender kiss from her husband. Yet she received neither. Since *that* night, Endre had been distant and, at times, short with her. He had not even once entered her bedchamber.

Perhaps it was she who needed to show affection. She wrapped her arms around him, but she embraced a statue—cold, rigid and utterly unfeeling towards her.

"I shall come find you as soon as I can. I promise," Endre said, his voice still subdued.

Margit pulled back a little but kept her hands on his arms. After failing him intimately as a wife, she could not think of any other way to make amends. "I'm sorry for leaving you. Yet I do not wish you to suffer. You must think of yourself."

He squinted at her. "What do you mean?"

"You...you are a young man. If I don't return from this journey, you must find another woman."

Endre's cheeks flushed instantly. "How can you say this? Do

you intend to abandon me?"

"No! I didn't mean to offend you. I only say that if anything happened to me—"

Margit paused, chastising herself for she had insulted him once again. Dropping her gaze to the ground, she mumbled, "I'm sorry. I speak foolishly sometimes."

Endre failed to reply, which increased her embarrassment. She breathed a sigh of relief, however, when she saw Adnan approach with his mule and a sturdy donkey in tow.

"Good morrow to you!" Her friend's voice rang with cheerfulness and excitement. Behind him, the sky already brightened with the colours of the new day.

He handed Margit her bow and quiver, a pair of throwing knives as well as a shiny new sabre made by Ahmed. She smiled, thankful for his reassuring presence. She placed the knives in her saddlebag. After hanging the sabre and quiver to the saddle and the bow across her back, she turned to watch her husband.

Silently and sullenly, Endre loaded and secured her bundle of clothes, rolled blankets and a sack of food supplies onto the back of the donkey. "All ready for you."

"Thank you," Margit mumbled, her soul painfully heavy.

Without looking at her, he helped her mount Csillag.

"Farewell, sir." Adnan extended his hand towards Endre, but the latter left him hanging for a moment.

"Look after my wife," he said sternly.

"Of course."

Endre finally took Adnan's hand; but instead of shaking it, he tugged Adnan towards him. "Peasant!" he hissed into his ear. "I trust you are a good man. But if you do anything to sully her honour, I shall rip your head off!"

Margit gasped at Endre's sharp tone.

Adnan recoiled, eyes wide and frightened. "I'd never do that. Have you forgotten I swore on my faith's Holy Book?"

"Time to go," Margit intervened before the atmosphere turned more hostile. She had other, more worrying thoughts on her mind than to be distracted by her husband's jealousy; a long, arduous and perilous journey into the unknown lay ahead.

17

A Dangerous Journey

After Belgrade and the Danube faded into the distance, Margit's heartbeat grew unsteady as she and Adnan headed northeast for she was travelling even farther into strange lands. The cool, refreshing air which filled her lungs on the first day of her journey lightened her mood while sticking to the main roads quietened her anxiety. But in the early afternoon of the second day, the gentle wind blew no more, and the sun burned in the middle of the sky. Sweat poured down Margit's body. Csillag panted and snorted under her, his pace reduced to a slow tread.

She turned to Adnan. He did not fare any better. With a laboured movement of his hand, he kept drying his brow while he blew air out of his puffed cheeks.

To Margit's relief, a forested area appeared in the distance. At last they could rest there awhile.

The shade of tall and leafy trees offered shelter from the unrelenting force of the sun. The animals grazed happily, and Adnan fell asleep at once, chin drooped to his chest and back resting against a thick trunk.

Thirsty, Margit reached for her waterskin. It felt light in her hand. She needed to replenish.

With both her and Adnan's waterskins slung over her shoulder, she ventured into the forest, which extended far beyond what she initially thought. Despite the cooler air under the canopy of trees, she grunted from the effort as she picked her way through the dense vegetation.

At length, the babbling of water reached her ears.

Margit stopped and listened. Where was its source?

The sound came from a lower level.

As she peered ahead, patches of blue sky flashed through the rustling tree leaves. Rushing forward, she came to the crest of a slope.

Below her feet, a drop of about two men's height revealed a clear brook, which tumbled over rocks and stones. A trodden forest path ran along the stream and then curved around thickets left and right.

Thankfully, the sloping ground was covered in grass. Margit sat down, ready to slide. But the sound of approaching horses drove panic into her. Just as a group of riders emerged from around the bend of the path, she pushed herself up and dived behind a tree trunk at the brink of the drop. Scarcely daring to breathe, she listened.

Splashing and snorting replaced the clopping of hooves. The riders must have stopped to let their horses drink. The men's banter was loud enough for Margit to discern they spoke in Turkish. Pity Adnan was not there to translate their words.

Suppressing her fear, she braved a glance in their direction.

What were the Ottomans doing inside the Hungarian kingdom? In this part of the country, the Danube formed a natural border between Hungary and Ottoman-occupied Serbia. But the river was over a day's ride farther to the south. And those men wore ordinary clothes and displayed no military insignia or banners.

As they finally trotted away, they split into two groups, each taking a different direction.

Scouts!

Breathing hard, Margit waited until the sound of hooves had ceased. She slid down the slope to the brook and filled the waterskins. Uneasiness gnawed at her stomach. Pulse drumming in her ears, she clambered up the incline, ran back to Adnan and shook him awake.

He rubbed his eyes. "Something amiss?"

"Ottoman riders."

"What?" Adnan leapt to his feet. "Here?"

"No. We are safe. But I think they are scouting the area for an imminent attack. We must ride back to Belgrade and inform the authorities."

His brow creased with disapproval. "Are you mad? We've travelled for two days and now we just go back?"

"If an unexpected raid happens, innocent people will die. I'm sure you don't want that."

"What if they see us and kill us? We're well hidden here. Let's wait it out."

"I shall go," Margit said decisively. "You can stay if you prefer."

"Wait! You're so impatient." He scratched his chin, deliberating. "Let's ride to the next village and send a message to Belgrade from there."

Margit mulled over his suggestion for a few moments. He was right.

And so, they hastened back to the main road and towards the next settlement. The village was small: a handful of farmhouses spread along a single street, hemmed in by fields of wheat. A fortified mansion—clearly the home of the landowner—stood in the distance. His tenants took the warning seriously and alerted their lord, who sent a messenger to Belgrade. Although satisfied with her good deed, disquiet still nestled in Margit's heart as she and her friend resumed their journey. What if they ran across the Turks again?

***

Margit and Adnan rode for another four days and spent the nights in village inns. Even when indoors, they kept watch over each other. One would sleep first and the other would stay awake, and vice versa until daylight when they set off again.

During this time, Margit noticed how Adnan sometimes stared at her with wistful eyes. Possibly realising she saw this, he would turn his gaze to the sky. Whenever they happened to be in proximity, his hands shook slightly, and his face reddened. And just like while they were in Szabács, he never took the time to stop and pray to his God. When Margit asked him if he needed to do that, he dismissed her with a shake of his head.

On the seventh day of travelling, they entered the Banat of Temes.

Having left the Serbian-speaking lands far behind them by now, they found themselves in a territory with Wallachian population. The terrain had also changed. The expansive, flat plains had given way to a hilly landscape with forests, streams and narrow valleys. Margit was glad for the blankets Endre packed for her as the nights grew colder and the air took on a bitter chill whenever the wind picked up.

The villages and settlements now came farther and farther apart until, eventually, the two friends went a whole day without finding anywhere suitable to spend the night.

Thus a sheltered spot on the side of a wooded hill became their camp.

Despite the cold, they could not light a fire lest they attracted unwanted attention. They tethered the animals to a tree and laid the blankets on the ground. Adnan went to sleep first while Margit kept watch.

Sitting quietly, she wrapped her cape around her and looked at the cloudless sky. The waning crescent moon still hid behind the other side of the hill, letting the elaborate shapes of the various constellations shine brightly. Margit started to count the little lights but soon gave up and just admired the beauty of the night sky. Those stars had been up there since God created the world. They were the ones which had guided her Magyar ancestors from the vast plains of the East to their new homeland. The stars were also, according to the old myths of the Hungarian and Székely people, the place where the warriors went after they died. Those warriors would come back one day to defend their homeland when she was in danger.

Perhaps her father's spirit lived among them, too. If only he would return to help her with her mission. Margit strained to remember his face, yet only faint memories lingered. But a sensation of safety and peace enveloped her just as it had when he was with her.

As her weary eyes fluttered close, an otherworldly realm

unfurled before her. The imposing figure of a knight in full plate armour stood mere paces away. Surrounded by an eerie glow, he brandished a longsword in one hand and a battle axe in the other. Blood dripped from both weapons, its ominous sound echoing as it hit the ground. A shield with her family's coat of arms rested against the man's leg.

Margit searched his face.

Who are you?

Her gaze was drawn to the long red hair peeping from beneath his helmet, and her mouth fell open.

Father!

A chill shot down Margit's spine. He must have heard her call for help. Yet the image before her was not one of safety and love. Rage streamed from him, overwhelming her and stealing her breath. Why was he so angry? Was it against her or against those who harmed him?

He dropped the sword and took a step towards her, his armour clanking and his size looming like a giant shadow.

Now he had something else in his hand, which he threw to her.

Margit looked down. In her lap lay the severed head of an unknown young man, his face blood-streaked and his glassy eyes open wide as though staring into the horrors of Hell.

Heart pounding, Margit awoke with a scream.

Adnan's hand clamped over her mouth. "Shhh!"

Margit gasped for air as soon as he removed it.

"Turks," he said, pointing down the hill.

A line of riders, some of them carrying torches, were on the march, dragging dozens of captives behind them.

Margit brought her hand to her lips. "*Úristen!* They *did*

attack."

But instead of Belgrade and the border area along the Danube, they had raided much deeper into Hungarian territory, to the east. Of course. The small villages and settlements in the Banat of Temes were less protected than Belgrade and the Southern Country. But what would happen to the people? If the Turks wanted to kill them, they would have done it already. So, the obvious answer was they were going to sell them as slaves.

Guilt stabbed at Margit's heart. If only she could help those unfortunate souls. But it was not possible with only Adnan and her against so many men.

As the lines of people crept closer, Csillag's uneasy whinny drove fear back into her. Just one look up from the soldiers would mean capture. Margit crawled towards the animals on shaking limbs. She rose to her knees and rubbed the horse's tense neck.

But then, chaos erupted from below: anguished wails and yelling, followed by running footfalls that dislodged stones and clumps of earth. Was someone trying to climb the hill?

Csillag tossed his head. His hooves scraped the ground.

The mule brayed, and the donkey kicked.

Arrows whooshed through the still air.

Margit jumped up and flung her arms around Csillag's sweaty neck, murmuring, "Hush, my boy. Stay calm."

Adnan rushed to help, urgently trying to shush the mule and donkey. But the little devils only raised their voices in distress.

"They're coming," Adnan whispered.

She froze.

We are doomed!

Csillag's ears flicked back and forth. Margit's heart leapt each time he flinched.

Below them, the thump of two—nay, three—bodies. Screams of terror as blades flashed in the torchlight. The soldiers' attention thankfully diverted to restraining the panicked captives.

Those frantic moments dragged like hours of torture until the commotion died down, and the unholy procession resumed its sorrowful march.

At last, Csillag's muscles slowly relaxed, and he lowered his head.

As if taking cue from him, the mule and donkey also settled.

Yet Margit did not dare move. Only when the last flickering torch faded into the darkness did she allow herself to breathe freely. Still shaking, she collapsed onto the blanket.

"We're safe. God's great," Adnan said in a low voice as he sat beside her. "But tell me now: why were you screaming?"

Margit's heaving bosom trembled. "I had a strange dream. My father appeared to me, and he was furious. He threw someone's head at me. I don't know what to make of this. It was frightening."

"D'you think he's angry with you?"

"I think not. He looked more like he wanted revenge."

"And you'll give him that," Adnan reassured her. He pulled his cape around him. "Go to sleep. I'll keep watch."

Margit lay on her back and closed her eyes. But the sad image of the wailing captives and her father's looming shadow haunted her mind for a long time until exhaustion finally plunged her into a dreamless sleep.

A touch on her shoulder jolted Margit awake. Like stretched

strings of shining beads, slivers of sunshine pierced the thick foliage of the trees, shimmering in front of her bleary eyes.

She blinked and slowly raised herself.

A new day had dawned, but the events of the previous night lingered in her head like the whispering echo of a long-passed storm.

"Those poor souls," she said pensively.

She stood up and walked to the end of the ledge. "The bodies still lie there." She crossed herself. "One is a child."

"We must bury them," Adnan said.

Margit shook her head. Somewhere, not far from here, perhaps their loved ones were already mourning them. "No. We must take them home."

They loaded the young woman and the girl on Csillag and the man on the mule. Guiding her horse by the reins, Margit trudged absently on the forest path, her soul heavy with sadness. Adnan did not seem to fare much better as he led his mule with a darkened face and lips pressed together.

Fortunately, the raiders had come from the direction Margit and Adnan were headed, so their journey was not interrupted. But travelling on foot now slowed their progress because they needed to stop more often and rest.

The sun shone high in the sky when they reached the next settlement—a village bearing the scars of the previous night's Ottoman raid.

Margit halted and looked around. Although the houses made of earth stood intact, many reed or straw roofs and wooden fences still smouldered. People's belongings, broken utensils, tools, baskets and empty sacks of grain lay scattered across the ground.

The stench of smoke and dead animals turned Margit's stomach. She covered her mouth and nose with her hand.

Shouts and sobbing drew her attention away from the devastation. Some of the surviving inhabitants were burying their dead while possibly lamenting the loss of their livelihoods.

Brandishing makeshift wooden clubs, two elderly men in threadbare clothes blocked Margit and Adnan's way and addressed them in a foreign language.

Alarmed, she turned to her friend. "Neither Serbian nor Hungarian. Do you understand them?"

"No."

Margit recalled Imre's description of the areas she needed to traverse and the people she would meet on her way to Transylvania. "They must be Wallachian."

She took two cautious steps towards the men. "Look, we brought your folks." She pointed at the dead bodies on Csillag and the mule.

A deathly hush descended. Quiet like ghosts, the villagers—most of them of advanced age, probably abandoned by the raiders because they would not fetch a good price as slaves—emerged from the shadows of the wrecked dwellings and sheds. They huddled together, pale-faced and shaking, their eyes glued to the three bloodied corpses.

Breaking from the group, a hunched old woman tottered towards Csillag, her withered hand extending in the direction of the dead woman and child. Her trembling lips barely formed the words, "Irina... Lumina..."

A heart-wrenching wail erupted; so loud that Margit wondered how such a frail creature had the strength to release it. She rushed to support the old woman before she collapsed to the ground.

Clutching at each other, an elderly couple approached the mule and gazed at the man's body in frozen silence. Their son, perchance?

All it took was a few moments for the whole group to dissolve into sobs and sighs.

Though no words were shared, Margit and Adnan lowered the bodies, allowing their families to embrace them one last time. Then prayers were said, and shovels were put to work.

The rest of the day passed in silent labour, helping the villagers gather their scattered belongings and any surviving livestock. And when night fell, the grateful folk shared what little food remained with her and Adnan.

Against sorrow's lingering shadows, the weary but peaceful faces around the fire gave Margit comfort in seeing how her small act of kindness had the power to rekindle this grieving community's resilience in the face of such soul-crushing tragedy.

18
Homeland

When Margit and Adnan set off the following morning, leaden clouds hung from the sky, and the rumble of thunder carried from the distance. It was not long before thick raindrops pelted them and furrowed rivulets on the dirt road.

They rode in brooding silence, only exchanging a few words about finding shelter. Adnan stared ahead with a tormented gaze, hands fiddling with the reins of his mule. Were his thoughts still haunted by the harrowing village scenes and the anguished cries that also echoed in her own memory? No matter how much Margit willed herself onwards, her soul remained trapped in that place of grief.

Their damp clothes clung heavy with rain and sadness as they entered a small town. At the local inn, Margit's silver denars secured a separate stall for the animals and a private chamber for her and Adnan, while most of the travellers were accommodated either in the stables, the covered courtyard or the area of the tavern. And for a few copper coins, she secured a brazier and a wooden frame to hang their wet clothes.

They supped apart, each sitting on a stool on either side of the frame. But the silence weighed like an iron ball on Margit's chest. Behind a hanging shirt, she could just discern Adnan's sorry shadow hunched over his bowl. The poor lad still seemed to carry the woe of those strangers; perhaps he even blamed himself for being unable to ease their suffering.

Time to put all this behind us.

She pushed the two shirts apart and stuck her head through. "Hey. How do you fare?"

For the first time that day, he turned to look at her. His eyes lit up, but he still did not speak.

She rose, carried her stool across and sat beside him, smiling with the intent of easing his discomfort. "It doesn't seem the accursed rain will stop anytime soon. While we bide here, I can teach you Hungarian."

He raised an eyebrow. "Why?"

"Because it's the formal language in Szentimre, my estate. Unless my cousin and his mother have turned it into a Saxon manor."

Adnan cocked his head. "What's a Saxon?"

"It's how we call those from the German lands who settled in Transylvania two centuries ago."

"There are Germans in Transylvania?"

Margit chuckled at her friend's ignorance. Yet it was not his fault that he had not received an education. She would not know this either but for her tutor's lessons and Erzsi and Imre's detailed accounts of her family history. "Yes. Many different people live in Transylvania: Magyars, Saxons, Wallachians, Jews, Cumans. And in the mountains to the east, there are the Székely lands."

"See...what?" he said, failing to pronounce the strange word.

"Székely. A brother tribe of the Hungarians who speaks the same language, only a different dialect. My father was of Magyar, Saxon and Székely blood. My mother half-Magyar, half-Polish. My cousin's mother, that horrible Anna, is a Saxon too."

Adnan stared at her wide-eyed and puffed his cheeks.

Margit smiled. "Did you think you were the only one of mixed blood?" She pointed at her head. "The red hair comes from my father, who inherited it from his Saxon grandmother."

His stunned expression was so amusing.

"Now, enough with the history," she said, giggling. "Let us learn Hungarian."

After long and arduous hours, during which Adnan's face flushed again and again, he still struggled to pronounce the new words. Deep lines formed on his brow, and his mouth twisted into odd shapes. But Margit was patient and thorough, and she made sure he slowly and steadily learned the few phrases he needed to know at that point. She would teach him more later once in Szentimre, where he would also listen to the language daily.

And when this was out of the way, she spoke about a serious subject. "While we are there, you must hide your faith."

Adnan frowned. "Yes. Truth is, I don't remember the last time I prayed or fasted." He lowered his head. "My father always scolds me because I'm not that devoted. But after seeing how many people the Ottomans slaughter and enslave, I don't wish to share their faith."

"This pleases me, my friend." Margit patted him on the shoulder like she had seen other men with their companions. "But you know, we Christians have been killing each other for centuries. Look who Mátyás has been fighting all these years: the German emperor and the Polish king, who are trying to take his throne. They'd rather see Hungary suffer and be brought to her knees by the Ottomans so that they can just march in and take everything.

And I'm sure it wasn't a Turk who killed my father."

"So, you're not a believer either?"

Margit wagged her finger at him. "Oh no, I *do* believe. What I mean is that people can be good or bad regardless of their faith."

"Wise words, m'lady." Adnan stood up, stepped his right leg back and bent his knees gracefully while holding his imaginary skirts off the floor.

Margit raised her hand and pretended she was going to hit him. "You, silly ass! Men bow or go down on one knee. They don't curtsy like damsels."

As their merry laughter filled the chamber, the blood warmed in Margit's veins. Whatever hardships lay ahead, facing them would be easier with such a steadfast friend by her side.

***

The heavy rain continued for another day; but even when it finally stopped, they still could not travel. They waited two more days for the flood waters to recede before resuming their journey.

Determined to make up time, they travelled from first light until nightfall and stopped wherever that happened to be.

Fifteen days after they left Belgrade, they passed Hunyadvár—the majestic castle residence of the king's late father, its pointed towers piercing the azure sky—and then the stone fortress of Déva, spread out like the wings of the *Turul* bird atop a steep hill. As they continued northeast, the rolling hills gave way to thickly forested mountain ranges, narrow valleys, raging streams and crystal waterfalls. There were no towns or villages, only small settlements of sheep and cattle herders and the odd fortified church. Sometimes the trail was so unclear that Margit feared they were lost in the wilderness.

By sundown, they came across a young shepherd, who pointed them in the direction of Szentimre. "On the other side of that mountain."

On hearing her father's language, even with a vulgar accent, Margit flung her arms around the astounded boy but recoiled instantly, struck by his pungent stench of sheep.

She turned to Adnan. "We are not too far. We shall be there tomorrow."

Later that evening, while her friend prepared their camp for the night, Margit knelt on the ground and inhaled the scents of her homeland. It was as though she had entered a new world. Even the air felt different: refreshing, fragrant, familiar.

She clawed a lump of grass and earth and squeezed it in her closed hand, letting the moisture penetrate her skin and spread renewed vigour through her body.

Unable to still the furious beating of her heart, she barely slept that night. She woke Adnan up before the sun had risen over the mountain ridge. They saddled the animals and rode away as fast as the terrain allowed them.

The last barrier between Margit and her estate was a narrow pass through the mountain. A cascade of water ran through ancient rocks and crashed into a frothy stream, which flowed along the trodden path for a while and then disappeared into an opening in the ground. The smell of wet stone and earth lingered in Margit's nostrils long after leaving the waterfall behind.

High above, a golden eagle flew in the direction of Szentimre, his shrill cries asserting his dominance over the rough landscape; or, perhaps, extending a proud welcome to Margit as she was about to reach home at last.

A mile or so farther, the valley widened, eventually leading to a fertile plateau, which extended as far as the next mountain range in the distance.

The fresh wind created ripples on a sea of wheat to the left. Grassland occupied the space directly in front of Margit, split cleanly by a narrow dirt road. Apple orchards graced the land on the right in patches of dark green. Margit and Adnan passed small farmhouses, scattered in the beginning but in bigger clusters later on. Then they came across a stud farm, where spirited foals pranced about their paddock under their mothers' watchful eyes.

And beyond that stood the walls of a town.

All the activity on the ground—farmers and merchants going about their everyday business, animals grazing, people coming and going through the town gate, dogs barking, children playing— brought about a warm sense of nostalgia within Margit. Was this an old, forgotten childhood memory? Before everything changed and chaos ensued?

"Look!" Adnan's high-pitched exclamation startled her.

Following the direction he pointed, she lifted her gaze, and her jaw dropped.

On the top of a luscious hill, the castle of Sasfészek, surrounded by mighty stone fortifications with watchtowers at the four corners, gleamed like the purest gem in the midday sun. Bright red tiles on the pointed rooftops of the towers and keep contrasted with the pure white walls, creating a most vibrant image.

Margit had dreamt of Sasfészek for years; yet she never imagined it so beautiful, so breath-taking. "My home." Warm tears formed in her eyes.

"It's truly grand," Adnan agreed.

Margit composed herself quickly. She had to keep the pretence, the male disguise. Tears were not a part of this. She straightened herself in the saddle.

One last doubt flashed in her mind before proceeding. She ran her hand down the front of her body. Whether it be her own efforts to prevent her breasts from growing or mere fortune, she had been 'favoured' with an almost flat chest.

She turned to her friend for reassurance. "Can I pass as a man?"

Adnan surveyed her carefully and nodded. "As a young lad, yes. Just make your voice a little deeper and harden your gaze when you look others in the eye."

He was right. A woman's modesty had no place in her game of deception. She must be bold.

Her heart was beating like a drum when she stood at the town gate.

As if awoken from a long slumber, two halberd-wielding guards, their only armour a leather cuirass, scrambled from the shadows of the arched entrance to block her and Adnan's way.

The younger one, with a pockmarked face, spoke Hungarian with a foreign accent. "State your names and your business."

"Saša Lazarević," Margit replied and then introduced Adnan by the Serbian assumed name they had agreed upon. "And this is Stefan Danilović. We come from Belgrade, looking for work. Here is a reference from Lord István Bátori, the Judge Royal."

She handed the wary-looking guard the letter.

The man scrutinised her with narrowed eyes. His gaze hardened as it fell on Adnan. "Serbians? You're a long way from home."

"I'm half-Hungarian," Margit said, drawing his attention back to her. "My mother was from Hunyadvár."

"You speak the language well," the guard said while he examined the document, eyes running over it left to right and back again.

"It's upside down," Margit said, looking down her nose at him.

The soldier pinched his mouth before signalling for the two of them to follow him.

He led them into the sentry house: a narrow, tower-like building at the side of the gate. There, they waited until a strongly built armoured man of middle age, with a weather-beaten face and a scar running across his left cheek from the end of his nose towards his ear, entered.

"Captain Károly Dóczi," he said in a gruff voice, letter in hand.

He gave Margit and Adnan a long, careful look before returning the document to her. "You don't look like soldiers. Yet you bring glowing recommendations by one of the highest-ranking men in the kingdom. Did you really fight in Szabács?"

"Yes, captain," Margit replied, standing straight as an arrow. "I'm a good archer and rider. My friend can fight well too, and he is a fine blacksmith."

"Where did you come from?"

"Belgr—" Margit stopped herself. "I mean...Nándorfehérvár," she continued, stressing the Hungarian name of the city over the Serbian one.

"And why did you come here? Surely, you could find work there or join the royal army."

Margit held her chin high. "I'm proud to have Transylvanian blood, sir. I always wanted to return to my mother's native land and offer my services. As soon as we arrived in Hunyadvár, we were directed to Szentimre. A lot of skilled soldiers and knights who fought in many renowned battles came from here. This place is held in high esteem for its military tradition."

"Really?" The captain appeared more surprised by her words than suspicious of them. "The field commander will be glad to hear this." He fell quiet for a moment. "You're both in luck. We need a blacksmith, and we're presently recruiting mercenaries. Lord Szilágyi provides soldiers for hire to the king and to the voivode of Transylvania."

Margit's back stiffened. Surely, this lord was her cousin, Márton, who would be twenty-seven years old by now.

"Find somewhere to stay," the captain said. "Come back in the morn. I'll take you to the castle to meet the garrison commander. Despite the letter, we must still test your skills before we hire you."

19
The Test

As Margit walked the cobbled streets of the town of Szentimre, her heart palpitated in anxious anticipation. She was home at last, standing on the land taken from her so violently fourteen years prior.

But when her eager strides led her to the town square, it all felt so alien to her. She glanced about, seeking something—anything—that could prod her recollection.

The church bells rang for nones. A flock of startled doves took flight from the fountain central to the square and scattered across the sky.

Of course! The fountain.

Margit would come here to feed the birds and splash her hands in the water.

She closed her eyes, and the memories rushed back.

Market day.

Safe in her father's arms, Margit's eyes popped wide, her senses stimulated by the feast unfolding around her.

The sweet aroma of rosemary, sage and mint blended with the smoke of the fires roasting pork and fowl on spits. A woman proffered a fresh pie. Traders and peddlers hawked their wares; people bantered; children shrieked joyfully; chickens clucked; dogs barked. Overflowing stalls lined the main street and town square. The colours of fabrics, foodstuff, pottery, jewellery created a vibrant live embroidery.

On a stage across from her, a gypsy band played the liveliest tune. A bare-chested man swallowed fire. And then her favourite: the juggler, in his fanciful clothes and pointy shoes, keeping one apple in the air while catching the other two.

"Closer, Daddy!" Margit would squeal, her heart brimming with wonder.

"Yes, *kincsem*," her father would indulge her, his freckled face wearing a radiant smile, his forest-green eyes sparkling as he looked at her.

People would part to let them pass, heads bowed in respect. "Good day, m'lord. And lil' lady."

A sob rose in Margit's throat as she was overwhelmed with the profound joy and deeply buried grief that came with finally recalling this precious memory of her father.

The familiar face, the lively and welcoming images, however, quickly faded away. A crushing sorrow displaced the excitement which had filled Margit's breast before. "Why is it so different?"

"What's different?" came Adnan's voice.

She swept her arm across the grey and sombre image in front of them. "This. It's not the town I remember."

There were no gypsies and no juggler. The stage lay empty and half-collapsed, its planks rotting. Stale and mouldy smells lingered around. The streets were busy; yet the atmosphere teemed with fear, not mirth. The people went about their business in an eerily quiet way, hunched and scurrying from one place to another. No banter or gossip, no laughter filled the air. Even the voices of the merchants promoting their wares were subdued.

Was it perhaps because of all the soldiers crawling about sullen and heavily armed? The captain had said Márton supplied mercenaries to the royal army, so this should be expected. But why so many of them? Surely, they should be fighting battles instead of roaming the streets of Szentimre and driving unease into people's minds.

Margit clenched her teeth.

I promise you, Father: One day, I shall bring back joy and happiness to our land.

She beckoned Adnan. "Never mind. Let us find lodgings."

With the two inns being full, they were directed to a townhouse. The owner, a Saxon fabrics merchant with a thick blonde moustache and an even thicker accent when he spoke Hungarian, offered them his loft to rent. The space was adequate: a sleeping area with two separate beds and, behind a thin timber-framed partition, a sitting and eating area with hearth, a table and two stools.

Margit and Adnan left their belongings there and the animals in the stable and went to the nearby tavern for a meal.

The innkeeper's wife brought them some tasty pottage, cheese and freshly baked bread. She was Hungarian, but when Margit tried to start a conversation with her, she only responded with a stern look.

"No one seems friendly," Margit said to Adnan while they were getting ready for bed that night. "It looks like Márton has the people scared with all these soldiers about."

"We'll soon find out why. Now, let's sleep. I'm spent."

***

Following Captain Dóczi the next day, Margit and Adnan rode up the winding hill path towards Sasfészek.

A pair of goshawks circled above the castle, their piercing cries beckoning Margit's attention to a formidable sight. Perched upon the unforgiving terrain, her ancestral home—an Eyrie indeed— filled her with a profound sense of awe. At the height of three men, its mighty curtain wall appeared fused with the bedrock underneath, seemingly emerging from the rugged embrace of the cliffs themselves. In the presence of such grandeur, Margit's soul stirred with a mixture of reverence and belonging as if the castle's roots reached deep into the core of her being.

When she crossed the gate under the raised portcullis, an irresistible force impelled her forth into the echoes of her childhood. Her heart swelled with memories again. How many times had she run around the courtyard chasing a cat or played hide-and-seek with Endre in the stables? How strong her father's shoulders felt as they carried her! Watching the world from above, she would shriek with delight while coiling strands of his long red hair around her fingers until his voice, firm yet affectionate, gently prompted her to stop. She would chuckle at the servants and stable hands, who busied themselves with their daily chores. She would cover her ears to block out the hammering on metal coming from the smithy. And she would stubbornly plant her feet on the ground to resist Erzsi's efforts to pull her into the chapel for mass.

But the real gem of Sasfészek stood there before Margit's eyes: the four-storied stone keep where her innocent younger self lived, shielded from the perils of the world by its sturdy walls. Sunlight glinted on the glass of a window on the second floor. Was that her bedchamber? She could not recall. Yet a feeling of warmth and familiarity coursed through her veins and brought a smile to her face.

Attached to the side of the keep, the long, single-level great hall was adorned by a colonnaded portico. Margit did not remember anything of that building's interior. A place for the 'grown-up folk' as Erzsi used to say, where her father received and entertained his distinguished guests.

Margit let out a pensive sigh. Her father's image only lived as a memory inside her. And just like the town of Szentimre, a gloomy shadow lingered over Sasfészek now. Although the servants still bustled about, their voices were muffled by the sound of soldiers' boots and swords as they drilled in the courtyard and trod the battlements.

"We're preparing for war," Dóczi's voice interrupted her thoughts. "The Ottomans are marching against Moldavia with a large force, and its prince, Stefan, has asked King Mátyás for help. The king has sent the Judge Royal to Transylvania to muster troops."

Of course. This justified the large military presence in Szentimre. But the good news was that Bátori was in the province. Would Margit meet him again, perchance?

Inside the barracks, she waited for the garrison commander's arrival.

"His name is Pál Balog," Dóczi explained. "He's also the castellan, looking after the estate when the lord is absent. We have one more senior officer, the field commander János Bocskai. He's the one leading the men in battle as the lord himself never goes on campaign."

On hearing Balog's name, Margit shuddered. He was her cousin's 'lackey,' as Imre called him, who resented her father for demoting him.

At that moment, the very man entered. Of middle age but older than Dóczi, he had wavy black hair bestrewn with wiry strands of grey. Bearing the lines of an aggressive disposition, his face would have looked wholly fierce were it not for his ridiculously sized moustache, which drove away all fear of him from Margit's mind.

"These are the men," Dóczi said to him.

Balog's brown eyes peered at them under bushy eyebrows. "How old are you?"

"We are both eighteen, sir," Margit replied.

"Commander!" he corrected her and then stared at Adnan's puzzled face. "Why is your friend not speaking? Has he lost his tongue?"

"No, commander. He doesn't know Hungarian. But I'm teaching him, and he will learn soon."

Balog eyed them suspiciously. "Mmmm...I don't know," he said to Dóczi while pointing at Adnan. "This one looks like a Turk or Tatar." And inclining his head towards Margit, he scrutinised her more intently. "And this one looks like a woman."

"I am not a woman, commander," Margit said. She raised her eyebrows and chin. "I merely inherited my late mother's fair looks."

Balog let out the loudest snort.

"They're highly recommended by the Judge Royal," Dóczi said, struggling to maintain a straight face.

Balog finally stood back. "Yes, yes... I suppose appearances can be deceptive. Bring them to the field. I must test them."

On a flat, grassy area of several acres extending from the town walls to a stream which traversed the miner's village farther down its course, the training field buzzed with activity. Soldiers practised on quintains and scarecrow-shaped wicker pells, hurling insults at their imaginary opponents or words of encouragement to their mates in various languages. Arrows whistled through the air and thumped into round targets which dotted the field. Other men grappled or fought with training weapons in two lists, their armour rattling and their swords and shields cracking with each hit. Forming circles and squares at the commands of their captain, the light cavalrymen trained their steeds in battle formations. The horses' snorting, whinnying and puffing added to the pandemonium.

Amidst all this, Margit and Adnan's armour turned many heads and aroused derogatory comments and suspicious looks, thus validating Balog's already doubtful attitude. "On which side did you fight in Szabács?" he said.

"Why do you ask, commander?" Margit responded while she attached the mail aventail to her helmet.

He flicked his hand dismissively towards her and Adnan. "Turkish armour and helmets."

Expecting this question, Margit had rehearsed the answer in her head many times. "Ah! Loot from Szabács. Us being poor lads, we can't afford to have armour made. So, we use what we can find."

Balog snorted.

Margit bit her tongue to prevent herself from answering back. She had already detested this man before she met him, and now his condescending behaviour vexed her more.

"This way," Dóczi said, thankfully drawing her attention away from the castellan.

Margit and Adnan followed the two officers to the closest list.

"Hans! Ladislav! Approach!" Balog ordered two soldiers: a German bear of a man and a less brawny but still strong-looking Bohemian. "Let us put these two lads to the test."

Adnan was first.

Leaning over the wooden barrier of the list, Margit watched him anxiously as he fought the Bohemian with a blunted sword and defended himself well. When the German came at him with an axe, her friend showed great strength and agility, parrying the hits and evading the blows. Eventually, the much taller Hans struck Adnan on the shoulder. This left him shaky and disoriented, and he finally collapsed.

"Good enough for a blacksmith," Balog noted. He swung around and addressed Margit, "Your turn now."

"I fight this skinny...thing?" the German jested in broken Hungarian, tapping the haft of the axe against the palm of his mail-gloved hand.

"Hey, go easy on him," his Bohemian comrade added. "It's only practice."

Reluctantly, Margit climbed over the barrier. Hand-to-hand combat was her least favourite skill, but she needed to prove her worth. Here, on her own land, she must honour her father, her ancestors, her people. She put on her helmet and readied herself.

Like with Adnan, Ladislav attacked her first. Although Margit's heartbeat thumped in her ears, she stood with legs hip-width apart —one slightly ahead of the other—balancing on the balls of her feet. She squeezed the handle of a round shield in her left hand and a training sword in the right.

Ahmed's instructions swirled in her mind:

Raise shield arm to protect the head. Parry with the sword's edge. Keep your balance.

Shield up, kneel, hit opponent on the leg. Rise, block strike with the shield and push the other's weapon away from his body. As he opens up, hit him on the shoulder or head.

She was a hand taller than the soldier, so she took the advantage. And when he went for a stabbing move, she simply sidestepped.

This went on and on. Out of breath, Ladislav retreated, leaving the field to Hans.

The big German raised the training axe, intending to bring it down on Margit's head. But he simply sliced into thin air.

"Whoa! This one is fast," came Balog's excited voice from behind her.

Hans' second attempt she blocked with the shield. The muscles in her arm almost tore, absorbing the force of the blow. She screamed and jumped back, out of range. Sweat was now pouring down her back like an angry stream. How long had she been fighting? Too long, certainly. Her breath was ragged, coming out in gasps. The steel helmet and aventail weighed a ton.

Hans roared with the third hit. His whole body rose from the ground and fell on her shield, breaking it in two. She crashed to the ground, sword lost from her grip. The German's eyes glinted. He bellowed again and raised the axe.

All her defences gone, Margit kicked hard and swept his feet from under him. The man tilted sideways and fell with a clang.

Within an instant, she was on top of him, her knife against his throat.

"You won! You won!" Somewhere in Margit's blurred vision, Adnan was waving wildly at her.

The Bohemian grabbed her arm and hauled her to her feet.

"Damn you!" the German groaned as he picked himself up.

"Well done." Dóczi extended his hand to Margit. "You may not be big and strong, but you can hold your ground."

She shook his hand and then fell to her knees, gasping for breath while the world spun around her.

Less than an hour later, they were in the archery field. Despite the throbbing in her left arm, Margit steadily planted arrow after arrow into the centre of the target.

"This is tedious," Balog said. "Can you shoot on horseback?"

"Yes, commander."

"Very well. I'll give you a moving target." He looked around, and his gaze stopped at Adnan. "Hey, you! Come hither."

Eyes wide with concern, the young man approached.

The castellan thrust a round training shield at him. "Strap this to your arm."

Margit translated the order into Serbian.

Balog turned back to her while pointing at Adnan. "This is your target. You must hit the shield three times while you both ride at a gallop."

Margit's breath stuck in her throat. "What?"

"You heard me."

She cast a desperate look at Dóczi, but the captain's face

remained dispassionate as he brought Csillag to her.

"Such a fine horse. Pure white is so rare," was his only comment.

Thick fog clouded Margit's mind until Adnan held her by the wrist. "Don't fear. You know you're good. I trust you with my life."

She stared at him, her body still numb, and waited until he had securely tied the leather bracers around her forearms.

After he finished, Margit put her arms around the horse's head and rested her forehead against his. "*Kedves Csillagom,* be on your best behaviour. I need your help as never before."

"Move!" Balog slapped her shoulder. "We don't have all day."

Heart banging against her ribs, Margit mounted the horse. She pulled the archer's ring out of her satchel and placed it around her thumb. She took a few deep breaths to calm herself. The smallest error could be fatal.

Adnan rode away first on a palfrey that Balog had given him, and Margit followed.

Urging Csillag to a gallop with her heels, she caught up and flanked her friend from his right. She pressed her legs against the sides of the horse for balance and drew three arrows out of the quiver. Letting go of the reins, she nocked the first arrow with her right hand while she held the other two in the fingers of her left.

String pulled and held into position with the ring; forefinger pressed lightly on the nail of the thumb; anchored at the side of her mouth. Ready.

But the bouncing of her body in the saddle troubled her heartbeat and unsteadied her hands.

Come on! You have done this before... Yes, but only on a target, not on a person. Not on my dear friend.

Margit blinked to clear the tears of frustration forming in her eyes.

Concentrate!

She grunted. Too late. Chance missed. As the field was hemmed in by the stream, they had to move in a circle. Adnan wheeled the horse around.

She must try again. "Steady!" she ordered Csillag and tightened her legs around his sides again.

He responded eagerly, keeping a level pace.

Margit exhaled loudly as she watched her small target bob up and down on Adnan's arm. No time to waste. They were running out of space and would need to turn around again soon.

Empty your head. No thoughts.

She fixed her eyes on the shield, marking its movement. Bow raised, she aimed again and took the shot. The arrow flew with the slightest hiss and lodged itself into the bottom half of the target. She nocked again without looking at her hands, pulled the string and released. Success. Third one now. As she had got closer to Adnan, the force of her last hit unhorsed him.

Margit shrieked. Had she struck him?

But Adnan immediately stood up and signalled to her that he was unharmed. "Here! All three," he shouted, waving the shield aloft with the arrows stuck in it.

Officers and soldiers cheered and clapped when the two of them returned.

"You're both hired," Dóczi said. "You need more combat training, but you should be ready to fight in a month or two."

Margit did not remember how she returned to their lodgings. Her mind was absent, her head spinning, and Adnan's soothing words were just a distant jumble.

She slumped on the bed. Her voice came forth hoarse and broken. "I nearly killed you...nearly killed you."

The belt and helmet fell from Adnan's hands. "But you didn't. Not a scratch on me." He sat beside her and spoke softly, "My heart bleeds to see you like this. You should be looked after with love and devotion, not live the rough life of a soldier."

But that was the path she had chosen. Until she became the lady of the estate, she needed to steel herself and endure whatever Fate was about to throw at her.

20
Meeting the Devil

Late July 1476

With the sun on its descent, an amber glow spread across the sky above the mountains which shielded Sasfészek. A flock of birds flew towards the forested slopes to roost for the night. The summer heat still lingered as Margit waited for Adnan to finish his work at the smithy.

Even after a month, she still had not seen her cousin. Neither had she entered the keep, which was guarded at all times. Her daily regime was so strict that she spent most of her time on the training field practising with the archers, sword fighting and executing battlefield manoeuvres with the light cavalry.

With all these obstacles, how was she to find the evidence she needed to clear her father's name and avenge his death?

"If only I had presented myself as a kitchen hand, a cleaner or a page," she grumbled while battering the pell with her sabre in the castle courtyard. "I would be in the keep by now."

She stopped to catch her breath. Although she wore gloves, her hands were sore and full of blisters. But she did not mind. Like her father, fighting was in her blood. She had proven her worth. Still, neither the captain nor the castellan had allowed her to join the garrison.

Perhaps it was for the best, she thought, as five guards gathered to watch her with folded arms. Were they about to start on her again?

Memories of her Belgrade playmates attacking her rushed upon her recollection. An outsider back then; an outsider now— even in her own home.

"Using our pell again, *madárka*? Who gave you permission?" a guard rebuked her as if she had stolen something valuable from him.

Why did they call her 'little bird'? She was as tall as them.

"Why don't you answer, sweet boy?"

"Fair like a lady."

Their taunting words did not bother her, but there was an evil glint in their eyes.

Worst of all, the sergeant of the guards—a pig-faced man called Ferenc Bakó, who always stank of ale—smacked his lips in her direction.

Despite the apprehension spreading inside her, Margit clenched her hand around the hilt of the sabre and gritted her teeth.

She must not show any weakness.

They closed in on her from three sides.

Moving away from the pell, Margit raised the sabre and assumed a fighting stance.

"Oh, you wish to fight us?" the sergeant scoffed. "We'll crush you like a fly."

He unsheathed his weapon and lunged at her.

As if having a mind of its own, her sword arm whipped the sabre towards him. The tip touched his throat before his sword reached her. Fear steeled her voice. "You have no authority over me. I am one of the lord's mercenaries. If you harm me, he will be furious."

Bakó's face turned purple. No doubt, the muffled giggles and whispers from his men wounded his pride. He lowered his weapon and stepped back.

"Saša!" Adnan called from behind.

Daring not a glance at him, her eyes fixed on her tormentors, sabre at the ready.

"Here comes the Turkish spy," a guard said.

The sergeant spat on the ground. "Heathen scum."

Though Adnan would not have understood their Hungarian words, he must have sensed the danger because he stepped beside her, dagger drawn and pointed at the men. "Stand behind me."

Eyes still on the soldiers, Margit and Adnan moved back with cautious steps.

A wicked grin flashed across the sergeant's face. "We'll let you go this time." He pointed his sword in her direction. "But if you ever use our pell again, you'll be punished."

Once at a safe distance from the brutes, Margit and Adnan turned back from them and walked away, ignoring their taunts, teases and shrill whistles.

"Have those men bothered you before?" Adnan said while they strode down the hill path.

"Yes."

He stopped in his tracks. "Why didn't you tell me or the captain?"

"That would only infuriate them. For now, they have done me no harm. It's just words."

"Be wary." He was about to continue walking when he slapped his forehead. "Oh! I almost forgot. We've orders to be on the training field at dawn."

"Why?"

"The lord—your cousin—will make an inspection."

Margit's back stiffened. She had waited so long to meet Márton. But now that the time finally arrived, was she ready to face the demon who had haunted her life?

***

In the early-morning mist, the soldiers gathered on the training field. For the first time, Margit could see the full size of her cousin's mercenary forces: the men-at-arms and knights in well-polished plate armour; the infantry in mail shirts and open-face sallets, equipped with crossbows and halberds; and the brightly clad light cavalry made up of two distinct groups: the Serbian and Hungarian *huszárok* armed with sabres, lances and axes, and the Székely mounted archers. About a hundred and fifty men in total, ready to offer their services to the kingdom's Judge Royal.

The news of the Turkish attack on neighbouring Moldavia had alarmed all Transylvania; but although Bátori was already trying to raise troops, he was facing delays. As Captain Dóczi explained, the king wished to keep the well-trained royal army with him and had ordered Bátori to muster any soldiers he could out of the local Hungarian nobility, the Székely Seats, the general population of Saxons, Wallachians and Serbians, as well as any mercenaries like those of Szentimre who were available within the province of Transylvania.

"I hope they don't pick us," Adnan said to Margit.

The two of them stood in a separate group of twelve new recruits.

She brushed off the notion with a shake of her head. "They will not. We are still new."

Margit had a more pressing thought on her mind: Márton. After being away for a long time, he had only returned the night before to make this inspection. With the gold and silver mine in the king's hands, Márton's main source of income were the mercenaries. He would not miss the opportunity.

"Here they come!" Adnan's words set her heart racing.

She raised her head to catch a good view of the six men, who stopped only a few paces away. Balog, Dóczi, the Serbian captain and the Hungarian captain were on foot; the other two men on horseback.

The first of the riders was middle-aged and wore a mail shirt with steel plates over his shoulders and arms.

"He must be the field commander, János Bocskai," Margit whispered to Adnan. "And the younger one is Márton."

Unlike the armoured figures around him, her cousin donned refined attire: a short-sleeved, apple-green brocade *mente* revealing a similarly coloured silk *dolmány* underneath. Gilded spurs adorned his knee-high, blood-red riding boots. Atop his shoulder-length chestnut hair rested a brown felt hat with a feather pinned on its upturned brim. His well-trimmed beard, ruddy complexion, upright posture and air of pride and confidence completed a striking image.

An involuntary grunt escaped Margit's lips. Anger and envy pinched her heart. Her cousin had thrived on stolen wealth—hers...

"My lord!" Sergeant Bakó's voice from behind drew her attention away from Márton. "You must administer justice!"

Dragging a barefoot boy by the arm, the sergeant brushed past her and approached Márton.

Barely six or seven years of age, the child wailed and pleaded for mercy. Blood and mud stained his face.

"Coward," Margit hissed. "Find someone your size."

Adnan dug his elbow into her side. "Shhh."

In the meantime, Bakó shoved the boy to the ground in front of her cousin, making his horse shy backwards.

"What is the meaning of this?" Márton yelled, his shrill voice piercing Margit's ears, while he struggled to steady his horse.

The sergeant stood upright with his chest puffed as if he were to announce a grand achievement. "This thieving urchin stole a fresh loaf of bread from your kitchen, my lord. But I caught him."

Márton's face creased. He leaned over and screamed at the child, "How dare you steal from me?"

"Mercy, my lord!" the boy squealed, in floods of tears and trembling like a frightened bird. "My sire's dead. My poor mother has the fever and can't work. My little sister is starving, but we've no coin."

"That is not my concern. You committed a crime." Márton straightened himself in the saddle. "Sergeant! Cut off his finger. And if he is caught again, he will lose a hand."

Seeing Bakó unhook a small axe from his belt, Margit leaned forward, but Adnan held her back.

"Not here, you fool!" Márton shouted at the sergeant. "Take him away!"

"Yes, my lord." Bakó bowed and retreated, tugging the boy

behind him.

Searing pain ran through Margit's heart.

How can you be so cruel, cousin? He's only a child...only a child...

In a booming voice, Commander Bocskai read out the names of the companies chosen to link up with Bátori's troops: one hundred and twenty soldiers in total. Szentimre's contribution to the Royal Judge's campaign into Moldavia was significant.

"We're not going to war," Margit said, smiling.

But before she and Adnan were dismissed, Balog approached the field commander and Márton and talked to them in low tones. He then nodded to Captain Dóczi, who addressed Adnan. "Stefan Danilović! The men will need a blacksmith to maintain their armour and weapons."

Margit's stomach tumbled. "Oh, no! No!"

Alarmed, Adnan leaned in her direction. "What did he say?"

"They need a blacksmith."

The colour drained from Adnan's face.

"Collect your gear and follow Captain Marosi's infantry unit," Dóczi ordered him.

The world dimmed around Margit. She clasped her friend's wrist for a moment, but her strength abandoned her. His hand slipped away, leaving her forlorn.

Barely a heartbeat later, the captain's words stabbed her like the sharpest blade. "As for you, Saša Lazarević, come with me."

"What?" she mumbled, still dazed.

"Come with me," Dóczi repeated, louder now.

She followed him absently until they stood in front of the other two officers and her cousin.

"Ah, here you are!" Spittle flew from Balog's mouth. "Fortune smiles on you today."

Fortune?

Margit clenched her fists so tight that the fingernails clawed into her palms.

This time it was Commander Bocskai who spoke to her. "We don't send new recruits to battle, but we'll make an exception."

The longer Margit stood there, the more her legs trembled, and the faster her pulse throbbed.

"You have shown impressive skills with the bow, and you own a fine horse. You're perfect for the mounted archers' unit. Go find Captain Dokić of the light cavalry. He's Serbian, like you."

Margit bit hard on her lip, her heart about to crack. "I was in a siege before but never in an open-field battle."

And then, like a clap of thunder, her cousin's voice forced the air out of her lungs. "You want to be a soldier, don't you? Isn't this what you are here for?"

His grey-blue eyes stared down at her, their iciness penetrating the very core of her soul. It took a massive effort to restrain herself from drawing her knife and plunging it into his kidney. She would go for his chest, but it was out of reach.

Finally dismissing those dark thoughts, Margit lowered her gaze until it fell on Márton's hands. Only his right held the horse's reins. The left hung by his side, its little finger badly distorted. It looked as if he had lost the use of it.

"Well, answer me!" he barked.

"Yes, my lord." Her eyes narrowed with the rage swelling inside her.

"Then shut your mouth and do as you are ordered, or I shall

have the skin stripped from your back!"

Margit swallowed hard. The tension was so thick she would choke on it.

"Come with me, soldier," Dóczi intervened.

Just at the right time.

Walking away after the captain, she barely caught Márton say to Bocskai, "If he is as good as you say, make sure you demand a high price for him from Bátori."

"Son of a whore," she muttered.

"Beware!" Dóczi turned and glowered at her. "You are new, and you don't know how things work here. But be sure of this: any insubordination towards the lord or the officers, and your head will end up on a pole."

Margit raised her hand. "I apologise, Captain."

Her legs still shook, the remnants of fear coursing through her veins. A chilling image gripped her heart. The memory of her dream resurfaced. The severed head her father had tossed into her lap bore a disturbing resemblance to her cousin.

Questions flooded Margit's mind, each one more distressing than the last. Was it because Márton deserved such punishment for stealing her land? Or was it her father's desperate attempt beyond the grave to convey a hidden truth—that Márton was somehow responsible for his death? Surely, he could not be; he was only a boy of thirteen at the time. Could he have participated in such a terrible crime? But then, why not? The way he treated both her and the poor child had proven how dark his soul was.

Yet what hurt her most was that with the cruellest of twists, Fate had thwarted her plans. Just when she finally met her real enemy, he had sent her away from the estate. Perhaps he had even sent her to her death.

21
On the Battlefield

Margit wiped the sweat from her forehead. She gulped down two mouthfuls and handed the waterskin to Adnan.

"Never seen so many freckles on your face," he jested.

Too exhausted to laugh, she only let out half a smile. Riding for days on end was gruelling in the August weather. Her face was so hot and dry that she thought her skin might crack like the parched soil of a desert. On top of this, there was the constant chattering and shouting of men in all those different languages, the rattling of metal armour, the creaking carriage wheels, the barking dogs, the snorting and neighing horses, the clopping of their hooves—a cacophony bordering on the unbearable.

They had now joined the rest of the Hungarian army and the Serbian units attached to it near the Moldavian border. The Wallachian forces under Prince Stefan's cousin Vlad Dracul the Third were there already, and the two armies merged. But they still had some way to go until they met with the prince's troops, already fighting the Ottomans inside Moldavian territory.

Although her bleeding for that month had not come yet, Margit had to face other problems of her female nature. The men could simply turn their backs and relieve themselves at the side of the road while she had to hide behind bushes or wherever else she could find cover. Untying the points of the hose before pulling it down was a nightmare too. And while the soldiers could just strip and wash themselves in a stream, she could not do the same. When they crossed into Moldavia and made camp for the night, Margit felt like emptying a bucket of water over her. She could not tolerate the smell of her unwashed body any longer.

There was the possibility of an encounter with the enemy the next day, and so the men went to rest early. Only a few sentries guarded the camp. Margit avoided their attention and reached the Royal Judge's tent. Bátori stood outside and talked to another man, who spoke Hungarian with a strong Wallachian accent. Margit's recent stay in Szentimre and her mingling with the people there had helped her distinguish the various tongues and accents by now.

The two men were surrounded by soldiers, so she waited until the Wallachian had left before she approached Bátori.

"Let the lad pass. I know him," the commander ordered the guards.

She followed the Judge Royal into his tent. "Was he Prince Vlad?"

"Yes. The king kept him prisoner for years. But he has released him now and wants to put him on the Wallachian throne as an ally."

"I have heard so many stories about him. He looks fearsome."

Bátori chuckled. "Do you know Vlad is distantly related to you? Through marriage, of course, not blood."

"Really? How?"

"He's wedded to one of the Szilágyi women. The king's first cousin."

Margit's interest quickly faded into shoulder-shrugging.

Unfortunately, high-ranking family connections alone were not enough for her to reclaim her estate. She must fight for it.

Bátori's tone turned serious. "And what in the world are *you* doing here?"

She gave him a brief account of her exploits thus far.

Taken aback, he spoke with fatherly concern. "Why would you put your life in such peril?"

"I could not avoid it, Lord Judge. Had I refused, my cousin would have punished me severely."

He shook his head. "You should have sought a different kind of work, not that of a soldier."

"I have regretted this now. I thought they would employ me as a castle guard. Perhaps I should have kept my archery skills secret."

Bátori nodded, but the look of disquiet was still pinned on his face.

Affecting her most charming smile, Margit spoke in a low voice. "I have a favour to ask. I have not washed for weeks, and I —"

"Of course, dear lady." Bátori's tone rang with amusement. "I shall order my servants to prepare a bath for you, and I shall make sure you are not disturbed."

It was not long before the bath was ready. Margit asked the servants to leave before she undressed. Although they were female, she did not wish to reveal she was a woman in case they gossiped about it.

Immersing herself in the clean, lukewarm water, Margit felt as if she were in heaven. She scrubbed away the weeks of dirt, washed her hair and then sat back and closed her eyes. She did not fall asleep, just stayed there inhaling the relaxing scent of herbs and enjoying the silence.

But the peace and serenity was interrupted by whispers coming from the other side of the tent partition behind her.

Margit plunged neck-deep into the water with an unavoidable splash. She warily turned her head around. Two male shadows stilled for a moment and then withdrew from sight.

Who were they? And how much of her had they seen? The thought of being exposed filled her with dread. She trusted the Judge Royal, but...

Hastily, she dried herself, dressed and stepped into the other part of the tent. There was not a soul there.

***

Thick black clouds shrouded the late afternoon sun. The humid air clung to every exposed part of Margit's body. Now and then, the distant clap of thunder echoed from the north.

The Serbian and Székely mounted archers hid behind the trees in the wooded valley of the Siret River, on Moldavian land. The scouts had returned with information that, pursued by sections of Prince Stefan's army, the Ottomans were retreating towards the south of the country.

Twisting Csillag's reins in her right hand, Margit waited with her comrades as the columns of enemy riders and foot soldiers passed a hundred paces away. Bow clasped in her left hand, she strove to keep her breathing in check. Her first real-life battle as a mounted archer.

Csillag twitched under her as if he sensed her unease. She bent forward and whispered in his ear, "Steady now, my sweet boy."

He bobbed his head, then tossed it from side to side, snorting and making the two ponies on either side back away.

Forefinger raised to his lips, the sallow-skinned Székely archer on Margit's left shot her a disapproving glance. Whether due to her Turkish-style armour, her fine horse which seemed fit for a wealthy knight, or simply because she had come out of nowhere with little battle experience and yet could out-shoot most of them, the men had not accepted her as one of their own. This isolation unsettled her deeply now. The soldiers had their assignment to work as a group; but if the need arose for close combat, her fate rested solely in her own hands.

At the captain's sharp command, the first line of archers and crossbowmen broke cover. Arrows and bolts split the air, a deadly rain unleashing hell on the Turkish rear guard.

The second row followed.

Then Margit's line advanced. Despite her thrashing heart, most arrows hit their marks.

Confused, the enemy soldiers turned to engage, cutting themselves off from the rest of their army. The battle-hardened *huszárok* fell upon them. At a short distance back, Margit watched the bloody struggle and only shot arrows when the Ottomans pressed too close.

Soon, farther along the riverbank, the main Turkish force fell into disarray and blundered into the Hungarian and Wallachian heavy cavalry formation. But with a veil of mist and darkness cloaking the valley, both sides disengaged and withdrew.

Joy swelled in Margit's chest. They had carried the day.

She joined her comrades as they caught up with the Moldavians and camped together.

After sundown, the mist turned into sheets of rain. Such was its force that the river overflowed its banks and prevented the Ottomans from moving too far away as they also had to camp for the night. The next day, another battle would surely take place.

Hood pulled up, Margit made her way to the blacksmith's tent. There she found Adnan still hammering away at this late hour, his familiar figure comforting against the glow of several oil lamps.

She sat quietly on a stool and watched him until he finished his work. For now, the warmth of his smile and the shelter of canvas would keep the downpour and her uneasiness at bay.

"I'm glad you're well," Adnan said, after stowing his tools. "I was concerned."

"You need not be. I can look after myself. Besides, we only skirmished today."

They chatted about inconsequential matters until she parted from him with great reluctance. Being near Adnan brought a sense of safety and peace amidst the wilderness. His words soothed her weary spirit.

These pleasant thoughts swirling in her head, Margit trudged through the mud back to her tent.

The rain had finally stopped, and everything was quiet. Yet a strange feeling prickled the back of her neck. She held her breath and listened. At the sound of someone's footsteps, she spun around and glimpsed a shadowed figure duck behind a tent.

Despite her exhaustion, she rushed after him. But when she turned the corner, he was gone as if swallowed by the darkness and endless rows of tents.

The morning dew still glimmered on the trampled grass, and the musty smell of the river's swollen waters lingered in the air when the army engaged with the Ottomans the next day.

For Margit, the intermittent harassing and skirmishes were now a familiar game. She felt safe loosing arrows from a distance, avoiding the clash of steel.

Yet by late afternoon, these small encounters erupted into full engagement. Ahead rang the clamour of battle: the clang of metal, the men's bellowing war cries and the horses' neighing as the armoured cavalry collided with the Janissary ranks.

It was not long before the fighting engulfed Margit and her comrades.

"Enemy on the left!" the Serbian captain screamed, his voice echoing among the trees of the grove which covered the mounted archers' position.

Hidden in the undergrowth, the Turkish infantry pounced on them so swiftly that they drew steel, lacking time to nock arrows.

Margit reined Csillag in to avoid the fray as the men engaged.

But no...

Two Turks closed in, sabres flashing. Margit bared her own blade and drove the horse forward with her heels. Clutching the reins in her left hand, she leaned right with her sword arm extended. Csillag's galloping speed powered her strike. She severed the first man's arm below the elbow in a spray of crimson.

The impact almost unhorsed her and hurtled the contents of

her stomach to her throat. She screamed, fighting for balance. The second man loomed before her eyes. She jerked the sabre at him, but her waning strength just sent him to the ground.

Margit wheeled Csillag around and moved to finish the attacker before he found his feet. But a fierce *huszár* burst from the copse like an avenging angel and took him on in her stead.

Thank you, Lord!

"On your right!" a disembodied voice warned her.

Pulse roaring in her ears and breath coming in gasps, Margit barely glimpsed a lone Ottoman rider charging towards her.

"Run!" she screamed at Csillag, the enemy in pursuit.

Clumps of muddy earth and vegetation flew under her horse's hooves, each stride precarious as she guided Csillag left-handed while clasping the sabre in her right.

She glanced back. The man was inexplicably upon her, swinging his axe.

Urged by the last shreds of blind desperation, Margit bashed his arm. The weapon flew from his grasp.

Her next blow knocked the helmet off his head.

But before she knew it, the Ottoman pounced and pushed her off the saddle. Margit crashed with a shriek onto the grassy ground.

Now straddling her waist, the man punched her face before his hands closed around her throat.

Dazed, Margit stared into his blue eyes and saw a frantic fight to survive. As scared and as young as she was. Probably a Serbian, Wallachian or Hungarian boy abducted by the Turks and forced to serve them. In a different world, he would endeavour to court her now, not kill her.

The pressure on her throat brought her back to reality. She struggled for the knife on the side of her thigh, but his grip tightened, and the world began to fade.

She was a child again, crying and calling her father. And by a miracle of God, he heard her. For he appeared there in his splendid plate armour, brandishing his axe and screaming in rage. His warhorse's hooves pounded as he galloped to her rescue.

The soldier released her and stood up to face this new threat. It must have been some blow that hit him because it severed his head in one clean sweep. The head rolled by Margit's side, his body dropped atop her, and blood spurted onto her face.

Margit shoved the lifeless burden away. She sat up desperately and glanced about.

The sight of her saviour stole the breath from her lungs: a knight in full harness of blackened German plate armour astride an ebony steed moved in a circle around her. Blood stained the blade of his longsword. A short-shafted iron *Morgenstern* hung from his saddle. The visor of his sallet was closed. Instead of a family crest, the Hungarian royal coat of arms adorned his short tabard.

Margit's jaw dropped. Before she could utter a word, he wheeled his courser and disappeared into the forest nigh.

Alone again, she trembled uncontrollably. She pulled the helmet off her head and shut her eyes. An invisible hand clutched her throat, plunging her into a violent whirlpool. She gagged and choked. Violent convulsions in her stomach ejected its contents from her mouth.

At length, the debilitating sensation passed, and she could breathe freely again. Perhaps it had all been a dream. But when her eyes met the mangled body of the enemy soldier still lying there, the image of the mysterious knight returned and made her pulse race. Everything seemed strange and unreal. Was it her brush with death or something about the knight that left her so rattled? He had appeared from nowhere to save her before vanishing like a spectre. The heavy cavalry fought far from there; so, who was he? A real man or a supernatural entity? Was his sudden appearance the result of her appeal to her father? That thought sent a shiver down her spine. The old legends of the dead warriors returning to help their country in times of danger fascinated her, but she knew they were only myths.

There must be another explanation.

She crawled about to retrieve her bow and sabre.

Her legs shook so violently that she needed a gigantic effort to rise to her feet and maintain her balance. Her head spun; her throat was raw and sore. She wiped the blood off her face with a trembling hand and tried to call out for her horse, but the voice drowned in her throat.

Up and down her chest went as she wheezed with every breath.

Where are you, Csillag?

She prayed that he had escaped harm.

Neighing and snorting from the direction of the grove preceded the rhythmic pounding of hooves.

Heart gripped with sudden apprehension, Margit turned to look, but a thick mist covered her eyes. She blinked again and again, hoping they were not enemy soldiers.

At last her vision cleared, and she beheld the knight emerge on his prancing courser with Csillag in tow.

Margit inhaled with relief, bow and sabre falling from her

hands.

Thanks be to God!

The knight swung his leg over his horse's neck and jumped to the ground. He approached in long strides and brought Csillag to her.

Margit stumbled backwards. He stood too close. With her helmet out of reach, all she could do was lower her head lest he recognised her as female.

Her breath halted as he stepped forward and swept her off her feet with one chivalrous move. His firm grip sent foreign thrills rippling through her trembling body. Was this desire perchance? Lust? For the first time, she relished in her vulnerability as a woman held in the strong arms of her mystery rescuer.

The knight sat her side-saddle, befitting a lady, upon Csillag and fastened her weapons to the pommel with care.

Still dazed, Margit kept her head down, barely hearing his horse trot off. She pressed her hand on her chest as her heart galloped like a wild stallion and her breath came in ragged gasps.

Then, all at once, her strength abandoned her. She slid from the saddle and collapsed to the ground in a heap.

Sometime later, in the spreading twilight, Margit staggered about blindly, searching for the way back to the camp. The excitement of her rescue had ebbed away, replaced by despair about her current precarious situation. Her stomach churned, and bile rose to her already burning throat. The skin on her neck was swollen and sore to the touch. Even a simple act such as swallowing turned into torture.

Every crackling of leaves and twigs under her feet, every shadow flitting by in the bushes sent waves of panic through her. Had the enemy retreated or were the Turks still hiding, ready to pounce and devour her like a wounded doe?

Holding on to the pommel of Csillag's saddle, she put all her faith in her companion to lead her to safety. And proving that their bond was something extraordinary, the horse slowly found the way.

The familiar sounds of campfires, human activity and chatter marked the end of the agonising search. With her head still plagued by dizziness and her eyesight clouded, Margit barely made it to Adnan's tent and fell to her knees.

He rushed to hold her up before she crashed on her face. "What happened?"

Too weak to speak, Margit pointed at her bruised and swollen neck.

"I'll summon the surgeon," he said, but she seized his arm and shook her head.

He eyed her with surprise. "No? Why?"

She touched her chest.

Adnan nodded. "Oh, you fear he'll discover you're a woman. Then show me where you're hurt, and I'll look after you."

Margit smiled at him in gratitude. But even such a slight effort was too much, and she fell into his arms, exhausted.

22
Chasing a Shadow

Autumn 1476

Margit's body and voice recovered within a few days, but her mind was still in turmoil. Many things did not make sense. The Judge Royal had ordered her to refrain from fighting and rest instead. How did he come to know about her injury without her or Adnan informing him?

And who was the dashing knight who had saved her life? There were no royal army soldiers or officers in this campaign. He stood alone in the king's coat of arms. His tall and well-built frame, his mastery with the sword, his impressive armour and magnificent stallion set him apart as an exceptional warrior.

Margit could not shake his image from her mind. The tender way he had held her in his arms and placed her on the saddle hinted at a recognition of her femininity. How she longed to uncover the face hidden behind the closed visor!

The screeching, grinding sound of metal against the whetstone startled her, and she dropped the weapon she was sharpening.

Adnan stood over her with folded arms. "What's the matter with you? You'll destroy the sword. You're no help to me."

Margit looked up while hope fluttered within. "Have you brought good tidings?"

"I've asked about him. Some say he's a mercenary; others that he's a knight of the royal household; or an envoy bringing the king's orders to the commanders here."

Spurred on by a passion that grew with every beat of her heart, she rose to leave. "I must look for him myself."

Adnan caught her by the wrist before she took a step. "How? There are thousands of men here. I've walked the camp many times but haven't seen him."

With an abrupt move, Margit freed herself. "I shall search every tent, every nook and cranny of this camp. I shall not stop until I find him."

Adnan tapped his finger on her forehead. "Think! He didn't speak or show his face when he saved you. Perhaps he doesn't wish you to know."

Margit exhaled through clenched teeth. Adnan was right. She was chasing a shadow. But the unanswered questions and the allure of her unknown saviour continued to haunt her, demanding resolution.

***

Soon the campaign achieved its aim. Suffering minimum losses, the allied armies finally chased the Ottomans out of Moldavia, and Prince Stefan returned to his country's capital within a few weeks.

But their mission was not complete yet. Once Bátori's troops withdrew to the Transylvanian town of Brassó in September, they remained there until new instructions from the king arrived. Now the orders were to invade Wallachia and reinstate Prince Vlad to the throne.

Yet a month later, Bátori was still waiting for cannons and more soldiers before continuing the campaign.

"Let's return to Szentimre," Adnan said to Margit while they were idling. Sheets of rain pelted their tent and pooled on the grounds of the camp. "Your purpose is to take back your land, not to march into battle and die in some god-forsaken place. Speak with the Judge. I'm sure he'll let us leave."

She shook her head. "No. I fear my cousin will punish us if he doesn't receive his pay for our services."

"You fear your cousin? Or you hope to see your black knight again?"

"Ha! What do you know?"

"You're in love with him. I can see it on your face."

Margit's cheeks heated instantly. "I am not!" Yet her hasty response was more of an effort to convince herself rather than her friend.

Adnan chuckled. "Oh, admit it. You blush bright red ev'ry time you speak of him."

"I do not!" She pressed her cold palms against her cheeks.

"I don't believe a word you say."

Margit folded her arms and looked away as heat continued to flood her face. How could this happen to her? Even now, two months later, the mere memory of the stranger sent desire twirling through her veins like a potent wine. This was not the feeling she held for her husband or her friend. She had not seen the man's face, yet she longed for him. He could be ugly, ancient, deformed— it did not matter. His raw, commanding presence had enthralled her, body and soul, as irresistible as a siren's song.

She slapped the side of her head.

Enough with these thoughts!

In tough and dangerous times any weakness could be fatal. With a new campaign looming, only a clear mind would keep her safe.

***

As the well-rested army left Brassó and marched through the southern Carpathians towards Wallachia, Margit felt overwhelmed by a landscape so different from the large plains of Belgrade and the Southern Country where she grew up. Here at the edge of the Hungarian kingdom—this land plagued by incessant conflict for centuries—rugged mountains and vertiginous passes alternated with primeval forests and steep valleys while stone fortresses and outposts perched precariously on verdant hilltops and rocky outcrops. The wind murmured through rustling tree branches like the whispers of ancient warriors watching their descendants from afar. Startled by the marching boots of men, herds of red deer scuttled away to hide in the thickets. And above the soldier's steel helmets, golden eagles swooped downward and then soared again, their shrieking calls echoing on the slopes.

In early November, snow had not arrived yet. The yellow and rusty colours of the season contrasted with the deep green of the grass and fir trees, and the grey of the bare mountain rocks. The fresh air in her lungs and the cool moisture on her skin invigorated Margit. Whether stirred by elation or her father's passion for the fight which ran in her blood, she was proud that, despite the harrowing moments she experienced on the battlefield, she had done well to survive.

What would her life be like if she had been born a man—and a nobleman at that? Perhaps she would have been stronger and capable of enduring the onerous responsibilities of a landlord as well as honouring the duty of a warrior to his king and his homeland.

Her thoughts were interrupted by the order to stop and make camp at the last village on the Hungarian side of the border. The place was as wild and beautiful as any other in the area, except... Margit's eyes opened wide and a sigh of wonder rose from her chest. Because on the top of a steep, forested hill stood the most breath-taking fortress. Her own Sasfészek looked like a child's construction compared to that castle.

She turned from this sight to a Székely archer. "What is it called?"

"Törcsvár in Hungarian. Bran to the Wallachians," he replied in a flat voice as if he were talking about something ordinary. "It's a border and customs post, guarding the pass below that leads into Wallachia."

Margit cast him a disdainful glance and turned her gaze back to the magnificent edifice. With its walls merging into the edge of the cliffs and shooting up towards the sky, Törcsvár appeared naturally impenetrable. Like Sasfészek, the fortress shone brilliant white, with pointed rooftops of bright red tiles. The king's standard flew high on the towers, asserting his authority over the landscape.

Bátori, Prince Vlad and the other commanders received permission to spend the night in the castle, but the army camped around the village at the foot of the hill. There they could eat, replenish their supplies and take a good rest before entering Wallachia.

Margit sat in the blacksmith's tent with Adnan awhile. Evidently apprehensive of what was to come on the other side of the border, he scolded her for her stubborn refusal to return to Szentimre. But she would have none of it.

"Endre's right," Adnan said with a hint of bitterness in his voice. "You're so wild. Perhaps it's because you grew up without parents. You always do what you please." He let out a deep sigh. "Truth is, I envy that."

A lump formed in Margit's throat. The last time she saw her husband seemed so long ago. His unwavering devotion only magnified the weight of her guilt. She had failed to give him the love he deserved. And to make matters worse, her body now yearned for the mysterious knight though she was aware that their paths might never cross again.

Margit shook her head to disperse those sad thoughts. "It's late. I must go." She rose and left without another word.

The quickest way back to her tent passed through the edge of the sleeping village. Only the moonlight and a few standing torches—unattended and dying at this hour of the night—guided her steps.

Burdened with weariness and disquiet, Margit traipsed down the narrow dirt path traversing a cluster of houses and barns. Except for the murmur from the camp in the distance, the only sound that disturbed the silence was the rustling of dead leaves under her boots.

What awaited her the next day, she did not know. Another battle perhaps? Another encounter with death?

No, I must not think such thoughts. What good are they to me but put more fear in my heart?

She gritted her teeth and pressed on.

The rustling grew louder, carried by footsteps coming from the opposite direction. Something brushed by her side. What was it? Man or spirit?

She spun around to see a white tabard on the back of a tall figure. The meagre light let her but a glimpse of the Hungarian coat of arms bobbing up and down as he strolled away.

Margit's hairs stood on end at the back of her neck.

The only soldier who wears the royal coat of arms is...

"Hey! Wait!" she called after him.

The stranger quickened his pace, but Margit gave chase, sliding on the soggy fallen leaves.

She forced herself to halt to find her footing. But when she raised her gaze, he had disappeared, lost in the darkness.

Where did he go?

Margit's eyes searched about, falling on a turn into an alley around a stone barn. If he was not on the main path anymore, he must have gone down there.

A part of her filled with apprehension. It was unwise to venture into an unknown area on her own. But another part urged her on. She would not miss her greatest chance to find out if her knight had returned.

She hurried towards the alley. Before she knew it, someone grabbed her from behind and slammed her face-first against the building's rough wall. A strong hand clamped on her neck.

Margit fought to turn her head but to no avail. His other hand grabbed her right arm and locked it behind her back.

"Let me go!" she hissed, determined not to cry out in pain. But, inadvertently, her next words came forth at a higher pitch. "You are hurting me."

Whoever he was, he pulled back momentarily as if taking heed; but then, less forcibly, he pushed her against the wall anew.

"What do you want?" Margit said, deepening her tone now.

He took some time to respond. "I wish to protect you." His voice was a mere whisper. The only certain thing was that he spoke Hungarian.

Protect me?

The man's firm grip awakened a memory. A strange feeling coursed through Margit's body. "Why would I need protection?"

"Because of who you are."

Who I am?

Tension froze Margit. The only one who knew this was the Judge. Had he betrayed her secret? Or did the stranger lie, trying to make her reveal herself? "I don't believe you unless you tell me who you think I am exactly."

"A noble lady the Judge Royal is very fond of."

So it *was* Bátori's doing. Margit grunted. "Then tell me who you are too."

He did not answer.

Even through his gambeson and tabard, she could feel the taut muscles of his arms and chest pressing against her shoulders. His stature, his strength—all familiar somehow. Margit could not hold back any longer. She needed to know. "Are you the knight who saved me before?"

"Yes."

Oh, if only she could see his face! She struggled to turn around, but he held her neck tighter and pushed his knee against her lower back while his breath blew warm into her ear.

Margit's skin turned to gooseflesh, her breasts swelled, her nipples hardened. A fiery prickle shot down her spine.

What's happening to me?

Amidst a storm of confusing emotions, she fought to restrain herself. Perhaps she could use this urge to her advantage and discover who he is. "If you wish to make love to me, let us go into the barn."

Silence. He pulled back a little. And then came his reaction. "What?"

Margit's face twisted against the stone wall as his force came hard on her once more. Her mind racing, she responded breathlessly, "You're touching me in an inappropriate way. It's plain as day that you desire me. So, let us lie together."

"Are you trying to trick me?" he said, still in a whisper.

Damn! I can't deceive him.

"You are a wedded woman," he continued. "Why commit a mortal sin?"

He even knows I am married?

"Don't tell me you are concerned about my soul," she sneered. "And yes, I love my husband with all my heart; that's why I need someone like you to teach me how to please a man."

The stranger's hand twitched on her neck as his breath caught for a fleeting moment. "Do you always have your way?"

"Yes, all the time."

"Well, not this time."

He dragged her away from the wall and, still keeping a tight grip on her neck and arm, made her turn to the left. "Look!

Someone's coming."

He shoved her forward, back onto the main path.

For a moment, Margit tried to peer through the darkness, but she quickly realised she had been fooled. By the time she turned around, he was gone.

"Son of a whore!" She sank against the wall, trying to regain her composure.

Her arm was still sore and so was her neck, but that did not bother her at all. Her heart was beating at a frantic rate, and her entire body throbbed with fiery excitement. That stranger had dared to assert his power over her, instead of crumbling under the force of her nature. After Endre, Adnan, Ahmed, István Bátori and even the king himself, who all fell for her charm and fiery disposition, she had finally met her match.

23
Tears

By late morning, the mist had barely lifted as the army marched through a narrow gorge, its rocky slopes rising vertically towards the heavens. The noise of men and animals reverberated in the stony silence and bounced back into Margit's ears as a dull echo.

Holding Csillag's reins, her hands trembled. Not from the cold but from the scouts' reports that the enemy—Vlad's Wallachian rival Basarab Laiotă and his Ottoman allies—knew of their movements and had gathered a few miles away, ready to stop their advance.

Attached to the baggage train, Adnan was not beside her anymore. Instead, the Serbian and Székely light cavalrymen had been her taciturn, stern-faced companions since they left Törcsvár. Could she trust them with her life?

The urgency of the preparation for the upcoming battle had diverted Margit's mind away from the mystery knight. Her quick search around the camp the night before and in the early morning did not produce any results. He had disappeared again although an unknown man-at-arms on a black courser accompanied the Judge Royal and Prince Vlad, a long way behind her. No matter how many times Margit glanced back, she caught only a glimpse of him: dressed in a black gambeson and a short-sleeved brigandine, his face hidden behind the half-lowered visor of a sallet.

Could it be him?

An irresistible force drew her to him like a moth to a flame. She needed an excuse to leave the marching line.

"Captain, I..." Her voice stuck in her throat, drowned by the sudden murmur of hundreds of men as the front lines of the army exited the gorge.

What's happening?

"Prepare for battle!"

The soldiers rushed ahead, spilling into the open terrain and sweeping her forward with them.

The enemy was there, already in formation, their banners flapping in the wind and their cries and drums creating an ear-splitting racket.

"Infantry! Frontal attack! Cavalry at the flanks!"

Margit strung her bow and opened the lid of the quiver.

A group of Székely riders encircled her. "Come with us!"

Chest tightening with worry, she glanced at the Serbian captain.

He nodded.

Margit rode with them through the trees, skirting the enemy flank. The chaos of battle flashed in the corner of her vision as she pressed Csillag onward. Weapons clanged; horses roared; men cried out, their voices melding into a distant din.

Soon they reached higher ground and took cover in a thicket overlooking the battlefield. A cunning yet precarious move. What had they planned? Attacking from behind gave them an edge; but they were sorely outnumbered.

The Székely group leader addressed Margit. "Your arrows may not pierce armour, but they can serve us in another way. Hide behind the trees and strike at the horses. Bring the men down for us to finish."

She glared at him. "I shall neither cripple nor kill horses. Men yes, but horses never!"

"You dispute my orders?" His face flushed red with anger. He raised his flanged mace above Csillag's head, making him twitch under her. "You do what I order you, or else *your* horse dies."

Faced with a worse threat, Margit nodded reluctantly.

Another rider attached two quivers to her saddle.

So many arrows? Are they expecting me to shoot for hours?

The leader signalled for the men to spread out and for Margit to follow him to a small opening in the tree line. "Start here and move to the right."

Margit dismounted and steadied her breath, pushing all distractions from her mind. Settled at last, her hand loosed arrows with practised ease. Horses and men dropped to the ground. Within moments, her comrades charged down the slope, weapons drawn. Confusion spread among the enemy troops, now attacked from two sides.

Slowly stepping to the right, Margit kept releasing arrows that felled beasts and men alike. Though proud of her skill, pity pierced her heart. So much senseless agony and death. Severed limbs, wretched screams of the wounded and dying, circling carrion birds. Blood soaked the earth. Merciless Death descended to claim those souls.

Tears of conscience blinked back, Margit steeled herself. She was a soldier now. This horror must not sway her.

Csillag's sharp whinny snapped her concentration back. Heavy footsteps crunched behind her. Six Ottomans surrounded her, blades gleaming. One wielded a war hammer.

No chance of escape.

At least, save Csillag.

She slapped his rump. "Go!"

He took off, slamming into an enemy man and hurling him to the ground. His bones cracked as he fell.

Five left.

Margit dropped the bow and drew her sabre. The world closed in around her. She could not defeat them all. Was this the end?

God, forgive my sins.

Her thirst for revenge and retribution had led to this lone moment. She would be gone and become nothing more than a memory.

With the fury of the doomed, she countered the first, the second, the third strike, locked in a deadly dance of Fate.

Then hooves thundered, and a feral scream sent the birds flapping from the trees.

Her dark knight had come.

No time to watch as another blade sliced the air near Margit's face. She lashed out, spraying blood while the knight also cut the Ottomans down.

"Behind you!" he shouted.

She barely turned halfway when a crushing force slammed her helmet. Pain shrieked through her skull; metal clanged in her ears. Time distorted as she fell.

The image of the knight galloping towards her, his *Morgenstern* raised high, flashed before her eyes.

A body crashed beside her.

Then darkness swept her away.

Sometime later, when Margit briefly surfaced to consciousness, she found herself strapped against the knight's chest as he rode at a reckless pace. Although barely two hands' breadth away from his face, she could not make out his features. A dark cloud enveloped her and gradually turned the indistinct images into blackness.

***

A cool drop fell on Margit's parched lips; another on the tip of her nose; then on her cheek, soothing her burning skin and throbbing head.

Water?

The liquid trickled into her mouth. Its saltiness stung her tongue.

Tears... Who cries over my broken body?

With great effort, she forced her eyes open. A man's blurred outline appeared, leaning over her.

Was he real, or was she dreaming?

His face became clearer and clearer until she recognised him. "Father. Why are you crying? Am I dead?"

"You are not dead, *kincsem*." His voice caressed her like a breath of cool morning air. "But you must fight to stay alive. I know you can do it. You are strong."

She blinked. How could her father look so young?

But anything can happen in a dream.

"Oh, Father, I miss you so much."

Now, it was she who wept. And then his hand touched her

cheek, surrounding her in safety and solace. She knew he would always be with her; he would always watch over her. She smiled with the last of her strength until exhaustion dragged her into oblivion once again.

24
The Awakening

A dark-brown crucifix on the wall opposite greeted Margit as she awoke. Still in a trance, she studied it until the realisation slowly sank in that she had emerged from a long and deep sleep.

Lying on a hard bed, she felt aches spreading over her body. Her head throbbed. Despite the discomfort, she reached for her brow and touched bandages wrapped tightly around it.

Confused, she scanned the room. Bare white walls and ceiling; a narrow black door; a small table in the corner. Sunlight on the wall to her right hinted at a window but turning her head proved too painful.

Where am I?

She attempted to lift herself, but her arms refused, and she dropped on her back again. Searing agony lanced through her skull and made her groan. A sudden wave of dizziness overwhelmed her. Within moments, panic seized her, and a scream tore from her throat.

The door creaked open. A woman of middle age in a nun's grey habit, linen wimple and veil entered.

"Calm yourself, child."

Margit fell silent and eyed the woman with some wonder. The nun sat on the edge of the bed and touched Margit's forehead. "The fever's gone." She moved her hand to Margit's chest. "Breathing and heartbeat are normal. The good Lord has spared you."

"Who are you? Where am I? And what happened to me?"

"This is the monastery of Szent Erzsébet." The nun crossed herself. "I am Sister Kinga. You were brought here two weeks ago with a serious head injury. My sisters and I looked after you and prayed for you day and night. You fought in a battle, we were told. Why would a young woman like you go to war?"

Margit pressed her lips together. She would reveal nothing.

"Very well." The nun sighed. "You don't wish to tell me who you are. I shall respect that."

"The man who brought me here. Who was he?"

"Alas, we don't know. He only said he was an officer of King Mátyás' army, and he had carried you all the way from Wallachia."

"He saved my life."

"Indeed. We were impressed by the way he bandaged your head. He seemed to care a lot about you."

"Is he still here?"

"No, he stayed for the first night and then left."

Margit let out a frustrated exhalation. The knight had eluded her again. "I must go," she said abruptly. "I have something very important to do."

"No! You must rest. You have been unconscious for many days. Your brain was swelling when you were brought here. We had to bore a small hole into your skull to relieve the pressure."

Margit shuddered. "What?"

"Don't fret, child. In an area plagued by wars, our monastery has dealt with battle injuries for many years. Your head will heal in time. You just need to rest and do what we say."

Margit resigned to the notion that she could not do otherwise.

Even the limited movements she made brought about more nausea and dizziness.

A hint of a smile graced the nun's weathered face. "I was informed that two young men have been waiting patiently for you to wake up. They were not allowed to stay on the grounds of the monastery, but I shall send for them now."

Two young men? Adnan must be one. And the other? Endre, perhaps? Or...

"You are fortunate," Sister Kinga continued. "You have people who care deeply about you. It's not too late to turn your life around."

They helped her sit up on the bed and then embraced her—first Endre, then Adnan. Their devotion warmed her heart. Sister Kinga was right. Margit was lucky to have them. And most of all, lucky to be alive and intact, her memory whole. How narrowly she had escaped death! The realisation shook her profoundly. War was not for her. She had lost sight of her true purpose. And now she would have to wait even longer to heal.

A novice nun brought hot broth. Since Margit was too frail to care for herself, Adnan held the bowl while Endre fed her with a spoon. No words passed among the three, their bond transcending speech.

After eating, Margit felt a little better. "How did you know to find me here?"

"Bátori," Adnan said. "We won the battle, and we were to march on. But he ordered me to go to you. I've brought your horse. He was lost but found his way back to the camp in the end."

"Thank God! Poor Csillag. He must have got such a fright that day."

"Bátori sent me a message too, and I arrived two days ago," Endre added. "I was so afraid I would lose you."

He kissed her cheek while cradling her face in his palm and looking fondly upon her.

Seeing him gaze at her like this invoked a faint memory. She pulled back from her husband's touch, that distant recollection prompting her to seek an answer. "I need to know something. Did I wake up at all while you were here? Even for a moment or two?"

Adnan shook his head at once, but Endre hesitated. "No," he said quietly. "Why do you ask?"

Was I dreaming then?

Through the fog of pain, Margit recalled a man leaning over her; a man who wept and touched her face so tenderly. At first, she thought he was her father, but his tears and caresses felt too real for any dream. If not Adnan or Endre, then who? A shiver ran through her. Could he have been her mysterious knight? Why would he care for her so? And what drew her to him in such a powerful way? She choked back a sob, emotions swelling.

"Margit, what's the matter?" Her husband's voice pulled her back.

"Nothing. Just dizzy. I need to rest."

"Of course." He helped her lie down. "We shall return later."

Alone once more, she shut her eyes. That blow had made everything so clear. Life was too short and precious to waste on fighting other people's wars. She must fight her own battle for Szentimre.

Whoever her rescuer might be, she thanked him. Though his

enigmatic figure still lingered in her mind, she needed to accept the possibility that he would never see him again.

***

Endre returned the following afternoon. A darkness had settled in his eyes, replacing the smile that lit them the day before. "I didn't tell you yesterday because you had just awakened, and I didn't wish to distress you." He took a deep breath. "My father passed a week after you left."

"Oh, Endre! I'm so sorry." Tears stung Margit's eyes, and sorrow gripped her heart. "You know I loved him very much. He was like a father to me. I owe him my life, really. And it pains me more because I caused his suffering."

He raised his forefinger. "Never say that again! I told you many a time: it was not your fault. It was meant to happen."

Margit dried her tears, but the guilt would never leave her.

"I have contemplated our affairs seriously," Endre said. "My father had dedicated his life to honouring and protecting your father's legacy. Even at his deathbed, he begged me to be strong and continue his work. And so, I must do my duty. You carry a heavy burden, and I need to be by your side until you win back what was taken from you. But to do that, I must become your equal first. Otherwise, I shall always be known as the husband of Margit Szilágyi-Bátori and not as Endre Gerendi. Do you understand?"

"Nonsense! I have never thought of you as inferior to me."

"Yes, but this is not how the world will see me. I am only a knight's son while you carry the blood of two of the most powerful families in the kingdom. I must prove myself worthy of you before I share your title and your land."

Margit's stomach tightened in anticipation of what he would say next.

"I have made a start," he resumed. "After my father's passing, I had our marriage validated. As you remember, everything was done in secret, but now all the papers have been made official. Then I went to see the king. Obviously, he can't give me a title for nothing, so I offered to do whatever necessary to earn one."

"But you have already proven your loyalty by serving him all this time. What else does he need?"

"That was only to have my father pardoned and released from prison. Now I must do it for myself."

"And what did the king say?"

Endre straightened himself and looked her in the eye. "He appointed me as an officer in his army. If I do well and survive long enough, I can receive a higher commission and the nobility title that comes with it."

"But this also means you must go to war again."

Endre let out a light laugh. "Says the lady who has been fighting the Turks for the last three months."

Margit could not help but smile at his comment. "Well, it's over now. No more fighting for me."

"Good. At least, I shall not need to worry while I'm far away."

Margit's face twitched. More than likely, she would not see him for a long time. An inexplicable melancholy settled about her heart. Well past his nineteenth year, Endre had changed so much: taller now, with broader chest and shoulders and taut muscles in his arms. The deep crease between his eyebrows and the tension in his features made him look weary and aged before his time.

"So, when do you leave?" she said.

"In the morn. I only waited to make sure you are well before I set off."

"Where will you go?"

"Wherever the king sends me. But please, remember this: no matter where I am, I shall always be with you in spirit."

Margit covered her mouth with her hand, fighting back a new wave of sadness.

Endre kissed her on the cheek. "Look after yourself, *szívem*. I have found lodgings in Brassó for you and Adnan to stay after you leave the convent. When you have fully recovered, send me a message. I promise I shall come to take you to Nándorfehérvár or Szentimre, or anywhere else you wish to go."

25
The Incident

May / June 1478

Against the deep green of the forested mountains, the now familiar sight of Sasfészek sent a warm wave of excitement through Margit's body. Her heart brimmed with the sweet anticipation of seeing a long-lost loved one again.

A year and a half after her injury, gone were the debilitating headaches, exhaustion and spells of dizziness and confusion, which had marred her long road to recovery. The pains she had endured as she endeavoured to regain her fighting and archery skills were now a distant memory.

But she would not have made it without the support of the two men in her life. The thought brought a smile to her lips.

God bless them both.

Adnan for having the kindness and patience of a saint, putting up with all her episodes of frustration and bouts of anger without a word of annoyance or complaint. And Endre for providing her with everything she needed: from lodgings and coin for her expenses to hiring an instructor to help her rebuild her combat skills.

Because of his increased military duties, her husband had only visited her twice. Each time he looked different, both in his appearance and behaviour. Always in a nobleman's solemn attire, he had lost his boyish charm and wore a serious expression as if carrying the weight of the world on his shoulders. He did not talk much and restrained from expressing his emotions.

Anxiety and guilt crept into Margit's mind. How could she forgive herself for causing this gaping distance between them? She had pushed Endre away for fear of conceiving a child. She had abandoned him and his ailing father, blinded by her thirst for revenge. She had no time for him, no regard for his plight. And then, during the few weeks before her injury, she had even desired another man—a faceless stranger.

Margit blinked away those thoughts. After nearly two years of diversions since leaving Belgrade, she had finally returned home for good. No more distractions. Szentimre awaited, the blood of her ancestors calling her back to embrace her destiny at long last.

She rode through the town gate with Adnan by her side. The guard at the entrance remembered them, and so did Captain Dóczi. "Where have you been all this time?" he said, his voice laden with genuine concern. "I thought you were dead."

Margit explained what had happened before asking if she and Adnan could have their places back in the castle.

"The blacksmith will surely be glad to have his assistant, but I don't know about you. I'll speak to the castellan and see if he can put you on guard duty since you can't fight wars anymore."

Margit smiled. The captain was certainly a compassionate man. He could have sent them away on grounds of their long absence, but he was kind enough to help them instead.

They returned to their old lodgings, vacant since the mercenaries of Szentimre still fought in some faraway land.

The next day, they were both informed they had employment: Adnan in the smithy and Margit as a castle guard. Glad tidings for her because she would be positioned closer to her relatives and would have a greater chance of starting her investigation soon.

***

Margit had not asked Endre to escort her because she did not wish to drag him all the way from the north-western border, where he was serving the king, to Brassó and from there to Szentimre. Instead, once settled, she wrote to let him know she had arrived safely and was looking forward to seeing him whenever he could visit her.

During the following weeks, her duties were mainly on the watchtowers and the castle gate but also at the keep entrance. Her cousin was clearly obsessed with security. He never went out without bodyguards and always placed several soldiers around his residence.

Guarding the keep was Margit's favourite duty because it gave her the opportunity to observe who came in and out of the house. Márton was not at home much. He travelled between his three estates—Szentimre and the other two belonging to his mother. But when he was in residence in Sasfészek, he held meetings with his advisors and always stormed in and out looking vexed, barking orders at servants and soldiers.

On the nights Márton was home, a mysterious woman would arrive after sundown and leave at dawn. Although Margit only saw her in the hours of darkness or at first light, she noted the lady's rosemary scent, rustling silk gown and curly red hair, which she covered with a hood only after stepping out of the keep. As Márton had no wife, Margit assumed the woman was his mistress or a hired companion to warm his bed at night.

Of Aunt Anna no trace could be found. All enquiries yielded no clear answer; only that she was still alive yet unseen for several years. Some thought she resided in another of Márton's estates, but no one could say for certain.

***

One night in late June, Margit stood at the bottom of the stairs to the keep after her shift. The castle complex was unusually quiet. Normally, there would be guards pacing the courtyard, the odd servant finishing up chores or a stable boy filling the horses' trough with water for the night.

Perhaps fate had given her this chance to find a way into her cousin's residence.

She glanced up to ensure the guards at the entrance were not watching her. It was impossible to enter through the great hall because the building stood directly in the soldiers' line of vision. With her body close to the wall, she stole around the keep from the opposite side and followed the downward sloping path that brought her to a cellar in the lower ground floor.

Not a soul there. Margit shook the lock, but it did not move. Of course. Valuable supplies were stored there. Why did she expect the cellar to be unlocked?

With the sour taste of disappointment in her mouth, she crept along the wall until the slope turned upwards, leading her to the kitchen. She cast a quick look about and then pressed her ear to the door. Not a sound. Holding her breath, she pulled the metal latch, and it opened.

"Stop, thief!" came a gruff voice.

Margit jumped. The voice was familiar.

The man grabbed her from behind, drew her away from the door and slammed her, face first, against the wall. "Who do we have here?"

Margit retched at the potent stench of ale and some other disgusting odour issuing from his mouth. She tried to free herself, but the weight of his body kept her pinned to the wall.

And then she remembered. He was that horrible man, Sergeant Bakó, who had tormented her before with his nasty words and obscene gestures.

His arm clamped tighter around her body, just above the waist. *Dear God, make him stop!*

What if he touched her breasts? Would the binding fool him? Perhaps not... Cold sweat formed on her back. "Take your hands off me!"

Bakó let out a creepy laughing sound. "Oh, it's you, *Madárka*. What are you trying to steal?"

"Let me go, or I'll scream!"

"No, you won't." With his free hand, he covered her mouth. "Why are you sneaking about the lord's house at this hour? You're no mercenary anymore. You're one of my men, and I've every right to punish you."

His arm edged dangerously upwards. Margit could not let herself be caught. Not after the hardships she had endured to get closer to her cousin.

She bit his finger with all her might until she tasted blood.

Bakó screeched and loosened his grip.

Margit ducked, turned around and drew the knife that she always kept strapped to her leg. She grabbed his man-parts and held the blade against them.

"Oh, don't hurt me," the sergeant squealed.

"Move away, or I shall cut you!"

"Yes, yes. Keep your voice down."

Heartbeat thudding in her ears, Margit shoved him against the wall and sprinted to the gatehouse. The taste of blood still lingered in her mouth. She spat out in disgust.

A guard approached, but she stopped him with an abrupt movement of her hand. "Keep away from me! I feel very sick, and I need to go home."

The soldier stood aside to let her pass.

Panting and wheezing, Margit ran to her lodgings and clambered up the stairs to the loft.

"What happened?" Adnan mumbled, awakened from his sleep.

Still gasping and shaking, she fell into his arms until she eventually calmed herself and told him everything.

***

The sun was barely up the next morning when Margit received an order to see the garrison commander presently.

Her face turned cold, and a cloud covered her eyes. She clasped Adnan's arm. "What am I to do? They will punish me."

"Let me go with you," he said in a soft, reassuring voice. "I shan't let anyone harm you."

At the gatehouse, Margit's stomach knotted as her lowered gaze trailed across the grey flagstones until it met two pairs of feet in front of a table. She slowly raised her eyes. Balog and Dóczi. No sign of Bakó.

The castellan glared at her with flushed cheeks and eyes like burning coal. "You pulled a knife on your sergeant. You will be severely punished."

She coughed from the choking feeling in her throat. "He attacked me, commander."

Balog's eyebrows knitted. "He caught you trying to break into the lord's residence. Why?"

Margit pressed her hand against her stomach to still the turmoil that swirled within. How was she to justify her actions? She blurted out the first excuse that came to her mind. "I was hungry and merely looking for food."

"Do you take me for a fool?" Balog thundered. "You are but a lousy liar!"

Margit bit her lip hard for fear of saying anything else that would worsen her position.

In desperation, she turned to the captain.

He's a good man. He should say something now.

But instead, Dóczi looked away as Balog announced, "Ten lashes to be administered immediately."

Horrified, Margit staggered backwards, but Adnan's swift arms steadied her.

"Commander! Punish me instead," Adnan interjected in reasonably good Hungarian. "My friend's injured in the head and can't take pain."

"Your friend is a soldier, damn you!" Balog yelled, spit flying from his mouth. "Does he expect to go into battle and not be subjected to pain?"

"Sir," Dóczi interfered, "may I speak with you?"

As the two men exited, Margit turned to Adnan. Once again, he had put himself in harm's way to protect her. How could she live with the shame?

"Why?" The word came from her mouth in a whisper, all but lost to the heavy footsteps of Balog and Dóczi returning to the room.

The castellan looked somewhat calmer now. "Blacksmith," he said to Adnan, "I shall allow you to take the punishment, but this is the one and only time."

Adnan bowed his head.

Margit squeezed his arm, but he smiled reassuringly.

"Now, come along. Both of you," Balog ordered them.

Margit watched in horror as the whip sliced Adnan's back. Blood oozed from his ripped flesh. Tied to a post in the castle courtyard, he endured the ordeal, face twisting in agony; yet not a single sound came from his lips. A small crowd of soldiers and servants had gathered to watch, their expressions ranging from malicious satisfaction to a mixture of pity and discomfort.

"Four...five..." the punishing guard counted impassively.

Only halfway.

Tears streamed down Margit's cheeks. She turned away, unable to witness more.

Balog grabbed her neck and forced her to face the brutal spectacle. "This is all *your* doing. You are a goddamn coward to let your friend suffer for you."

Margit growled, her cornered fury rising. She already despised the castellan for she believed he had a hand in her father's murder. His present cruelty augmented her hatred.

His time will come. He will pay for everything.

Another man she would make pay was Bakó. The sergeant stood at the front of the crowd, legs apart and arms folded, watching with a crooked grin on his face. Margit glared at him, and he reciprocated with an obscene gesture.

"Nine. Ten." The whip's savage sound ceased at last.

The soldiers untied Adnan, and he crumpled to the ground, broken.

Margit started towards him, but Balog seized her arm and dragged her to the gatehouse.

"Take the blacksmith to his lodgings," Captain Dóczi ordered his men and followed Balog and Margit.

They returned to the same room where they stood earlier in the day. What in the world did the castellan want from her now?

He eyed her from top to toe. "I've always suspected there is something peculiar about you."

Margit's back stiffened. "What do you mean, sir?"

"How old are you?"

"Twenty."

"Your voice is too high, and you lack manly features. Only moments ago, you wept like a girl."

How was she to reply to that? Her eyes shifted to Captain Dóczi, expecting an intervention from him, but he only looked on blank-faced.

"Crying like a girl? I am a man, commander," she replied in a shaky voice.

"Then you will not mind pulling down your hose and proving this to us?"

"What?" Dóczi finally reacted.

Balog ignored him, boring into Margit. "If you speak the truth, you have nothing to fear."

Knees buckling, she desperately sought an excuse not to undress. "Well, commander...I am not a woman. But I am not a man either. At least, not a full man."

Balog's confused-looking eyes opened wide. "Eh? Explain yourself!"

Panic flooded Margit, but inspiration struck. "Turkish raiders abducted me when I was a boy. They sold me as a slave to the governor of Smederevo. One of his wives liked me and took me into the harem. The women grew fond of me and wished to keep me there."

She sucked her lower lip, feigning an expression of sadness as if her tortured past had returned to haunt her. "But the governor would not allow a man among his wives. He had my...man-parts cut off."

A gulp, and then a sigh. "So, my voice will never change; I shall never have a beard; I shall never be a real man. A few years later, I escaped. I wanted to make my captors pay. That's why I became a soldier, trained hard and swore to fight the infidels until the day I die."

She held the castellan's gaze steadily. "So, I could show you what I look like down there, but—"

"No, don't!" Balog's face creased in disgust. "I believe you."

Relief coursed through Margit.

A miracle!

She murmured thanks to God under her breath.

"You will not be a guard any longer," the castellan continued. "I can't afford any more incidents like that. You may work with your friend in the smithy, but you are relieved of your duties as a soldier."

With her confidence restored, Margit could even jest now. She assumed a disappointed expression. "Oh, commander! You know what a good archer I am."

"This is my order!" Balog slammed his fist on the table. "You are dismissed."

Feet barely touching the ground, Margit flew home to Adnan.

She found him lying face-down on the bed and groaning in pain. To ease her own suffering as much as his, she cleaned and tended to his wounds.

But she knew he would be scarred for life.

"I'm so sorry," she said, voice full of regret.

With several moans, he turned and looked at her, his eyes wet and bloodshot. "Don't be. I'd do this for you again and again."

Margit kissed the top of his head. She wanted to cry but was unable to summon tears. Being assaulted and then narrowly escaping flogging and public humiliation that would reveal her identity should have shattered her. Yet she felt only hollow relief at escaping intact.

But witnessing Adnan suffer for protecting her cut far deeper. His love was unconditional while hers could never be what he desired.

When this was over, she would find a way to repay his sacrifice; she would ensure he lived a peaceful life away from the pain she had caused him. It was the least she could do for a friend who willingly walked through hellfire at her side.

26
The Way In

Despite the pain, Adnan returned to the forge a week later because the elderly blacksmith had fallen ill. He put on a brave face and worked without complaint. Margit gladly helped him. For the first time, she felt safe. She was not out on the march, fighting in some distant place or lying in bed injured.

Dóczi came to the smithy around midday. Sweating in the intense heat, he removed his hat and dried his brow. "Good day to you."

"And to you, sir," Margit replied. "Do you need anything fixed?"

The captain glanced about and then spoke in a low voice. "I apologise for what befell you and your friend. I couldn't stop Balog, but I told him Sergeant Bakó is an outright knave who deserved what you did to him. I knew you were different, and I feared you wouldn't survive the punishment. Thanks be to God, the castellan allowed your friend to take your place."

Margit bowed her head. "Thank you, captain. You are a good man, and I shall never forget that."

"I had a wife and a son," he said, sadness darkening his eyes. "He would be eighteen if he were alive. A fine-looking lad, just like you. He and my good woman were slaughtered during the Turkish attack on Várad in '74. There hasn't been a day since that I don't think about them. I wasn't there to protect them."

This must be the reason he is so kind to me.

"I'm sorry for your pain, sir. Nothing worse in the world than losing a child."

The captain nodded. "If you ever need anything, talk to me."

Margit did not ponder long. "If you don't mind me asking, sir, were you here during the time of the previous lord? Do you know what befell him?"

"No, I only came here after my family was killed. Why?"

"My mother worked in this castle when she was young." Margit's cheeks heated in the lie, but she continued without hesitation. "She had only the best words to say about Lord Sándor and his lady. I wonder how his nephew came to inherit the estate. He doesn't strike me as a kind person at all."

Dóczi frowned. "You should keep your opinion to yourself. If the lord suspects anything, you'll be in serious trouble. I must go now before my visit is noticed."

Heart heavy, Margit returned to the smithy's rear, where Adnan had just set down his tools. He took off his leather apron and washed the day's grime and smoke smudges from his hands and face.

Drops of water glittered in his dark hair as he ran his damp fingers through to tame some unruly strands.

"It's repast time," he said. "I'd close the workshop, but since you're here, will you stay? You can rest when I return."

Margit eyed him with curiosity. It was unusual of him to be so attentive to his appearance. "Where are you going?"

"Only to eat."

"Really? Did you spruce up for that?"

Adnan did not answer, just looked away.

Was he hiding something?

"I don't believe you," she insisted. "Who are you going to see?"

"Nobody."

But his reddened face only confirmed her suspicion. "I think you are going to meet a damsel."

Adnan looked away again, making Margit chuckle. "Oh! Adnan has a lover."

"Never say my real name," he said, placing his hand across her mouth. "You don't know who's listening." He stepped back and folded his arms. "And no, she's not my lover. Only a girl I like. I must go."

He started for the door, but Margit stood in his way. "You have kept a secret from me? I shall not let you leave until you tell me who the fair maiden is."

Adnan exhaled sharply. "Ilona Kovács, the kitchen maid."

"Good choice. You will never go hungry." She finally stepped aside. "Don't forget to bring me some food."

Adnan's face was beaming when he returned to the smithy an hour later. He handed Margit a wrapped parcel containing a slice of still warm bread, a chicken leg, a morsel of cheese and an apple.

Without thanking him, she feasted on the delicious food. But her curiosity was as big as her appetite. "Tell me," she said, chewing on the chicken leg, "did you kiss her?"

Adnan's smile turned into a frown. "No. She doesn't know I like her."

"Only the house servants and the officers are allowed to eat in the castle kitchen. She must care for you if she feeds you every day. Why don't you tell her?"

He did not reply. Instead, he put on his apron and picked up his tools.

Poor Adnan! His inexperience makes him too timid.

"You are too shy, my friend. Women don't fancy shy men. They dream of being courted passionately. You must tell her how you feel."

"Yes, yes... One day."

"Not one day. Now. You're a grown man. You need a woman. Not only for company, but for other—"

Adnan made a face at her. "Enough!"

Margit giggled. "Only teasing you."

She fell silent and continued eating. But then, a revelation came: "This damsel could be my way in."

"Your way in to what?"

"My cousin's house. She works in the kitchen, where the servants take their meals. I'm sure if there is any gossip about Márton and Anna, she would know. And if she lets me in there, I shall have access to the rest of the keep."

Adnan dropped his hammer on the bench. "No! Don't do this. You'll cause her trouble."

Of course, he wanted to protect the maid. But Margit could not miss this unique opportunity to learn more about her cousin and, possibly, about what had happened to her father. "Don't fret. She will not be put in danger. Just take me with you tomorrow and leave the rest to me."

***

When Margit and Adnan entered through the exterior door the following day, the castle kitchen was all but deserted. The men and women who worked there had finished cooking the main meal of the day and were relaxing in the courtyard before the big rush.

Platters, bowls, baskets and pots, brimming with mouth-watering food and spices that made Margit's stomach grumble, lay on the work benches which lined two sides of the room. Across from the entrance, a blackened cauldron—big enough to hold an entire pig inside—was suspended above the crackling open fire of the hearth. Plates and cups piled atop a wooden chest, while brass and steel utensils hung from hooks on the walls. And the sweet aroma of wine in earthen jugs wafted in the air.

Only a maid remained inside, cleaning the large table in the centre of the room and setting it for the meal.

Margit nudged Adnan and formed the question silently with her lips.

At his nod, she observed her friend's love interest keenly.

The rosy-cheeked maiden appeared to be about eighteen years of age. She wore a neat brown woollen kirtle and a linen bonnet with strings tied under her chin. But a few curls of shiny black hair had escaped their confinement and swung merrily at the sides of her neck as she moved. Beyond her lovely features, feminine grace emanated from her shapely body.

Unexpected jealousy twinged at Margit's heart.

Ilona pivoted at the sound of their footsteps, shielding her eyes from the sunlight that streamed through the doorway.

Recognition lit her face, and she beamed a sweet smile at

Adnan. "I've kept the best bits for you," she chirped, hurrying over with a parcel tidily wrapped in linen cloth.

"Thank you, Ilona," Adnan said. "You're an angel."

About to hand him the food, Ilona's fingers stilled upon noticing Margit. Inhaling sharply, she dropped the little bundle and covered her trembling lips.

Unable to decipher the girl's peculiar behaviour, Margit retrieved the parcel and passed it to Adnan.

The maid's arms fell to her sides. She gaped at Margit with wide, enraptured eyes.

A confused-looking Adnan hastened to fill the uneasy silence. "This is my friend, Saša," he said, in his attempt at Hungarian. "He...works with me in the...blacksmith...place."

Ilona's rosy face turned crimson as she spoke in a faltering voice. "Glad to...make your...your...quentance...sir."

"Acquaintance," Margit corrected the girl and bowed her head to conceal her amusement.

Silence again. Ilona's eyes were still glued on Margit. A silly smile spread on her face while her fingers played with a lock of hair.

Margit thought the awkwardness would choke her. She coughed, jolting the kitchen maid out of an evident reverie.

"Forgive me. I have a...lot of work...to do," Ilona stuttered. "Come a little earlier tomorrow. I'll have something ready for you to eat here." And with the broom now in hand, she swept the already spotless floor.

What strange behaviour!

Once outside the kitchen, Margit could not contain her curiosity. "What's the matter with her?"

Adnan's face creased. "Don't you know?"

Margit slapped her forehead.

Of course! But why?

"You're just too fair-looking for a man," Adnan sighed, throwing his hands in the air. He stomped his way towards the smithy.

"I'm sorry!" Margit hurried after him. "At least, you have nothing to fear. It's not like I would steal her from you."

Adnan stopped in his tracks and turned around. He wagged his finger at her. "You'll break her heart when she learns the truth. How are you going to live with that?"

Margit smiled reassuringly. "Do not fear. I shall not cause her any harm."

Ilona came to the forge that afternoon and every day thereafter. She kept bringing utensils for fixing and knives for sharpening even though they had the equipment to do that in the kitchen. Ignoring poor Adnan, she hovered around Margit like a moth attracted by lamplight and hung on her every word.

27
On the Inside

Mid-July 1478

The early-evening breeze rushed through the open door and windows and touched Margit's face before dissipating inside the kitchen. After a sizzling summer's day, it brought relief and coolness, together with the sharp but refreshing scent of the pine trees from the surrounding mountains.

"Hard day tomorrow."

Ilona's voice yanked Margit out of her daydreaming. She shifted on the bench by the table. "Why?"

Even though no supper had been cooked that night due to the lord's absence from the estate, the two of them were still in the kitchen: Margit hoping to gain access to her cousin's house after the rest of the workers had left for the day; and Ilona, evidently, because of her fascination with 'Saša'.

"The voivode comes tomorrow with his retinue," the maid said. "Twenty in total. God help us!"

"I can help too."

Ilona's face lit up. "Yes! We could do with another pair of hands. But beware: you'll be stuck here from dawn 'til late at night."

"I don't mind."

"Thank you, dear Saša. You're always so—" She scratched her

head. "What's the word? Chivelous? Like the knights of the old times in my grandam's stories."

Margit laughed. "Chivalrous."

"Yes, that."

Ilona smiled and fluttered her eyelashes. Over the last few days, her amorous behaviour had turned giddier and giddier.

Margit caught Ilona's dainty hand and gently moved it away from her shoulder, on which it had so eagerly nestled. "I wish to help with serving the food."

This would allow her to stand close to her cousin and observe him. And perhaps her aunt would make an appearance. If she were in the castle, that is.

"I assume supper will be served in the great hall?" Margit continued.

The maid bobbed her head. "Yes." A mischievous smile sparkled in her eyes. "I've heard the voivode has his niece with him. He's trying to arrange a marriage between her and Lord Márton."

Margit raised an eyebrow. "Really?"

"He'll fail, though. Like all the others before." Ilona shrugged her shoulders. "Unless the girl has the right colour hair."

Margit cocked her head towards the maid. "What do you mean?"

"The lord fancies redheads only."

Margit found this strange but did not dwell on the detail. It was time she set her plan in motion. She swung her legs over the bench, stood up and looked Ilona straight in the eye. "Can you take me to the great hall?"

The girl's face flushed instantly. "Oh, no! We're not allowed in there."

"Why not? The lord is absent. No one will be watching. And if, perchance, anyone sees us, we shall say we went there to see how the table will be arranged for tomorrow's feast."

Receiving no response, Margit feigned her most charming smile. "Please."

Ilona pressed her lips into a thin line and tapped her forefinger on her cheek. "Mmmmm... Very well." She rose and took Margit's hand.

They slipped through the kitchen's interior door into a shadowy passage beyond. Margit's anticipation grew, her heart thrummed with both excitement and trepidation at what awaited within. Up a short flight of stairs and along another corridor their footfalls echoed until Ilona pushed open a heavy, groaning door.

As they emerged into the great hall, Margit's chest brimmed with wonder. She surveyed the chamber with eyes and mouth open wide to absorb every detail of the treasures that lay there. Sasfészek was not simply her ancestral home but her inheritance too—a legacy connecting her ancestors to future generations through her.

Although smaller than the great hall in King Mátyás' palace, an air of grandeur filled the space. Tapestries lined two of the walls, their colours so vivid that they seemed about to leap out of their golden-threaded borders. In a strange, but by no means sacrilegious, blend of Christianity and pagan Magyar legend, the first tapestry depicted The Last Supper while the other displayed the Wondrous Stag chased by the hunters Hunor and Magor.

What inspired hands had crafted these? Enraptured, Margit reached out to stroke the lush fabric, sending ripples through the hanging with the stag. Her fingertips tingled. Between the two, this was her favourite scene.

To her left, arched windows let the languid sunlight flood the hall and cast vibrant stained-glass shadows that danced across whitewashed walls. Margit's eyes chased the multi-hued shapes, falling at last upon the vaulted ceiling, decorated in splendour with intricate carvings on its wooden beams.

Her gaze shifted across the chamber, heart swelling at the Szilágyi of Szentimre crest of sculpted marble ensconced above the fireplace. Margit bowed her head, sparing a moment to pray for the souls of her ancestors, men and women, who had built and defended this haven time and again.

The family coat of arms appeared also on a banner hanging from the cornice of the wall on the right, beside the flag of the *Siebenbürgen*. Whether out of pride or for show, her cousin seemed to honour both his Magyar and Saxon legacy. A third flag, that of the kingdom of Hungary, proclaimed the family's loyalty to the Crown. Margit sneered. The Szilágyi family's loyalty certainly; but what about Márton's?

Ilona nudged Margit out of her thoughts. "I see the tables are already in place."

The main dining table, made of solid wood, stood on a dais central to the hall. Margit counted seven high-backed chairs along its side; the middle one the most ornate. Márton's surely.

This will be my seat one day, with Endre by my side.

She turned to Ilona. "I assume the lord and his guests will sit there. Who will sit at the side tables?"

"The officers, the voivode's knights and his niece's maidservants."

"Of course," Margit mumbled absently. The seating arrangements were inconsequential. Only the knowledge of her family and her childhood memories mattered.

As she turned her back to the tables, her eyes fell on a display cabinet standing in the corner by the door to the kitchen. Her jaw dropped. How had she missed that?

A full suit of armour—old-looking, scratched and dented—with the family crest engraved on the breastplate was mounted on a stand inside the cabinet.

Why is it here and not in the armoury or my cousin's chamber?

"Tell me, Ilona, does the armour belong to Lord Márton? Does he wear it? I heard he never goes to war."

The maid shook her head. "It's not his. It belonged to the previous lord, his uncle. And so did the weapons."

Margit's breath caught at the sight of her father's knightly equipment: the *misericorde*, the cross-hilted sword, the spiked horseman's axe and the cavalry shield. His coat of arms adorned them all although the colours of the crest painted on the shield had faded with time. For a heartbeat, Margit thought she saw bloodstains on the axe's blade. Real or imagined? It mattered not; the grief of her loss tore through her anew.

Tears flooded her eyes and then flowed unchecked as she took in the relics of the man she barely knew; the armour he wore and the weapons he wielded in life, now remnants of his valour and love for his homeland.

Turning swiftly, she wiped her cheeks before Ilona glimpsed her sorrow. She shifted her gaze elsewhere—anywhere but on the lingering imprint of her father's ghost in this hall. There would be time to grieve when she would do so freely. For now, she must keep her eyes dry and steel her heart and spirit lest she raised suspicions and questions impossible to answer.

"Let us explore further," she blurted out.

Ilona furrowed her brow. "No, we can't. We shouldn't even be here."

"Come! It will be our little adventure."

Margit extended her hand and again faked the sweetest smile she could.

Her gesture, possibly combined with the fact that the lord was away and most of the servants had given themselves a day of rest, must have changed Ilona's mind. She took Margit's hand.

The door moaned as they pushed it open. Margit found herself in a small ante-room, strikingly spartan compared to the hall. As she roamed through the rest of the house, she saw hardly any decoration, in stark contrast to the splendour of the great hall.

Coming to the entrance area, Margit climbed the stone staircase to the floor above in long strides ahead of Ilona. A corridor lit by a row of vaulted windows had a series of rooms on the other side. Margit nudged the first door open. Despite Ilona's discouraging mumble, she entered.

Damp and must assaulted her nostrils and made her grimace. The air was stale. Carpeted from one end to the other, the chamber lay empty but for an old table and a wooden chest shoved in one corner. Dust particles floated in the feeble light, and cobwebs swayed between the table legs.

An inexorable pull drew Margit to the trunk. Lifting its lid revealed children's faded toys within: dolls, balls, soldiers, animals, a couple of tiny wooden swords.

As her fingers brushed these relics, an eerie chill crept through her bones. The world fell away until only she existed, suspended in an endless void. Then a horrifying vision flashed: a girl—herself—pinned helplessly to the floor as a hand crushed her chest. Another hand under her skirts...

What is this?

Revulsion clenched Margit's gut. Her legs buckled, and she staggered backwards onto the unforgiving wall. Pain exploded through her shoulder, jolting her back to the present. Gasping, she steadied herself against the solid stones.

The vision evaporated, but an indistinct unease lingered in its wake. Had something happened to her in this chamber? An echo of evil certainly lurked there though its source eluded her.

"What's wrong?" came Ilona's voice.

"Nothing. I only felt a little dizzy. It's too warm and stifling here."

"It's not. Perhaps you're ill. Come, let's go."

Ilona's hand steadied her as they left the room. But halfway down the stairs, Margit heard a scream; loud and clear—a shrill cry of anguish and despair, coming from an upper floor and piercing her soul.

"Did you hear that, Ilona?"

"Hear what?"

"A scream."

"I heard nothing. You must have imagined it. Let's go!"

Ilona rushed down the stairs, pulling her along.

Lost in a haze, Margit hardly recalled returning to the kitchen. A shiver of dread crept down her spine, leaving a trail of icy sweat in its wake as chilling questions beset her troubled mind.

What unspeakable horrors had unfolded in that chamber? What creature had unleashed that bloodcurdling scream? In her desperate effort to unravel her forgotten past, had she inadvertently awakened the demons which now howled in her head?

28
Revelation

The castle had been bustling with activity since sunrise the following day. The aroma of fowl, pork, hare and other game roasting on spits outside the kitchen made Margit's mouth water even though she had already broken her fast.

Banishing the dreadful echoes of the past night to the back of her mind, she entered the kitchen, which was packed with servants scurrying around. Vegetables boiled in cauldrons in the hearth, their earthy smell mixing with the sweet scent of fruit pies in the oven.

"Oh, you're here," Ilona chirped. A broad smile lit her face. She shoved a knife into Margit's hand. "Start chopping the herbs. Then slice the cheese."

Time flew by until nones, when soldiers and servants lined up in the courtyard to welcome the fourth most powerful man in the kingdom of Hungary: the Voivode of Transylvania, Péter Vingárti Geréb. This man was a first cousin of King Mátyás on his mother's side.

Margit grunted in disgust.

Another one of my relatives. Yet it's my cousin who hosts him. In my home.

At the back of a group of servants, she stood on the tips of her toes to catch a glimpse of the man, who arrived with his retinue and his niece, a skinny blonde-haired maiden, not much older than fifteen years of age. They had been escorted all the way to

Sasfészek by Márton and his knights.

"Why are you idling about?" came Ilona's sharp voice. Either burdened with too much responsibility or possibly feeling important, Ilona had been ordering Margit around all day.

But Margit did not complain. She had offered to be there, and she would do anything for a chance to stand close to her cousin in the great hall during the big feast.

After more hours of cooking and preparation, food was finally ready to be served at vespers. In their splendid attires, Márton and his guests returned after service in the chapel and headed for the great hall.

Dressed in a boy servant's clothes, Margit put on a linen coif with its strings hanging loose on either side of her face. "How do I look?"

Ilona straightened the coarse wool tunic, which had gathered in folds at Margit's waist. "Perfect now."

Margit entered the great hall hesitantly. Movement and noises assailed her from all directions as she stopped to survey the scene.

The tables were already set and heavy with all that lavish food the cooks and kitchen hands had prepared. With several standing torches burning beside the tables and a multitude of lamps and candles, there was not a dark spot in the chamber while a wave of warmth—nay, heat—enveloped Margit, shooting hot flushes across her face.

Exactly as Ilona had described, the castle officers, the voivode's retinue and his niece's maidservants sat at the two side tables below the dais. When they did not stuff their mouths with food and drink, they chattered and giggled merrily.

At the head table, her cousin had settled into the middle seat. To his right sat the voivode, his niece and his senior knight. To Márton's left: the red-haired woman who visited him at night, an unknown nobleman and Balog.

Servants scurried back and forth, almost colliding with Margit as she ventured towards the centre of the hall.

"You, there!" Evidently anxious, the head cupbearer beckoned her urgently.

Margit approached cautiously. What did the man want from her?

"One lad is ill. Help serve wine. Now!" he barked and rushed off.

Though taken aback by his abrupt manner, Margit seized the opportunity.

After stumbling up the dais, she regained her composure and smoothed down her tunic. She stood near Márton, body straight and hands clasped behind her back. Caught as if by an irresistible force, her eyes constantly shifted towards her cousin. But fearing her swelling abhorrence might escape onto her countenance, she turned her attention to the voivode's niece.

Amidst the lewd jests and coarse laughter of the other guests, the young lady kept to herself, head low and hands trembling as she nibbled on her food. Indeed, she looked like a lamb about to be led to slaughter.

Poor damsel.

Margit wished her cousin would reject her as his bride. The maiden would probably be humiliated briefly, but this would be a hundred times better than a lifetime of misery with a man who, more than likely, would never treat her with respect. And the evidence was there, in plain sight: Márton's mistress sitting beside him.

Shameless!

The orders to fill the cups with wine came thick and fast. Back and forth Margit hastened, obeying the cupbearer's commands without complaint. To her, the biggest reward was to stand close to her cousin and observe his behaviour.

As she leaned over to serve the nobleman on the other side of the red-haired woman, she noticed the two wore matching silver wedding bands and conversed in intimate terms.

My cousin uses another man's wife for his pleasure?

Margit shuddered inwardly with disgust. Her eyes fixed on the nobleman. He was neither old nor ugly, just ordinary-looking, well-dressed and quiet. He must have known that his wife lay with the lord for he shot hateful glances at Márton and pressed his clenched fists on the table every time Margit's cousin whispered in the woman's ear or touched her hand.

The more Margit studied the scene, a strange, foreboding chill crawled over her. A future tragedy, perhaps? Why she felt this, she did not know.

In a gruff and demanding voice, Márton repeatedly summoned her to pour wine into his ornate gilded goblet. Margit clenched and unclenched her teeth, wishing she could slip poison into his drink. But what good would that do to her? She still needed to find her father's murderer.

As the hours passed, her cousin descended into a drunken state, not unlike many of his guests. Some men became so boisterous that the voivode's niece, her face growing redder than the wine served at the table, stood up and excused herself.

Márton leered at the girl as she walked out of the hall; but the moment she was out of sight, he winked at his mistress.

"What do you think of my niece, sir?" the voivode said, barely making himself heard over the hubbub.

"Oh, she is delightful," Márton replied without looking at the man for his eyes were still fixed on the other woman. "But I need time to think about your offer. I shall send you my reply in due course."

From the tone of his voice, Margit could tell he was not interested. He resumed his drinking and laughing with the red-haired lady, making her husband's face twist in anger and change a number of colours.

I don't know how this gentleman restrains himself against such an affront.

On his part, the voivode did not seem to approve of his host's behaviour either. He pushed his chair back. Its grating noise on the dais drew Márton's attention back to him. The voivode excused himself and left the great hall, followed by his people.

Margit was filling Márton's cup for the tenth—or twelfth?— time when he suddenly turned to her. She recoiled, spilling the wine on the table and on him.

Her cousin whipped his arms up in the air. His voice cut her right through to the core. "Damn you, boy!"

Margit's face burned. Her pulse thudded in her temples, and her voice faltered. "I'm so...sorry, my...my lord."

Oh, how she resented saying this!

Without thinking, she picked a handcloth from the table and patted the wine stains on his velvet doublet.

Márton grunted and seized her hand. "How dare you touch me?"

The cloth fell from Margit's grasp. Fear, like poison, envenomed her quivering heart. A dark and menacing figure formed before her eyes. She had seen that vision before.

God help me!

Márton's voice took on a shade of evil beyond words as his grip tightened around her wrist. "You have such slender hands. Like a woman's," he muttered as if she was his only intended audience. "Who are you?"

Panting now, Margit turned away. The marble fireplace, the flags, the tapestries... Any other sight but him.

Márton yanked at her. "How dare you look away when I speak to you?"

Cold sweat dripped down Margit's temples.

Dear God, make it stop.

She forced herself to turn back to him.

How different he looked now. Gone were the arrogance and disdain of the day she first met him. Weariness marred his countenance, and a shadow covered his bloodshot eyes as he squinted to scrutinise her face. "Take off your cap!"

She removed the coif slowly, unable to steady her free hand.

Márton's stare fixed on her hair.

Margit attempted to wrest herself out of his grip, but her move made him squeeze her wrist so hard that she thought her bones were about to snap. Her teeth dug into her lower lip. She must stem the tears of pain lest they infuriate him more.

His gaze shifted back onto her face. Something akin to recognition flickered in his eyes. "Have I seen you before?"

Despite multiple shivers running down her spine, she had to give a quick answer to avoid further investigation. "Yes, my lord. I was one of your soldiers."

"You were?" Márton looked her up and down.

"Yes. I was wounded in battle and cannot fight anymore. But I can make myself useful as a servant."

"Useful?" he croaked. "Consider yourself fortunate that I have guests. I would have you whipped otherwise."

His mistress tapped him on the shoulder. "My lord, leave the poor lad in peace."

Márton snorted and let go of Margit's hand at last.

God bless you, lady!

Still trembling, Margit stepped away from him. In the corner of her eye, the cupbearer signalled to her to calm herself. She rubbed her swollen, red wrist to ease the discomfort.

Soon, more and more guests staggered out of the hall, including the red-haired woman's inebriated husband, who flung his handcloth onto the table and cursed under his breath before departing.

Márton and his mistress were the only ones left at the table. He raised his hand to summon the cupbearer, but the lady objected, "No, my lord. You've had too much wine."

A violent expression consumed his features. "Shut your mouth, Ágnes!" He banged his fist, making plates and cups rattle. "You sound like my mother."

"You are weary, my lord. You must rest well and then consider the voivode's proposal," the woman continued, clearly fighting back her fear. "You must do your duty and wed that lady."

Her bravery startled Margit.

"My duty? Damn my duty!" Márton gnashed his teeth, a thick vein popping on his neck. He swept his hand across the hall. "I did not wish to live like this." He stood up abruptly and raised his goblet. "Here is to my accursed family," he spluttered and then turned his gaze to his distorted little finger. "They gave me a noble name and a life of pain."

He swayed back and forth and would have fallen on his back if the cupbearer and a servant had not caught him.

"My dear lord!" Ágnes pleaded. "You scare me."

Márton flung off the two men and scowled at her. "You will betray me too. Like everyone else."

"I shall wait in the bedchamber," she said in a subdued voice. With skirts gathered in her hand, she hastened out of the hall.

Márton shifted his vehement glare to the servants. "Begone! All of you!"

Men and women stopped whatever they were doing, bowed and withdrew.

Dreading to remain alone with her cousin, Margit turned around to leave too, but he seized her by the arm.

"I blame you, boy," he said, slurring each word.

Margit's stomach tumbled. What else was he to accuse her of?

Márton winced and let go of her. "Your red hair reminds me of an old enemy. He was a great warrior. He was also the man I hated most in the world."

Enemy? Warrior?

"All the bad things in my life happened because of him." Márton flung his arm towards an invisible person. "He had a knack for stirring up turmoil in other people's souls. My father wasted his life hating him. My mother wasted her life lusting after him. My first image of 'love' was of him fondling his wife like a common whore in the upstairs corridor. And when I told him I loved his daughter and wished to marry her, he crippled my hand."

A gasp stole the air from Margit's lungs.

What is this I hear?

Oblivious to the facial expressions which might have betrayed the disorder of her mind by now, Márton pointed at the display cabinet with a trembling finger. "This is why I still keep his things therein."

Margit looked in that direction.

Does he speak of my—

"I see them every day, and I say: perhaps you were a hero a long time ago, but what are you now?" He let out a sinister laugh. "Another corpse rotting in Hell. You will never hurt me again."

He speaks of my father! My father crippled him... Because Márton loved...me?

Repulsion slithered inside Margit's body. Like a thick cloud of gloom, disbelief overspread her mind. Her legs gave way, and she staggered backwards, barely able to keep her balance.

Her cousin's outburst was the first evidence of what had happened that fateful evening, sixteen years earlier. Could he have been her father's murderer? The thought brought the contents of her stomach to her mouth. Her body burned with anger, and she balled her fists. If only she had the courage to grab the axe from the cabinet and smash his head...

The sound of the door slamming made her jump. Márton had stormed out, leaving her alone in the great hall. Her body drained of all its strength, she collapsed in a chair and remained there until she finally calmed herself.

Later that night, after cleaning and tidying the kitchen, Margit sat down next to Ilona, exhausted. Everyone else had left.

"Thank you for helping," Ilona said with a tired smile.

"My pleasure. But I must go now."

"Wait!" In an unexpected move, the maid sat on Margit's knees. "I didn't thank you properly."

Lips puckered, Ilona leaned over.

Even though she had no more strength left in her, Margit jerked her head away just in time. The girl's kiss landed on her cheek instead.

After a brief, awkward silence, Margit spoke as gently as she could. "I shall take my leave."

"Of course," Ilona mumbled and stood up, cheeks reddened and gaze dropped to the floor.

29
The Night Visitor

Margit spent the following morning under the bedcovers, brooding over the previous evening's events. She wished to avoid Ilona, too. The kitchen maid's fascination with 'Saša' had grown so much that Margit did not know what to do.

Yet it was her cousin's behaviour which troubled her the most. The revelation that he loved her and wished to marry her when she was a child shook her to the core.

Márton harboured so much hatred against her father. From what Erzsi had told her, his mother, Anna, had been behind some horrible events that transpired for many years. It came as no surprise that her son would grow up to be like her. Perhaps Margit's father had a good reason to punish Márton so severely. Now that Margit thought of it, Erzsi had never spoken of that incident. Why would her godmother hide something so important? Was it because she did not wish to bring back a bad memory?

That must be it.

Perhaps her cousin's punishment was related to the vision Margit had in that empty room of the keep. She closed her eyes and forced herself to return there.

Breaking through the fog of her forgotten childhood, memories leapt upon her.

Yes, it was Márton. His wolfish face leaned over her now; his hand pressed hard on her chest. Her throat constricted; her breath turned into desperate gasps. His other hand fumbled with her skirts, reaching for the most intimate part of her body. Her stomach swirled, about to expel its contents violently... Searching around for help, her eyes fell on another boy... Endre... He was there, too. He had tried to stop Márton, but her cousin punched him. Brave little Endre. Blood oozed from his nose, streaking his lips and chin.

And then, before her cousin could complete his terrible deed, the door burst open. A giant in her eyes, her father hauled Márton off her and hurled him to the floor.

"I'm here, *kincsem*. You are safe. I'm here. I'm here," her father said, his voice a comforting blanket; his arms a fortress protecting her from all the evils of the world. Still, she could not stop crying...

Margit shivered in the bed, her entire body drenched in sweat. Fear, shame and guilt assaulted her from within. Blanket clenched in her hands, she gasped and coughed and retched. Her head pounded. Heat rushed to her face. Fever parched her mouth, dried her eyes, boiled her brain.

Tortured by flashing images of that incident, she eventually sank into a heavy stupor. Her sense of time slipped away. During brief moments of dazed consciousness, she heard Adnan's muffled voice, but she could not respond. Dread paralysed her limbs, and little by little, the world collapsed around her, sucked away by a mysterious and frightening force.

Alone in the empty chamber of her mind, she stared at a white wall until shadows gathered like black clouds before a storm. Murky as the waters of a swamp, they transformed into a grotesque figure. An invisible, giant foot stamped on her chest.

The warm sweat turned icy, piercing through every pore of her skin. She curled in a corner, trembling and unable to control her chattering teeth.

All her fears banded together, bent on her destruction. Thunder rumbled. Gnarled arms and hands with distorted fingers grew out of the shadowy apparition and reached towards her. Emitting the stench of death, a ghastly mouth gaped, ready to devour her.

Margit pressed her hands against her ears.

Please, please, I beg of you. Leave me in peace. I can't bear it. I can't live anymore.

The floor she was lying on broke, and she began to sink.

But then the blinding flash of lightning tore through her dark enemy. Brilliant white, with the wingspan of an angel, a dove chased away every bit of blackness until the room brightened and the ground stopped moving under her.

The bird hovered over Margit for a moment, and as she raised her grateful eyes, it transformed into a woman; fair and radiant, now a familiar figure.

Mama!

"I'm here, *kincsem*."

Shedding rivers of silent tears, Margit fell into her mother's open arms.

"Calm yourself, my child. Let me take your bad dreams away."

Like the lightest breeze, her mother's airy hand caressed Margit's face and hair; then slid down her chest and rested on her heart. As if by a holy miracle, all life's fears, worries, burdens, regrets, shame and guilt rose off Margit's breast.

Her mother gently moved away and gazed at her with a loving

smile. "Go now in God's peace. Live your life. Give your love to those who deserve it." She winked. "And trust your husband with all your heart."

Despite the relief flooding Margit's body, sadness stabbed deep in her soul. "Mama, please, stay a little longer."

"My work is done, *kincsem*. You are strong now. Broken no more."

Her image flickered.

Margit reached out for her mother in wild desperation, but she faded away.

Margit awoke with a gasp. Around her, the blue light of dawn seeped furtively into the chamber. Her mind still dazed, she lay on her back and inhaled deeply.

Someone's soft breathing reached her ears. Adnan slept in a chair beside her, his head tilted to one side. She smiled, always grateful for his reassuring presence.

In the cool air flowing through the open skylight, a cathartic wave washed over her. Gone were the fever, the dryness, the pain in her head, the tightness in her chest.

Yet she was unable to move for her body was drained as if she had fought the hardest battle of her life.

Her mother's encouraging words still lingered in Margit's mind. She clung to them like a lifeline fortifying her spirit.

Sleep took her gently this time, leading her into a brighter world, where she felt free from the ghosts of her past and ready to face the future with strength and determination. She was a different person now.

When she opened her eyes again, the last light of the day created shadows on the wall. But they no longer menaced her.

A joyous face appeared.

"Adnan."

"Margit! At last! Welcome back to the land of the living."

She turned her head right and left. "How long have I been lying here?"

"Two days. Burning with fever and mumbling like one possessed." He touched her forehead. "But the fever's gone now."

Feeling much better, Margit sat up and ate the light supper her friend prepared for her. Then she related the events of her cousin's banquet to him. But she never spoke of the horrible incident from her childhood.

"D'you believe your cousin killed your father?" Adnan said.

"After listening to his raving speech, I'm sure he wished my father dead. But I have no proof he did the deed. Oh, I wish I could just stab his black heart and get done with it! Having to face this ordeal until I find evidence will drive me to madness."

"God's great, Margit. He'll show you the way."

As night fell once again, she lay down and pulled the covers over her. Adnan extinguished the rushlight and went to bed too.

Sometime later, a knock on the door awoke Margit, but she was too tired to move. Despite her protest, Adnan got up and opened the door. A sliver of lamplight shone through the opening and onto Margit's face. Although only a meagre flame, it blinded her in the darkness of the chamber. She hid her head under the blanket.

"I must go out awhile," Adnan said.

"At this hour?" Margit peeped from behind the blanket. "Be

wary."

"Don't fret. All's well."

He left the chamber, closing the door behind him.

His naked chest pressed against her back while his hand caressed her thigh and hip under the nightshirt. Her mystery knight had appeared to her in a dream, the most scandalous dream ever. Margit could not see his face as she lay on her side, and he was behind her. But for some strange reason, she knew it was him. A stream of warmth surged through her veins. Her body tensed with delicious anticipation.

But it was not a dream anymore. His breath on her neck, the prickling of her skin... All real. Was he truly there?

His touch affected her like a potent spell, rendering her powerless. She swallowed to bring much needed moisture to her throat. "How did you find me?"

"I always find you," he said in the lightest of whispers.

Margit moaned as he playfully bit her shoulder, the side of her neck, her ear. Stubble grazed her skin, sending ripples of excitement down her spine.

Fully awakened now, it finally dawned on her that she was about to commit a mortal sin. "Stop! I can't betray my husband."

He ignored her, raising panic inside her. "Stop and reveal yourself, or I shall scream!"

"No, don't scream!" Now that he spoke a little louder, his voice sounded familiar. "And you have not betrayed your husband because *I am* your husband."

Margit's face heated with embarrassment. "Endre! You scared

the life out of me!" She turned around and slapped him on the head.

He seized her wrist. "Never hit me again! We are not children anymore."

She fought to free herself, but his grip was too firm. With a swift movement, he was on top of her, pinning her hands down over her head. "Your body is so hard. It feels like I'm in bed with a man."

Margit scoffed. "How do you know?"

"You have a sharp tongue, dear wife. And you are too wild. It's about time someone tamed you."

"Tamed me?"

Her curiosity piqued, she let him kiss her deeply, pull the nightshirt over her head and toss it aside. Strangely, she felt no shame in exposing her body this time. It was that dreadful event from her childhood which had tainted her intimate moments with her husband until now. Neither she nor Endre was to blame.

As his hands, mouth and tongue lingeringly explored every part of her, Margit's skin burned with overwhelming desire, which consumed her flesh and sent her head into a spin. Her mother's words echoed in her mind. "Trust your husband with all your heart."

Yes, she did trust him now. Gone were all her fears, her inhibitions. Her soul healed from past experiences and pain, she surrendered.

For the first time, she accepted her husband with hungry eagerness. Urged by the sounds of his passion and the tensing of his body, she dug her nails into the tight muscles of his back, clinging to him in unspeakable bliss until their heartbeats became one. She thought her breath stopped for the briefest moment as her body convulsed, and she panted as if she had run many miles.

With an intense moan, Endre pulled away just in time.

"You remembered," Margit whispered, still out of breath.

"Of course, *szívem*. No children before we become the lords of Szentimre." His kiss cooled her parched lips.

They lay side by side for a while, both sweating and spent.

Endre was the first to break the silence. "Why did you speak of betraying your husband?"

"Oh, never mind. I was half-asleep and babbling."

"You thought I was someone else, didn't you?" A hint of bitterness tinged his voice.

"No!" Margit protested, but her cheeks were on fire. Thanks be to God, he could not see her face in the darkness.

"Don't lie. I know about the 'black knight' who rode to your rescue. I'm sure he caught your fancy."

Margit clenched her teeth. "Who told you that?"

"Oh... Ummm... The Lord Judge."

"The Judge?"

How curious! It did not make sense.

"Of course, I could not have you lust after a stranger. I had to get better in this game," Endre said.

"It's not a game. He is only a fantasy. You are real." She ran her hand down his chest, relishing the warmth of his skin. "But tell me, how did you learn to please a woman this much? Or are you just so jealous of a simple fantasy?"

"I visited a brothel."

She sprang upright on the bed. "What?"

"When you left Nándorfehérvár, you told me I could—"

The blood shot to Margit's head. "Yes, I told you to find another woman. But only if I happened to die. How could you when I still live?"

Endre sat up too and put his hand on her arm. "Hey, calm yourself. I didn't do anything with those women. I swear. I only talked to them and took their advice. By God, I wasn't sure if I would please you, but it seems..."

She curled her lip. "Do you expect me to believe you?"

"Believe what you wish. I tell the truth."

His steady voice revealed sincerity and eased her concerns. "Very well. I trust you," she said.

A knock on the door made both pull the bedcovers over them.

"It's I, Adnan. May I enter? I need to sleep."

"Yes," Endre answered.

"Adnan!" Margit exclaimed. "Were you outside all this time? Did you—"

"Yes, I heard everything. And so did the whole town."

"Pay no heed," Endre said to her. "He is jealous."

"How dare you?" Adnan burst out. "I've been looking after her all this time. Where were you when she needed you? When she was fighting the Turks in foreign lands; when she was injured and at death's door; when she was attacked by a drunk soldier; or when she barely escaped flogging for fighting back at him? And now, you just walk in here to claim your prize?"

"If you have an issue with me, peasant, let us settle it like men tomorrow."

"Stop this nonsense!" Margit interjected. "You are both very important to me, and I don't intend to lose either of you in a duel."

Adnan got into bed and did not speak again.

But Endre did not stay quiet. "Who tried to harm you, Margit? He will die by my hand."

"Calm yourself, husband. No harm was done to me. Instead, I gave the man such a fright that he will not bother me again."

***

When Margit woke up the next morning, Adnan had left, and Endre still slept beside her. Through the skylight above, sunshine flooded the chamber and enveloped him in a golden mist.

The more Margit studied him, the more different he looked from what she remembered. His body was now hard-trained and muscular, faded scars hinting at deeds of valour. A darker shade of blonde, his hair was cut tight at the sides and back but longer on the top. A few days' stubble shadowed his jaw. All this combined to make his otherwise gentle features look rugged. This was neither her childhood companion nor the shy adolescent she had married, but someone entirely different: a strong and confident man, who had slowly won her heart and had now conquered her body, too.

One night many years earlier, Erzsi—a little tipsy—had spoken to her about a lovers' passion that her parents shared, which went beyond marital duty. It was the glue which held their marriage together for so long. Margit had been born of that passion. It ran in her blood. And now, it had been awakened, thanks to Endre. They were not merely husband and wife any longer; they were lovers.

She lay back on the pillow and closed her eyes, trying to seal the enchanting image of him into her mind. Everything around her was so calm that she drifted back to sleep.

When she awoke again sometime later, she was alone. She put her clothes on hastily and rushed into the next room, eager to find Endre. He was there, fully dressed, his face washed and shaved, sitting at the table and breaking his fast.

He rose and bowed his head. "Good day, my lady."

"My lady?" Margit sneered. "Last night you called me a man."

Endre raised an apologetic hand. "Only in jest. I hope you were not offended."

"No. I took it as a compliment. I have always wished I were a man."

His chuckle made her fold her arms and look at him askance. He had never been one for jokes. This new Endre was a mystery to her.

She joined him at the table. "So, what news do you bring?"

"We defeated the emperor's forces in Austria last autumn but could not take Vienna. Perhaps next time. The king has now secured peace with Emperor Frederick and is negotiating with Władysław, the Polish king's son, over Bohemia. When this is achieved, he will turn his attention to the Ottomans."

"Have you been home at all? How are your mother and grandmother? And Erzsi?"

"They are well. Erzsi misses you. She asked to travel with me, but I did not think it safe for her to be here."

"I miss her too. I have no one to wag the finger at me and reprimand me for misbehaving."

She let out a nostalgic sigh, not only at the thought of Erzsi but also for the carefree years of her childhood. Nothing would be the same again.

"There is something else I wish to tell you," Endre continued.

"What?"

"I am now a knight in my own right. And a captain of the royal army. I have a hundred cavalry soldiers under my command on the battlefield."

Margit smiled. He had achieved so much for a young man of twenty-one. "You make me proud, husband. But most of all, I'm glad that you came to see me. I have missed you."

Her words brought a broad grin to his face. He must have relished the notion that he was not her inferior any longer.

The sun's reflection on something shiny drew Margit's attention.

Propped against the wall under the skylight, Endre's sword nestled in a leather scabbard with polished metal fittings. Margit rose from the table and crossed the room. She drew the sword and swung it around. It felt slightly heavier than she was comfortable with. Its edges and tip were razor sharp. A masterfully crafted longsword, no doubt.

She turned to Endre. "Did Ahmed make this for you?"

"No, I had it made in Buda by one of the king's blade smiths."

"Splendid. And where is your armour? I'm dying to see it."

"I have not come here in an official capacity, and I did not wish to cause a stir riding into Szentimre as a royal army officer. I only came to see you and hear your news."

She related to him what had happened since she arrived at the estate for the second time.

He apologised for not being by her side during those difficult times, but she assured him she completely understood his reasons.

Endre clasped her hands in his own and looked her in the eye.

"The king appreciates my education and knowledge of languages. He has sent me to Transylvania on a mission. The Turks have grown restless lately, and the instability in Wallachia after Prince Vlad's death worries Mátyás. I am to inspect the main fortresses and towns outside of the Székely Seats and Saxon lands and record their military capability and readiness. So, I shall be in the province for one or two months. After I present my report to the king, I shall return to help you. I promise."

Margit shook her head, her heart heavy with the knowledge that he must leave again.

Sensing, perhaps, her disappointment, Endre drew a piece of paper from his belt pouch. "Here is the list of all the places I am to inspect and the dates when I shall be at each one. I shall never be more than three-or four-days' ride from here. So, if you need me, you will know where to find me."

Endre handed her the paper and took a deep bow. "I must take my leave now."

Margit flung the paper onto the table. "Why in God's name are you so formal with me? We have known each other since we were babies."

"I wish to show respect to you, my lady wife."

"You needn't do that. I know you respect me. You make me feel I have gained a noble husband but lost my childhood friend."

"I shall always be your friend."

She saw a smile flicker on his face, which warmed her heart, if only for an instant. "Must you leave now?"

"My men are waiting in Déva. We are to start the inspections today."

Margit stepped in his way and threw her arms around his neck.

"Surely they will not mind waiting a little lon—"

Before the last word left her mouth, Endre kissed her deeply. They were both out of breath when he pulled away.

"I am yours," he said and, taking her by the hand, led her back to the bedchamber.

30
The Prisoner

As soon as Margit entered the castle kitchen the following evening, Ilona dropped the broom and ran to embrace her.

"Saša! You disappeared for days. Stefan said you were ill, but he wouldn't let me visit you."

Margit disentangled herself as gently as she could. "Oh, it was nothing serious. You need not fret."

"I've...mi...missed you," Ilona stammered, blushing.

Margit forced a grin. This fascination always put her in an awkward position, but she still had not thought of a way to tell the maid that she was not interested or, more importantly, that she was not a man.

"You're so different." Ilona ran her hand down Margit's arm. "Any other man would've tried to bed me by now."

The creaking of the internal kitchen door offered Margit some respite. A guard barged in, looking anxious. "What are you doing, wench?" he shouted at Ilona. "It's time. Have you forgotten?"

"No," the maid replied hurriedly. "I'll go to her now."

The soldier slammed the door behind him.

Curiosity sparked inside Margit. "What's the matter?"

"Nothing. The head cook is ill today, and I must do something in her place."

Perplexed, Margit inclined her head towards Ilona.

The girl's face reddened. "Oh, I'm not allowed to tell you."

What was so secret that the maid was too afraid to reveal? "You can talk to me. I shall not tell anyone."

Ilona seemed to ponder, rocking her head from side to side. "Very well. You can come with me; but only because I fear going there on my own. Promise you won't say anything, no matter what you see or hear."

"Yes, I swear to God."

Intrigued some more now, Margit waited, arms folded, while the maid took a wooden bowl and filled it with the leftovers of the day's supper, still stewing in a big pot over the dying fire in the hearth. What would this mystery pertain to?

They left the kitchen and walked through the corridor to the main residence. After traversing the great hall, the anteroom and the entrance hall, they climbed two flights of stairs. Margit had not ventured this far before. The opportunity to see more of the keep raised her pulse.

The staircase and corridor on the second floor were as austere as the rest of the building. On one side, a series of arched windows let in the last light of the day while hanging lamps illuminated the other side of the corridor.

They turned around a corner and came face-to-face with a yawning soldier guarding a chamber. As soon as he saw them, he stood to attention.

"I brought the lady's supper," Ilona said.

Margit's eyebrows shot up.

Lady?

"What's *he* doing here?" the guard hissed, pointing at Margit.

Ilona lowered her head. "After she screamed at me last time, I'm afraid to go in alone."

"I'll go with you."

"And who will stand guard here? I see your comrade deserted you."

The soldier let out a huff. "The rascal went to piss again. Very well. You can both go in. But no talking."

"Yes, of course."

Keys jingled as the guard searched his belt for the right one. He unlocked the door and pushed it open. Then he stood back at his position.

Margit followed Ilona into the chamber. Her eyes searched about with eager curiosity. In this untidy room, where a jumble of small furniture, utensils, clothes, jewellery and loose fabrics lay scattered, her attention was drawn to a canopied bed resting upon an elevated platform.

Bathed in the orange light of the setting sun which entered through a window, a woman sat slumped at the foot of the platform with her legs stretched out. Long and dishevelled grey hair framed an emaciated and wrinkled face, shadows accentuating her sunken cheeks. Dull and unblinking, her stare was fixed at that same window, perhaps her sole portal to the outer world. A mere long chemise, tattered along the hemline and at the edges of the sleeves, covered her gaunt body. Black with grime, her bare feet protruded from her clothing. Equally filthy and skeletal, her hands were shackled together with a long chain, granting her only minimal freedom of movement.

The stench of unwashed body odour, sickness and urine pervaded the air.

Margit's stomach tightened. What had this woman done to deserve such punishment?

Ilona approached the stranger on tiptoes and placed the bowl on the floor. She then stepped back and stood beside Margit.

"Let's go," she whispered, perhaps afraid the prisoner might hear her.

"Who is she?"

Ilona shushed Margit with a wave of her hand and then pulled her arm. But an overwhelming force kept Margit's feet stuck to the floor.

The woman took the bowl and stared at it awhile, her lips moving without producing any sound. She raised her head slowly as if it were too heavy for her scrawny neck. When her eyes met Margit's, an expression of fear distorted her face. She recoiled and dropped the bowl, spilling the food all around her.

Ilona tugged at Margit's arm. "Let's go."

Fascination with the woman's strange behaviour would not permit Margit to move a limb or look away.

The prisoner trembled, dropped her eyes to the floor and, as though breathing out her last breath, she remained as motionless as a statue.

"Please, let's go!" Ilona's voice rang of despair.

At last yielding to her friend's plea, Margit turned to leave the chamber. But then, the woman mumbled in a raspy voice, "I did not want you to die... I loved you."

The words struck Margit like a thunderbolt, paralysing her.

Who does she speak of?

"For the love of God, move!" Ilona squealed.

There was momentary silence, and then the old woman whispered, "Sándor."

Margit spun about to face her. "What did you say?"

The prisoner's eyes grew wide and flashed with a wildness of nature beyond human. She raised her knobbly finger at Margit and let out a series of gasping noises before shrieking, "What do you want from me, Sándor?"

Just then Margit realised she had left her hair uncovered. Although perplexed by such ominous words, the fear of being recognised made her snatch the coif from inside her belt and plant it on her head. "You are mistaken, lady. I'm only a servant."

The old woman covered her face with her hands and began screaming in the Saxon language.

The guard burst into the chamber and, grabbing both Margit and Ilona by their arms, he dragged them out before locking the door.

The wailing continued from the inside. It did not sound human anymore. It echoed in Margit's ears like the cry of a wounded animal.

This was the scream I heard before!

"Look what you've done, you fools!" The soldier waved his fist at them. "Now she won't stop for the whole night. Thanks be to God, the lord's away, otherwise we'd all be flogged."

Tears streaked Ilona's face. "Please, let's go!"

Margit clambered down the stairs after her friend and flew through the rest of the house until she reached the kitchen.

Ilona sobbed uncontrollably, her shoulders shuddering, up and down, back and forth.

Only after Margit caught her own breath did she draw her friend into her arms. "Forgive me. I know you had a fright. But you're safe now. Calm yourself."

Though Margit comforted Ilona with a reassuring voice, her mind was transfixed by the prisoner. The woman's words reverberated inside her head. It was only now, as her thoughts cleared, that she wondered if the stranger was none other than Anna herself. She looked the right age, spoke Saxon and called out the name of Margit's father—this only Anna would have known. And she was locked in a private chamber, not in the dungeon as a common criminal. But who would have locked her there? Márton?

Like a draught of frosty air gushing through an open window, such a possibility made Margit shudder. Yet for what cause would a son imprison his own mother? How long had she been there? Evidently enough time to have plunged her into the depths of insanity.

31
A New Destiny

Even three days later, the prisoner's words—her aunt's words—'I did not want you to die' still haunted Margit. Had Anna witnessed her father's murder? Or worse, had she played a part in it? And why did the woman react so strongly upon seeing her? Anna could not have recognised Margit dressed as a man. Yet, despite her evident madness, she must have noticed something which reminded her of Sándor; something which had conjured painful memories and caused her outburst. Was it Margit's face or, more likely, her red hair?

Another mystery Margit could not decipher was Anna's imprisonment. At the banquet, Márton had told his mistress that she would betray him like everyone else. Had his mother done something so traitorous to justify her harsh punishment? Whatever the reason was, it only deepened Margit's abhorrence of her cousin.

If only she could talk to Anna. But this was impossible. After the incident, a rumour spread among the servants that the mad woman kept banging on her door and screaming that the previous lord of Szentimre, dead many years now, had returned. The guards did not allow anyone near Anna's quarters. Even her food was now brought to her only by one of them.

Craning her neck, Margit looked up from the courtyard

towards a terrace on the second floor, surrounded by a crenelated parapet. Was that near Anna's bedchamber? Yes, it must be. She vaguely remembered a door leading to an outside space. But with the keep not directly connected to the curtain wall, there was no access to that spot from the outside. Margit slammed her fist against her hip.

Damn! I shall never have another chance.

"What are you doing?" Ilona's voice startled her.

"Oh, nothing." Margit sought an excuse to avoid being dragged into doing kitchen chores after a hard day's work in the searing heat of the forge. "I'm tired and stopped to catch my breath. I must go."

The maid pursed her lips, concern darkening her usually cheerful countenance. "Come to the kitchen. I wish to speak with you."

Margit grunted a reluctant assent and followed her. At least, with the sun low on the horizon, the air had turned cooler.

"Such a lovely eve," Ilona sighed before opening the door.

The kitchen was deserted and already tidy.

Margit stayed the maid by the wrist. "If there are no chores to do, why have you brought me here?"

Ilona pointed at the bench. "Sit."

Curiosity and apprehension twitched within Margit as she obeyed the request. Perhaps the girl wished to talk about the incident with Anna. How would she answer her?

After a long silence, Ilona finally spoke. "I'm sure you know how I feel about you."

Margit winced.

Oh, no. Not this again.

Ilona leaned forward—attempting to kiss her, no doubt—but Margit turned away.

This fascination business must end. "I'm not the right person for you," she said bluntly. "My friend Stefan likes you. He's a good man. He will look after you."

Ilona's face dropped, and her voice came forth in a whimper. "But I don't love *him*. I love *you*."

Pushing her sympathy aside, Margit forced herself to turn her heart to stone. "I like you as a friend. Nothing more."

Ilona slumped on the bench, eyes welling as her brows knitted and her lips trembled. "Please. I've never been with a man. Can you, at least, lie with me just one time and make me happy as a woman, even for a few moments only?"

"No. I'm sorry."

"My body burns with desire. Don't you feel anything at all when I touch you?"

Ilona whipped one arm around Margit's neck and yanked her towards her whilst she put her other hand between Margit's legs and squeezed. Or tried to squeeze.

She immediately jumped up, eyes and mouth wide open. "There's nothing there!"

Margit looked away. What was she to say? Perhaps she could fool Ilona in the same way she had deceived the castellan. "I told you I am not the right one for you."

Ilona looked at Margit with apparent disgust and confusion. "What happened to you?"

"The Turks."

With narrowed eyes, Ilona scrutinised Margit, her gaze lingering on Margit's chest and the front of her neck. After a deep swallow, she shook her head. "No, no. You lie."

"Why do you say I lie?"

"You're a woman!" Ilona shrieked, hands clasping her head. "How didn't I see this before?" She pulled at her hair. "How was I so blind?" Her arms now fell lifelessly by her sides. "Oh, dear God, I've made a fool of myself."

Burdened with guilt, Margit stood up and reached out to hug her.

But Ilona recoiled as if she had been burned by fire. "Don't touch me!" She collapsed on a stool and buried her face in her hands. "I'm so ashamed...so ashamed."

Margit spoke softly to soothe the maid's anguish. "Calm yourself. It was an honest mistake. And the blame is upon me for I deceived you. I apologise."

Ilona raised her head and took many deep breaths. After drying her tears, she looked at Margit. "Will you, at least, tell me who you are and why you lied to me?"

Margit shook her head.

"Don't fret," Ilona insisted. "I shan't tell anyone."

Margit still hesitated. Could she trust the maid? "You swear?"

"Yes!" Ilona crossed herself. "On everything that's holy."

It was a serious oath. The muscles on Margit's face relaxed. "I have been sent by the king on a secret mission."

"King Mátyás?"

"Yes. And that's all you need to know."

Curiosity sparked in Ilona's eyes. "What's your real name?"

"I can't tell you that. You must still call me Saša."

"And what of your friend, Stefan? Does he know who you are?"

"Yes, he's helping me with the mission."

"Are you two…lovers?"

Margit blushed. "Lovers? No, only friends. I have a husband."

By now, Ilona appeared to have overcome her surprise and embarrassment. A soft smile spread on her face. "I accept your epology."

"Apology," Margit could not help correcting her.

Ilona dismissed the interruption with a flick of her hand. "You were just doing your duty." Her face took on a look of renewed vigour. "If you tell me what your mission is, I'll help you. I don't wish to be a lowly kitchen maid all my life. Perhaps if I give good service to the king, my position can change?"

Margit paused again. She could do with some assistance. But reveal the whole truth to Ilona? She was not certain.

"Don't fear," the maid said. "I swore to keep your secret."

Weighing her friend's earnest responses and sworn oath, Margit decided to put her faith in Ilona at last. "I'm here to investigate the death of the previous lord of Szentimre."

Ilona's face brightened. "Oh, Saša! Both my grandam and my father worked for Lord Sándor and his lady. They'd be so glad to meet you."

***

The vermilion glow of the early evening enveloping the town of Szentimre brought silence with it as people retired to their homes for supper. But now and then, a gentle wind carried the muffled sounds of talk and laughter from the main gate, where the guards told stories and jokes to pass the time.

Struggling to contain the flutters of anticipation, Margit followed Ilona as they edged around walls and stole silently across alleys until they arrived at the kitchen maid's house.

Inside the modest but tidy abode, an old woman was sitting by the hearth, her hunched figure cast in the glow of the fire and the light of the descending sun through the window. Even though it was summer, the mountain air must have felt chilly to her.

Hands clasped tightly in front of her, Margit waited by the doorway while Ilona embraced the woman, rekindled the fire and lit a tallow candle on the windowsill.

"My grandam, Mária," Ilona said, and then, addressing her grandmother, she pointed at Margit. "This lady has been sent by the king to talk about important business at his request."

Two eager strides was all Margit took to approach this woman, her only hope of uncovering a mystery that tormented her for so long. Was she going to have answers at last?

Despite her advanced years, Mária pushed herself up and bowed to Margit. "It'll be my honour to serve the king."

"My grandam was the head cook in Sasfészek for many years," Ilona continued. "She knows all about the previous lord and lady of the estate."

At the mention of her father and mother, Margit's heart palpitated wildly.

Mária raised her forefinger to her lips. "Shhh! You know we're not allowed to speak of the previous lord, Iluska. On pain of death." Mouth pinched, she sank back in her chair and waved Margit away. "You seek the only thing I can't help you with."

The spectre of failure impelled Margit to kneel in front of the old woman and take her leathery hand in hers. "I must know what happened to Lord Sándor. I mean, the king needs to know. His Majesty understands an injustice was committed here in his name and now wishes to make amends."

"How can he make amends?" Mária's voice quavered with a combination of sadness and anger. "What's done is done, and nothing will bring the man back from the grave." Her wrinkled face creased even more.

"Mistress, I beg of you. It's very important," Margit pressed on.

Mária looked away. But after a moment, she turned back to Margit and peered as if trying to scrutinise her face.

A sharp intake of breath, and the woman's eyes opened wide. "Unless—" Her voice hinted of hope this time. "Come closer."

Still on her knees, Margit leaned forward.

With a rushed wave of her hand, the woman sent Ilona to fetch the candle from the windowsill and shine it on Margit's hair and face. In a heartbeat, Mária covered her mouth with her hand as tears poured down her cheeks. "My lady! God hasn't forsaken us. You have returned."

The light of the candle danced in Ilona's trembling hands.

Margit sprang to her feet, hand braced against the nearest wall for support. "What did you say?"

Kneeling with difficulty, Mária clasped Margit's free hand and covered it with kisses.

Margit twitched at the wetness of the woman's tears and her faltering voice. "Oh, I'd recognise you anywhere, *kedvesem*, even amidst a crowd of thousands. You have both your parents in you."

"Who do you speak of, grandam?" Ilona interjected.

Disbelief mingling with curiosity filled Margit's chest. "How do you know me?"

A sad smile formed on the woman's face. "Erzsi would bring you and little Endre to the kitchen when you were bored with your playing. You loved to taste my sweet pies and sugared plums. Oh, merciful God! I feel as if I'm back there again, looking at your merry faces."

Cheeks heated with joy and relief, Margit hastened to help Mária sit down in her chair again. "Tell me, mistress—"

"What in the name of God is this?" Ilona interrupted. "Who are you?"

Fuelled by pride now, Margit could not hold back. She straightened her shoulders and spoke with authority. "I am Margit Alexandra Szilágyi-Bátori, the daughter of Sándor and Margit, the previous lord and lady of Szentimre."

The candle slipped out of Ilona's hands, its flame extinguished as it hit the floor. She dropped to her knees. "Forgive this wretched kitchen maid for the offence, your ladychip!"

"Ladyship," her grandmother scolded her. "I thought I'd taught you better."

Margit hauled Ilona to her feet. "Don't be silly. You caused me no offence."

She turned to Mária. "My cousin doesn't know I am here, and it must remain this way. I have come to find evidence that my father was not a traitor and that he was unlawfully killed, or rather murdered."

"Oh, there's no doubt about that."

"Can you tell me more, please?" Desperate for answers to long-held questions, Margit pulled a stool and sat next to the woman while Ilona returned the candle to the windowsill and joined them, sitting cross-legged on the floor.

Mária did not know what had transpired in the great hall the evening Margit's father died. But she described its aftermath in great detail: how the king's soldiers took over the castle; how they came into the kitchen and held the servants captive until the next morning; how they terrorised the people of the estate, trying to find out where the lord's daughter was hiding. And after the soldiers left, and the locals buried their dead, Szentimre was never the same.

Márton and Anna steadily eliminated any resistance against their rule. They banned any talk about the events of that night and dismissed those of Sándor's advisers who had remained loyal to him after confiscating their money and revoking their privileges. Although they handed the mine over to the king, they still treated the miners as their property and taxed them heavily for living on the estate land. Then outsiders arrived at their behest: Saxons to set up shops; Germans, Bohemians, Serbians and others to form their mercenary troops for hire. Many of the poorer local Hungarian and Wallachian tenant families, who had lived here for generations, were oppressed so hard that they were forced into servitude or left the estate.

"They tried to wipe our memories," Mária continued, "and most of the younger people have forgotten. But there are still some of us who remember, and who have been praying for a miracle. You're our miracle, my lady; the only one who can save us."

Margit pressed her hand to her heart. Her stomach churned, and the pulse thundered in her ears. She had come to Szentimre for her own reasons; but now she realised those people—her people—were desperate, and she was their only hope.

Her thoughts were interrupted by the appearance of a man in the doorway.

Ilona clambered up and rushed to embrace him.

"My son-in-law, Gábor Kovács," Mária explained. "Iluska's father. He was a castle guard. But after he was wounded that evening and then dismissed, he's been working as a miner."

As Ilona lit another tallow candle on the eating table, Margit noticed the man's clothes and boots were caked with dirt.

"We have a visitor," the man mumbled. "I'm sorry if my appearance offends you. I'll go clean myself."

"Please don't apologise," Margit said. "I am not offended. Sit down and rest. You work hard. You must be tired."

The man washed his hands and face in a copper basin and sat at the table. Ilona served him his supper.

Many thoughts swirled in Margit's head. If Gábor was a soldier at the time of her father's death, could he enlighten her some more? Had he, perhaps, seen her father on that fateful day? Could she trust him though? As with Ilona and Mária, Margit was taking a dangerous gamble. Was it worth it?

Unable to decide, she remained silent, leaving it in Fate's hands.

After the man had eaten, Mária spoke to him. "Son, after so many years, God has answered our prayers."

The man regarded her with some wonder. "What do you mean?"

"This is our little lady." The old woman pointed at Margit. "Our dear lord's daughter. She has come to save us all."

Margit's heart leapt to her throat. She clenched her hands anxiously. What would be his reaction?

"Is it true?" Gábor said.

At Mária's nod, he sprang up and immediately knelt at Margit's feet, bowing his head. "I'm at your service, my lady."

Flattered by such treatment, Margit blushed but quickly gathered herself. In dire need to press on with uncovering the truth, she helped the still stunned man back to his seat and asked him to relate the events of that night.

"I was one of the last people to see your lord father alive," he started his narration. "He was with his friend, Imre Gerendi, in the keep when he ordered us to let the king's soldiers in. When I came out, I saw my former commander, Pál Balog, enter with a royal army officer, Lord Márton and Lady Ágnes. I waved at the soldiers, and they marched into the courtyard. All of us guards, we remained at our posts. It wasn't long before we heard shouting, then a woman's scream and more shouting. After that, silence. A sergeant ordered the royal soldiers into the keep. I heard Balog yell from within: 'He killed the captain! Treason against the king!' The soldiers attacked us. We fought back, but they were too many. I escaped and rushed into the keep to see with my own eyes."

Gábor paused to wipe tears; yet it was Margit's heart which ached with poignant sorrow.

"The young lord and his mother were gone," he continued, "but I could still hear her screams coming from the upper floors. Master Gerendi wasn't there either."

"He had left to take me out of the castle at my father's request. God bless him, he saved me," Margit said, sparing a thought for Imre's soul. But she needed to know more. "What happened then?"

"In the great hall, the officer lay on his back, a sword through his heart. My lord beside him, face-down in a pool of blood. Another bloodied sword near him." Gábor shifted in his chair and tilted his head to one side, his voice turning reflective. "Now that I think of it again, it all looked strange. As if someone had moved the bodies on purpose."

Margit raised her hand to her neck. Her throat tightened, blocking her breath. She could feel her father's pain; the agony of his last moments; the darkness covering his eyes. What were his dying thoughts? Were they filled with dread for leaving his little daughter behind, alone and vulnerable?

Dear father, wherever you are, know that I am safe...that I have not forgotten. Your sacrifice was not in vain.

Gábor's trembling voice drew her back from the edge of an abyss of grief. "Fear gripped me. I ran to the kitchen to get my mother-in-law out. The soldiers already had the servants on their knees. Someone attacked me. I fought back but got injured and fainted. I woke up at home, in bed. I recovered from my wounds, but my soul will never be whole after what I saw."

His clouded eyes fixed on Margit's face. "Such a horrible crime, my lady. The young lord and his mother told us your father and the officer fought each other. But I never believed that story. My lord was a man of honour, not a traitor. If he had fought the officer, it would've been solely to defend himself."

The question tormenting Margit's mind for so long finally came forth, "Who do you think killed him?"

"Oh, I wish I knew. The only thing I can say is it wasn't Lady Anna. The way she wailed—"

"So, it was either my cousin or Balog."

Margit's teeth cut into her lip as she fought to suppress her tears. This was not the time for crying and mourning. She had a duty to perform, not only to her dead father but to his people as well. Her destiny had become bigger than she had ever imagined.

***

After talking to Mária and Gábor, Margit now knew much more about her father's murder.

First, Anna had been a witness. Although she initially ruled the estate in a ruthless manner until Márton came of age, the event must have scarred her inside, affecting her mind. For what other reason would her own son hold her prisoner? Was he afraid that, in a fit of madness, she would reveal the truth? Out of the three parties, she seemed to be the weakest. And because of her torment, she would, perhaps, be willing to confess at the promise of freedom.

Second, Márton's hatred of his uncle still simmered under the confident and cruel front he struggled to maintain. Could he have been the murderer despite his young age? In his previous encounters with Margit, he had proven that he had the motive, and based on Gábor's narration, he had been given the opportunity, too.

As for Pál Balog, he sounded like the most likely culprit, being a grown man, definitely stronger than a thirteen-year-old boy. Margit remembered Imre saying Balog held a grudge against her father for demoting him. Yet there was a long way between holding a grudge and committing murder. But what if he had been paid by someone to do it? In fact, the castellan was hard to decipher. He either pretended very well, or the event had left him unaffected, and he believed his conscience was clear.

Margit hated all three of them and would sooner see them dead and buried. But she needed to be patient. Proving that her cousin had been involved in her father's murder would probably be enough to give Szentimre back to her. It would not, however, clear her father's name. She needed to show to the king that he was innocent. But all she knew was that Mátyás held a letter in his possession, which led him to believe that Sándor had rebelled against him. She suspected the document was forged, but how could she prove that?

Her father's advisers might have known about the letter. But what had become of them? When Margit asked Gábor, she received a distressing answer:

"All but one blamed your cousin and his mother. Within three months, they were dead: poisoned, stabbed, drowned. And the only one who had kept his position—Kálmán Havasi, the treasurer —took his own life though he was favoured by Lady Anna."

Margit's stomach tightened. Now she could see why the people of the estate were so subdued and glum. With all of her father's advisers out of the way, they had no one in authority to turn to. Little by little, they must have given up any thought of resistance and succumbed to the cruel treatment of their new landlords.

Yet Gábor's reassuring words lit a glimmer of hope inside her soul. "But they'll stand by your side when you lead them, my lady. I know they will."

After that day, whenever she could, Margit walked the streets of the town and villages, the country and forest paths, the fields and paddocks. She followed the banks of streams and surveyed the ponds, wells and watermills. She stopped to observe and speak with farmers, herders, gamekeepers, butchers, bakers, miners, millers, weavers, smiths, shopkeepers. This was her land and her people. She needed to know their joys and worries, their hopes and fears. For one day, she would become their protector; the one to give them a better life.

32
The Human Side of a Monster

Late October 1478

The metallic sound of swords split the dense, foggy air and echoed in the stillness of the early morning.

Margit's hands closed around the hilt of the longsword. Was she mad to be out there, at the edge of the forest, while the estate's residents slept in their warm beds or attended the Sunday Prime service?

Grunting and panting, she parried her husband's hits but staggered under their force. A step back gave her only brief respite before Endre swung at her again.

The blades met in the middle and stalled for a heartbeat until Endre slid his all the way down to the hilt. Despite the grinding noise piercing her ears, Margit held her ground with gritted teeth. But not for long. Still pushing hard, Endre twisted his wrists to the side and knocked the sword out of her hands.

The momentum swept Margit sideways. A hefty blow to her ribs took the air out of her lungs and thrust her to the ground.

She slammed her fist on the hard earth. The armour kept bodily injury at bay but could not counter the damage to her pride. On seeing her husband raise the sword over her, she extended her arm to request a break.

Endre lifted his visor. "The battle will not stop for you to take a nap."

Margit uncovered her face and shot him an irritated glance. "Damn you!" She pushed herself to her feet.

"Mind your language! You will soon become the lady of this estate. You must behave as such."

He struck her on the chest with the edge of his blade. The blow was not too strong, but it hit her coat of plates with a clanking sound. She slipped and fell on her backside.

Endre burst into laughter. Margit chuckled, too, as he hauled her to her feet.

"Go again!" He took his position opposite her with both arms extended and holding the sword.

"No. I'm exhausted. Truly. I do much better on horseback with a bow in my hand."

"Very well. Take a rest, and then you can practise archery."

They took off their helmets and mail gloves and sat side-by-side on the ground.

Margit rested her head on Endre's breastplate. The light touch of his fingertips tracing the outline of her mouth set her blood on fire. If only the night would come sooner so that she could surrender to the all-consuming passion of their love. A love which had caused the unthinkable: she had now accepted her womanhood and did not resent her body anymore.

She raised her head, her lips seeking his. And when the fervent kiss ended, she smiled. "I should thank the king for my happiness."

During his inspection of Szentimre at the end of the summer, Endre had examined the production and revenue of the mine and discovered extensive corruption. Although appointed by the king, the manager was taking bribes from local craftsmen and merchants to sell gold and silver to them at a lower price, without the permission of the owner of the mine: the king. As a result, only half of the precious metal production was sent to Mátyás.

As soon as Endre informed the king, Mátyás ordered him back to Szentimre to rectify the problem. He was to escort the new manager, advise and guide him during the first few months of his tenure. He also had to ensure that anyone offering bribes or requesting favours was caught and dealt with promptly.

Endre's new post allowed him to stay in Szentimre for the coming months. He took a house in the miners' village and hired Margit as his assistant. At last, they could live together. But even though behind closed doors they were husband and wife, as soon as they left their home she had to pretend she was Endre's male cousin.

Margit's parting with Adnan left a poignant emptiness in her heart. At least, it was some consolation that her friend did not remain lonely for long because Ilona soon bestowed her affection on him. Despite fearing his father's disapproval, Adnan changed his religion so that he could marry her. Margit and Endre arranged for him to be baptised and became his godparents. He took the Christian name István, which was the Hungarian version of his Serbian alias, Stefan. Margit had chosen this for him because it was her brother's name, and she loved Adnan like a brother.

Endre shifted his body, jolting her back to the present. "We should move towards the valley. The fog is too thick for shooting arrows here. I shall fetch the horses and our equipment."

As he disappeared from sight, Margit closed her eyes and breathed in the fresh mountain air. It was chilly, but she liked that.

The sound of approaching horses startled her. It did not come from the direction she would expect. She peered through the fog but could only discern the outlines of the riders.

"Why, look who's here," a disturbingly familiar voice said. "*Madárka.*"

Sergeant Ferenc Bakó and four guards lined up in front of her.

Margit sprang up, longsword held tight in her hands. "Don't come near me!"

"What's the matter?" Endre's voice came from behind and brought some reassurance. With Zora and Csillag in tow, he stood beside Margit.

"This is private land," the sergeant said. "You have no right to be here, wielding weapons."

Endre dropped the horses' reins and stepped in front of Margit, his hand clenched around the hilt of his sword. "I am the king's envoy. If you do anything against us, you will be in serious trouble."

Bakó sneered and gestured to his men to surround Endre and Margit.

"This is private land," he repeated, stressing each word. "It matters not who you work for. You may not bear weapons without my lord's permission. But I'm willing to let you go,"—he bent forward in the saddle and lowered his voice as if he were about to utter conspiratorial words—"if you hand the red *madárka* over to me."

"Who is *madárka*?" Endre's eyes followed the sergeant's gaze. "What? No! He is my cousin. Why would I hand him over to you?"

"Cousin?" Bakó snorted. "I see no family resemblance."

"None of your concern. Leave us in peace, now!"

"You give me no choice. I'll arrest you."

Endre spoke to Margit in Serbian, "Is he the man who attacked you before?"

She pressed her lips together. This confrontation could get much worse if she answered.

"I assume he is." Endre unsheathed his sword and glared at the sergeant. "Stay back, or I'll kill you!"

"No one is killing anyone!" came a voice from the fog.

Indistinct shadows emerged, shaping into the form of several riders: Márton, his knights, the voivode of Transylvania and the latter's retinue.

"My lord!" Endre re-sheathed the sword and stood straight. "I am Captain Andrej Lazarević, the king's envoy. You were away when I arrived, and we haven't been introduced yet. I am here to advise the manager of the mine. Your men are harassing my assistant and I."

Márton shot a furious look at the sergeant. "My family has fought and bled for Hungary and the king. We have been loyal to the Crown for generations. How dare you obstruct His Majesty's representative?"

Margit's face twitched.

How hypocritical.

Márton and his father had not shed a drop of blood for their homeland. It was *her* father who did and his ancestors before him.

"Forgive me, my lord," Bakó squeaked, looking like he had wet himself. "We're leaving now." He signalled to his men, and they trotted away.

Márton turned to Endre with an affected-looking smile. "Pardon me, captain. I am Lord Szilágyi, your host. And this is my distinguished guest, Péter Vingárti Geréb, the Voivode of Transylvania."

Both Endre and Margit bowed—to the voivode, of course, not to Márton.

"By way of apology, I wish to invite both of you to my banquet after the vespers service," Márton said. "I trust you will attend."

"We shall, my lord. Thank you," Endre replied.

As her cousin disappeared back into the fog, Margit's blood boiled. He was still the lord of the estate, and she had not been able to do anything about it. How much longer did she have to wait until she wiped that smirk off his face?

***

The banquet Margit attended as a guest differed greatly from the one she had attended as a servant a few months prior. The mood was sombre: no entertainment, no drunken jokes, no laughter. Even the number of guests was limited.

Only the head table was set, with Márton sitting in the middle. To his right: the voivode, his knight and the man Margit thought as Ágnes' husband. Endre, Ágnes and Margit sat to Márton's left.

Margit's interest was piqued when the woman's husband—much calmer than at the previous banquet—introduced himself as Béla Havasi, Márton's treasurer. Margit wondered if this man was related to Kálmán Havasi, her father's treasurer; the one who had committed suicide a few months after her father's death.

Halfway through the main course, Márton stood up, raised his goblet and addressed the voivode in a dispassionate voice. "I wish to announce that I have accepted to wed your gracious lady niece. I shall travel to Gyulafehérvár with you to discuss the date and the necessary arrangements."

The voivode regarded him with raised eyebrows as though he had not expected the announcement.

After that, silence descended. Now and again, Margit caught Márton seeking his mistress with his eyes. Shadows flitted across his face in the candlelight and accentuated his gloomy expression. What was on his mind? Surely, he had accepted the match for political reasons—a common occurrence among the nobility. Still, in his case, something else seemed to bother him. Margit watched as he exchanged a furtive glance with Ágnes and then sighed. His hand trembled bringing the goblet to his lips. Did he truly love this woman? Was he, perhaps, an ordinary man after all, capable of showing normal, human emotions?

During the time she spent in the estate, Margit had noticed that Márton was not respected. He was feared. People obeyed him, but no one wished to be close to him. Even Ágnes looked fearful in his presence. He seemed alone, living in the shadow of a better man—Margit's father, a man loved and revered as a war hero and as a leader.

"Well, sir, I shall retire now." The voivode's voice drew Margit's attention away from her cousin. "Thank you for your hospitality."

Margit and the other guests rose and waited until he and his knight left the great hall before sitting at the table again.

"We should leave too, my lord," Endre said. "We do not wish to impose on your generosity."

Márton touched Endre's forearm. The same affected smile appeared on his face. "No, please stay. My treasurer and I would like to discuss your inspection of Szentimre and the mine." His quavering voice came at a higher pitch than usual. "We never had a representative of the king staying with us for such a long time." A light laugh escaped his lips. "We wish to know if you have discovered issues we should be concerned about."

Reluctantly, Endre was drawn into a long conversation with Márton and Béla. Margit listened until the clank of Ágnes' spoon dropping on the plate startled her. She turned to the woman, who covered her mouth with her hand and shuddered. "Are you well, lady?"

Ágnes nodded. Having only nibbled at her food, she pushed her plate away and pressed her hand on her stomach.

Did she feel ill, or did she simply dislike the food?

Until that night, Margit had not thought much about Ágnes. But after closely observing her now and bringing to mind her cousin's behaviour at the previous banquet, Margit began to view her in a different light. Perhaps the woman had no choice. Márton must have exerted full power over her. If she refused him, he would do something bad to her husband or to her.

"You are a learned man." Márton's words to Endre made Margit turn to the men again. "Your knowledge of military matters, management and finances is astonishing. And for a Serb, you speak Hungarian perfectly. Not a hint of a foreign accent."

"I am also fluent in German, Latin and Polish and have a fair knowledge of Wallachian."

Margit smiled to herself, pride filling her chest. Her husband had worked so hard to rise above his station. As a boy, he had always been diligent and dedicated to his studies; whereas all she ever wanted was for the lessons to end quickly so that she could go to Ahmed's yard and train.

"If you were not in the king's service," Márton continued, "I would ask you to work for me; even though I dislike your appearance." He made a circle with his hand around his own face and then pointed at his hair. "It is so...peasant-like." He let out a nervous laugh again.

In light of how badly Márton treated his peasants, was this a jest or an insult? Margit leaned forward to have a better view of her husband's reaction.

The corner of Endre's mouth twisted into a crooked smile. "My lord, I can assure you short hair and a shaved face make a soldier feel more comfortable under all the heavy armour."

Márton grimaced. "My apologies. I meant no offence."

"None taken."

Margit sat back and shook her head. Another instance of her depraved cousin's inability to connect with people; another reason this volatile and possibly murderous man would be so lonely. Though Margit was nothing like him, she was no stranger to loneliness. She had experienced it before: in Belgrade when Imre was in prison, Endre served the king and Dragoslava shunned her. And then again, after her head injury, when the days felt so long as she waited for her body to heal. But neither that momentary sympathy nor the close family connection she shared with Márton were enough to dampen the hate she carried inside her heart.

33
Breakthrough

December 1478

Wrapped in her warm cape as she and Endre rode in the fields below the castle hill, Margit took in the wild beauty that surrounded her. Even in the dead of winter and despite nature's sombre mood, there was always something to marvel at in Szentimre: the ancient, snow-covered mountains guarding her native land like an army of giants; the evergreen trees standing tall and defiant against the wind; the snowflakes dancing in the morning light; the horses' hooves crunching on the pure snow; the fresh air that filled her lungs and made her feel alive.

But as she approached the town, her gaze was drawn to the streaks of frozen blood staining the white ground. She followed them with her eyes. A few paces away, near the base of the fortification wall, lay the body of a woman, half-eaten by wolves.

Margit shuddered and turned away in horror.

It was still early, not a soul around.

Curiosity now leading her, Margit dismounted; and so did her husband. They approached the terrible sight.

Endre crossed himself. "It must have happened during the night. The wolves got to her quickly. She looks frozen solid." He glanced around and then up. "She is close to the wall, and I don't see any footprints though fresh snow could have covered them.

Did she fall?"

Some strange sensation whispered to Margit otherwise. She leaned in closer. Most of the woman's face was missing, but her curly red hair gave Margit an inkling of who she might be.

"*Úristen!*" Seized by sudden terror, Margit staggered back. Her legs gave way, and she fell backwards on the snow.

Endre flung his arms around her and lifted her back up. "What is it?"

"Was she pushed, perchance?" Margit said without realising it.

"Pushed?" Endre seemed more horrified by this notion now than he was at first witnessing the corpse. "What makes you think that?"

Although afraid to touch the body, Margit observed it even closer.

The silver wedding ring. Yes...it is her!

"She's Ágnes Havasi!"

"Ágnes Havasi? The treasurer's wife?"

"Yes," Margit mumbled, her hairs standing on end and her eyes still glued to the mangled body. "We must alert the guards. And her husband, of course."

The official verdict was suicide. A night guard said Ágnes suddenly appeared on the battlements, in a distressed state. He enquired what troubled her, but she pushed him aside, ran to the edge and jumped. The soldier did not alert anyone for fear that he would be held responsible.

Because Ágnes had taken her own life, the Church rejected her. She could not be buried on holy ground. Although Margit understood the graveness of the sin, her heart ached at the thought that the woman's soul would never rest in peace.

She and Endre helped Béla Havasi bury Ágnes in the pine forest. No priest and no representative of the landlord attended. The only prayer to accompany her send-off to the next world was said by Endre.

The sight of Béla sobbing endlessly at his wife's grave touched Margit's heart. He must have truly loved her though she had not been faithful to him.

***

Life returned to normal after that incident. The situation at the mine improved. Production levels increased, and no more illegal deals with local tradesmen took place. By now, Endre had more free time to spend with Margit, planning their next step.

However, they had hit a frustrating impasse in gathering information to help their case. Except for Ilona's father and grandmother, no one in the estate was willing to talk. After much deliberation on what course to pursue, they agreed their only hope was to spirit Anna away from the castle and convince her to confess in front of the king. Not a simple task by any means. What's more, the woman was half-mad. Would she be able to testify? And would the king believe her?

As for the letter that Margit's father had supposedly written to Mátyás, they needed to look for it in the royal correspondence archives and compare it with some other documents they had in their possession.

Then, two weeks after Ágnes' death, Béla appeared at Margit and Endre's temporary abode.

Although the treasurer's face looked hot and flushed, tiny icicles had formed on his eyebrows. He carried a leather satchel, which he placed on the floor before brushing the snowflakes off his cape.

He fixed Endre with imploring eyes. "I apologise for disturbing you, sir." His voice trembled. "I need to speak to someone in authority." He seemed to struggle against his emotions, which piqued Margit's curiosity. "But I don't trust my lord's officials. You work for the king, and I hope you will see that I come to no harm after what I have to say."

Endre invited him to sit on a high-backed cushioned chair by the fire. "Of course, Master Havasi. I have no affiliation to Lord Szilágyi, and I promise I shall not inform him of anything you tell me."

Béla's worried eyes turned to Margit.

"Do not fear, sir," Endre reassured him. "You can trust my assistant." He gestured to Margit to sit beside him on a bench across from their visitor. "Please, speak freely."

Perched on the edge of her seat, Margit leaned forward intently.

The treasurer inhaled sharply. "I'm certain my dear wife didn't kill herself. She was murdered."

His words struck Margit like a thunderbolt.

I knew it!

She turned her wide eyes to Endre, who shared the same astonished look.

"And," Havasi continued, "the soldier who testified that he saw her jump, lied. This is also why no one notified me that her body lay there all night."

Endre inclined his head towards the treasurer. "Murdered? By whom?"

"Lord Márton."

Margit's hand flew to her mouth to stifle a gasp. Had her cousin's cruelty no bounds?

"Even if he didn't commit the crime himself," Béla said, "he paid someone else to do it."

Endre fixed the man with a serious stare. "This is a grave accusation. Do you have proof?"

Still reeling from Havasi's claim, Margit held her breath, waiting for his response. But Béla's lips trembled, and he looked away.

Margit's heart sank like a stone. Was he hesitating because he did not know them well, or had he perhaps regretted his words already? Surely, her and Endre's support during his darkest hour would have provided him with some confidence.

Speak, man!

The crackling of the fire was magnified by the silence.

Tension clenched Margit's stomach.

At length, Béla looked Endre in the eye. "Over the last few years, the lord has taken many women from the estate to his bed. But he obsessed over Ágnes' red hair."

Again, his voice cracked. "We were already married and had a daughter when Márton offered an arrangement. He wanted Ágnes as his mistress. In return, he promised to make me his advisor and pay me well for my services. He would also give her gifts of jewellery, clothes, perfume and anything else she desired."

Havasi's face creased into a grimace of anguish. "I certainly didn't wish to share my beloved with another man. She didn't want to do it either, so we declined the offer. Márton became so enraged that he threatened to destroy our family. He took away my land and ancestral home and forced us to move to Szentimre."

Margit twitched in disgust, her hands gripping the edge of the bench.

That vile man did the same to me. He tried to violate my body and then stole my land.

"We had no choice," Béla said with a sigh. "Ágnes had to make herself available to him any time he called for her, even in the middle of the night."

Oh, how Margit felt the treasurer's pain. Another family whose life had been plundered by her cousin.

"This must have been distressing for you both," Endre remarked and encouraged Béla to continue.

Havasi nodded, his face now dark and pensive. "There was also another part to the arrangement. Ágnes was not to conceive a child by either him or me. Of course, the lord didn't want an illegitimate child, but he wouldn't allow her to have one with me either. Out of spite, perhaps." He lowered his head as if the weight of grief and anger settled heavily on his shoulders. "For five long years, my dear wife suffered terribly. He didn't harm her body, but he broke her spirit with his violent outbursts of jealousy."

What a monster!

Margit pressed her fists on the bench as she remembered Márton's revolting behaviour to the woman during his drunken rant at the first banquet he had held for the voivode.

And Havasi resumed, "So, when he announced his betrothal,

we took our chance. Ágnes felt that continuing relations with him was disrespectful towards the lady he was to marry. To force his hand, we decided to have another child. Ágnes revealed to me that she was pregnant the day before she died."

The treasurer covered his eyes with his hand. He sniffled and looked at Endre again. "The happiness I saw on her face when she told me—" He choked for a moment, then drew a deep breath. "She did not kill herself. We were to live as a family again. She went to see the lord and tell him. And that night she died."

Béla's words shuddered to a halt as tears came unbidden now and sobs escaped his lips.

Innocent blood on my cousin's hands.

A feral growl rose from Margit's throat. Revenge's spark roared to a conflagration in her chest, scorching away any doubt. She would ensure Márton paid for his depravities at long last.

Endre put a friendly hand on the man's shoulder, but regret darkened his face. "I believe you. And I'm sorry for your loss. She was certainly a brave woman, and you were a loving husband. However, I fear your suspicions are not enough to condemn the lord."

Margit cast Endre a hardened look. What proof did he need?

But, for the first time, determination marked Béla's features and a deep crease formed on his brow. "My beloved *will* have peace." He retrieved his satchel. "I knew my words alone wouldn't be enough, so I brought something that could destroy Lord Márton in a different way."

Heart drumming, Margit leaned back. Could justice be found at last?

"Really?" Endre breathed, mirroring her keen anticipation.

"Yes, sir. But I can't say anything more unless you swear on your honour as a knight and as an officer of the king that my daughter and I will not be harmed."

Margit nodded vigorously, willing her husband to agree.

"Of course," Endre said. "I swear I shall protect you both."

Without further hesitation, Béla took a neatly folded but yellow-stained document out of the bag.

"My uncle, Kálmán Havasi, was Lord Márton's treasurer. The only one of the previous lord's advisors who had kept his position, favoured by both Márton and his mother. No one could understand why he killed himself. Only I knew the truth. Unmarried and with no children of his own, Kálmán loved me like a son and made me his heir. The day before he died, he confessed he was carrying a crushing burden. He told me if Márton ever threatened me, I was to use a letter he handed me—a letter so important that it could destroy the lord. Only a lad of nineteen and too busy chasing maidens, I didn't pay attention to my uncle's words. I hid the document but never opened it, fearing its contents would put me in danger. But I shall stay silent no more."

Margit stretched out her arm, but Endre pulled the document out of Béla's hand before her.

Fidgeting, she peered over her husband's shoulder. The letter had the Szilágyi of Szentimre seal stuck to it, but the seal was broken. Her pulse quickened while Endre unfolded it and glanced at its contents.

"I looked at it before I came here," Béla said, "but I don't understand much. It's in Latin, I believe."

"Yes, Latin."

"What does it say?" Margit pleaded, the pitch of her voice high in her urgency to discover the document's damning content. Retribution was so close—she needed to know.

But Endre left her guessing. As he read the letter, excitement lit his face. What had he found?

"I shall help you avenge your wife," he said to Havasi, "if you promise to help me bring Lord Márton to justice for another crime he possibly committed a long time ago."

Which crime? Does he mean my father's—

Margit jumped to her feet, struggling to restrain herself from snatching the document from her husband's hands.

Endre pointed at the letter. "This could be the missing piece of evidence I was looking for. Do you swear you will tell no one else about it?"

Chewing her lip in impatience, Margit leaned in to hear the treasurer's response.

"Yes, I swear," Havasi declared.

"Are you willing to testify in front of the king about how you came to possess the letter, who gave it to you and why?"

"Yes."

"Give me the letter!" Margit interjected, her burning cheeks reflecting her mounting frenzy to know it contents.

She almost kicked Endre out of frustration when he motioned her to stay. He stood up and extended his hand to Béla, who shook it without hesitation.

"Now, Master Havasi," Endre said, "I would like to introduce you to someone."

Margit froze. What was her husband about to do?

Before she opened her mouth to protest, Endre spoke. "This is my wife, Lady Margit Szilágyi-Bátori, the daughter of Sándor

Szilágyi, who was the previous lord of Szentimre."

Havasi's eyes almost popped out of their sockets. "This is a lady?"

Taken by surprise, Margit cast her husband a panicked look for putting his faith in a stranger. But Endre's smile and nod allayed her fear.

She stood straight and assumed an air of authority befitting her status. "You have trusted me with your secret. Can I now trust you with mine?"

Havasi sprang up and bowed his head, his voice trembling. "Of course, my lady."

"I have come here in disguise to investigate my father's murder. I believe my cousin played a part in it."

Endre handed the document to her at last. "This is the letter your father wrote to the king, pleading with him to reconsider his decision to take over the mine. There is nothing traitorous in it. Your aunt and cousin must have stolen it and then forced Kálmán Havasi to write the fake, disrespectful one, imitating your father's handwriting and signature. As a treasurer, Kálmán could also get his hands on his master's correspondence seal."

Those evil vultures! They are the real traitors.

Clenching her teeth, Margit examined the letter. She could only understand a few words and phrases here and there. If only she had paid more attention during her Latin lessons! Her father's neat handwriting flowed before her eyes, making her tense muscles relax. His voice rang in her ears clear and steady, speaking words that came straight from the heart.

"If we take this letter to the king and compare it with the forged one, I'm sure we shall see the difference," Endre continued.

Holding the document to her swelling chest, Margit smiled. After so many setbacks, the time to defeat her enemies and clear her father's name had finally arrived. "Thank you for this, Master Havasi. I cannot express in words how much it means to me."

"Always at your service, my lady. I shall pray for the day to come when both my wife and your father will be avenged."

Then Endre spoke to the treasurer in a serious tone. "You must take your daughter and anything valuable you can carry and leave Szentimre immediately. I shall give you directions to my house in Nándorfehérvár and a letter for my mother to give you shelter. You must stay there and wait for us. My wife and I are about to cause havoc here, and we do not wish you and your child to get caught in the middle."

Margit gaped at her husband. The thrill of vindication competed with the dark anticipation of an upcoming storm.

What did Endre have in mind?

34
Fighting the Ghosts

Christmas Eve 1478

Thick clouds covered the night sky, concealing the moon and cloaking the landscape in darkness. The icy wind, which whistled by Margit's ears, numbed her limbs and made each breath painful. Knee-deep, the pristine snow, along with the thick hillside brush, impeded her and Endre's climb. She stopped now and then to find her footing.

Endre offered his left hand—his right holding a metal lantern. "Make haste! We must be in and out before your cousin's banquet ends."

Margit grunted while she disentangled herself from those accursed thorny bushes, which threatened to tear her clothes and graze her hands. Still, she refused his help.

The light of the lantern provided little comfort in the vastness of the castle hill slope. Finding the exact spot of the entrance to the secret tunnel added to Margit's frustration. Although they had located it after many days of exploring as they prepared their daring plan, the darkness had turned their task more difficult. So much precious time wasted already.

Margit quickened her step, only to slip on something and fall flat on her face. The icy snow stung her skin. "Damn!"

With great effort, she pushed herself to her knees.

Endre turned to her. "Are you hurt?"

The lantern was in her face. "Move that away from me!"

He extended his free hand again. This time, she took it. The sureness of his grip eased her disquiet.

Yet after a little while, she lost her patience again. "Are we ever going to find this tunnel?"

"I have been counting the steps. We are close, I think."

"You think? You are the one who told me to hasten because we are running out of time."

"Oh, here it is!" A hint of gloating coloured his voice.

Of course. Always so clever.

Endre raised the lantern, revealing a long, dark hollow spot on the cliff-face. They pushed aside the branches of more bushes, and there it was: an opening so narrow that it barely allowed one person to enter sideways.

He squeezed in first. A moment later, he called for her.

Against the rock Margit trailed, dislodging frozen specks of dirt. They irritated her throat as she inhaled. She suppressed the cough, anxious to exit the tight space.

Soon she found herself in a chamber-like area. After replacing the dying candle in the lantern with a new one, Endre moved the light about this cavern, which could fit at least four or five people. The smell of damp earth assaulted Margit's nostrils.

Before she knew it, Endre's lantern disappeared around a turn. Rushing after him, she stumbled into the arched entrance of a tunnel with steps carved into the rock.

Although they were in an enclosed area, air still flowed through somehow, guttering the flame dangerously low.

With an impatient urge, she pushed Endre aside and climbed

the stairs: one, two, three...twenty and bang!

She collided with something that felt like an iron grill gate. "Argh!"

But the pain did not distress her as much as the realisation that their path was blocked. Imre had told her about the gate, but she hoped it would be unlocked. "Pity the key was lost."

"Do not fret. I came prepared." Endre handed the lantern to her and unhooked a small hammer from his belt. "Keep the light steady."

The intermittent clanging reverberated in the emptiness of the tunnel.

Margit winced. "Make haste before the entire castle hears us."

To her relief, the rusted lock snapped after only a few attempts, and the gate groaned open.

She returned the lantern to him and continued to climb the stepped path through the cave until she reached a dead end in a chamber enclosed by brick walls. The ground underfoot felt flat and smooth.

"According to my father's description, this must be the lower level of the keep," Endre said. He held the lantern aloft.

Margit looked up. From the reach of the glow, she perceived a shaft which rose above them with a narrow, spiral staircase leading upwards. "Yes, it seems we are inside the building now."

Her stomach tightened with both anticipation and apprehension. From what Imre had told her, this was the secret way into her father's bedchamber—the last part of her journey.

The ascent grew steeper as the risers between the steps increased and the treads narrowed. Drenched in sweat and breathing heavily, Margit wondered how in the world Imre had got them out of the castle on the night her father died—all four of them: two women and two small children—without anyone falling down and breaking their neck. Their descent into what resembled a bottomless pit must have been frightening. But she was going up now, and it was not so dangerous. Yet her knees ached, and her thigh muscles burned with the effort.

The higher she climbed, the more the old memories tormented her mind in terrible flashes: the light of a candle creating fluid shadows on the rough walls; the icy hand of fear gripping her heart as she bobbed up and down in Imre's arms; his breath, heavy and hot against her neck; the sweat wetting her hair as she lay her head on his broad shoulders; Endre's whining voice—the steps were too steep for his little legs; Dragoslava's suppressed sobs; Erzsi's prayers... And only one thought swirling in Margit's mind: *Where's my daddy?*

Assailed by those images of gloom, she stumbled. Dizziness overtook her. "I can't...I can't..." Her body tilted precariously to the side. *I'm going to fall...I'm going to die...*

Strong hands restrained her. She was in Endre's steady arms. "I got you, *szívem*," he said, his voice equally steady and reassuring.

With his support, she sat down on a step. Fear still throbbed inside her. "Were you scared on the night we escaped?"

"Of course. I was only a child, like you."

Margit sighed. "I remember everything now."

"It's in the past, *szívem*. We are not children anymore. We are stronger now." He extended his arm to help her stand up. "Come! We must hurry."

The time it took to reach the top felt like an eternity. At the end of the steps stood a low doorway. They stooped to avoid hitting their heads against the ceiling. Endre felt about the wall until he found a cranny. "Here's the lever."

Clenching her teeth to withstand the piercing pain in her leg muscles, Margit knelt and peered through a thin crack at the bottom of the doorway. "No light."

Endre pulled the lever. The false wall in front of them sprang inward and revealed an opening into a bedchamber through the panelling. A long time ago, Margit's father slept there. Now her cousin probably occupied it as the lord of the estate.

With only their lantern's illumination to guide them, they fumbled their way to the chamber's door. They stood by and listened. Distant murmur, mingled with music and laughter, rose from the great hall, two floors below. The Christmas banquet was in full swing.

"I shall leave this here. The light would draw attention," Endre said and placed the lantern on the floor.

They stepped into a torch-lit corridor and drew their swords slowly. The last obstacle to their endeavour lay ahead: the two guards outside Anna's room. Those soldiers were not allowed to drink ale or wine while on duty, and so they had to be fought off; preferably one at a time.

Endre hid around the corner from them and flung a coin in their direction. The metallic sound echoed in the silence.

"Who's there?" a voice said in Wallachian.

"Why are you standing here?" the other guard responded. "Go and check, you fool!"

Margit held her breath as footsteps approached. But the

moment the soldier turned the corner, Endre hit him in the face with the pommel of his sword. The man staggered momentarily but did not fall until Margit hit him on the back of the head, and he crashed to the floor at last.

"Hey! What happened? Hey!" came the anxious voice of his comrade.

A brief silence. And then the second guard came flying down the corridor, only to be met by a blow to his face. As he fell on his back, Endre straddled him and punched him a few more times until he passed out.

He used the men's boot laces to tie their hands and gestured to Margit to go ahead.

She grabbed the bunch of keys from the guard's belt and hastened to the door. After trying a few keys, she unlocked the door to Anna's room and let herself and Endre in.

Surrounded by darkness, barely broken upon by the haze of two tallow candles in wall sconces, Anna was sitting at the side of her bed, staring at the sky through the window. Lost in whatever world her thoughts lingered, she did not seem to notice Margit and Endre's presence.

"I shall wait outside in case anyone approaches," Endre whispered in Margit's ear. "Be quick." And he exited quietly.

"Anna!" Margit called in a soft but determined voice.

As if snapped out of a spell, the woman turned around and squinted. "Who's there?"

Margit stood in the light of the candle.

"It's you again!" Anna rasped. "What do you want from me? Are you back to torture me? All of you, ghosts and demons. Leave me in peace!"

She covered her face with her chained hands and let out a wail that froze the blood in Margit's veins.

Margit stepped cautiously towards Anna, praying her words would have enough force to deceive her aunt. "I have come to take you out of here. Save you from this prison. I promise you will be free. No one will harm you anymore. Come!"

She extended her hand and waited.

The woman raised her head slowly. Horror distorted her face. "You are dead. Both of you. And now you appear as one to have your revenge?"

"What?" Margit squirmed. Erzsi had told her Anna lusted after Margit's father for many years and tried in vain to break his marriage. And then, after Margit's mother died, Anna attempted anew. But failing to seduce him, she schemed to steal his land for the benefit of her son. Erzsi was convinced that Anna had somehow caused his death.

But what was going on in the woman's disturbed mind now? Had she noticed Margit's resemblance to both her parents? Was it guilt and regret for her past actions that troubled her? She seemed unable to distinguish between reality and whatever tormented her haunted mind.

Shouts came from the corridor and then the clash of metal. Margit's hand flew to her mouth. They had been discovered. Would Endre be able to fend off the threat on his own? She took a step back, dithering whether to go help him or continue to convince her aunt.

Perhaps encouraged by the scuffle noises outside, Anna growled like a rabid animal. She sprang up and pounced. Sharp nails dug into Margit's cheek, and the chain of the shackles slammed against her jaw. Margit screeched and pushed her aunt to the floor. Anna curled into a ball, hissing and breathing heavily.

Margit pressed her hand on the side of her face. The broken skin stung like hundreds of needles. Although her chin throbbed, her teeth had not broken from the impact, thanks be to God.

No more noises echoed from the corridor, but running footsteps approached.

The cold hand of fear seized Margit's body. Was it her husband or the guards? She clasped the handle of her sword, ready to fight if needed.

Endre burst into the chamber. "What happened? Are you hurt?"

Margit released her grip on the sword. She shook her head, her eyes still fixed on her aunt.

Anna rose to her knees. She screamed and wailed again.

"Enough!" Endre said. "I stopped another guard, but if more of them hear her now, our efforts will be in vain."

He stepped behind Anna, hauled her off the floor and locked his arm around her chest. His other hand balled into a fist, he pressed his thumb under her chin, causing her to faint.

Margit gasped. "Are you out of your mind? You could have killed her."

"Trust me. She is not dead." His harsh tone softened as he continued, "We can't wait any longer. Now help me drag the guards into this chamber. We must lock them here."

When they finally exited the cave, the frosty wind slapped Margit's face.

"Adnan should be here by now," Endre said.

He whistled twice, and thankfully the response came soon. The dark figure of their lantern-bearing friend hastened towards them.

Adnan helped Endre carry the still unconscious Anna to a two-passenger closed carriage at the foot of the hill. After they laid the woman on the seat and covered her with a fur blanket, Adnan broke her shackles with his tools and bound her wrists and ankles with rope.

Glad to see the two horses tied to the back of the carriage, Margit stroked Csillag and Zora's heads.

"We must go," Endre said. He climbed to the driver's seat, fastened a lantern next to him and took the reins.

With a heavy heart, Margit embraced Adnan. "Thank you. I don't know what I would do without you. I wish you and Ilona would come with us."

"I must stay." His voice quavered. "She doesn't wish to leave her family behind. But I'll pray to see you come back soon. As the lady of the estate."

Margit bit hard on her lower lip, fighting back the emotion as she moved away from him.

"Hey!" he said suddenly, making her turn around to look at him again. "I've a favour to ask."

"Anything."

"Please visit my father. Tell him I'm sorry I haven't come to see him for so long. Tell him I love him, and I think of him all the time. But don't say anything about my conversion and my marriage to Ilona yet. I'll be the one to do it."

"Of course."

"Make haste!" Endre interrupted them. "We must go."

Margit cast a last look at Adnan and patted him on the shoulder. "I shall see you soon, God willing."

A screech clawed into Margit's brain like a hawk's talons. Still heavy from sleep, her eyes refused to open until a hefty kick against her shin made her jump in her seat.

"What the devil?"

Although the bumpy ride had lulled the exhausted Margit into the land of dreams, it must have awakened Anna. Still screaming, the woman threw the blanket off and thrashed her bound legs and hands about in the cramped space of the carriage.

"Stop!" Margit shouted, covering her ears.

To no avail.

She grabbed her aunt by the shoulders and pushed her down on the seat. But Anna kicked again, at which Margit's feet slid under her, and she collapsed face-first onto the carriage floor.

Before she could get up, Anna's knees dug into her back as she clambered over Margit's prostrate body to reach for the door.

An icy gust rushed in. "No!" Margit stretched forward, catching the edge of her aunt's chemise. "Stop!"

Anna's bound feet kicked at Margit's face.

Despite the pain and the temporary dizziness, Margit pulled with all her might.

Her aunt fought back.

But at length, the door slipped out of Anna's grasp, swung wide, bounced on the carriage exterior and slammed shut, striking the woman on the head.

The carriage shuddered to a halt. Both Anna and Margit

crashed against the base of the seat, but Margit quickly gained the upper hand and held her aunt down.

After a moment of silence, the door flung open, and Endre's angry voice gusted in together with the freezing wind. "What's the matter?"

"She tried to jump," Margit said.

Endre motioned her to move before he climbed in, lifted Anna off the floor and forced her down on the seat. "Are you out of your mind, woman? Trying to kill yourself?"

Anna shrieked, and evading his grasp, she dived for the open door.

Strangely, Endre did not stop her.

In the faint blue light of dawn, Margit watched her aunt's body fly forward, only to crash face-first into a snowdrift.

Endre stepped out and plucked Anna from the snow. He swept his arm across the frozen landscape. "Look around you, lady. Where do you wish to go in this wilderness? You will freeze to death."

Though her head, back and ribs still hurt, Margit jumped off the carriage and approached her aunt. "I am your niece, Margit Szilágyi," she said as she wiped the melting snow from the woman's scowling face. "Sándor's daughter. And this is my husband, Endre Gerendi."

Anna recoiled. The same image of horror twisted her features once again.

"Calm yourself, aunt," Margit made every effort to sound gentle and reassuring. "I swear, we shall not harm you."

Her expression now resigned and dejected, Anna shivered and sobbed silently.

Margit covered her with the blanket. "We shall look after you. Take you somewhere warm and safe." She turned to her husband. "We must continue."

Endre lifted Anna into his arms and placed her on the seat while Margit leaned over her. "If we untie you, will you promise not to escape?"

Tears still streaking her pale face, Anna finally nodded.

Anna did not speak during the rest of the journey to Belgrade. She stared out of the carriage window although, from time to time, Margit caught her steal a glance in her direction and then turn away with a grimace. At night, when they stopped to rest at various inns along the way, Anna cried herself to sleep.

When they arrived at Endre's house two weeks later, the reunion between Margit and Erzsi was an emotional one. The woman, now grey-haired and weary from all the sleepless nights she spent worrying about her beloved goddaughter, was in floods of tears. Her only consolation throughout this time had been Endre's visits and his letters, which informed her of Margit's welfare. But Erzsi's mood instantly changed when she saw Anna, and she chastised Margit for bringing 'the evil woman' into their lives again even though it were for a good reason.

On her part, Dragoslava offered Margit a more restrained reception as if only a day had passed since they last saw each other. Béla and his child were there too. Relieved to see Margit and Endre, Havasi urged them to take him to Buda to testify against Márton in front of the king.

But before they could do that, they needed to convince Anna to talk. In an effort to entice her, and notwithstanding her godmother's protests, Margit gave the bedchamber she shared with Erzsi to her aunt. The glaze-tiled masonry stove always kept the room warm, and the window let plenty of sunlight in.

Although she and Erzsi kept a close eye on Anna, they never restricted her freedom to wander around the house and the garden. They took her for walks in the city, which she seemed to enjoy because she paused to breathe in the air of the open space many a time and even cracked a smile. But she still refused to talk, only mumbled to herself in the Saxon language now and again.

"I beg of you, Aunt." Margit clasped her hands under her chin but fought hard to hide the despair in her voice. "I understand he's your son, and you don't wish to betray him. But he doesn't deserve your loyalty. Look how he treated you. He locked you in a room for so long, chained you and fed you scraps. I promise I shall let no one harm you again."

Margit's words were in vain. Anna stared at her with frightened eyes as though she were looking at a ghost.

Despite having Béla's help and her father's letter, Margit needed Anna as a witness to confirm who had killed him. This would ensure the murderer's punishment and would convince the king to return Szentimre to her possession.

After three months with no result, Erzsi thought of a possible way to persuade Anna. She and Margit went to merchants and tailors in the city and had an elegant silk gown and red leather shoes made for Anna. They also bought her a beaded necklace. Margit helped her put these on, and then Erzsi tied Anna's hair with colourful ribbons and livened up her cheeks with red powder and her lips with balm.

Margit held the looking glass in front of her aunt. Anna grinned as she stared at her reflection.

"You look so much younger," Margit lied. "I shall take you to the palace, and everyone will admire you. Even the king will be impressed."

Those words seemed to have a sudden effect on Anna. "The palace? Truly?"

At last!

Her spirits lifted, Margit smiled. Finally, she had broken through a first brick in the wall of silence which had surrounded her aunt for so long. "Yes. You are your old self again. Like back in the good times."

Anna ran her fingers down her gown, feeling the smooth, pure silk. After looking askance at Margit, she twirled a few times and let out a raspy laugh as the fabric swished. The veil of uncertainty faded from her face. "Will you...really take me to...the palace?" Although her voice was hoarse and faltering, her eyes gleamed with joy.

Margit grinned. "Yes, I promise. But I need your help first."

Anna's face darkened. Other thoughts seemed to cross her mind. She clutched her skirts as if she wished to rip the material apart. Her voice rang of suspicion. "Why would you take me to the palace?"

Quelling her impatience, Margit paused to choose her words carefully. Yet there was no subtle way to approach the subject. "The king believes my father was a traitor. You know very well that he was not. I must clear his name."

Anna released her grip on her gown and took a step back. A deep crease formed between her eyebrows. "And what will happen to me after I reveal the truth?"

The words gushed from Margit's trembling lips unchecked. "So, you know what happened. You know who murdered my father."

Silence.

Margit waited, her heart racing, until she could wait no more. "Please, tell me!"

At the hurried shake of Anna's head, dread sank in Margit's stomach like a stone. She clasped her aunt's hand. "How can you live with such burden on your conscience? Confess and free yourself."

Anna withdrew her hand. "What will happen to me then?"

Margit hesitated. Would she lie and reassure the woman that all would be well? It was not up to her, really. "That will be the king's decision," she said sternly, frustration simmering within but never reaching the surface. "I have liberated you from Márton's prison, but I can't promise you anything more."

After various emotions battled on her face, Anna turned away. "Then I can't help you."

Margit felt an angry fire rise to her head but restrained herself from lashing out at her aunt. She summoned every bit of her will to persuade the woman. Perhaps somewhere, very deep down indeed, in Anna's inner world there was a glimmer of decency. Or regret for covering a crime for so long. Or even a fear of divine punishment in the afterlife. Any one of those would do.

Again, she took hold of Anna's wrist and squeezed fiercely. "Search deep within your soul, Aunt. I hope there is a trace of dignity still hiding there."

But Anna's vacant stare shattered her. Letting go, Margit

fought to keep despair from taking hold within. "I know about the fake letter to the king. I'm sure you and your son caused my father's death. Telling the truth is the only way to earn God's forgiveness; the only way to stop the ghosts tormenting you. You wish those ghastly visions gone, do you not?"

Anna bobbed her head several times. Shaking, she stepped back and sank onto the bed. "I loved Sándor," she said, her breath quickening with each word. "I never wished him dead."

Margit's chest tightened. Would she finally have her answers? Now that her aunt was, at last, standing on the brink, Margit needed to press on, no matter what the cost. "Yet he died because of your scheming. This is why you must tell the truth."

Though Anna looked away, her hoarse words descended like a snowslide from a mountain, ruthlessly exposing the bare rock beneath. "I gave money to Balog. He bribed the treasurer to forge the letter. We lied to the king about Sándor's insubordination." She paused and pressed her hand against her forehead. "The plan was to have him arrested for defying the king's orders. I would then plead with Mátyás not to imprison him but confiscate his estate instead and grant it to Márton. And as a condition for saving him from a life sentence, I would make Sándor marry me." She turned to Margit, eyes wet and pleading. "This was all I wished. Believe me."

White-hot fury seared Margit's veins, yet she kept silent lest she impeded her aunt's confession.

Anna's breaths came out in gasps and sobs. "My own son betrayed me!" she squealed. "He hated his uncle because of Miklós' death and because Sándor had crippled his hand. He just drew the knife and—"

A ghastly pallor now spreading over her face, Anna clutched her head with tensed hands and pulled at her hair. Dislodged ribbons flew off and slowly fell to the floor like ashes after a deadly fire.

Despite the trembling of her own insides, Margit steeled herself to face the most painful moments in her life. "Please, tell me what my cousin did," she hissed through clenched teeth.

The wailing cries pouring louder and louder out of her aunt's mouth sent chills down Margit's spine.

"He...he...ran the...the knife through," Anna continued in desperate gasps. "I watched Sándor bleed to death in front of me... How horrible... I could do nothing to help him... Then Balog murdered the army officer to silence him."

Monsters! Devil's spawn, all of you!

Burning bile choked Margit's throat. She staggered to brace herself against the wall as her own heavy breathing and Anna's mourning howls filled her ears. After so long, the brutal truth had demolished her defences.

At length, her aunt's uncontrollable sobbing subsided. Her croaky voice grated in Margit's head. "Márton wanted to throw his body off the castle walls for the wolves to eat. At that moment, it dawned on me that I had raised a monster. I pleaded and convinced him it would be a terribly un-Christian act to haunt him for the rest of his life. In the end, he let me place him in the family crypt. I tried hard to continue with my life for a few years, but it was all in vain. Your father's spirit plagued me. I saw him everywhere, covered in blood and glaring at me."

Margit's heart pounded. Disgust and horror displaced the glimmer of decency in Anna's merciful act to save her father's body.

No! Márton is her son. She raised him hateful and depraved. The crime falls equally on her shoulders.

And Anna continued, "Márton was afraid I would crack and reveal his crime. That's why he locked me in that room." She raised her head suddenly and looked Margit in the eye. "But you know, it was your mother's bedchamber. Soon, her ghost replaced Sándor's. She appeared to me every night and said horrible things. She hated me so much."

Heat flooded Margit's face. She could not restrain herself this time. "Could you blame her?" she spat. "You tried to steal her husband."

Anna's gaze wandered about the room. "I was jealous. He was all that I ever dreamt of finding in a man. And she had him in her bed. I lay with him a single night, and it was worth more than all the years I spent with Miklós, my lawful husband."

"Stop!" Margit covered her ears against Anna's vile insinuations. "I don't wish to hear any more!"

Anna's face twisted into a wry smile. "Why? Do you think your father was a saint? He knew how to make a woman scream with pleasure."

"How dare you?" Margit raised her shaking fist. "Another word about this, and you return to Márton."

Yet the woman did not flinch. "You are your father's daughter. The same fire burns inside you."

Anna's taunt found its mark. Pride briefly surged inside Margit before cold hostility took hold. There was nothing genuine in her aunt's expression, only mockery. Margit stepped back and squared her shoulders. "We shall leave for Buda in the morn. Prepare yourself."

35
Justice

May 1479

In dazzling sunlight, the palace complex buzzed with activity. Masons, builders and labourers scurried about, climbing up and down the scaffolds, carrying materials, hammering, plastering, painting while they sang and joked to make their toil more pleasant.

But Margit paid no regard to the architectural miracle unfolding around her. After hearing Havasi's and Anna's testimonies and examining her father's letter against the forged one, the king had summoned her, Endre and her aunt to the palace to announce his judgement.

Margit flew through courtyards, alleyways and corridors, leaving Endre and Anna a long way behind.

Outside the king's audience room, a spindly young clerk fixed her with a stern look.

Margit inhaled deeply to compose herself. Although her future depended on this meeting with Mátyás, she must not show any signs of impatience. She tidied her hair, smoothed down her tunic and swept specks of dust off her hose.

She lifted her head, only to come within an inch of the clerk's sour face. "For the love of—"

Despite his raised eyebrows, the man's voice was devoid of

emotion. "You may enter."

He escorted her into the audience room, bowed to the king and took his leave.

Awe flooded Margit as she beheld the magnificence surrounding her: oak-panelled wall sections alternated with colourful tapestries; frescoes adorned the vaulted ceiling, gilded patterns glimmering on its ribs; marble-coated pillars sparkled in the radiance spilling through towering arched windows.

The air was perfumed by rosemary oil and incense that burned in metal cauldrons on tripods, their vapour twisting upwards to meet the flames of scented candles in two wrought-iron wheels hanging overhead.

For a heartbeat, Margit discerned the rhythmic scratching of a scribe's quill on paper somewhere nigh.

Her mind flew back to the great hall in Sasfészek.

If only I had the chance to bring it to life like this!

Her feet glided on the polished black-and-white chequered marble floor as she approached the king.

Armed with menacing halberds, two guards stood like solid columns on either side of His Majesty's gilded throne, the splendour of their shiny plate armour matching the opulence of the room.

"Dear cousin," Mátyás said.

Margit knelt and bowed her head to hide her wide grin. What a delight it was to hear the king call her *cousin*!

"You are still in a man's attire," he continued. "It seems this has become a habit of yours."

Her cheeks heated with embarrassment. "Forgive me, Lord King. As I have yet to receive your wise judgement, I must remain in disguise."

"Very well. You may rise now."

Only now did Margit realise that Mátyás' voice sounded hoarse and strained.

She stood up and raised her gaze to him. She did not expect the king's pitiful sight.

Drawn and pale, his face was so thin that his nose protruded like a beak, shadowing his hollow cheeks. His eyes were clouded, dark crescent marks under them, and blinked as if they could not stand the brightness of the chamber. Even the light diadem appeared a heavy burden on his slightly trembling head.

Was it illness or worry that plagued him?

"Have you come alone?" he interrupted her observations.

"No, Lord King. My husband is—"

At that moment, the clerk announced the arrival of Endre and Anna.

Endre bowed deeply and went to stand beside Margit while a shaking Anna curtsied as much as her age would allow her.

"Very well...very well," Mátyás mumbled, straining his eyes to look at the newcomers. "Sir Gerendi, it pleases me to see you again. Many of my people abandoned me over the years. You could have done the same after I imprisoned your father. But your unwavering loyalty will not be forgotten."

Endre bowed again. "I am honoured to serve you, Lord King."

A hint of bitterness in her husband's voice pinched Margit's heart. Endre could have abandoned her for the same reason. Yet he stood by her despite his own suffering.

But that was in the past. Margit fiddled with the buckle of her belt. Her breath quickened with anticipation. Would the king's praise for her husband be followed by a positive outcome to her petition?

To her dismay, Mátyás addressed her aunt next. "I shall begin with you, Lady Anna." He cleared his throat, but his voice still came forth cracked despite the solemn words he uttered. "For your scheming and participation in the murder of my relative, Sándor Szilágyi of Szentimre, in the year of our Lord fourteen-hundred-and-sixty-two, you are hereby ordered to abandon your earthly possessions and enter the Dominican nunnery on Hare Island."

Anna's shriek tore through the vastness of the audience room. She turned to Margit with brimming eyes. "You promised you would look after me. How can you take me from one prison and send me to another?"

Despite searching within for compassion, Margit found only fury at her aunt's crimes. Anna deserved no mercy. Only God could forgive her.

Emotions rising to a storm inside her, Margit wished to respond, but Mátyás took the words out of her mouth. "How ungrateful of you, Lady Anna! I have offered you a chance to eternal life: the time to redeem yourself and wash away your sins with fasting and prayers so that you can face your Maker with a cleansed heart and soul."

Anna fell to her knees, hands clasping her head. "No! No! Your Majesty, I beg of you. Anything but this. I'd rather die."

Although Margit longed to condemn her aunt further, she watched coldly as Anna's screams made the king squirm on his throne. He gestured to the royal guards. "Take her out of my sight!"

Anna's wailing faded as the soldiers dragged her out of the

chamber.

A chill settled over Margit's raging heart. Justice was served though she could find no comfort until her father's name was cleared. She turned to the king, praying his next words would at last bring the relief she so urgently needed.

Evidently distressed, Mátyás rubbed his forehead. A young page, who had been standing by a side door, rushed to wipe beads of sweat from the king's brow with a cloth. Then he retreated as swiftly as he had appeared.

Notwithstanding her sympathy for Mátyás' misery, Margit shuffled her weight impatiently from left to right several times.

Make haste, Lord King! Give your decision. I can't bear the wait.

Endre's hand squeezed her arm and anchored her. Grateful, she nodded to him, and he let her go. She squared her shoulders and gazed at the king.

Eyes downcast, Mátyás beckoned the scribe with an unsteady hand.

When, at length, the king looked at Margit again, the wrinkles under his eyes deepened, and a shadow flitted across his face. "I cannot bring your father back or ease your pain. But I accept that in my youthful inexperience, I was deceived like a fool and made an error of judgement." His voice faltered, and he hurriedly dried a tear with his finger. "I have barely slept since I heard your aunt's confession."

"Lord King—" Inner turmoil made Margit choke on her words.

Mátyás stayed her with his raised hand. "The first of these documents is a pardon—issued *post-mortem,* alas—clearing Sándor Szilágyi of Szentimre of the charge of treason and restoring his title and his land in Hunyad County, in the province of Transylvania."

At the king's behest, the scribe handed two letters to Margit. She clutched them to her chest as if to stop her heart from bursting out. To her, they were the most valuable treasure in the world.

Did you hear that, Father? You are innocent. You can stand proud.

All those years of struggle and strife, all the perils she had endured, they were worth every moment. Even if the king did not offer her anything else, it was enough.

"The second is a charter which acknowledges you, Lady Margit Szilágyi, and your husband, Sir Endre Gerendi, as the rightful lords of Szentimre. Your first cousin, Márton Szilágyi, has been found guilty of your father's murder and has been stripped of his titles and land. His other two estates in Transylvania are also to pass to your possession."

Try as she might, Margit could not control her trembling body. Trusting the precious documents to her husband's hands, she sank to her knees and clenched her fists, nails digging into the skin of her palms. She wanted to scream and cry a river of relief. Her chest convulsed, resisting her effort to hold back. A whirlpool of emotions choked her. She brought her hand to her throat. But loathing to show weakness in front of the king, she sniffled hard to drown the sobs that threatened to consume her entire being.

Feeling untethered from reality, she barely heard Endre's words over the thumping of her heart in her ears. "Lord King, this charter does not address the subject of removing Márton from the estate and bringing him to justice."

At last brought back into herself, Margit searched the king's face.

Mátyás' countenance finally hardened with resolve, his voice now steady and determined. "I have dispatched an order to Lord Bátori to assist you. He is the new voivode of Transylvania. Wait for his word."

36
Best Laid Plans

Late July 1479

Fuelled by the determination to reclaim her destiny at last, Margit pushed aside the bush branches which impeded her ascent towards the secret tunnel. Unable to use a lantern for fear of being seen, she held Endre's hand as they made their way uphill in the meagre light of a waxing crescent moon.

Recent events flashed through her mind. Despite Mátyás' deliberation, Bátori never sent her a message. For what reason, she did not know. One thing was certain: she had wasted valuable time awaiting his support.

Adnan and Gábor were the only friends Margit could rely on. During a moonless night, she and Endre had sneaked into Szentimre on foot and spent three days hiding in a barn while Gábor watched the movements of the night guards. Following the annulment of his betrothal to Péter Vingárti Geréb's niece due to the king's decision, Márton obviously expected Margit to appear at any time, and so he had ordered his men to check anyone entering the estate.

"Almost there. Are you ready?" Endre's voice, calm and serious as ever, recalled her out of her deep thoughts.

Her hand brushed across the pommel of the sword in her belt and clenched around the hilt of the dagger strapped on her thigh.

"Yes. Let us go."

The only thought on her mind was how she would capture her cousin as soon as she burst into his bedchamber. This would be her biggest moment, the one she had been waiting for all her life...

But no sooner had Endre raised his head above the last ledge below the cave than he slid back down. He grabbed Margit, startling her by the sudden force, and pinned her against the rocks. His hand clamped over her mouth.

Faint voices came from above. Guards? But how? Not knowing the existence of the secret passage, Gábor must have neglected to observe that part of the castle hill.

Endre pushed her down into a clump of bushes. Though thorns scratched her face and arms, she stifled a groan.

The voices grew louder, followed by footsteps dislodging loose pebbles as someone approached and stood on the ledge above her and Endre.

"Are you sure?" a man said in Hungarian. "I can't see anyone."

Crouched beside her husband, Margit held her breath. Did Márton know about the tunnel? Or had she perchance not closed the secret door properly when they abducted Anna?

"It's probably some fox or squirrel," the same voice said.

The footsteps faded away.

When silence returned, Margit and Endre picked their way carefully down the slope until they reached the bottom of the hill.

Out of breath, Margit sat down. Their plan had failed, and they did not have an alternative. Humiliation and anger scorched her cheeks. "What are we to do?"

"We must leave and think of another plan," Endre said in a low voice, glancing about warily for possible threats.

"Leave? And go where?"

"The mine. It belongs to the king. Márton has no authority there."

Margit's heart sank. She did not wish to give up, but her husband was right.

They barely eluded the patrol teams, which were criss-crossing the estate all night. Avoiding the miners' village, they climbed the sloping path to the mine. Endre knew the manager from the time when he helped him restore production and fight corruption there.

Indeed, the man let them hide in his cottage.

Margit sent a message to Adnan with Gábor the next day, and her friend came presently. Despite the smile on his face, he seemed concerned about her safety. It would only be a matter of time before Márton found out that she was hiding right under his nose. The four of them could not take on the whole castle garrison, plus all the mercenaries who were stationed in the estate.

"Write to Bátori," Endre suggested. "Perhaps the king's letter never reached him. This time, we must ensure he receives it."

She did, and the manager of the mine undertook to deliver the message to the voivode in person. As the king's employee, he could not be searched by Márton's soldiers.

Three days passed, and nothing happened. On the fourth morning, Gábor came to Margit and Endre, panting and wheezing. "Márton knows you're here. He's sending soldiers."

The news hit Margit like a thunderbolt. "How?"

"Don't forget he was expecting us," Endre said. "I'm sure he has spies everywhere, possibly here in the mine as well."

"The workers are on your side, my lady," Gábor reassured her. "I suggest you come to see with your own eyes."

Margit and Endre followed him to a cave-like chamber at the entrance of the mine. Some fifty men had gathered there, armed with tools that could easily turn into deadly weapons: axes, knives, shovels, chisels and hammers. There was a general murmur among them, which Gábor quelled by raising his arm.

As the men's eyes rested on her, Margit clasped her trembling hands behind her back and stood upright with her chin raised. "I assume you know who I am."

"Yes," replied one man, who looked to be in charge. "Many years ago, we served your lord father. But now we work for the king, and we receive our wages from him. We're no financial burden to Lord Márton, and yet he mistreats us."

Margit nodded. "I'm well informed of your plight."

"And we've been informed of your intentions." The miner glanced at the hardened faces of his fellow workers. "We pledge to stand by you, Lady Szilágyi, if you promise you'll treat us fairly."

This show of solidarity heartened Margit. Gone was the shaking of her hands and the tightness in her stomach. She walked right into the middle of the crowd and spoke at the top of her voice:

"I promise that when I take back my inheritance, I shall look after you and your families. You don't know me, but I swear I shall strive to prove myself to you. Having lived as a refugee for many years, I have known poverty and injustice. I have also fought for Hungary as a soldier, and I shall fight now again next to you for justice!"

She had barely finished her words when a massive cheer erupted. She looked at Endre, who stood among the crowd with a broad smile on his face. And only then did she realise she had just delivered her first speech as a leader. Her chest swelled with pride.

But only a moment later, Gábor's gasping voice drove the fear back into her soul. "They're on the way. Get ready, men!"

Margit turned to the direction he was looking. Three columns of riders emerged from the town in the distance.

Moving silently, the miners spread along the ridge of the hill, weapons at the ready.

Margit fiddled with the hilt of her sword. It had been a long time since she was in a battle, and truth be told, she was dreading it. But she had to lead by example. All those men were strangers to her; yet they were prepared to sacrifice their lives defending her.

She glanced at her husband, who stood beside her. He looked calm, holding his bared longsword in front of him, its tip resting on the ground.

Everyone around her was silent. But then, all of a sudden, gasps and cries of disbelief.

In the valley below, Márton's soldiers were not heading for the mine but riding towards the miners' village instead.

Why?

"The cowards do not wish to face us," Endre said. "It seems they plan to hold the miners' families hostage to make us surrender."

Margit clenched her fists. "Let us go help the people, then."

"The soldiers will reach the village before us. We may save some people, but we can't save them all."

The look on the men's faces changed from that of determination to worry and then panic. A wave of whispers spread across their line.

"Do not fear!" Endre spoke to them with a voice of authority.

"They will not harm anyone until they have delivered their message."

The soldiers surrounded the village, carrying torches. A few moments later, the distant gallop of a lone rider grew louder and louder until he appeared at the far end of the hillside path.

Margit turned to Endre. How stone-faced he looked! Did he know what to do, or was he trying to hide his fear? "What is your advice, husband?"

"I don't know. These are *your* people. It's *your* decision."

You jest?

Endre was the one with the most military experience. Why did he ask *her* to decide?

Standing at a safe distance, Márton's messenger shouted, "Margit Szilágyi! Surrender, or we shall burn the village to the ground and kill anyone who dares to resist!"

A deathly hush descended upon the crowd of miners.

Margit looked hard at their distressed faces. Some of them lowered their heads or turned away.

"No, no. I shall not let innocent women and children suffer on my account. I shall give myself up."

A sigh of relief rose in unison from dozens of mouths around her.

"Stand down!" she ordered the men and walked to the front. "I surrender. Tell the soldiers to withdraw from the village."

The messenger signalled to his comrades. The riders retreated, gathered at the entrance of the village and waited.

Endre handed his sword to Gábor. Turning to Margit, his smile did not reach his eyes, which darkened with worry. "I applaud you, my dear and brave wife. You have made your first important decision as a leader, choosing to sacrifice yourself to save your people."

Was he taunting her? But no... There was an unsteadiness in his voice as he spoke such grave words. "It tears me apart to let you walk into such peril alone. I shall go with you." His tight jaw belied the reassurance he was evidently attempting to project.

"Why?" was all she could utter in her astonishment.

"Szentimre is my home, too. And as your husband, I shall forever stand by your side."

***

Margit grunted as the soldier chained her to the wall of a cell in the castle dungeon. That hateful Sergeant Bakó stood by and watched. The light of a lantern accentuated the repulsive way he leered at her. Everything about him made her skin crawl.

The guard ensured that she had been secured and then looked at his superior. Bakó waved him away and approached Margit. "You've just made my day, wench. I'll enjoy seeing you suffer this time."

Margit glared at him. "Don't touch me!"

"Do you think you can scare me?" he scoffed. "Just look around you: here's me, free to do whatever I wish with you; and there's you, chained to the wall and not a knife in sight."

He lunged at her. Before Margit had the time to react, he slammed her face against the rough wall. Her lungs constricted from the crushing pressure of his body against hers. "You will regret this!" she hissed.

Clenching her neck in his sweaty hand, he let out a creepy, laughing sound. "I'll snap you like a twig."

But a thunderous voice made him let her go at once. "What the devil are you doing?"

Despite her discomfort, Margit turned around.

Márton and Balog stood at the cell door.

Fear twisted the sergeant's face. He fell to his knees. "Forgive me, my lord! I was only trying to frighten her."

Dark like the Devil's countenance, Márton's face twitched. "You filthy scum! You are nobody. A worm crawling in cow dung. How dare you touch my noble cousin?"

The sergeant wailed desperately, pleading for mercy.

"Kill him!" Márton ordered Balog, his voice sharp like a dagger.

The castellan looked lost. "Pardon, my lord?"

"You heard me. Do it now, or I shall take *your* head."

Although Margit hated Bakó, she felt her stomach turn violently while a terrified Balog drew his sword, locked his arm around the sergeant's neck and cut his throat with an abrupt movement.

"Take him away!" Márton barked.

After stepping over Bakó's still convulsing, blood-gushing body, he stood face-to-face with Margit.

They glared at each other like two animals fighting for territory.

"You lived on my land, took my money, sat at my table!" he growled. "You lied, spied, hid and waited for the right time to strike. But I caught you."

Margit's rage burst forth like a scathing torrent. "You are a cold-blooded murderer and a tyrant! You killed my father, destroyed my home, my life; you made me a refugee. You imprisoned your own mother to silence her. You murdered an innocent woman and her unborn child. And you have terrorised the people of the estate for years."

Márton recoiled. Had any of her fierce words struck true?

He took a deep breath and continued in a calmer manner, "You did not need to run. I would not harm you. I did not wish to take Szentimre from you." His voice quavered. "I wished to share it with you...because...because I...loved you."

"You loved me?" Disgust churned in Margit's gut for a moment, then surged up her throat and gushed from her mouth. "Is this why you tried to hurt me when I was a child?"

"When you were a child?"

"I remember what you did to me." Margit's eyes darted to his crooked finger.

His expression changed as a semblance of guilt seemed to claim his features. "No! I swear to God. I was stupid and ignorant. I didn't know right from wrong." He raised his distorted left hand in front of Margit's face. "Your father made sure I would never forget what I did."

"If you feel any kind of remorse, let me go and give yourself up. Mátyás knows what you did to my father, and if you harm me, he will hunt you to the ends of the world."

All remorse vanished. Márton sneered. "The king has more important things to worry about."

Evil passion glinted in his grey-blue eyes as his gaze slithered down her body, making her twitch. He leaned unwelcomely close. His breath burned her cheek. Then taking a lock of her hair, he rubbed it between his fingers. "You will look so beautiful when your hair grows long, and I put you in a gown. *Drágám*, you will shine brighter than the sun."

Sick with revulsion, Margit jerked her head away. "Keep your filthy hands off me!"

Márton grimaced but did not relent. His hissing voice dripped venom. "You will never take this land from me. You will destroy the king's letter and inform him that you have forgiven me everything. In return, I shall let you live in the castle." He released a hoarse, sinister laugh. "And I shall make you mine."

Margit gasped. "You mad son of a whore! You know that the moment you take these chains off me, I shall kill you!"

"No, you will not." A wicked grin overspread his face. "Don't forget I also hold your husband prisoner." He caressed the hilt of the dagger hanging from his belt. "If you refuse me, I shall carve his heart out of his chest with my own hands. Before your very eyes, preferably. But if you do what I ask, I swear I shall not harm him. He will still be in prison, but he will stay alive. For how long depends entirely on you."

Margit reeled under this devastating blow. Rage and fear jousted inside her like two bitter enemies. Márton had found her weakness. Would she surrender to save Endre?

No. I shall not give in so easily. There must be another way.

She pressed her lips together.

Evidently realising that he would not receive a reply there and then, Márton raised three fingers in front of her face. "You have three days."

"Go to hell!"

"Oh, *drágám*, I have already been there and back," he said in a bitter whisper. With that, he turned around and walked away.

37
The Confrontation

In the meagre rushlight left in the cell, Margit stared at Bakó's bloodstains on the flagstones. Even though the wicked man deserved punishment, her cousin's cruelty was excessive. She squeezed her eyes shut, but the gruesome images still seared her mind, and her stomach churned.

A little later, a guard brought her food, but she kicked the plate away in disgust. Soon, the light died, and darkness enveloped her. What time of the day was it? Exhaustion pulled at her limbs. Chains barely allowing enough movement, she collapsed and fell asleep.

She thought she was dreaming when a voice addressed her, "Wake up, lady!"

Was this another nightmare?

Margit blinked against a lantern's blinding light. Captain Dóczi loomed over her.

"What's the matter?" she mumbled.

He hung the lantern on a wall bracket, then grasped her arm and dragged her to her feet. On wobbly legs, she tottered, but his firm hands supported her.

Hope sparked inside Margit. Dóczi had helped her before. She searched his face; yet she could not decipher his dispassionate expression.

Even the tone of his voice was restrained, revealing nothing. "You fooled us all, lady, with your sad story about what the Turks did to you when you were a 'boy'."

Margit sighed. "I had no choice."

The captain unchained her from the wall, but her weakened body lacked the strength to fight her escape.

He shackled her hands behind her back. "The lord demands you."

All hope drained from Margit's body. "Please, don't take me to him."

"I have my orders, lady." He gripped her arm, digging his fingers into her flesh. "The voivode's army is outside the town walls. Your cousin plans to use you as a hostage."

"Lord Bátori, at last!" Margit shrieked. A sudden spurt of energy burst through her body. She addressed Dóczi with a steady voice, "Captain, don't do my cousin's bidding. He's nothing but a murderer and a usurper. This land belongs to me. Both the king and the voivode are my relatives. I promise I shall bestow my gratitude on you in the best possible way if you release me."

The captain's arms fell by his sides. He looked away.

Silence stretched out, its burden crushing Margit's chest.

At length, Dóczi pressed his hand on his forehead. "God forgive me." He took a key out of his belt pouch and unlocked Margit's shackles. And bowing his head, he said, "At your service, my lady."

Margit stared at him, wide-eyed. But soon, a dreaded thought stalled the breath in her throat. "My husband! Where is he?" She grabbed Dóczi's arm. "Tell me!"

The captain led her to another cell at the far end of the dungeon.

Endre was chained to the wall. Now placed in a recess, Dóczi's lantern revealed her husband's pale face and dark marks under his eyes.

But as soon as Endre saw her, he smiled. "Margit! Thank God, you are safe." He looked her up and down. "And you are free? How?"

She pointed at the captain. "This good man is on our side. And Bátori's army stands at the town gates."

Endre raised his chained hands in front of Dóczi's face. "Release me!"

But the captain shook his head. "I can't. The lord holds the key."

"Damn you, Márton!" Margit spat on the floor. "Captain, can we break the chains?"

Dóczi struck the metal with the pommel and then the blade of his sword. No matter how many times the clanging reverberated around the walls, the metal did not shatter. "We need a strong tool, my lady. Hammer or pincers."

"The smithy," Margit said.

"It'll take time. Your cousin will suspect something's amiss."

The fear of failure punched Margit's stomach. "Captain," she ordered Dóczi, "get those tools and free my husband."

"Yes, my lady," he obliged and departed in a hurry.

Margit flung her arms around Endre's neck and crushed her lips against his. "Márton will try to escape through the secret tunnel. I must stop him."

"Margit, no!" Endre pleaded as she pulled away.

In wild desperation, he moved towards her, yanking at his chains; but the unyielding bonds restrained him.

"Don't worry, husband. Adnan will help me."

"Margit! Margit!"

Endre's cries faded away as she dashed out of the dungeon and stepped into the courtyard.

The glaring sunshine jarred her and brought a sting to her eyes and nose. As her vision cleared, scenes of chaos unfolded before her: castle guards rushed about, shouting and scrambling to take their posts.

Her regained freedom and thirst for retribution propelled Margit forward. Through groups of soldiers, she jostled and elbowed her way to the smithy just as Dóczi came out with the necessary tools.

Adnan jumped up from his stool, relief flooding his face. "Margit! You're free. God is great!"

"I need weapons! Now!"

He pointed at a counter.

She grabbed a sword, strapped a knife to her right leg and placed an open-face helmet on her head. "Come with me. Time for revenge, at last."

Heart racing, she ran to meet her destiny.

An eerie silence hung about the unguarded keep. Margit and Adnan barged in, blades at the ready, and slammed the heavy door shut.

"Secure the door to the great hall," she ordered him.

"What the devil is going on?" Her cousin's voice came from the floor above. He stood on the wide step at the turn of the staircase with Balog by his side, both with their swords bared.

Márton's face hardened as soon as he saw her. "Dóczi was meant to deliver you in chains."

"Well, he's not on your side anymore."

Both hands clenched around the handle of her sword, Margit assumed a fighting stance. Let him come. She was ready.

But instead of Márton, Balog attacked her first.

"I'll take him," Adnan said, drawing the castellan away.

Her cousin had not moved but simply watched from above.

No time to waste. She must capture him now, or else...

With sure strides, Margit charged up the stairs until she came to the step below him. "Give yourself up, cousin. The voivode's army is outside."

"I know I am a dead man." The wicked glint had returned to his eyes. "But I shall take you with me. Since you rejected my proposition, I shall never let you have Szentimre."

Holding the weapon with steady hands, she took the final stride onto the wide step. "I *do not* intend to die today, cousin."

Márton withdrew momentarily and then lunged at her.

Raising her sword just in time, Margit parried his hit, but its force made her stagger backwards.

Steel rang out as blades crossed in a deadly clash. Crippled left hand notwithstanding, her cousin displayed impressive fighting skills. Margit continued to block and evade his strikes. But little by little, she was driven back towards the edge, her heels barely balancing above the lower flight of stairs. One wrong move, one slip, meant a bone-shattering plunge.

Damn these steps! How did I end up so cornered?

Her mind raced, seeking a solution while blows rained down. One foot braced on the lower step, then the other, she retreated carefully.

Halfway down, Márton suddenly kicked out instead.

Agony exploded in Margit's stomach as his boot connected with brutal force and drove the air from her lungs. In a blinding flash, the sword fell from her numb fingers, and the world spun wildly as she tumbled down the unforgiving steps. Each one struck like a hammer blow, wrenching another ragged gasp through her shattered ribs.

At the bottom of the staircase, she scrambled to crawl away through shrieking pain, elbows scraping against the floor.

A feral snarl rent the air and sent fresh terror through her veins. Teeth bared in a madman's rabid hiss and eyes ablaze like hellfire, he launched at her.

Is it truly going to end like this?

With a desperate cry, Margit summoned the last shreds of her strength and kicked hard against his knee just as his flashing blade descended with murderous intent.

He howled and fell onto his back. His blade clanged away across the flagstones.

Vision blurring against the pain, Margit pushed herself up on all fours, crawled over and straddled his chest, knife to his throat. Her pulse roared. The moment she craved since childhood had arrived. Vengeance was now within her grasp.

Then the world fell away. Time stopped. Even her breathing stopped. It was just the two of them, suspended in space. Her eyes narrowed, fixed on Márton's face. His arrogance had melted, his evil grin vanished, his ruddy colour faded, leaving only naked fear in their wake. Her blade nicked his skin, and a scarlet thread trickled free.

In her mind's eye, the vengeful scene played out: the wet pop of steel through flesh, the hot gush of arteries, the gruesome gurgling… One push would end him. So simple.

But what would that make her? The same as him: a ruthless murderer, a damned soul. How would she live on with that burden upon her conscience? This was not justice, but rage. She would not sacrifice her soul, no matter how vile the foe. Some battles could only be lost to win the war within.

Brought back into herself, she noticed Márton's shut, trembling eyes. Sweat trickled down his face. Or were they tears? "Will you surrender?"

"Yes! Yes!" he rasped.

Margit's chest heaved with relief. She moved the knife from his throat.

But then, the blade clattered away as she rolled off him. The metallic sound of her helmet hitting the floor shrieked through her ears. Reality spun sickeningly.

Now Margit lay pinned beneath Márton astride her stomach, his legs pressing hard into her sides. She screamed for air against the crushing agony. Only one desperate thought filled her mind. "Father!"

"Oh yes, you will see him soon," Márton sneered. He increased the pressure against her ribcage while his good hand locked around her throat, cutting off her breath.

Weak and squirming, Margit had only moments before oblivion, and then death, claimed her. Frantically, she fumbled outwards. Her hand closed around a familiar object.

With every last scrap of her might, she thrust the knife through Márton's gambeson and into his flesh. He screamed as she ripped the knife back out, warm blood spilling over her hand.

Snarling, she plunged it in once more.

With a howl, he tumbled away and collapsed by her side.

Relief flooded Margit as the choking pressure instantly ceased, and the searing pain in her ribs subsided.

A crashing sound came from the distance. Running footsteps rang out; and then the sickening crunch of a foot blow against flesh and bone.

Through a watery veil of tears, Margit discerned a tall figure above her.

"*Szívem*? Talk to me!"

My dear husband.

Endre was on his knees, leaning over her; one hand on her shoulder, the other cupping the side of her face.

Her throat raw as if she had swallowed nails, Margit croaked the only question on her mind, "Is he dead?"

But oblivion claimed her before she could comprehend the answer.

***

The light breeze caressed Margit's face. When she opened her eyes, she found herself in a strange place. A chamber unknown and yet so familiar. Daylight spilled through the open door of an outside terrace.

She had been there before. Yes... It was where Anna languished as Márton's prisoner. Only that now it was clean, bright and airy. The same room where her mother died giving birth to her, a score and one year earlier. Her life had come full circle.

Whispers drew her attention to the two men sitting by her side: the two men she loved most in the world.

Endre leaned over and kissed her on the forehead while Adnan held her hand tightly. A smile of relief shone on their faces.

"What happened?" She could barely hear her own faint voice. The burning pain in her ribs returned, and every breath hurt.

"Dóczi went to meet the voivode's men," Endre spoke first. "He was amazed at what he saw. Armed with mere tools, scores of miners, farmers and labourers stood beside the soldiers, chanting your name. The town gate was open. The people of Szentimre lined the streets, cheering at Bátori's men. Márton's guards and mercenaries did not resist."

"Was Bátori with them?"

"No, but he had given his men orders to protect you. They told me the king's letter was misplaced during the change of voivode, and it never reached him."

Margit smiled. Even with a long delay, her relative had honoured his promise.

Her neck creaked as she turned to Adnan. "And you? Your arm is bandaged. Were you hurt?"

"Oh, only a scratch. I lost a bit of blood, but no harm done. I won't say the same about Balog."

"Did you kill him?"

"For a garrison commander, he's a lousy fighter. I beat him to within an inch of his life. But he'll live, and he'll pay for his sins. The soldiers arrested him."

"And Márton?"

Endre exchanged a glance with Adnan and then lowered his

head. "He survived."

Margit closed her eyes as the terrifying moments came back to mind. "Oh, Endre, I couldn't kill him. Despite everything, I couldn't do it. I hate myself for showing weakness."

"You are not weak, *szívem*. Quite the opposite. It's easy to kill someone you hate. Sparing their life shows one is a better person."

Her entire body trembled. "And then he pushed me to the floor and tried to strangle me. Oh, I thought I would die." Her voice cracked. "I cried out for my father. This strange urge for action overtook me. It was as if he heard me and guided my hand to find the knife. The next thing I remember is someone standing over me. Was it you?"

"Yes. I admit I was tempted to take Márton's head, but I kicked him in the face instead and let Bátori's men arrest him. If he is not executed for what he did, I'm sure he will rot in some damp dungeon, contemplating his horrible deeds. You are safe now, *szívem*. He will not hurt you anymore."

Margit let out a prolonged sigh. At last, she would have peace.

"We shall let you rest," Endre said and departed with Adnan.

Not long after, the figure of a woman appeared by the terrace door. Her loose blonde hair and blue velvet gown adorned with golden embroidery flowed in the breeze.

Comforting warmth flooded Margit's body. Was this a dream, or was she awake?

Mama!

A loving smile graced the woman's face. And spreading her arms, she transformed into a dove of the purest white and flew away.

38
A Funeral Long Overdue

Late August 1479

Fewer than a dozen souls sat in the castle chapel that morning, a month later. Margit walked towards the altar, leaning on her husband's arm. Pain still racked her body and grief burdened her heart. But the task she had to perform that day was long overdue.

Her father never had a proper funeral. After barely managing to save his body from being thrown to the wolves by Márton, Anna had it placed in a simple wooden coffin in the family crypt. There had been no service. No one mourned him, except for the woman who, ironically, had brought about his demise.

As soon as Margit felt a little better, she and Endre had gone to the crypt to make sure her father's body was still there, and that Anna had not lied. But when Endre lifted the coffin lid, a gigantic, stomach-twirling wave overwhelmed Margit.

Her father, a strong and fine-looking man full of life, his eyes shining whenever he beheld his little daughter—that was the image she wished to seal forever in her mind.

Margit dared not look. Averting her eyes, she only asked in a shaky voice, "Is it he?"

Endre took a long time to reply. "I think so. These are the remains of a tall man with red hair."

Even Endre, who always kept a cool head, seemed forlorn.

When he put the lid back in its place, sorrow shadowed his face. Did he, perhaps, think of his own dead father?

"I'm sorry for asking you to do this," she mumbled.

He did not respond, just took her by the arm and helped her climb the steps back to the chapel.

Those painful moments flashed before Margit's eyes as she stood in front of the people who had gathered to attend the funeral: Erzsi, Adnan, Ahmed, Ilona, Dragoslava, old Mária, Gábor, Béla Havasi and Captain Dóczi. Although the people of Szentimre wanted to be there in their numbers, Margit had not invited anyone else. As grateful as she was to all who had helped her, she only wished to share this poignant occasion with those closest to her.

After a deep breath, she nodded to Endre. He moved a step away and bowed his head as she started to speak.

"I was not fortunate to know my mother, and I remember little of my father. Over the years, I heard so much about him. I know that he was not perfect; yet to many people, he was a hero. To me, he was just my dear father. He loved me and protected me, and I owe him my life. Seventeen years ago, a terrible injustice was committed against him, and he was snatched from this world too soon. Together with those who supported me in this journey, I fought hard for a long time to clear his name and honour his memory so that he can finally rest in peace beside his beloved wife and son."

When Margit finished her speech, a respectful silence filled the chapel.

Looking at each one of her friends, Margit saw the affection on Adnan's face, the respect on Ahmed's, the admiration on Ilona's and Gábor's, the bittersweet smile on Dragoslava's, the pride in Erzsi's eyes. She had grown up without her parents, but now these people had become her family, and they held a special place in her heart.

***

"Ah, here you are!" Endre said. "I have been looking for you."

Sitting under a pine tree at the edge of the forest and looking into the distance, Margit did not acknowledge him at first. But as soon as he sat by her side, she rested her head on his shoulder.

"You have taken your revenge, and you have just sent your father to his last resting place. Yet you are still in a man's clothes," he remarked with a hint of bitterness. "I don't remember when I last saw you in a gown."

She smiled. "It's so strange. I have spent many years pretending to be a man, and now I don't know how to live as a woman. And all this inheritance of mine. How shall I manage it? I'm scared."

"That makes two of us."

Margit sat up straight and looked at him askance. "I don't believe you. You are always so calm and wise. You know everything about anything."

"Don't fret. You will learn too."

Margit turned from him and remained silent awhile. Her thoughts mingled with admiring the view of Szentimre from above. Hard to believe that such a peaceful place had been the scene of so much pain and heartbreak. But that was all in the past.

The future was in her hands now.

"I need to visit the other two estates," Endre said. "I am concerned about the one in Szeben. Rumour has it that a Turkish attack is imminent on the Saxon lands. I don't know how much of it is true, but Bátori has been gathering troops."

Like a needle, worry prickled her heart. "Don't tell me you are going to war again. You are a landlord now, for the love of God! You don't need the mercenary's wages."

"I shall fight if I am needed. I must protect my homeland."

Heart in her throat, Margit reached for his hand. "I understand you will defend our home if we are attacked; but please promise me that you will resign from your army commission and your obligations as an officer."

"Very well, I shall," Endre said with a sigh. He, too, sat up straight. "Do I have a choice? If I don't do as you order, you will kick me in the balls like you used to."

Margit's cheeks heated in an instant. "I never kicked you in the balls! Only in the knee."

39
The Mystery Knight

13 October 1479

It was not yet dawn when shouts and banging on her chamber door awakened Margit. She sprang upright, covered in sweat. Her heart raced like a galloping horse.

She stretched her hand over the other side of the bed. Empty. It had been so for many weeks. Away in Szeben, Endre was organising the defence of their other estate. Unfortunately for the people of Transylvania, the rumours about a Turkish attack had proven true.

More banging. "My lady! Rise! Messenger!"

Messenger at this hour? Was Endre in danger?

Bare-footed, Margit jumped out of bed and stumbled to the door, her chemise clutched in her hands.

The man she came face-to-face with was panting as he shoved a letter into her hand. "From your lord husband. Urgent." With that, he departed like a gust of wind.

Adnan and Ilona rushed to her from the other side of the corridor. Adnan handed her his candle. "What's amiss?"

"The Turks and the Wallachians of Basarab the Younger have attacked the Saxon lands." Margit gulped back her fears. *"Battle is imminent in the area of Kenyérmező. Send as many men as you can afford. The situation is critical."*

She raised her head after reading the message aloud. "I can see

Endre's hand was shaking when he wrote it." She looked at Adnan's concerned face. "Tell Bocskai to gather all the soldiers bar fifteen guards, who must stay here to protect the estate."

"Of course."

As he turned around to leave, Margit thrust the candle at Ilona and rushed after him. "I shall lead them."

Adnan stopped in his tracks. "What?"

"I must help my husband. He's in great peril."

Behind her, Ilona gasped.

"You wish to go to battle?" Adnan said and switched to the Serbian language. "Are you out of your mind?"

"Don't you dare try to stop me!"

Adnan shook his head. "Very well. I'll go with you then."

"No, you must stay here and look after the defence of the estate."

"Dóczi can do that. Besides, you give me no choice. I must go because if anything happens to you, Endre will kill me."

***

Many hours later, when Kenyérmező came into view, the battle already raged with savage intensity.

The plain by the Maros river swarmed with soldiers and horses. Banners, tabards and armour flashed as the opposing armies crashed against each other like waves breaking upon rock.

The screams of men and beasts melded with the jarring cacophony of steel while arrows rained through the smoke-choked air. The stench of burning wood, spilled blood and animal droppings assaulted Margit's senses. And as fog, smoke and dust obscured the sun, the lurking shadow of Death descended to claim his tithe of flesh and blood—of human sacrifice.

Margit reined Csillag in to survey the field. The Serbian light cavalry—allies of the voivode—on the left flank had all but collapsed. The agile Akinjis and pike-wielding Wallachian foot soldiers were pushing the riders towards the middle section. In the centre stood Bátori and his troops. His men had advanced too far and ended up engulfed by the enemy.

"Where are our soldiers?" Adnan's shout raised concern in Margit's heart.

Squinting, she spotted the banner of Szentimre only a stone's throw from the voivode's forces. "There! Let's go!" She drew her sabre.

Margit and Adnan fought their way through a mass of soldiers, friends and enemies alike. But when she got closer, she still could not find Endre.

Where in the world is he?

She gestured to commander Bocskai and the reinforcements she had brought to join the rest of the Szentimre men.

"Look!" Adnan shouted. "Bátori's in trouble!"

Violently unhorsed, the voivode was struggling to stay on his feet and fight off the blows of a dozen enemies who had surrounded him. Presently, a knight in full plate black armour jumped off his mount and rushed to Bátori's side. Wielding a mighty longsword with both hands and moving like a whirlwind, he kept the Turks at bay albeit temporarily.

Margit's chest convulsed. She had no doubt. He was her saviour, her mystery knight. Settled in her new life, she had forgotten about him. But here he was again, as dazzling as before, but now in mortal danger.

Time to return the favour.

Bátori and the knight were isolated. Dead bodies lay around them while more and more Ottomans rushed at them like a tidal wave. The voivode took a hit on his leg and faltered. His companion also staggered under the pressure of fighting too many men simultaneously.

Driven by a strange, uncontrollable force, Margit re-sheathed the sabre and, heels dug into Csillag's sides, she urged him to a gallop towards the two lone figures. She dropped the reins and prepared the bow.

One, two, three, four... The arrows flew and hit their targets with precision.

Beside her, Adnan did the same.

The enemy onslaught stalled. The brief pause gave just enough time for more Hungarian soldiers to come to the two men's assistance.

Margit continued to loose until she ran out of arrows. But by now, she was already beside the kneeling voivode.

She leapt off her horse, pulled him up and dragged him away from the melee.

Recognition flickered in Bátori's bloodshot eyes. "What are you doing here?"

"Looking for my husband. Have you seen him?"

"There."

"Where?" Her eyes desperately searched around.

"In the black armour."

Margit's knees almost went from under her. "What? He can't

be."

The knight turned back and lifted the visor of his sallet. His face twisted. "Margit! Go home!"

"Endre?" she gasped.

The stranger she had so long dreamed of and desired was her husband? How was this possible?

"Watch out!" Adnan's scream jolted her back to reality just as a Wallachian soldier lunged at her with a bloodied sword. With an instinctive move, she sidestepped and evaded the hit. At the same time, her friend jumped behind the enemy and pierced him through.

Endre's face flushed. "Leave! Now! This is no place for you. You will die."

"Too late."

Endre cursed—the first time Margit had heard him do so.

"Where the devil is Kinizsi?" Bátori bellowed behind them.

"Sir, we just passed him on our way here. He should arrive at the far side of the battlefield soon," Margit replied.

"Damn!" the voivode groaned, clutching his wounded leg.

A fresh wave of enemies surged towards them. But the Hungarian response was immediate. A score of men formed a shield with their armoured bodies to protect the voivode. An ever-growing pile of the dead stood as the only barrier between the two sides. Arrows and bolts were flying in all directions.

"Go find Kinizsi and tell him to hurry!" Endre shouted to Adnan. "We can't hold them any longer."

Margit handed Csillag's reins to her friend. "Take him with you. Make sure he's safe."

Endre placed Bátori's arm around his own shoulder. "You must leave the fight, my lord. You are in danger."

But the voivode valiantly refused. He would never give up the fight. He steadied himself and pushed Endre away.

"I can't abandon him," Endre said to Margit. "Not after what he did for us. But you must go now. Your last chance."

Margit shook her head. "No! This is my homeland too. And as you wife, I shall forever stand by your side."

He had told her the same words when she was about to give herself up to her cousin's men at Szentimre. If he stood by her then, she was going to do the same for him now. No chance she would desert him. "I shall stay."

Endre shook his head. "Very well. If this is what is meant for us, let us kill as many heathens as we can." He unhooked the *Morgenstern* from his belt and handed it to her. "Use this. Better than your sabre."

Margit clenched her fingers around the weapon's haft. "I'm ready."

Endre grasped her wrist and squeezed it. She turned around. Their eyes met for a heartbeat, but it felt like a lifetime.

"I love you." His tender whisper reached her ears despite the clamour of battle.

Her chest heaved. He had said that many times before. But for some strange reason, at that precise moment, the tone of his voice carried all the immeasurable pain of saying farewell.

Tears stole to Margit's eyes. "I love you too... Forever." The first time she had uttered these words. But now she meant them with all her heart.

She blinked to clear her vision and crossed herself.

Dear God, let us survive this day. I promise that hereafter I shall live in peace, dedicating my life to my husband and to the good of my people.

Unlike her previous battles, where she fought pretending to be someone else, she entered this one as her true self—as a woman. And while she once did it for coin or because she was pressed, this time she was about to charge into the fray wholeheartedly to defend her homeland.

Bátori screamed at his men to advance. He raised his sword and, despite his wounds, threw himself at the wall of enemy soldiers. Endre pulled the visor shut and moved right next to him. Margit followed, only a step behind.

The chill of the night barely affected Margit. The sweetness of victory, thanks to Lord Kinizsi's timely intervention, warmed her and those around her as they celebrated together: Hungarian, Serbian, Wallachian, Saxon, Székely, commanders, noblemen, knights, ordinary soldiers and peasants. They had lit fires all over the battlefield and were eating, drinking, singing and dancing. Although their own dead had been buried, the bodies of their enemies still lay around. A gruesome spectacle. But in such turbulent times, death was part of everyday reality. Short and precious, life had to be lived and cherished at every opportunity. No one knew what the next day would bring.

Sitting by the fire and with Csillag nuzzling her shoulder, Margit watched Endre and Adnan. Careful with their drinking, the two men remained sober, still discussing the battle. Their friendly —nay, brotherly—chat made her smile. Whether for her sake or simply because Adnan loved another woman now, Endre had finally made peace with him.

Margit took several swigs from the wineskin. It numbed the pain of her injuries and lifted her spirits. It transported her to a place of joy, where she could gaze the harsh world in a different light; where she could feel proud of defending her land and continuing her warrior bloodline.

The squeeze of someone's hand on her arm awakened the soreness. Kinizsi's firm grasp hauled her to her feet.

"Lord Bátori has been praising you all night," he said, slurring his words. "I think the old fool is in love with you."

He dragged her to the spot where all the commanders and high-ranking noblemen were sitting, including a heavily bandaged Bátori.

"We have a lady soldier here," Kinizsi announced. "Her father fought with János Hunyadi and Mihály Szilágyi in Varna and Nándorfehérvár, and she thinks she can match his bravery."

Margit's response was fuelled by pride and the effects of wine. "And I fought with King Mátyás in Szabács, and with István Bátori and Pál Kinizsi in Kenyérmező!"

The men cheered and drank to her health.

"You're a true daughter of this land," Kinizsi said and raised his hand towards the sky. "Your father watches you proudly from above."

Margit's heart brimmed with an unusual combination of sadness and joy.

How strange life is! The one time I fought as a woman, they have, at last, accepted me as one of their own.

"Will you be my wife?" a nobleman shouted, making Margit's cheeks heat with embarrassment.

"The lady already has a husband," Endre interfered as he stepped beside her. "Me!"

"I envy you, sir!" the same man jested, and they all burst into roaring laughter.

Endre led Margit away by the hand. "Pay no heed to them. They are drunk."

"Oh, cheer up, will you? You are always so serious."

She wrested herself free, threw her arms around his neck and planted her lips on his.

Endre responded with fervour but then pulled back. "Have you no shame, wife? There are people around." Despite his reprimanding words, the tone of amusement in his voice put her mind at ease.

She laughed and whispered in his ear, "I know you are my mystery knight."

His eyebrows shot up. "Oh, you finally uncovered my secret."

"Why did you do this?"

Endre assumed a serious tone. "To punish you for treating me like a pitiful boy and never showing me true love. I created the mysterious knight to stir your feelings and make you see me as a real man—even though you didn't know I was that man."

"A well-deserved punishment indeed," Margit admitted, mirth and self-reproach filling her chest. "But why did you not tell me?"

"I didn't need to. You gave me what I wished for: your unbridled passion."

Her face flushed. "Oh!"

Embarrassment aside, she had more questions. "Where did you hide this fine armour? And what happened to your fierce black courser?"

"The harness I kept in the armoury after we moved to Sasfészek. As for Sárkány, my beautiful horse and battle companion, he died in the Austrian campaign two years ago. His loss caused me great sadness."

Margit nodded pensively. "Yes, I can understand."

She moved away from Endre and sat on the ground.

He sat beside her.

Gazing at the starry sky, Margit let out a deep sigh. "My dear father has always watched over me. For he knew from the moment he chose you as my husband that you would always protect me."

Endre drew her towards him until she rested her head on his shoulder.

"You saved my life," she continued, "and I'm so grateful. But you also let me make a fool of myself."

"Do you refer to the time when you wanted us to make love in a barn? I should have been insulted to hear that my wife desired a stranger. But the truth is, I felt weak at the knees when you said you loved your husband with all your heart."

"You, rascal!" She raised her hand, but he stopped her mid-air.

"Calm yourself, *szívem*! I shall make it right by you. There is a village nigh, and I'm sure we shall find a barn somewhere. What do you say? I can cover my face too if you wish?"

Excitement warmed Margit's cheeks. "Yes! We must go now." She sprang up, grabbed his hand and pulled him to his feet. "There is no better time to conceive a child."

40
A New Life

Mid-May 1480

On the terrace outside her bedchamber, Margit breathed in the fragrant mountain air. Below the castle hill, the town of Szentimre buzzed in the balmy early evening as people in the streets and main square savoured the last of the day's sunshine. Farther ahead, beyond the walls, the farmers and labourers had finished their hard work for the day and were returning to their homes.

Such peace and beauty!

Margit flicked aside the strands of hair that the breeze kept blowing into her eyes. Although long hair was something she had grown accustomed to by now, the floor-length clothes still bothered her. So awkward and heavy. Would she ever get used to her new life as the lady of Szentimre?

Smiling, she smoothed out her green silk gown over her round belly. Only a couple of months left until this little one came into the world. A gentle, warm wave of happiness enveloped her heart.

The shadows had grown longer in the twilight when the clopping of horses' hooves approached. Margit leaned over the parapet wall to catch a glimpse of her husband and Adnan arriving in the courtyard.

It was not too long before Endre stepped onto the terrace. He stood behind her and put his arms around her shoulders.

His stubble scratched her cheek, raising a much-missed tingle on her skin. So good to feel his body again and take in his comforting presence. "How did it go, husband?"

"The king will not give us the mine back. But he has entrusted us with its management. And as a reward, we can have fifteen percent of the production and sell it to anyone and at any price we wish."

"Great news!"

As she turned around, Endre surprised her with the most passionate kiss. "I have missed you," he said softly. "Both of you." He pressed his hand on her belly, perhaps hoping to feel the baby kick. But nothing happened.

Margit thought her heart was about to melt. She could not have wished for a more loving husband. "Your son is probably asleep."

"She could be a daughter."

"Trust me, you do not wish to have a daughter. Would you be able to handle another one like me?"

He chuckled. "You are right. One mad redhead is enough."

Margit ran her fingers through his hair, her eyes diving into his. "You know, there is Magyar, Székely and Saxon blood on my father's side; my mother was half-Polish; and you are half-Serbian. Do you think all this will make our child exceptional?"

"Our child will be exceptional simply because it is ours."

Another embrace. Another kiss. Their love was endless.

But then Endre pulled back and touched his forehead. "Oh, I almost forgot. István Bátori is coming for a visit tomorrow. He said you promised him a banquet."

"Tomorrow?" Heat rushed to Margit's face. "How am I to prepare everything at such short notice?"

"You have that wonderful housekeeper of yours. She will take care of it."

"Ilona? She's great, but she can be a little tyrant sometimes. The servants fear her."

"Can you blame her? She has a tough mistress. If she doesn't do things right, she will get an arrow on her behind."

"I don't shoot people anymore."

Margit raised her hand to give him a friendly slap like in the old times, but she hesitated. Endre seized the opportunity, got hold of her arm and twisted it behind her back. "Out of all the women in the world, I got the wildest one."

"You mean the *best* one!" With a swift movement, she spun around and freed herself from his grip.

Endre drew her back into his arms and kissed her on the cheek. "I shall take my supper now. I'm so hungry."

Margit turned to follow him, but movement in the corner of her eye made her stop.

With a high-pitched cry, a majestic male golden eagle swooped down from the mountains, swift as an arrow. And as he perched on the parapet wall, his unwavering, penetrating gaze met Margit's.

An otherworldly but loving feeling warmed her soul as if a familiar spirit had come home to rest. The eagle had returned to his nest—his *Eyrie*.

Tears flooded Margit's eyes. She placed her hand on her chest.

Father! You are home again. You still live in my heart.

After he surveyed his beautiful and beloved land for a few moments, the eagle spread his wings and, like another mythical *Turul* bird, soared into the fiery sky.

THE END

The Szilágyi of Szentimre (fictional) coat of arms.
Illustration by Sigrid Whelan. A variation on the 15th century
Szilágyi of Horogszeg family crest, adapted to suit the origins of
this novel's fictional family. The sun and crescent moon added to
this coat of arms are the symbols of the Székely people.

ACKNOWLEDGEMENTS AND THANKS

I would like to thank the following people who helped me on my writing journey:

My partner, Stephen Dunne, for his love and constant support.

My brother, George Vavoulidis, for reading the very first draft of my novel and encouraging me to continue.

Autumn Bardot, Edward Willis, Emily Cotton, Nicolette Croft, Gregory May and Kenn Allen for providing feedback on the opening chapters.

My alpha and beta readers for their valuable comments: Maria Avramidou, Yvonne Albericci, Elysée Yhuel, Anna Engels, Sherry Vernick Ostroff, Rebecca Mogollón, Róbert Bordás and Gábor Szántai.

Tarah Threadgill and Mark Andrew for the developmental editing.

Mark Andrew for the line editing.

Kathryn Helstrom for the copy editing.

Sigrid Whelan for the illustration of my protagonist's family coat of arms.

Paddy Shaw for the illustration and border patterns on the front cover.

Dee Marley of White Rabbit Arts/Historium Press for designing the front and back cover, interior formatting, and for publication assistance.

AUTHOR NOTES

Return to the Eyrie is the sequel to *Lord of the Eyrie*, which was published in January/February 2022 by Historium Press. If you liked this novel, please consider checking out *Lord of the Eyrie* as well to read the story of Margit's parents.

The main characters in this novel are fictional, but the historical, political, social and cultural background is real. Historical events—such as battles—have been altered to allow the participation of these fictional characters in them.

The dialogues of real historical figures and their interactions with the fictional characters are the product of my imagination. However, they are based on research of primary and secondary sources, and as such, they are not impossible or out of character.

Some liberties were taken with elements of the historical background for the benefit of the narrative. For example:

1. Adnan's infiltration of Szabács as a spy has been inspired by a detail from the poem *Szabács Viadala*, where an Ottoman soldier opens the gate of the fortress to the king's army after remembering he is Hungarian in origin. The fortress most likely fell as a result of direct assault after weeks of bombardment weakened the defences.
2. Although Muslims lived in the kingdom of Hungary until the late 13th century, they were assimilated over the following period. For this reason, I have used a plausible excuse for the Belgrade authorities to allow Ahmed and Adnan to keep their religion.
3. Apart from some general information on István Bátori's and Vlad the Impaler's campaigns in Moldavia and Wallachia in the autumn of 1476, I was only able to find very limited details. Therefore, the skirmishes and battles Margit participates in (chapters 21 to 23) were the product of my imagination.

4. In primary and secondary sources, there are two different versions of how Pál Kinizsi saved the day in the battle of Kenyérmező (chapter 39): one has him coming late to the battle and attacking the Ottomans from the rear; the other has him already present at a different part of the battlefield, holding his position against another section of the Ottoman army and only interfering when Bátori's forces were in mortal danger. I have used the first version.

In the Appendices, I have listed a selected bibliography of the primary and secondary sources that I used in my research.

HISTORICAL BACKGROUND

Much larger in size than the modern-day country, fifteenth-century Hungary extended from Southern Poland to Belgrade and from Croatia to Central Romania. By the middle of the century, neighbouring countries—which served as 'buffer zones' between the expanding Ottoman Empire and the kingdom of Hungary—had become 'vassals' of the Sultan, and the two countries ended up sharing a border. During that period, the previous raiding and plundering expeditions of the Ottomans developed into larger-scale invasions of Hungarian territory. The southern frontier (Croatia, Slavonia, Southern Transylvania and the parts of Serbia which were still under Hungarian control) was frequently attacked, and its defences were tested to their limits.

Transylvania in the 15th century

Fifteenth-century Transylvania was a semi-autonomous, multi-ethnic province, which comprised Hungarians, Wallachians, Saxons, Székelys, Slavs and other ethnic groups. Transylvania was ruled by a Voivode (military governor), who also held the title of Count of the Székelys. After an unsuccessful peasant rebellion in 1437 against increased taxation and the monetary policy of the government, the three 'privileged' classes of Transylvania signed an agreement to support each other against any future resistance. These were called the 'three nations' of the province, and they were:

1. The Saxons: people from various German territories who migrated to Southern Transylvania from the 12th century onwards, originally as border guards. Later on, more immigrants arrived, who held a variety of occupations, such as mining experts, merchants and craftsmen. Their population expanded quickly, and their areas became known as the *Siebenbürgen* ('Seven Fortresses'—which also became the German name for Transylvania in general) This name possibly derived from the fact that there were seven

major German towns in Transylvania.

2. The Székely people (pronounced Seh-ke-y): a Hungarian-speaking ethnic group living mainly in the 'Székely Lands' of Eastern Transylvania. They served as border guards and soldiers in the medieval kingdom of Hungary, and their main occupation was agriculture and animal husbandry. They lived in communities of various sizes, where the land was held and cultivated in common. Although they were not nobility, they were exempt from taxes in return for military service. Theories about their origin vary from the ones claiming they are descendants of Attila's Huns to those (more likely ones) stating they are early Hungarians who settled in the Carpathian Basin before the 'Conquest', i.e., the arrival of the Magyars in the Carpathian basin at the end of the 9th century AD.

3. The remaining lands of Transylvania belonged to the nobility, who were predominantly of Hungarian (Magyar) origin. In addition, a number of Wallachian (Romanian), Moldavian and Southern Slavic families who had become 'magyarised' and Catholic, were granted lands by the king for their military service and joined the ranks of the nobility.

Wallachia and Moldavia in the 15th century

A part of modern-day Romania, Wallachia was in constant internal conflict during the fifteenth century, changing allegiance between the Kingdom of Hungary and the Ottoman Empire. Princes from rival clans (the Dăneşti and Drăculeşti—both lines of the House of Basarab) fought each other for the principality's throne, sometimes aligning themselves with Hungary and sometimes paying tribute to the Sultan. It was not uncommon to see Wallachian armies fight on two different sides in battles between Hungary and the Ottoman Empire.

Medieval Moldavia occupied territories which are now split between modern-day Romania and the Republic of Moldova. Prince Stefan the Great was its most famous and most heroic leader during the late fifteenth century. Moldova also frequently switched allegiance between Hungary, the Ottoman Empire and the Kingdom of Poland. For example, during his early reign Stefan fought against King Mátyás (eg. in the battle of Baia, 1467) but later allied with him to expel the Ottomans from Moldavia (1476)

APPENDICES

1. Glossary of Terms

Akinji (Turk. akıncı): irregular light horseman of the Ottoman army. Akinjis mostly came from Anatolia and operated as raiders on the frontiers of the Ottoman empire and as skirmish units during battles. Their main weapons were bows and arrows, but they also used spears, swords and battle axes

Brigandine: a form of medieval body armour, made of overlapping small steel plates riveted to an exterior covering of canvas, heavy cloth or leather

Janissaries (Turk. yeniçeri): the elite infantry of the Ottoman army. Mostly made up of boys from the conquered lands who were enslaved and converted to Islam, the Janissaries underwent strict training and became the first modern professional standing army in Europe

Misericorde: a long, narrow dagger used to deliver a mercy stroke to a fatally wounded opponent in battle

Morgenstern (Germ. Morning Star): a mace-like weapon consisting of a wooden haft with an attached spiked ball usually made of steel or iron

Pavise: a large oblong shield usually covering the entire body, used by infantry and archers. Many pavises were brightly painted with the arms of the soldiers' units or the crests of their lords. The name comes from the Italian city of Pavia, where these shields were originally made

Sallet: a light 15th century helmet with a movable visor and an outward curve extending over the back of the neck. It was favoured by knights and infantry soldiers alike. Archers' sallets did not have a visor

Southern Country (Hung. Délvidék): the southern parts of the medieval Kingdom of Hungary, comprising areas which today mostly belong to Croatia, Serbia and Romania, with only small parts within modern-day Hungary itself

Turul: a mythological bird of prey (possibly a type of falcon) appearing in old Hungarian and Turkic tradition. It is one of the national symbols of Hungary

Voivode (Hung. Vajda): military governor. The Voivode of Transylvania was the fourth most powerful man in the medieval Kingdom of Hungary

Wondrous Stag (Hung. Csodaszarvas): a legendary stag in Hungarian mythology, hunted by the brothers Hunor and Magor— the mythical ancestors of the Huns and the Magyars. The hunt led the two heroes to a new land, which they made their home. The legend was used by medieval chroniclers to promote the idea of a common origin between Huns and Magyars

2. English translation of the Hungarian names in the story (approximate pronunciation in brackets)

In the novel, I have used the 'western' order of names for the convenience of English-speaking readers. In Hungarian, the order is the reverse: the family name precedes the first name.

First Names

Margit (Mawr-git, *a* like in call, *g* like in get) = Margaret
Endre (End-re) = Andrew
Imre (Im-re, *i* like in sit and *e* like in get) = possibly the Hungarian equivalent of the German name Emmerich / sometimes translated as Henry in English
Erzsi (Er-zhi, *zs* like the *s* in leisure) = Lizzie - full name **Erzsébet** (Er-zheh-bet) = Elizabeth
Márton (Mar-ton, á like in father) = Martin
Mátyás (Ma-tyash, *ty* like in courtyard) = Matthias
Ilona (I-lo-naw, *i* like in sit) = Helen
Gábor (Ga-bor) = Gabriel
Béla (Beh-law) – no English equivalent
Ágnes (Ag-nesh) = Agnes
Károly (Ka-roy) = Charles
Ferenc (Fe-rents) = Francis
Pál (Pal) = Paul
Péter (Peh-ter) = Peter
Mária (Ma-riaw) = Mary
István (Isht-van) = Stephen
Sándor (Shan-dor) = Alexander
Miklós (Mik-lowsh) = Nicholas

Family Names

Szilágyi (Si-la-dyi, *gy* like the *dy* in woodyard)
Bátori (Ba-to-ri)
Gerendi (Ge-ren-di)
Dóczi (Dow-tsi)
Balog (Baw-log)
Kovács (Ko-vatch)
Kinizsi (Ki-ni-zhi, *i* like in sit and *zh* like the *s* in leisure)
Havasi (Haw-vaw-shi)
Bakó (Baw-kow)

Place names

Fictional:
Sasfészek (Shawsh-feh-sek) = Eyrie
Szentimre (Sent-im-re) = Saint Imre

Real:
Banat of Temes: a county in the medieval Kingdom of Hungary—the area around modern-day Timişoara in Romania

Brassó: a major Saxon town in medieval Transylvania—modern-day Braşov in Romania

Hunyadvár: a town in Transylvania with a magnificent fortress built by King Mátyás' father, János Hunyadi (a powerful 15th century warlord, voivode of Transylvania and later governor of Hungary)—modern-day Hunedoara in Romania

Kenyérmező: a region in south-western Transylvania near the river Maros (Hung.) / Mureş (Rom.)—the area is called Câmpul Pâinii in Romanian

Nándorfehérvár: the Hungarian name of Belgrade, capital of Serbia

Szabács: the Hungarian name of Šabac fortress in Serbia

Szeben: another major Saxon town in Transylvania – modern-day Sibiu in Romania

3. Selected Bibliography

Primary sources

Antonio Bonfini: *A Magyar Történelem Tizedei (Rerum Hungaricarum Decades)*, Hungarian trans. P. Kulcsár (Budapest, 1995)

János Thuróczy: *Chronicle of the Hungarians*, trans. F. Mantello (Bloomington, 1991)

The Annals of Jan Długosz: A History of Eastern Europe from AD965 to AD 1480, trans. and abridged M. Michael (Chichester, 1997)

Szabács Viadala (The Fight for Szabács)—a poem commemorating the siege and capture of *Szabács* (author anonymous; date unknown but possibly around the time of the siege in 1476)
https://magyar-irodalom.elte.hu/gepesk/kkor/049.htm

Secondary works

Bánlaky, J., *A Magyar Nemzet Hadtörténelme (The Military History of the Hungarian Nation)* (Budapest, 1928)—online version: edited by Arcanum Adatbázis Kft. (2001) http://mek.oszk.hu/09400/09477/html/index.html

Engel, P., *The Realm of St Stephen: A History of Medieval Hungary 895-1526* (London & New York, 2001)

Fügedi, E., *The Elefánthy: The Hungarian Nobleman and his Kindred* (Budapest, 1998)

Horváth, R. & Neumann, T., *Ecsedi Bátori István: Egy Katonabáró Életpályája 1458-1493 (István Bátori of Ecsed: The Career of a Soldier-Baron 1458-1493)* (Budapest, 2012)

Horváth, R., *Itineraria Regis Matthiae et Reginae Beatricis de Aragonia 1458-(1476)-1490 (The Itinerary of King Matthias and Queen Beatrix of Aragon)* (Budapest, 2011)

Magyar, K., *A Középkori Budai Király Palota Fő Építési Korszakainak Alaprajzi Rekonstrukciója I (The Reconstructed Ground Plans of the Main Architectural Periods of the Medieval Royal Palace of Buda)*—article in *Budapest Régiségei 31, 1997,* pp. 101-120

Rady, M., *Nobility, Land and Service in Medieval Hungary* (Hampshire and New York, 2000)

Pálosfalvi, T., *From Nicopolis to Mohács: A History of Ottoman-Hungarian Warfare, 1389–1526* (Leiden, 2018)

www.hungarianottomanwars.com : online blog by Szántai Gábor

HISTORIUM PRESS

www.historiumpress.com